From the farthest reaches of the universe to the innermost workings of the human heart and mind . . . Let tomorrow's masters of science fiction and fantasy take you on a journey that will capture your imagination:

Scattered starfarers in the emptiness beyond the solar system try to stay connected and even find love in the greatest emptiness imaginable.

A half-human spellcaster must compete against other witches for a grand championship, but her greatest challenge may be confronting herself.

A washed-up reporter investigating a story on the Moon finds that the truth can be more dangerous than terrorism.

A detective tries to solve a murder in a world where a godlike computer can reprogram reality itself, at will.

In a dark, fantastic world, a scholar from a dying race takes an acolyte who holds secrets greater than the histories they study.

Far from Earth, a human envoy finds himself caught in a bloody religious war between two alien cultures, neither of which he can understand.

A hunter tracks addicts who have lost their souls inside a computer network and drags them back out, whether or not they are ready to face the real world.

Missionaries on a hellish planet try to impose peace between warring alien races, even if it means destroying the world's life cycle.

Survivors aboard a damaged sky city must use all their wits and resources to keep from sinking into the depths of a gas giant.

A veteran space-salvage worker must survive pirates, ruthless corporations, ghost ships . . . and a rookie partner.

An embittered field medic in an interstellar war must save a thousand lives before he can go home.

A young activist agrees to spread a terrible virus to save the world from a government conspiracy . . . but there may be more than one conspiracy, and she doesn't know exactly which side she's on.

An ancient, immortal woman in the old South finds that she can put an end to her eternal curse, but only if she kills a Yankee soldier she has nursed back to health.

These stories from the freshest, most talented new voices in science fiction and fantasy, are individually illustrated by the best new artists in the genre. You will definitely encounter these names again in the future—but you saw them first in L. Ron Hubbard Presents Writers of the Future *Volume XXVII.*

What Has Been Said About the
L. RON HUBBARD
Presents
Writers of the Future
Anthologies

What the critics have said about Writers of the Future:

"Always a glimpse of tomorrow's stars . . ."
— *Publishers Weekly* starred review

"Fortunately, for the past quarter century the aptly named Writers of the Future competition has been seeking out and recognizing rising science-fiction stars."
— *Sci Fi* magazine

"Not only is the writing excellent . . . it is also extremely varied. There's a lot of hot new talent in it."
— *Locus* magazine

"A first rate collection of stories and illustrations."
— *Booklist* magazine

"This compilation shows why the series continues to produce some of the newest talent in the genre. The number of authors and artists who have come through this competition is staggering."
— *Midwest Book Review*

From novice to professional: What Writers of the Future means to you as an aspiring writer, as relayed from some of our past winners.

"This Contest serves as one of those first rungs that one must climb on the ladder to success."

— Dave Wolverton
Writers of the Future Contest winner 1987 and Contest judge

"The Writers of the Future Contest was definitely an accelerator to my writing development. I learned so much, and it came at just the right moment for me."

— Jo Beverley
Writers of the Future Contest winner 1988

"That phone call telling me I had won was the first time in my life that it seemed possible I would achieve my long-cherished dream of having a career as a writer."

— K. D. Wentworth
Writers of the Future Contest winner 1989
and Contest Coordinating Judge

"I really can't say enough good things about Writers of the Future. . . . It's fair to say that without Writers of the Future, I wouldn't be where I am today. . . ."

— Patrick Rothfuss
Writers of the Future Contest winner 2002

"The Writers of the Future Contest has had a profound impact on my career, ever since I submitted my first story in 1989."

— Sean Williams
Writers of the Future Contest winner 1993 and Contest judge

"The Writers of the Future Contest played a critical role in the early stages of my career as a writer."

— Eric Flint
Writers of the Future Contest winner 1993 and Contest judge

"The Contest kept the spark and life of my science-fictional imagination going. I might have had little confidence before, but after the workshops, I received the great start that the Contest's visionary founder always hoped and knew that it could provide."

— Amy Sterling Casil
Writers of the Future Contest winner 1999

"It's hard to say enough about how unique and powerful this Contest can be for any writer who's ready to take the next step."

— Jeff Carlson
Writers of the Future Contest winner 2007

"The Writers of the Future Contest sowed the seeds of my success. . . . So many people say a writing career is impossible, but WotF says, 'Dreams are worth following.'"

— Scott Nicholson
Writers of the Future Contest winner 1999

"You have to ask yourself, 'Do I really have what it takes, or am I just fooling myself?' That pat on the back from Writers of the Future told me not to give up. . . . All in all, the Contest was a fine finishing step from amateur to pro, and I'm grateful to all those involved."

— James Alan Gardner
Writers of the Future Contest winner 1990

"The Writers of the Future experience played a pivotal role during a most impressionable time in my writing career. Everyone was so welcoming. And afterwards, the WotF folks were always around when I had questions or needed help. It was all far more than a mere writing contest."

— Nnedi Okorafor
Writers of the Future Contest published finalist 2002

"When I first set out to become a professional writer (ah, hubris), one of my key ambitions was to place in the top tier of the L. Ron Hubbard Writers of the Future Contest. . . . Without Mr. Hubbard's sponsorship, I wouldn't have had that fabulous, high-profile launch."

— Jay Lake
Writers of the Future Contest winner 2003

"The generosity of the people involved with the Contest is amazing, and frankly humbling. It's no exaggeration to say I wouldn't be where I am today without it, and that means I wouldn't be going where I am tomorrow, either. So, in a way Writers of the Future shaped my future, and continues to shape it."

— Steven Savile
Writers of the Future Contest winner 2003

"Knowing that such great authors as the WotF judges felt my stories were worth publishing encouraged me to write more and submit more."

— Eric James Stone
Writers of the Future Contest winner 2005

"I credit the Writers of the Future Contest as an important part of my career launch, and I highly recommend it to everyone who wants to establish themselves in the field of science fiction and fantasy."

— Ken Scholes
Writers of the Future Contest winner 2005

"The Writers of the Future Contest launched my career into several amazing trajectories, and I'm enjoying them all."

— David Sakmyster
Writers of the Future Contest winner 2006

A word from Illustrators of the Future judges:

"The Illustrators of the Future Contest is one of the best opportunities a young artist will ever get. You have nothing to lose and a lot to win."

— Frank Frazetta, Artist
Illustrators of the Future Contest judge

"I only wish that there had been an Illustrators of the Future competition forty-five years ago. What a blessing it would have been to a young artist with a little bit of talent, a Dutch name and a heart full of desire."

— H. R. Van Dongen, Artist
Illustrators of the Future Contest judge

"The Contests are amazing competitions because really, you've nothing to lose and they provide good positive encouragement to anyone who wins. Judging the entries is always a lot of fun and inspiring. I wish I had something like this when I was getting started— very positive and cool."

— Bob Eggleton, Artist
Illustrators of the Future Contest judge

"The aspect I personally value most highly about the program is that of working with my fellow professionals, both artists and writers, to accomplish a worthwhile goal of giving tomorrow's artists and writers recognition and advancement in the highly competitive field of imaginative endeavor—the only existing program that does this."

— Stephen Hickman, Artist
Illustrators of the Future Contest judge

"These Contests provide a wonderful safety net of professionals for young artists and writers. And it's due to the fact that L. Ron Hubbard was willing to lend a hand."

— Judith Miller, Artist
Illustrators of the Future Contest judge

L. Ron Hubbard PRESENTS
Writers of the Future

VOLUME XXVII

L. Ron Hubbard PRESENTS

Writers of the Future

VOLUME XXVII

The year's thirteen best tales from
the Writers of the Future
international writers' program

Illustrated by winners in
the Illustrators of the Future
international illustrators' program

With essays on writing & illustration by

L. Ron Hubbard / Mike Resnick / Robert Castillo

Edited by K. D. Wentworth

GALAXY PRESS, LLC

The Unreachable Voices of Ghosts: © 2011 Jeffrey Lyman
Maddy Dune's First and Only Spelling Bee: © 2011 Patrick O'Sullivan
The Truth, from a Lie of Convenience: © 2011 Brennan Harvey
How to View Art: © 1984 L. Ron Hubbard Library
In Apprehension, How Like a God: © 2011 R. P. L. Johnson
An Acolyte of Black Spires: © 2011 Ryan Harvey
The Dualist: © 2011 Van Aaron Hughes
Bonehouse: © 2011 Keffy R. M. Kehrli
This Peaceful State of War: © 2011 Patty Jansen
Sailing the Sky Sea: © 2011 Geir Lanesskog
Unfamiliar Territory: © 2011 Ben Mann
Medic!: © 2011 Adam Perin
Vector Victoria: © 2011 D. A. D'Amico
The Sundial: © 2011 John Arkwright

Illustration on page 21: © 2011 Nico Photos
Illustration on page 60: © 2011 Meghan Muriel
Illustrations on pages 76 & 503: © 2011 Irvin Rodriguez
Illustration on page 161: © 2011 Dustin D. Panzino
Illustration on page 173: © 2011 Fred Jordan
Illustration on page 245: © 2011 Frederick Edwards
Illustration on page 283: © 2011 Vivian Friedel
Illustration on page 314: © 2011 Scott Frederick Hargrave
Illustration on page 354: © 2011 Joey Jordan
Illustration on page 387: © 2011 Erik Jean Solem
Illustration on page 437: © 2011 Gregory J. Gunther
Illustration on page 460: © 2011 Ryan Downing

Cover Artwork: Mission © 2011 Cliff Nielsen

Interior Design: Jerry Kelly

ISBN-10 1-59212-870-X
ISBN-13 978-1-59212-870-9
Library of Congress Control Number: 2011926124
First Edition Paperback
Printed in the United States of America

CONTENTS

Introduction

BY K. D. WENTWORTH

---

*K. D. Wentworth has sold more than eighty pieces of
short fiction to such markets as* F&SF, Alfred Hitchcock's
Mystery Magazine, Realms of Fantasy, Weird Tales,
Witch Way to the Mall *and* Return to the Twilight Zone.
*Four of her stories have been finalists for the Nebula Award
for Short Fiction. Currently, she has eight novels in print, the
most recent being* The Crucible of Empire, *written with Eric
Flint and published by Baen. She has served as Coordinating
Judge for the Writers of the Future Contest and has now taken
on the additional responsibility as Editor for the Writers of the
Future anthology. She lives in Tulsa with her husband and
a combined total of one hundred and sixty pounds of dog
(Akita + Siberian "Hussy") and is working on another new
novel with Flint.*

Introduction

As Coordinating Judge for the L. Ron Hubbard Writers of the Future Contest, I have the best job in the world. It was created by L. Ron Hubbard in 1983 when he set up the Writers of the Future Contest and then first entrusted to founding Contest judge, the perceptive Algis Budrys. L. Ron Hubbard, a widely published and gifted writer himself, knew how hard it was for beginning writers to get their proverbial foot in the door. He understood what it was like to have talent and drive and stories that you were burning to tell. He wanted to give new writers a running start, launch their careers and then make us all richer with the stories that only they could tell.

Coordinating Judge is certainly not an easy job. It requires me to sift through an enormous number of entries each quarter, looking for the eight best which will become Finalists. These eight go on to be judged again by a panel of four of our distinguished Contest Judges. They select the winning three stories, which will receive a monetary prize, publication in our anthology and a trip to the annual workshop. Currently our judges are: Tim Powers, Jerry Pournelle,

Larry Niven, Anne McCaffrey, Kristine Kathryn Rusch, Dean Wesley Smith, Eric Flint, Mike Resnick, Robert J. Sawyer, Robert Silverberg, Dave Wolverton, Dr. Yoji Kondo, Doug Beason, Kevin J. Anderson, Rebecca Moesta, Frederik Pohl, Nina Kiriki Hoffman, Sean Williams, Gregory Benford, Orson Scott Card and Brian Herbert.

Most quarters, I find it extremely difficult to sort out those last eight pieces. Often, only a hair's breadth separates the eight Finalists from the ten Semifinalists. As L. Ron Hubbard recognized, there is so much talent out there waiting to be discovered. New writers just need encouragement and a chance to be read. From my own experience as a winner in the Contest, I know that the existence of a professional market where new writers are only competing with each other is incredibly valuable. It keeps beginners writing when they might otherwise give up, encouraging them to produce a story every quarter so that they have something to enter. L. Ron Hubbard understood that every story we write teaches us new skills and helps us travel just a bit farther down the road toward publication. Producing fiction regularly is one of the defining characteristics of an author who will go on to develop a professional career.

So, if it's that difficult, why do I say I have the best job in the world? It's because my job involves making dreams come true. Writers must work so hard to learn their craft, but then, once they've achieved a professional standard with their prose, they discover they have to work even harder to get published. It's not uncommon for them to give up just short of success. The Writers of the Future Contest was

3

created to find talented newcomers and give them that much-needed boost to their careers at the point when they most need it.

Actually, I tried very hard not to have this job. When Algis Budrys first approached me to become First Reader for the Contest, I told him no. I was working full time as a teacher, taking care of my mom and grandparents, serving on the con committee of a literary science fiction convention, and, oh, yes, writing books and stories of my own.

But Algis would not take no for an answer. He suggested that I do the First Reading for just one quarter in the summer when I was not teaching. I agreed and was promptly swamped, spending many long hours learning how to distinguish which stories I should read all the way through. Then, at the end of the quarter, when he said he wanted me to be the permanent First Reader, I said no again. Definitely not! I simply did not have the time. He just smiled that wonderful mischievous smile of his and said, "I hope to change your mind." Somehow, the boxes just kept coming to my house and I kept reading.

Algis knew what I would soon learn: helping new writers is addictive. A year later, I became Coordinating Judge when Algis retired. And, you know what? He was right. I love this job. I love finding great new stories each year and then sending them out into the world to be appreciated by fans everywhere. I love meeting and instructing the new writers who will write the books and stories that will become new classics we will all enjoy for years to come. I love having the chance to give back to the world at least some small measure of the joy that was given to me when I won in 1988.

The other best job in the world belongs to Ron Lindahn and Val Lakey Lindahn. They run the L. Ron Hubbard Illustrators of the Future Contest, which was created in 1988 as a companion to Writers of the Future, and teach the workshop that is part of the prize package. Again, the purpose is to find talented artists just on the edge of breaking out, recognize and commend their abilities, publish their creative efforts and instruct them on how to move up to the next level in their career.

Illustrator winners each illustrate one of the anthology's stories, then are transported to the annual Illustrators' workshop where Val and Ron Lindahn (and a number of our other Illustrators judges) dispense invaluable advice about how to develop and manage a career as an artist and keep inspiration coming. Unfortunately, as rare as it is, it is not enough to just have talent. Emerging artists must learn how to develop a portfolio and professional contacts, market their work and make it pay.

But Val and Ron and I would not have such fabulous jobs if it were not for all the talented folks out there honing their abilities as fiction writers and artists, waiting for their moment to step into the spotlight. Be assured that we are eager to read your stories and view your illustrations. We want to shake your hand on the stage as you receive your award and proceed to the next level in your career. We want to follow your success in the years to come.

So keep entering! I promise the best is just ahead.

The Unreachable Voices of Ghosts

written by

Jeffrey Lyman

illustrated by

NICO PHOTOS

ABOUT THE AUTHOR

Jeff Lyman was born in Sault Sainte Marie, Michigan, on the Canadian border—a small town that averages 180 days a year below freezing and eleven feet of snow. With little else to do during the winter, Jeff learned to read early. This helped him overcome tremendous culture shock when he moved to the outskirts of New York City at the age of seven. He doesn't remember the transition from Dr. Seuss to science fiction, but it happened early.

Though he has written throughout his life, Jeff finally decided to take writing seriously in 2004 by attending Odyssey, The Fantasy Writing Workshop. It transformed his life and vaulted his meager skills a thousandfold. Since then he has been published numerous times in small press anthologies and has assisted in editing the Bad-Ass Faeries series of anthologies, as well as others. This submission to Writers of the Future is his first professional sale.

Jeff graduated from Princeton University in 1994 with a degree in aerospace engineering. He currently lives and works near New York City as a mechanical engineer and loves climbing and burrowing into the forgotten crevices of the city.

ABOUT THE ILLUSTRATOR

Nico was born and raised in sunny Los Angeles and spent most of his time in his jungle-esque front yard. Nico likes to think of this front yard as the beginning of his artistic career. It was an incredible place where danger lurked around every corner and you never knew what magnificent treasures were to be found. That yard was the spark which ignited his imagination.

At the age of ten, Nico discovered Japanese anime through a promotional videotape (you may remember videotapes . . . ?) that somehow ended up in his mailbox. The tape was a Pokémon episode. That did it. He was hooked, which resulted in all kinds of personal problems (e.g., Pikachu-shaped birthday cakes and approximately 24,849 hours of life wasted on his Game Boy) but it also resulted in a passion for drawing, which, fed by his wonderfully supportive parents, soon became a craze, and subsequently a mania. He recalls spending seven or eight hours a day, seven days a week drawing on his summer breaks, and about 98.6% of all his class time being consumed with doodles.

His parents, recognizing his mania for what it was, decided that the best way to handle it was to channel it. He was enrolled in art classes and received how-to books for Christmas and was generally deluged with artistic encouragement. Then he met Ken Hellenbolt. Ken worked for Hanna-Barbera in the old days and would become a friend and artistic mentor. That's when Nico's drawing ability really skyrocketed. His art insanity reached a new peak when Ken introduced him to the work of Frank Frazetta. Frazetta's art touched Nico like none had before and right then he knew that's what he wanted to do.

The Unreachable
Voices of Ghosts

Max Getty's sail-ship passed the official outer edge of the Kuiper Belt at a tremendous velocity, sailing over the Kuiper Cliff where the density of asteroids and planetoids plummeted. Out here, the sun's influence was tenuous. Not that he noticed a difference or could tell that he was moving at all. Still, it was a milestone for which he had been waiting for fifteen years in his little two-room ship. He toasted himself with a tiny sip of fifteen-year-old Scotch (when purchased), now thirty years old, and went back to routine.

"Trap status," he said to the voice inputs, swiveling on his chair to look back at the sun. It was a bright star, and the computer had centered it in the rear screen so he could find it easily. It made him feel nostalgic, though he had bid it good riddance when he set out from near-Earth orbit.

"Trap status optimal." Data scrolled down Screen #4 on his left.

Around the *Odysseus,* an aura of twelve tethers extended, three kilometers of fishing line out to Aeolus traps bound to each end. Magnetic fields held the powerful traps open, but like mousetraps, they would clap shut at the slightest perturbation.

Max had deployed them years ago, still deep in the Kuiper Belt and long before they could possibly catch something. He wasn't really sure why he had bothered since he didn't want to catch anything.

He clicked a couple of toggles and reefed the sails slightly. The galactic wind fought the solar wind and eddies were warping his trajectory. Not that he really had a destination. There were no destinations out here. You sailed until you died or until you got lucky and caught a baby black hole.

The *incoming message* signal beeped twice. Max had his comm unit set on passive receipt, since he didn't want to talk.

A faint voice rasped from the speakers, as much white noise as speech. "Jennifer Gates here, signing off. This'll be my last general transmission to all you fishermen and women. I didn't have the luck of it, but here's raising a glass to you all. May you find a black hole in your nets and the sun at your face. I'll stay on for a month or two more, so, Michael Dunkirk and Oruna Miguel, keep talking to me."

Max checked the data log. The message had originated hours ago from very far out. Jennifer Gates was probably crying with her friends right now, contemplating suicide. He grabbed an empty shot glass with an image of the Hawaiian Islands on the side and raised it to the viewscreen in front of him. "For Jennifer Gates and all the cold stars shining. Let your eyes forever turn to the sun, your life to the solar wind."

He looked down at the empty shot glass. He hated the goodbye messages. A few came in every month, a constant reminder that the odds of anyone catching a baby black hole and turning their ship around were maybe one in ten.

He called up a tracking screen that showed the fishermen and women in this sector of the void. Hundreds and hundreds, their positions continuously tracked as their messages arrived. He located the bright dot that was Jennifer Gates. Her ship was clearly past the nebulous radius-of-no-return, so she had already sailed for months beyond the end of her road. She didn't *have* to kill herself. She could keep heading out until she died of old age, but who wanted that? Suicide was the norm.

Beyond Gates' bright dot sailed thousands of coffins, ships that had gone silent but not cold, still heading out. Their computers routinely broadcast their coordinates and the Ident numbers of fishers gone down to sea. At a radius very far out, even these began to wink out as their generators failed. A bare dusting, those with the most expensive isotope generators, sparkled beyond the *dark line.* Those faintest signals took weeks to drift back to the living fishers from coffins hundreds of years old.

Max sometimes gazed for hours at the constellation of sail-ships, both the active ones and the coffins. It was a wonder. So many years' worth of desperate people, so many failed dreams. He had pinged some of the coffins when he was still in the Kuiper Belt, requesting data packets of long-vanished conversations. They arrived, and he would sit in his chair pedaling his bicycle for exercise and listen to dead fishers talking about pretty much the same things that living fishers talked about now.

Political parties had changed, or conflicts or failures that had caused the despair necessary for becoming a fisher, but it was familiar. The corporations fed on that despair to fetch baby black holes for their stardrives. Why else sell the sail-ships so cheap? Anyone could go out into the void who wanted to go, so long as they offered their patron corporation first-right-of-black-hole-purchase at a set price.

Max hadn't fallen for that trap. He had purchased his own sail-ship outright with a powerful generator, a large hydroponic module and a powerful high-gain antenna so he could follow broadcasts from home. He even had two rooms, unlike the corporate giveaways with their single-chamber ships. He couldn't imagine being trapped in such a shoebox. The minimum trip was thirty years, fifteen out past the Kuiper Belt and fifteen back in if you happened to stumble on a baby black hole right over the Kuiper Cliff.

Well-wishing messages streamed into his receiver as the collective community bid farewell to Jennifer Gates.

"Halt all feeds," Max said.

His sail-ship fell silent save for the squeak of the bicycle pedals under his feet and his ragged breathing. He hated silence, even though he never talked to anyone, because then his ship felt like what it was. If he wasn't listening to idle fisher-chatter, he played music or 3-D immersion feeds his antenna picked up from home. He got the latest that Hollywood, Bollywood and France had to offer.

"Isolate the Kingfisher's signal and play," he said, not wanting to watch a movie or newsfeed right now.

Bartelmeus Jones, called the Kingfisher by pretty

much everyone, stood in direct contrast to Jennifer Gates. He was the most distant living fisher. He was ninety-seven years old and had been outbound for seventy-one of those years.

He joked that he was too chicken to kill himself, but Max knew that couldn't be the whole truth. Everyone out here had months of despair. Months so black that even the greatest optimists and greatest cowards found their fingers on the link to disable their CO_2 scrubbers. Hell, some folks killed themselves before they even reached the Kuiper Cliff, and only their coffins coasted out into the void. What a waste. And yet the Kingfisher rode on.

He clearly enjoyed his status as the patriarch of the scattered fishers. He liked giving advice and telling stories of victories and losses. He had known a lot of the long-silent voices from the coffins and had a great many stories to tell. The void wasn't as empty as it seemed, and seventy-one years was enough to accumulate tales of wonder.

Max hadn't liked him much in the early years after he passed Pluto. The Kingfisher's inability to catch a black hole or kill himself felt too much like failure, only with a running commentary. Bartelmeus was always "on," always talking. He was the white noise of deep space. But he had a way of growing on you and now Max tuned in to him often.

" . . . flared out his sails as far as they would go, and Rebecca Solange furled hers completely. It took him four and a half years to reach her, but woo wee, that was a union."

Max flicked off the feed. He'd heard variants of this one many times. Jack Kwon and Miriam Solange, out past the radius-of-no-return and very much in love, had jettisoned their Aeolus traps and linked ships, sailing outbound together before fighting and ending in a murder-suicide nine years later. That was before the sail-ships were outfitted with easy linking ports, so it was the first time anyone had tried it. It was common now for fishers to link ships. Well, common as in one every few years. It took a hell of a lot to overtake one another in the vastness of the void.

Max had a bunch of Kingfisher recordings on his data banks; many were variants of one another. He preferred the "seldom" stories—the ones told rarely or maybe only once. He had pinged a lot of deep coffins over the years, looking for ancient Kingfisher broadcasts stored in their fading memory. He'd even pinged the Kwon-Solange coffin, which was moving ever outward in union, but that one was dark. Kwon had recorded a number of rambling monologues before he killed himself.

Max unstrapped himself from his bicycle and puttered around the small cabin for a few hours, checking all systems. The generator was producing power optimally, and would for many years. He checked his wife's Swedish ivy plant, which had grown into a spider web of vines and branches over the past fifteen years. The nutrient drip at the main flowerpot was doing fine, as well as fifteen other drips at far-flung roots where the plant had attached itself to walls and ceilings.

Max hesitated over the hibernation box. Maybe it was time to go to sleep for a month or two, recharge the batteries. Most fishers lived this way, hopscotching through life. Four weeks awake, four to eight weeks asleep. Max didn't follow that pattern so much, both because he didn't mind being awake in the ship and because he knew from experience that he needed a minimum of three weeks to really shake off the effects of hibernation-torpor. Just when he was starting to feel his best, he was expected to jump back into the box.

He eased himself into the container, a tight fit under the best of circumstances, and started the cycle. In the moment that sleep took him, he felt like he was drowning. It happened every time.

The years passed in comfortable routine: awake/asleep, repairs on systems, lurking and watching the constant video chatter from so many new and old fishers. A few times a month there were going-away parties and eulogies; some months were worse than others. Every other month or so someone caught a baby black hole and there was much jealous rejoicing; some months were luckier than others. Max maintained his Aeolus traps, figuring if he was one of the lucky ones, he'd give it away. That'd make a story for the Kingfisher's arsenal.

Then, six years into his fishing run across the void, Max ran into the first major mechanical failure that he couldn't fix on his own. The computer yanked him out of hibernation early, alarm lights flashing.

Groaning, he sat on the edge of the box for several minutes trying to massage feeling back into his numb left side. He felt very ill, worse than usual. The drugs hadn't had a chance to metabolize. Then he shoved over to the alarm console and stopped the flashing lights.

The water reclamation unit was failing. It was working at about forty percent, chugging unhealthily. There was an annoying buzz coming from below the floor.

He unscrewed the deck plate over the unit and saw that the holding tank was about half filled with wastewater. Humidity levels were increasing in the cabin. He shut the system down and pulled the filters with his working right hand. They seemed fairly clean. They were supposed to be self-cleaning. He pushed them back into place, then replaced the belts on the transfer pumps because the old ones looked worn. He turned the system on again, and it buzzed just as loudly as before, maybe worse.

What to do, what to do? He wiped his hand across his forehead, trying to calm his breathing. He wouldn't last long without water. Though he had come out here for solitude and escape from the teeming billions back in-system, he wasn't suicidal. In the back of his mind, he'd always known he would die sometime, but he tried not to dwell on it. He called up the schematics for the unit and a troubleshooting guide, and despaired at the highly technical scroll and the replacement parts required. Apparently, the manufacturer assumed that the ship owner would have access to a port and a mechanic.

As Max wiggled and wedged his body down farther into the cavity around the wastewater tank, pushing aside silicone tubes and pressing against cold pipes sweating condensation in the new humidity, it suddenly occurred to him that he envied the Kingfisher. He didn't want to die. He wanted to be that voice from the void that went on and on like a sense of permanence while everyone else came and went. A second later, it occurred to him that he couldn't be the Kingfisher because he never spoke to anyone and had no stories to tell. In that instant, his self-imposed isolation struck him—the uncrossable gulf between himself and everyone else. He cried for the first time since his wife's funeral, and violent, jerking sobs tore through his body. He pressed his fist hard against his mouth and bit down, unable to stop the tidal force of tears.

When the fit abated enough so he could control himself, he blinked wet eyes against the diamond-bright glare of a hundred teardrops floating in front of the pit-lamps. He started to laugh. With the water reclamation unit on the blink, he'd have a hell of a time cleaning this up.

He pulled himself weakly from the aftermath and back into his little home. He didn't want to be alone anymore.

Strapping himself into his chair, he pulled the comm deck close to his body. He took one of the long, trailing vines of the Swedish ivy gently between his fingers and ran his thumb across a glossy leaf. He had made a promise to his wife at her grave that he'd never speak to anyone again, but maybe she would understand.

"This is Max Getty," he said with a voice he had hardly used in twenty-one years. "Ship *Odysseus*. You don't know me, but I need help. My water reclamation unit's failing and I can't fix it."

He sat waiting, scared, his wife's ivy plant in his hand, imagining the message streaming across the void. What would they think? He had never spoken to them, so would they even answer him?

Within minutes, and then over the following hour, he was extremely grateful as messages of welcome poured in from hundreds of fishers scattered hither and yon. He knew so many of them from thousands of hours of silent lurking, but now they wanted to know him too. He understood that he was a curiosity in their static world, but was surprised to find he didn't mind. He liked being the center of attention for a little while. He answered as many people as he could, though he was vague on his personal life from so long ago back in-system.

Hours sped by—there were so many hellos and helpful suggestions for his water unit that he didn't notice the time lag between individual incoming messages. But he grew tired, tired of smiling and tired of talking. His epiphany faded as his voice grew hoarse, and he craved a little of his isolation again.

"I gotta go, folks," he said. His cheeks had cramped from his fixed grin. "Not to be rude, but it's been a while, and this has been like jumping into icy water. Give me time to ease into civilization."

He unstrapped and pushed himself across the command module to his bunk/hydroponics room. He was still hibernation-sick and needed some normal sleep before tackling the repairs. The communications array unit continued to ping over and over, flickering from one face to the next as well-wishers said goodbye, ignoring the irony of overwhelming the overwhelmed.

Max squirmed under the webbing on his bed and closed his eyes, tracing the intricacies of the spreading ivy plant in his mind like a fractal. The messages would arrive for a while. His sign-off message hadn't even reached the more distant ships yet.

He must have dozed. He awoke to a woman speaking in the next room. She was using technical terms and a wide variety of cusses.

Untangling himself from the webbing, Max pushed back to the command module. There was an attractive forty-something woman on his screen; thick, curly, red hair was pulled back in a zero-G braid, bright green eyes focused on the camera. She had a bag of parts floating next to her head and a magnetic wrench in her hand. Max hit replay and her face appeared on screen from the beginning.

"Max Getty," she barked too loudly, "welcome to the dance. Maureen O'Shea here, maybe five years farther out than you. I didn't join the happy-happy pile-on because I figured that was the surefired way of scaring you back into your shell. But just between you and me, all the advice everyone gave you about your water unit is crap. Ignore it. I've put together a video of what you have to do, step by step, so slap on your virtual-goggles and I'll walk you through it. Of course, if I screw this up and butcher my own water unit, I'll be damned pissed at you and I'll probably be sending out a suicide-announcement inside of forty-eight hours. Got your goggles on? Good, because here we go. And stop looking at my ass!"

Goggles on, seemingly standing inside her tiny ship, Max couldn't help but stare at her backside while she disassembled her water unit to an unending stream of profanity. That was his formal introduction to Maureen O'Shea.

Max found that he enjoyed her virtual company so much that he had trouble following her instructions. He had to replay the recording three times and pause it frequently because she moved so fast. Together, they disassembled the entire filtration and reclamation unit and rebuilt it from the ground up using replacement parts he didn't know he had, or parts that were clearly not intended for the purpose.

Finishing up, surrounded by a haze of sweat and hot air, with old tears clinging to the walls, Max fired up the unit. It thrummed to life, rattled a bit, found its equilibrium and settled into a purr as sweet as the day he'd bought it.

Laughing with delight, he turned the air cyclers on HIGH and watched as sweat and tears were sucked into the intakes. He did a happy dance in the middle of the cabin until he bashed his knuckles on the edge of a storage box.

He had fixed the water unit and was no longer about to die; he had introduced himself to the community, for good or ill; he had met Maureen with the curvy backside; he had wrapped his knuckles in surgical tape to keep droplets of blood from floating through the cabin after the tears.

He had to respond to her. She was five years farther out? That was quite a distance.

He called up the constellation of fishers and located her ship from the Ident codes embedded in her message. A point of light brightened well beyond his own. He zoomed out. She was only a few years from the radius-of-no-return. But that point was subjective. Depending on her age, she could go several years beyond that radius before the return trip would be long enough for a death sentence.

Max paused her image on his screen and stared at it. She really did look like she was in her low forties.

But if she'd been flying for twenty-five or so years, she would have left home as a teenager. That was illegal. She had to be at least fifty. She looked *good*.

He washed up and shaved as he composed a response to her in his head. Resettling into his chair, he activated the single-point video feed. He hadn't ever used the virtual feeds and wasn't sure if the thirty-two surround cameras were working.

"Max Getty here, pleased to make your acquaintance." He stopped and hit delete. That was awful. She certainly wasn't so formal as that. He started the recording again and tried to put enthusiasm into his voice. "Max Getty here. Maureen, thanks so much! Worked like a charm. Who woulda thought to use a sock smeared in grease as a gasket? I'm babbling, but I'm out of practice with talking. I used to be pretty good at it. Um . . . just thanks."

He hit SEND and sat staring at the blank screen, hoping she'd respond and kicking himself for not sending a message that she might have wanted to respond to.

Determined not to hover, he set to wiping down all the walls where condensation had accumulated while the water unit was off. The receiver pinged in just under half an hour and he stared at it in a panic with his damp rag clutched in his hand. What would she say? What would she think of him?

"Max," Maureen's voice boomed out into the cabin. "Pleased ta meetcha. But you didn't have to shave on my account. Really. I didn't shave for you." She lifted a foot and tugged up her pant leg a few inches. "See? Oh, wait, I was trying not to scare you back into your shell, wasn't I? Damn. Flee, flee before me." She waggled her foot at the camera.

She sighed and leaned back in her worn chair, hands behind her head. "So you going to talk or what? You going to join us a little bit, or are you pretty much done? You don't look like a hermit, you know. You don't look like one of the crazies moldering away in their ships. So call me back. Let me know."

Max smiled and hit the REPLY button.

They quickly became friends, gossiping about this fisher or that, talking about their lives. Max stopped visiting the public channels as much in favor of communicating with Maureen. He'd often seen it happen to fishers, but it hadn't occurred to him that he might be one.

He and Maureen tried to carry on normal conversations with their sixteen-minute time lag, but that quickly became frustrating while they waited for each other's answers. So they began to write longer and longer replies, letters almost. They told stories to each other, made up or true, and went on 3-D tours of their ships to show each other items that were precious to them. They watched new vids from Earth and argued about them afterwards. They retold their favorite Kingfisher stories to each other.

Then the moment came that Max knew must come eventually—Maureen told him how she became a fisherwoman. The story came after she went on nostalgically for the inner system.

"Are you kidding?" Max fired back a bit too abruptly. "Don't you remember how crowded Earth is? And the Moon, and Mars, and Phobos and Deimos? You can see the ring around Earth in broad daylight now from all the asteroids towed in from the main belt. All those orbital mansions dug into old, mined-out rocks. Good riddance!"

"Let me tell you why I came out this way," she responded. "I got a good education at University College Dublin. They had this program where if you gave ten years of your life to Ireland after you graduated, they'd let you attend for free. I really wanted to get married and have my one kid allowed, but it didn't happen. Since I passed the exams, I figured what the hell, might as well go to school while I waited for Mr. Right. So there I was at thirty years old after my ten years, just starting out in the job market, no money, no status and no husband. I wanted my baby more than anything, but I couldn't afford the taxes."

Max was surprised by this hint at her age. She had probably spent a couple of years after she turned thirty trying to get money together. And yet, she couldn't be much older than fifty. She just didn't look it, and there were no rejuvenation surgeries out here on the sail-ships.

She smiled wistfully. "You know, I imagined my baby so often that she became real to me. Like she existed somewhere just waiting for me to get pregnant. And then when I couldn't, I felt like I'd failed her. Like maybe I killed her. I got suicidal."

Max couldn't see where she was going with this, except maybe the suicidal part. How did going out to fish and hopefully coming back a successful old lady help with breeding? Not that he condoned

24

breeding. The draconian measures enacted by most of Earth's governments were necessary. They were starting to have an effect, but there were still so many immigrants from the Moon and Mars that there was a net gain year to year.

"So I came out here," she continued. "Earth didn't have anything to offer me. I figured if I could score a black hole, I could go back, buy an apartment with a bit of a view and use the rest of the money to help other women qualify for their kid. If I couldn't be a mom, maybe I could be an aunt many times over." She shrugged. "Now I'm close to the radius-of-no-return. Not much time left for my dream. But you know what? That happens to ninety percent of us out here, so I'm not too down. I tried.

"But you. What happened to you back there? Your ship is bigger than all of ours and you didn't speak to any of us for over two decades. What do you want with the money if you catch a black hole, huh? You hate the inner system. You gonna buy an orbital mansion tucked into an asteroid? Hide for your few remaining years and then die alone above the teeming masses on the planet underneath you? What's your real story, Max?"

"I told my wife at her funeral that I wouldn't talk to anyone, ever again," he said. "After I bought the ship and made my arrangements to go, of course."

He couldn't use that old excuse of the promise to his wife anymore, because he'd broken the promise a thousand times over in the past few weeks. He still didn't want to talk about the past.

"I used to be someone famous," he said. "It doesn't matter who. I don't use that name anymore. I traveled everywhere, performed for millions every day. I loved it, the attention and the money and all that." He looked up at the sprawling net of ivy branches across the ceiling. The plant thrived after all these years.

"My wife was murdered by my fans. It was some splinter-fan group where everyone was mad I wasn't single and on the eligible lists. That's a simplification, but there it is. I suffered through the murder trial—six young women pleading with me to forgive them and then marry them because they were my true soul mates. That's when I realized humans are just animals, and I was a performing monkey. I thrived on fame, and they killed her because of it. I killed her.

"I have no interest in going back. I don't check my old fan groups because I'm afraid they're still hunting me." He shivered. "People weren't meant to live so crammed together. It does something to their heads."

"I guess," she responded quietly, "we're both out here grieving someone we didn't really kill, huh? Hell of a long way to go just to run away."

"I suppose," he said. "Maybe not far enough. It tore the heart out of me." He stopped and gripped his hands together to keep them from shaking. "You want to know a secret? I fantasize sometimes about catching a black hole and feeding my ship to it. Wouldn't be much of a meal for the little feller, though, would it? And I used to think I was so big."

"I know what you mean," was all she said, and then her transmission ended.

He didn't feel much like responding again himself. He felt like crap for saying any of those words aloud.

They didn't speak about it again, but the moment

brought them close together. In between hibernation spells, they talked constantly. She worked hard to draw him out of his shell, usually against his will. She forced him to participate in community chats and random social events. There were games of logic and games of luck, built around the necessary time lag in communication. There were costume balls where you had to make a costume out of whatever you had available on your ship, the more inventive the better. There were recipe competitions to see who could make the best-tasting muck from the food recyclers (herbs and vegetables from the hydroponics were not allowed).

All the while time marched on and Maureen's ship crept ever closer to the radius-of-no-return. Max tried to ignore it until the day he came out of hibernation to learn the Kingfisher was gone.

The radio waves were alive with chatter about it. People were upset at the passing of the only permanent fixture in deep space. Not just the Kingfisher, but his ship had gone silent as well. No known location, no response to pings. The popular theory was that his generator had finally failed. The immortal and indestructible Kingfisher had outlived his ship, if only by a few minutes. It was a stunning victory after seventy-eight years of failure, because he alone had never killed himself.

"Do you want to join ships?" Max asked Maureen abruptly, not long after. "Stay together on the ride out?"

"What, be another Kwon-Solange death coffin? I love you, hon, but like you always say, people weren't meant to live on top of each other like that. Besides, I don't want to live until my late 90s out here, telling the same stories over and over again to new fishers who are just going to die like their predecessors."

"I could catch you and we could join for a little while. Could we do that?" The Kingfisher was silent; Max couldn't bear to think of Maureen going silent too.

She took a long while in answering. "It'd be nice to see you in the flesh just once. Really nice. But I'm five years ahead of you. Even if I threw my sails out and used the galactic wind as a brake, it'd take you ten years or more to catch me. I don't have another ten years in me. I don't."

"Don't kill yourself."

"Not yet, hon. I'm still here, still talking."

They smiled at each other and went on as before, ignoring the eight-hundred-pound gorilla in the sail-ship.

Then, just about a year later, his computer woke him from hibernation with alarms. All momentous events seemed to happen during hibernation, when he was sick unto death. He was approaching sixty years old and his body wasn't so young as it once was. Soon he'd be at his own radius-of-no-return, when the journey back in would take longer than the years he had left.

He sat on the lip of the hibernation box and shook his left arm, which was always the side that went numb. Then he pushed over to the alarm console to see what calamity he'd be facing today. Say what you want about free corporate sail-ships, they were robust. Max had made more repairs on his boat than any other fisher he knew.

He stared at the alarm screen, trying to make sense of the flashing icons. Then he let out a whoop. One of his Aeolus traps had slammed shut, and the inertial magnets were registering a point-mass on the order of a million metric tons.

He did his usual happy dance, not caring how many times he bashed his knuckles into corners or how tangled he got in the ivy vine that had taken over the cabin. He located his now thirty-nine-year-old bottle of Scotch and took a big pull, then doubled over coughing and choking.

He wanted to tell Maureen, but she would be in hibernation for at least ten more days. There was no one else he wanted to tell. Maybe he could get her computer to override her presets and wake her up.

Or he could surprise her. He could use the black hole to fly out to her ship in short order. Link with her and fly both of their ships back in-system. Sure, they'd be very old when they got back, but she could still set up her charity with the money they made off the sale. And they could be together.

If they ever fought like Kwon and Solange, they could separate and let their momentum carry both ships back home separately. He'd still have saved her.

He carefully reeled the trap in close, then jettisoned his ship's rear cowl to reveal the fusion rocket that all fishers carried in their guts and dreamed about. He settled the black hole at the focal point of the rocket and adjusted his magnetic fields until it was stable. Then he fed it the Aeolus trap. His sensors registered a tiny burst of radiation as the black hole fed, not enough to propel the ship but enough to give him a better picture of the black hole's size and rotational velocity. He reeled in the other eleven traps and fed them in one by one, calibrating and adjusting the focal point of the rocket after each one.

He leaned back in his chair, staring at the view screen that showed nothing but the cold steel and aluminum rocket. He marveled that he had one of the primordial powerhouses of the universe nestled in the palm of his hand and he couldn't even see it.

How long until Maureen woke up? Too long. There was no time like the present to fire up the engine and see if it worked. He furled his sails in tight and rolled them into their interior compartments, then recorded a goodbye message for Maureen in case his ship exploded.

He ramped the generator slowly up to one hundred percent and deployed the electromagnetic ramscoop from the nose of the ship, then waited in breathless silence for something to happen. Was this region of space dense enough in ions to make the engine work? It had to be. People caught black holes and powered their ramjets all the time.

With a bang that rattled his teeth, Max slammed backward into his seat and hung on for the ride. He could barely think. He'd been weightless for decades, and he felt the nausea of tremendous acceleration distorting his body. He fought the G-forces just to extend his hand and hit the diagnostic button.

His coasting velocity had been well above the ramjet's minimum requirements, and the scoop was snatching ionized hydrogen out of the void like a charm. The ions sluiced down the magnetic field lines, compressed into a hot gas at the base of the scoop and shot out across the face of hyperdense gravitational fields at the edge of the black hole, fusing instantly. A plasma jet stretched behind the ship for miles in an explosive release of energy that shook the ship.

Max whooped, then gasped as the ship surged forward. The ejecta trail increased in intensity and length. He must be pushing through a denser pocket of hydrogen. Slowly, agonizingly, he made his way to his bed. The velocity-to-drag ratio should balance itself in a few days and the acceleration would decrease to a more comfortable level. Until then, he would just be miserable.

Two weeks later, when Maureen was up and about and drinking a lot of water to push the hibernation poisons from her body, he excitedly told her the news. She, in turn, was ecstatic for him until she realized he was coming to get her.

"You can't," she said, looking genuinely horrified. "You have to take it and head back in."

Gray shot through her red hair now, and laugh-lines limned her face. Max thought she looked beautiful. "I don't want to go back, remember?" he sent back. "The only way I'll go back is with you. Now spread your sails as a brake, because I'm comin' in hot. I bet I can reach you in under two years. C'mon, whatya say?"

"You're crazy. We'll never make it back alive. And what if we end up clawing each other's eyes out like Kwan and Solange?"

"We'll be flying faster than normal. My ship might

31

need more fixing than your corporate models, but her ramscoop is a sight to behold. With my bigger generator, it's two dozen kilometers wide."

"Now you're boasting about size?"

"I'm serious. I'm coming to get you, and I can pack on speed like you wouldn't believe. We'll be a success story, the anti-Kwon/Solange. Give these folks out here hope. Who knows, maybe everyone will fish in tandem after we're gone."

"What if you don't like me in person?" She was strapped into her chair, and she looked smaller than Max had ever seen her.

"Are you kidding? How could you think that? You've been alone too long; you've gotten used to it. You dragged me out of my shell, so now I'm dragging you out of yours."

She looked unconvinced. He was hurt by her lack of excitement, but figured she was scared.

He had to tell the fisher community soon after he told her, because his ship had gone red on everyone's screen as soon as he deployed his ramscoop. Congratulations poured in, a mix of joy and jealousy, as they always were. And then when it became clear another week later, that he wasn't turning, he had to tell the crowd about his rescue mission. He was heading for Maureen.

That saddled his idiocy with a romantic twist that enthralled the community. Most people cheered him on. His position was continuously tracked. Maureen's gradually slowing velocity was calculated as she braked against nothing more than the ethereal galactic wind.

He and Maureen tried to maintain normal conversations, but the excitement of the community was infectious. The chance to go home was overwhelming, though Max readily admitted he still had no interest in setting foot on Earth again.

A year and a half into the run, he diverted the ion stream away from the black hole to stop the fusion and used the scoop as a friction drag to slow himself. He was going too fast to use his sail as a brake—the filaments would have disintegrated under the pressure. Countdown timers appeared on the screens of the fisher community.

One year, ten months and eleven days after Max started his run, he caught sight of Maureen's tiny ship for the first time. He brought the scoop in tight to half a kilometer and his deceleration eased. By the time he was a hundred meters behind her, the scoop was gone and his sails were out for more precise steering.

"I'm here," Max said when he was above her, his velocity matched with hers. It was so nice talking to her without a time lag.

"Are you sure this is a good idea? I'm getting pretty old, you know. Set in my ways." She looked flustered.

A clunk reverberated through both ships as the automatic pilots clamped their docking ports together.

"Maureen, you old bat, I love you. I've loved you for years with no hope of ever seeing you. I'm old too, by the way, in case you hadn't noticed. Please, can I come in?"

"I guess." She gave a nervous smile.

Max grabbed his bottle of Scotch and pulled up the floor plates over his docking hatch. Pressing the release sequence, he watched as the wheel atop the hatch plate spun. The hatch opened with a hiss and he backed up. Maureen's hatch swung down a moment later with another hiss. He pulled himself through, careful not to touch anything. The metal was dangerously cold from space.

"Hello?" he said to the back of her chair. The light was muted in the chamber. Everything smelled musty, but he assumed that his ship stank too, only he couldn't smell it anymore.

She turned to face him slowly, sheepishly, and he was stunned to see a wizened old woman in the chair. Her fluffy white hair was pulled back in a loose ponytail.

"Hi, Max," she said, and it was her voice. Her nervous smile.

"Maureen?"

"Yeah, it's me." She held up her hands. "In the flesh."

"But how?"

"I'm eighty-two. I'm afraid I've been lying to you all these years. Projecting a somewhat younger image of me."

She smiled *her* familiar smile from the deep folds of her face. Max shook his head and smiled back. "Come here. Give me a hug."

She pushed up to him and they embraced and hung onto each other tightly, desperately. Her console beeped over and over again, as fishers queried what was going on. They knew the ships must be united by now.

"I just couldn't tell you," she said, her voice muffled

in his sleeve. "After a while I figured it didn't matter. I wasn't going home. Neither of us was."

Max kissed Maureen on the forehead and then on the lips. "I told you before, I'm in love with you. Nothing else matters."

Tears streamed from her eyes, floating in a glistening constellation.

"Stop that, love. It's a bear to clean it up. Relays could short out."

She laughed. "Can I see your ship?"

"Come on up."

"Wait a second." She pushed back down to her communications array. "Leave us alone, boys and girls," she said in the voice he knew. "We're busy."

They climbed into his ship, where she got to see what two rooms were like instead of just one.

All the rocket flight back through the void, past hundreds of fishers they knew so well, they were cheered on and waved forward. Messages were given to them to deliver back home. Prayers were requested for successful fishing journeys. Maureen was eighty-seven years old when they rocketed over the Kuiper Cliff and back into the denser regions of the asteroid belt.

Max steered them safely through. It wouldn't do to catch an asteroid in their ramscoop, and they passed Pluto not long after Maureen's ninetieth birthday. Together, they answered the friendly hails of the research outposts around Neptune and filed their proper reports with the flight authorities as they passed Saturn.

Two months shy of her ninety-eighth birthday,

Max brought the twinned ships in to dock at the massive commercial shipyards orbiting the Moon.

"Told you I'd bring you home again," he said to her, smiling down at her thin face. She lay in the bed, wrapped in netting to ease her body as they decelerated.

She glanced at the ceiling above them where the Swedish ivy swayed. "I'm dying. I can't believe that damned plant is going to outlive me."

"No, it won't. It's part of this ship. There's no way to get it out now. When they pull apart the ship to wrestle the black hole out, the plant will die."

"It's your wife's plant."

"It was part of my promise to her, never to talk to anyone again. After that, it was part of my memory of her." He sighed and looked up. "I'll take a cutting of it with me and replant it. You shouldn't discard memories. Especially good ones."

"Am I a good one?"

"The best. Thank you for coming with me."

"Thank you for rescuing me, though I didn't want to be rescued."

"Let's go collect our money and get ourselves a nice apartment."

"You are such a dreamer, Max Getty. I'm not going anywhere but a hospital for the terminally old."

"And you are a cranky woman, Maureen O'Shea. Cranky. Now come on. I hear there's a place on this station with more than three small rooms. Even a window where you can watch the Earthrise behind the Moon. I'll get you some new teeth so you can chew food."

She smacked him in the arm like she always did.

Max lifted Maureen and carried her from the ship as torch men began cutting the hull away from the black hole. They both looked back more than once.

Maddy Dune's First and Only Spelling Bee

written by

Patrick O'Sullivan

illustrated by

MEGHAN MURIEL

ABOUT THE AUTHOR

It didn't take long for aliens to find Patrick O'Sullivan and spirit him away from his St. Louis birthplace for hours at a time. If not for Andre Norton and the crew of the The Solar Queen, he might still be earthbound instead of in seat 5D, the elbow of his pencil-wielding left arm blocking the serving cart.

A software engineer and technology entrepreneur, Patrick is always on the move; one day on Arrakis, the next in Virginia, a few hours on Cyteen, then off to Dublin or Helm's Deep or Saganami Island or the Florida Keys or someplace new he's never been, like in print. This is his first published fiction, though he has written more than a roomful of technical documentation over the years (which might explain why he has to keep moving). Patrick never throws anything away even if he doesn't use it; the BS in engineering, the MA in Irish studies, they're both under this stack of printouts somewhere.

If he ever grows up, he'd like to see one of his novels spirit others away to alien worlds of adventure. He's been studying with the best, trying to discover the alchemical magic that will make it happen. *Every moonlit signpost, every manuscript written in blood seems to hint at the same formula: one part Writers of the Future, n parts elbow grease, just add readers and stand back.*

If n is a number short of infinity and the flight attendants keep the aisle clear, he might just work that magic. Eventually.

ABOUT THE ILLUSTRATOR

Art was Meghan Muriel's first talent. As early as age two, she would surprise her mother with sketches of horses running on and off the page, as if the images were snapshots taken of a much larger scene. Since then, pencil, pen and ink and acrylics have been her media of choice for illustrating all of the fantasy and science fiction stories she conceived and wrote down in her journal.

After high school, however, she put aside her artistic skill to pursue a degree in creative writing, and only after a ten-year hiatus did she dust it off again, when her husband, a Marine officer, came home from a tour in Iraq and announced that they should cowrite a children's midgrade fantasy adventure about a wily white weasel who is a professional kat herder in the magical land of OCKT (the acronym stands for "Overly Curious Kritters and Things"). The world turned out so fantastical and the characters so zany that she adopted a new medium: multimedia collage, targeting a colorful synergy of fantasy and reality. A set of these interior illustrations went on to place Finalist twice in a row in the Illustrators of the Future Contest before her current win. Meghan has also done sketches for the website of the popular talk show Coast to Coast AM, *and she has semipro sales, both in writing and illustration, in the webzine* NewMyths. *To this day, Meghan has no formal education in art, but believes firmly that with passion and the right drive, one can translate a thousand words into one heck of a killer picture.*

40

Maddy Dune's First and Only Spelling Bee

Maddy leaned her weight into the massive door of St. Anselm's Orphanage and shoved. It shoved back.

"Isn't anyone going to help me with this?" Her ridiculous family shuffled their collective feet.

"I don't like the smell of this place," Uncle Leo said. He mounted the stairs with a rolling, wobbling gait, as if he were still parading the quarterdeck of a ship.

"I don't like the looks of it." Emma mounted the stairs as well, basket in hand. Maddy's sister ran a gloved fingertip across the door latch. "Rather shabby." She pursed her lips and studied the resulting grime.

"Kill them all," her brother Rookhaven croaked. He hopped once on Maddy's shoulder before he hammered his gray-black beak thrice against the door.

"Do you have anything to add, Madame Aubergine?" Maddy said. Her father's familiar sprawled languorously in the basket Emma carried. The blue-black cat knotted a paw and steel claws gleamed in the dim lamplight. Madame Aubergine began to clean the fur between her toes.

A key scratched in the lock and hinges grated in the damp evening. The gas lamp above the doorway gave body to the shadows as the door moved inward a hand's breadth.

A rusty voice called out, "State your name and purpose."

"Maddy Dune, here for the Spelling Bee."

There was the sound of rustling papers, of labored breathing, of a pen scratching on parchment.

"No Maddy Dune listed."

"Madeleine Dune," Maddy said. "Of Mundane House."

"We have a Madeleine Oortsgarten-Quille."

"That's me," Maddy said. Adopted daughter of Eusebius Quille and Nadine Oortsgarten, both away on business. That Quille was away seemed bearable; when he was home, he was never fully there. But Nadine. She had promised to be here for the Spelling Bee. She had given her word.

"Very well." The door crept open with a squeal. "You may enter this way if you wish, but the human entrance is . . . Oh. How . . . extraordinary. Of course you must come this way."

Maddy swallowed the lump in her throat and clutched her purse tight in her fist.

Uncle Leo caught her sleeve. "You don't have to go in there."

Emma brushed a tear from Maddy's cheek. "You're as human as the rest of us."

"I'll look for you in the audience," Maddy said. She

squeezed her uncle's hand. She stood on her tiptoes and kissed her sister's cheek. She ran her fingers through Madame Aubergine's luxurious fur.

Rookhaven caught her earlobe and pulled her close. "Kill them all."

"I'll settle for outspelling them," Maddy said. She didn't have to listen to that little voice inside of her that whispered loudly enough for her brother to hear. She didn't have to kill them all.

Very few half-castes enter the contest," Sister Kale said. She was seated behind a table, processing Maddy's entry form.

"I see." Maddy shifted in her seat. Half-caste. She hadn't heard that one before. "I'm—"

"Don't tell me," Sister Kale said. "Let me guess." She studied Maddy as if she were viewing a beast in a menagerie.

Maddy stared back, examining a point on the wall behind the sister. From a distance, Maddy could be taken for a thirteen-year-old girl. Up close, people could see the truth. That's when they stepped back. All except Nadine. This would be so much easier if her mother were here. But she wasn't. Even though she promised.

"Red eyes . . . that glow," the sister said. "They don't belong in such a pretty face. Show us your teeth, girl."

Absolutely not. "My birth-mother was a Spectral Hound," Maddy said. "Captain Leonides Farrago and . . . my new family . . . they rescued me from crypto-naturalist pirates off the coast of Ghula."

"I asked you not to tell."

"You'd already guessed." Maddy chewed her lip and tried to imagine being elsewhere. Anywhere else.

"Yes, well. Near enough, I suppose." Sister Kale leaned forward. "Now show us those teeth like a good little beast-girl."

Maddy crossed her arms and glanced at Sister Kale. "I fail to see what this has to do with my entry in the Spelling Bee."

"Your eyes burn with an inner fire. I can see the flames," Sister Kale said. "How extraordinary!" She waved her hand. "Sister Blue, you really must see this. Sister Agnes—"

"Please," Maddy said. "The announcement said the contest is open to any student in Arduvulin City in the seventh through ninth books and—"

"Yes, of course," Sister Kale said. "But we so rarely get to examine such a . . . It's—"

"Outlandish," Sister Blue said. She examined Maddy's ears. "Though these seem nearly normal, Sister Kale."

"Uncanny," Sister Agnes said. She coiled a lock of Maddy's black hair around her fingers. "It is very fine. Not at all like fur. Get undressed, girl."

Maddy brushed the woman's hands away. "I will not."

"We need to know if you've dugs like a hound, or—"

Maddy growled and the sisters jerked back. She could kill them all. Except she had promised her mother. And Maddy kept her promises. Even if no one else did. "I'd like to go now and take my place," Maddy said, "for the Spelling Bee."

An officious-looking sister passed in the hallway

outside, shouting, "Five minutes, sisters! We need all the contestants on the stage now!"

The three sisters kept their distance. That always happened with people. Eventually. Maybe if she won the Spelling Bee, people would start treating her like a human. Maybe Nadine would forgive her, whatever it was she had done. She must have done something, otherwise Nadine would be here.

She wasn't going to win anything sitting in this chair. Maddy stood. "Right, which way is the stage?"

Maddy didn't expect there to be so many contestants. There were at least three dozen seated on the stage. Maddy took a seat near the back, next to a large cabinet of extravagantly carved mahogany. It was really quite an odd bit of furniture, taller than a tall man, wide as a parlor sofa in all directions and carved in a lattice so fine it was hard to see what was inside. Maddy was pressing her forehead to the cabinet, trying to see in when the referee called out.

"All rise for Its Royal Highness, Emperor of the Fogbound Realm, Sovereign of Arduvulin. Long may It reign."

There was a great deal of noise from the audience, some of it clapping. Maddy tried to find her family, but her view was blocked by a carved cabinet very much like the one next to her, but considerably larger, being carried on the bent backs of a dozen liveried men. As the cabinet passed, the noise of the audience grew louder until the cabinet was placed on a dais near the stage.

"My esteemed parent," the cabinet next to her said. "Doesn't It cut an imposing figure?"

"What?"

"Its Royal Highness," the cabinet said. "Clearly you've not met It before."

"No," Maddy said. "I don't—"

"Very few do," the cabinet said. "I am Its Royal Tanist. Its . . . progeny. You may call me Tan, Miss—"

"I, um," Maddy said. "I thought Its Royal Highness was so loathsome in visage that—"

"It needs spend Its days locked in the Nonesuch Palace," the cabinet next to her said. "Or in a box."

Maddy's cheeks burned. "I beg your pardon. I didn't—"

"Very few do," Tan said.

Maddy's tongue felt a dozen feet thick. "Your Royal—"

"Shhhh," Tan said. "It begins."

"But—"

"Quiet, please," Tan said. "If I'm to win, I need to know the rules."

If Maddy was to win, she needed to know the rules as well. She was going to win. Then Nadine would have to forgive her for whatever she had done.

"Attention," a man in the yellow and black costume of the Spelling Bee said. "We shall begin. The rules are simple. One must work one's spells unaided. One must complete one's spell correctly. One must not raise the dead or engage in sorcery of any kind. Bonus points will be awarded for originality, flair and emotional congruence."

"That's it?" Tan said. "This should be cake."

"Right," Maddy said. She surveyed the contestants. With the exception of two or three, they were all eighth or ninth book. She was just beginning seventh.

And they were all fully human. All except the creature in the cabinet next to her. Maddy shivered. "Cake."

"Algernon Adovado," the referee called, and a slope-shouldered boy of fifteen or sixteen marched to stand on an X marked near the center-front of the stage. He swallowed once and bobbed his head when asked if he was ready.

The first-round spells were trivial: make Greek Fire, shatter a wall of stone with sound, compose music from the murmuring of the audience. Tan had to do that one, and it was a strange and haunting song he produced, full of feelings that Maddy didn't like to think about, a single heart beating in a dusty corridor, the steps of a lone pilgrim across rainy cobbles, the creak of an empty chair, in an empty room, in an empty house. Now that she had, thought about them, that is, it was hard to concentrate. She looked for her family in the audience and found them. Rookhaven was perched on Uncle Leo's tricorner hat, peering to and fro. Madame Aubergine curled in Emma's lap. Leo waved when Maddy caught his eye. Emma cheered when Maddy was called to work her spell.

"Create the illusion of galloping horses."

Maddy repeated the challenge, stalling for time. "Create the illusion of galloping horses."

"That is correct."

Great. Quille had horses; they pulled a vast carriage and walked a stately mile. Uncle Leo had dray horses to haul the great wagons that trundled trade goods from warehouse to shipside. Maddy had never seen nor heard horses galloping. Except she had. When she was with her birth-mother, before she was stolen away. Maddy tried to recall the experience, but she had been a child. A very young child. She could either rely on the flawed recollection of a toddler or be eliminated in the first round.

Maddy began. From the crowd she drew the sounds of hammering hooves, the scent of harness and lathered flesh. She had some loose change in her pocket; it provided the essence of harness jingling. There was a draft in the great hall; Maddy channeled it to her purposes, amplifying it, bending it in on itself and converging it. The crowd grew louder as they felt the horses stream by. She added the sound of the hounds, her birth-mother's cries, her uncles and aunts of the pack. Maddy closed her eyes and refined, accenting and augmenting the vibrations in the air. She compressed the moisture of spent breath, building misty shapes of cloud. The crowd noise rose. She added the half-heard cries of the Huntsman and his pack. She amplified the scent of fear, the rush of unharvested grain against the thighs of the prey, the welling tears of terror, the whimper of despair. Maddy twisted and bent sound, and scent and touch; the grasping fingers of wind, the stumbling gait of the man, the twist of the backward glance, the leap, jaws open for the throat.

There. That was galloping horses. She opened her eyes.

The hall was empty, or so it seemed at first. Uncle Leo was standing in the aisle, cutlass drawn. Rookhaven flapped overhead, crying, "Kill them all, kill them all." Emma sat in her seat and smiled at Maddy, Madame Aubergine curled in her lap. A ring of men blocked her view of Its Majesty; their muskets were aimed at Maddy. The remaining audience crowded the exits, struggling to escape the hall. The stage was empty except for Tan's ornately carved cabinet, the curtain behind the stage torn down. A dozen Sisters of St. Anselm poured forth, burnished helms on their brows. Sister Kale held them back with a slash of her broadsword.

"The illusion of galloping horses," Maddy said. She pressed her palms against her face. She bit her lip. A tear ran down her cheek.

"There will be a short intermission," the referee said.

Maddy paced back and forth while the chaos she'd wrought was put to rights. Where was Nadine? She'd promised. Maddy didn't know what to do. She needed supervision. Now.

"That was fantastic," Tan said. "They ask for galloping horses and you give them the Wild Hunt."

Maddy slapped the cabinet before she remembered it held the heir to the throne. "Oh, no, sorry, Your Royal—"

"Tan," the cabinet said. "And that was truly spectacular, Maddy Oortsgarten-Quille. I see now why you didn't want to tell me your name."

"It's Maddy Dune," Maddy said. "Professor Quille and Detective Inspector Oortsgarten had no hand in the mess I've made."

"Oh, I wouldn't be so sure," Tan said. "They say Quille is the greatest enchanter who ever lived. Surely he taught you a thing or two."

Maddy laughed. "I can't understand half of what he says."

"The Detective Inspector—"

"Promised she'd be here for me," Maddy said. "I don't know what I did to anger her. I'm trying my best." They nearly had the audience settled back into their seats and the stage backdrop re-erected.

"Perhaps her duty called her away," Tan said.

"Not without saying something," Maddy said. "She's not that way."

"What way?" Tan said.

"Undependable," Maddy said. "That's my department." Maddy bit her nails as a sister herded a half dozen of the audience back to their seats. "I need her."

"Perhaps you only think you do," Tan said.

"Look around, man," Maddy said. She tried to peer into the cabinet.

"Please don't," Tan said. "Look, that is. Name me man anytime you wish. Few do, you know."

"Your . . . um, Tan—"

"Shush. As for the rest, you were asked to complete a task. You did. Better than anyone could have imagined."

"I scared the hell out of them," Maddy said.

"We do that just by being," Tan said. "Trust me. I know."

"That song you made. It was beautiful," Maddy said. It looked like the judges were taking their seats.

"I'm glad you liked it," Tan said. "I made it for you."

At the end of the second round there were only six left: two boys from the Cosmopolitan Day School, two Acolytes of the Sisters of St. Anselm, Tan and Maddy. The challenges were more difficult, focused on the enchantment of objects: make a chair dance, cause a clock to run backwards, that sort of thing. Maddy was weakest here. Such enchantments used up the enchanter's life force, aging them in the process. Her adoptive father, Eusebius Quille, refused her access to his library on permanent spells, and only the most trivial were covered in the seventh book. Maddy could make a broom sweep on its own accord; that was the limit of her skill.

Tan was challenged to ring the bells of St. Anselm's. He did, playing the same song he had played earlier. That tune of loneliness rang out across the city, and when Maddy dried her eyes, she found she wasn't the only one weeping. A single bell toned on, in time with her beating heart.

When her turn came, the audience was already headed for the exits. The referee looked at her and shook his head. He smiled when he read the challenge.

"Make a broom sweep on its own accord." A grim-faced sister darted out and handed Maddy a willow broom before she dashed away, stage left.

"Make a broom sweep on its own accord," Maddy said. She held the broom at arm's length. It was far from the best broom she had ever seen. It didn't look up to the task.

"That is correct."

Maddy watched the broom move back and forth like the clapper in a bell. She would make it to the third round, but it would be a hollow victory. The judges were afraid of her. They'd given her child's play to assuage their own fear. She was so tired, so very tired of being feared. That was the root of her loneliness. Only Nadine didn't fear her. That was why she needed her. Where was Nadine? The sound of the broom scratching across the stage tore at her. Surely there was something . . . Maddy stretched her consciousness out. She reached up and up, and there, she found them, the bells of St. Anselm's, still vibrating to Tan's song. She knew that song now, every note. She had been born with it playing in her heart. She tolled the bells slowly, in time with her sweeping broom. The sound resonated in her, stirring up memories she'd rather not think about. Somewhere there had to be an answer to that song, an antidote to the feeling that poured through her.

Maddy closed her eyes. She needed Nadine. If her mother were here, she wouldn't have to be afraid. Maddy imagined that, and slowly the music changed. Tan's song was still there, but another tune entwined it. It danced around it, holding it, not fighting it but redirecting it, answering it, an answer that negated the very question itself. There was no need for Tan's song, not really. It didn't have to be. Tan's song existed, there was no denying it. But it didn't need to linger there alone. Maddy knew that in her heart. Knew it now. She willed the bells to silence. She willed the broom to still. When she opened her eyes, she wasn't standing on the X. She was very far stage-right, the broom in her arms. She felt her face flush an instant before the crowd burst into applause. She'd been dancing with a broom.

You dance quite well," Tan said.

Maddy felt her face burn. "I had no intention of dancing."

"So much of what we do is without intent," Tan said. "I've been thinking of your mother."

"So have I," Maddy said. "She's never lied to me before."

"What makes you think she has in this case?" Tan said.

"She promised to be here, and she isn't." Maddy leaned her back against Tan's cabinet.

"I watched you dance," Tan said. "Did you learn those steps on your own?"

"Yes," Maddy said. "No. I don't know."

"Maddy," Tan said. "May I tell you a secret?"

"Must I keep it?" Maddy pressed her palms against the cabinet.

"I hope not," Tan said.

"What is it?" Maddy leaned her cheek against the finely carved wood.

"That song I wrote for you?" Tan said. "It was the only song I knew. Until today."

Maddy pressed her forehead against the cabinet and closed one eye. Perhaps then, she might see.

"Don't," Tan said. "I beg you."

Maddy jerked away as if the cabinet were on fire. "Very well, Your Highness." She stalked away to find a drink of water. By the time she had found a sister, they were calling for third round. Only an Acolyte of the Sisters of St. Anselm, Tan and Maddy had made it through.

Project your happiest memory," the referee said. This was the same challenge the Acolyte had received. That girl's memory was of playing with a clowder of kittens in the straw, only the image of a sister with a sack and the dunking pond in the distance marring the final moments.

Maddy studied the audience. They leaned forward in their seats. Uncle Leo sat back, his arms crossed, his face dark. Emma shook her head no. Madame Aubergine was awake. She stared intently at Maddy. Rookhaven hopped from foot to foot. Maddy didn't need to hear him to know his words. She searched the crowd for Nadine. Her mother had broken her word.

"Project my happiest memory," Maddy said.

"That is correct."

She studied the crowd. So easily swayed. They crawl before the Wild Hunt. They swoon before the dancing broom-girl. She glanced toward Tan's cabinet. She couldn't see inside. He wouldn't allow it. How bad could it be? Her prince had no idea what ugliness was.

"Very well."

Maddy was in her cage on the deck of the *Polyphemus*. It reeked of fear and waste. The sails were burning. Another ship was drawn alongside, grappling hooks holding the two together while men clambered aboard. The sorcerer who had bound her threw spells like rays of black sun fire about as a sure-footed woman leapt to the deck. Nadine Oortsgarten drew her sidearm. Around her men shriveled and burned.

A clumsy man followed her aboard, but when his feet struck wood, it was as if he were rooted to the spot. Eusebius Quille slammed his ashplant to the deck and the *Polyphemus* shuddered. Maddy howled and beat herself against the bars of the cage. The sorcerer turned his attention to Quille. Black fire burned in the sky, arcing upward, falling in sheets toward Quille only to pour around him and fall away in dark, burning sheets.

Maddy was distracted. Another man was boarding, a golden man with cutlass flashing and a young woman, parasol in hand, carrying a blue-black cat. Maddy bashed herself against the bars of her cage. A dark bird fluttered overhead. Maddy licked her lips and waited.

Captain Leonides Farrago carved a path through the crew with his cutlass. The smell of blood was past bearing. Maddy pounded again and again against her cage, and then Emma, the girl with the parasol, had her hand on the latch. Emma didn't see him, Maddy's guard, the one who had promised to do things to Maddy after she had her first blood, who whispered to her in the night, who petted her, laughing deep in his throat. Now he crept toward the girl, his steps behind her drowned in the cries of dying men. Madame Aubergine was a blue-black whirlwind, razor claws shredding the guard's face as he raised the boarding ax above his head. Emma turned at the sound, a fluid motion that terminated with a discharged pistol and a fountain of gore. Maddy licked her lips and howled. The bird Rookhaven alighted on the bars overhead. Maddy watched him and waited as Emma unlatched the door to her cage.

"Kill them all," Rookhaven crowed. Maddy's heart soared as her feet hit the deck.

Nadine pressed the muzzle of her handgun against the forehead of the sorcerer and fired. The undead thing blinked once before he shook his head and laughed. He was still laughing when Quille slammed him to the deck with a transfixion spell. Nadine worked the Undeath Hood over the sorcerer's head before he had a chance to stand. He was standing again by the time she actuated the plunger that sucked the hood tight about his skull and kept on shrinking.

Maddy paused long enough to bark out a cry of joy before she barreled down the companionway to the crew's quarters. He was here, somewhere, hiding among the other creatures too weak or insufficiently willful to earn a cage. A cage where the men could prod and tease her every moment of the day. Maddy could smell him. Maddy could see him, hiding between two packing crates. He discharged a pistol as Maddy advanced. The ball whizzed past her ear. She could taste his fear. Maddy smiled at the man who had stolen her away from the hunt. Maddy longed for the feel of his throat between her teeth. She burned for the taste of his pain.

That was where they found her, her new family. Even then, no one had the nerve to come near. Except Nadine. The Detective Inspector clapped the man in irons. Captain Farrago inched forward and dragged him away.

Maddy licked Nadine's blood-soaked hand and arched her back in contentment. She was safe. Safe and free.

Maddy faced the crowd, and for once, she didn't stifle the growl that swelled inside her.

"My happiest memory," Maddy said. Maddy bared her teeth. She imagined her fangs shone like ivory in the stage light.

No sound was to be heard but a young girl's soft sobbing.

Tan's cabinet was pulled carefully forward and positioned on the X.

"Project your happiest memory," the referee said.

"Certainly," Tan said.

A ruby-eyed girl danced with a broom. She moved as if she knew his every thought, as if together they shared that dark knowledge of the cage he was born to wear.

When the referee called the Acolyte of the Sisters of St. Anselm's for the fourth round, she ignored him. She sat, back to the audience, rocking side to side and whispering.

The referee placed his hand on the young woman's shoulder. "Really, miss—"

She turned, tears streaming down her face. "I brought them back." She stood. A moist and rotted sack dripped murky water onto the stage. "See?"

"You brought what back?" the referee said.

"The kittens," the Acolyte said, "from my happy day."

The bag had begun to writhe as if something large and powerful were trying to break loose. The referee stepped back. He jerked his head toward the opposite side of the stage. "We'll just put that over here." A half dozen sisters picked up their helms.

The sack twisted and made a tearing sound and the scent of corruption poured forth. A claw pushed out, then another. If those were kitten claws—

"Kill them all, kill them all," Rookhaven croaked. He swooped overhead just as the bag parted and its contents flopped out onto the floor. Not kittens. Grimfoxes. A half dozen of them. They swarmed the

Acolyte and the sack fell from her hand to transform, melding into the stage, shifting to open a black pool of emptiness. A withered hand gripped the edge of that black portal, then another. Someone was coming through. Something. The Acolyte had worked sorcery and raised the dead.

"Maddy, step back," Nadine said.

"Mom?" Maddy twisted around. Nadine's voice was coming from Tan's cabinet.

"I'm coming out," Nadine said. A crack appeared in the cabinet. It grew in size, a door, then the sound of the crowd made Maddy look away. The sorcerer was free of the portal-sack. He rained black fire on the audience almost casually as he made his way toward the cabinet of Its Royal Highness. A musket volley tore across the stage. Several balls struck the sorcerer and one might have struck Maddy if Nadine hadn't tackled her and pulled her down.

"What are you doing here?" Maddy said.

"I promised you," Nadine said. "And someone needed to guard Its Royal Tanist. A last-minute assignment." Nadine unholstered her handgun and unclipped the Undeath Hood from her belt. "Your father is with Its Royal Highness."

"Mom—"

"Stay back, Maddy." Nadine clambered to her feet. She cocked her firearm.

The sorcerer rained death down on the musketeers. They shriveled and burned in his dark fire.

"Mom—"

"Wait here, Maddy," Nadine said. "I'll be back in a moment."

More creatures were coming through the portal

now, Gray Men and Uncle Leo and Emma had their hands full.

There was nothing but a pile of well-picked bones where the Acolyte had been. The grimfoxes disappeared, one by one, through the cracked door of Its Royal Tanist's cabinet.

Maddy darted into the cabinet and kicked the door shut with her heel. She didn't need anything else sneaking up on her.

Tan was surrounded by grimfoxes. They shied away, unwilling to approach him closer. Yet. Maddy couldn't blame them. He burned from head to toe with a crimson flame that flickered and danced.

"Maddy, stay back," Tan said. "I told you not to look."

"You're beautiful," Maddy said.

"They can't hurt me," Tan said.

"They can hurt anyone," Maddy said. Grimfoxes were pure, cunning evil, shades of vile men too weak for sorcery, but too strong to die.

One of the grimfoxes noticed her. Then another.

"Maddy, go now," Tan said. "Leave. Hurry."

"No," Maddy said. Three of the grimfoxes were trying to get behind her. "Not without you."

"I can't go out there," Tan said.

"I can see that," Maddy said. One look at Tan and everyone in the crowd would feel as dirty and half-made as she did when they looked at her.

"Maddy—"

"There's only one thing to do." Maddy swallowed. "You may not want to watch."

"Kill them all," Rookhaven cried. He'd landed on Tan's cabinet. Tan's cage. "Kill them all."

MEGHAN MURIEL

"I'm sorry," she said. "It's what I was made for."

"No, it's not," Tan said. "Trust me. I know."

Rookhaven flapped away when Maddy growled. It wasn't just Maddy in the cage this time. This wasn't just another sick game. Someone needed her. Tan needed her. Needed her to kill them all.

There was no fifth round.

Maddy tried to sit up, but her Uncle Leo's strong arms stopped her. "You need to rest."

Eusebius Quille leaned on his ashplant and smiled. "Well done, daughter."

"A professional job, Sis." Emma patted Maddy's bandaged hand. Only Maddy's fingertips stood proud of the bandages.

Madame Aubergine padded on Maddy's pillow before she circled twice and settled in for a nap. Maddy felt at home in her room at Mundane House for the first time ever.

"Shoo, all of you," Nadine said. "I need to speak with my daughter."

They all left, except Madame Aubergine, who cracked an eye and settled back in, purring loudly.

"Maddy—"

"You were there for me," Maddy said. "That's all that matters. I'm sorry I doubted your word."

"I couldn't speak," Nadine said. "Anyone . . . Anything might have heard."

"I know that," Maddy said. "Now."

"Maddy—"

"I don't see how you can do it," Maddy said. "I can't think of anything else."

"Do what?"

"Guard Tan," Maddy said. "And then come back to the world."

"Its Tanist has . . . a winning personality. He's quite witty, and . . ."

"He burns like fire, Mother."

"Does he?" Nadine swallowed. "Quille does much the same, you know. For me."

"What does Tan look like to you?"

"Well," Nadine said. "I try not to look."

"Nadine—"

"Shush, dear heart, and listen." Nadine took Maddy's bandaged hand in hers. "Its Royal Highness and Its Tanist are cursed. When we look into their eyes we see our souls reflected."

"But he burns!" Maddy closed her eyes and remembered. "He burns with a magnificent fire."

Nadine's lips touched Maddy's forehead. "I have no doubt, daughter." She squeezed Maddy's fingers gently and touched her hair. "Who could help but love such a one?"

The door to Maddy's room opened and closed quietly when Nadine left. It opened and closed again shortly thereafter.

"Maddy?" Tan's voice was tentative and soft. Gentle fingers of fire touched her hand. Soft lips of flame brushed one fingertip, then another.

Maddy opened her eyes. Her room was lit with an endless, burning light.

Rookhaven landed on Tan's shoulder. He tugged on Its Tanist's blazing earlobe thrice and croaked out Maddy's inner thoughts, the ones she didn't dare voice. "Kiss them all! Kiss them all!"

62

"I will, bird," Tan said, "in time." Tan's lips brushed Maddy's fingertips and she felt an answering flame in her heart. "For now, two will have to do. Your well-armed relatives insist that Maddy needs her rest."

"I really don't," Maddy said.

"You do if you wish to join me for lunch tomorrow. There's a small ceremony, where I'm to pass the Spelling Bee Trophy to this year's champion. Apparently spelling grimfoxes back to hell earns a tremendous bonus in flair points."

"I could have killed them all," Maddy said. "But I didn't want to ruin my dress."

"A plausible story, Maddy Dune," Tan said. "We'll come up with a better one tomorrow."

"Or the next day," Maddy said.

"Or the day after that," Tan said.

"This could take forever," Maddy said.

Tan blazed with a brighter flame when the pounding on the door began. "All right, I'm coming out! Avert your eyes."

"See you tomorrow, Tan," Maddy said.

"Right," Tan said. "I like the sound of that."

"Me, too," Maddy said. "So get used to it."

The Truth, from a
Lie of Convenience

written by

Brennan Harvey

illustrated by

IRVIN RODRIGUEZ

ABOUT THE AUTHOR

Brennan Harvey has always enjoyed science fiction. The television shows Star Trek *and the movie* Beneath the Planet of the Apes *are two of his earliest SF memories. When a friend loaned him Robert Heinlein's novel* Friday, *Brennan started reading science fiction regularly. Years later, Mike Resnick's short story "Kirinyaga" ignited his desire for writing.*

In high school, Brennan's talent for writing was first recognized. He won a certificate for "composing an exceptional article for the CDC bulletin." In college, an English professor was impressed with Brennan's storytelling and submitted one of his short stories to the campus newspaper.

Brennan began writing fiction in 1998. He took creative writing classes and attended workshops, seminars, conventions and conferences. Brennan's first short story "In the Service of Others" was a Finalist in the L. Ron Hubbard Writers of the Future Contest in 2004. In the first quarter of this volume, his persistence finally paid off when he won first place. "The Truth, from a Lie of Convenience" is his first professional sale.

He finished his first novel EVE320 in 2009 and is currently working on his third novel, an untitled space opera.

Brennan lives in Huntington Beach, California. He is the organizer of the Long Beach Writers Meetup Group, a critique group in southern California. Brennan volunteers for the Southern California Writers Association and the online critique group SFNovelist.com.

ABOUT THE ILLUSTRATOR

Irvin Rodriguez was born in the Bronx, New York, the second youngest of five children. He was shown at an early age the value of hard work and creativity by his father. Pencil in hand, Irvin took on the world one drawing at a time, honing his skills the only way he knew how, drawing everything he could get his hands on.

The high school years were endured grudgingly until the day he met a friend who taught him how to airbrush and gave him his first job getting paid to make art. This experience expanded his knowledge of the art world and gave him the confidence and ability to experiment with different media and let his creativity take over. In 2006, Irvin began college at FIT as an illustration major, where he spent the next four years developing his abilities with traditional and digital media. His traditional foundations were learned under the tutelage of the painters from The Grand Central Academy of Art and the Guild Atelier.

Irvin's imagination is an untamed place that pulses with new ideas and images every minute of the day. Most days are spent drawing, and so are his nights, which leave little time for sleeping and eating. Luckily for him, he eats pencils and you can sleep when you die. Irvin loves nineteenth-century painting and illustration, SF and fantasy art and has a soft spot for a portrait. He hopes to soon share his beautiful imagery and love for fantasy in the entertainment industry.

The Truth, from a
Lie of Convenience

Marianne Summers scanned her image in the third cueing holotank, ensuring her displayed 3-D image looked presentable. In the one-sixth gravity of the Moon, she didn't need to tease her hair to give it any lift, but she did adjust her breasts, pulling them together to emphasize her cleavage. It was a trick every female newscaster knew, and she might as well take advantage of the forgiving gravity in Luna City and the gift it gave to her forty-five-year-old body. This ceremony she was covering might only be a one-time gig to pay the bills, but she wasn't taking any chances. Anyone could be watching, and this job might lead to more work—or even a permanent position for a news blog or network vlog.

The reminder beeped in her headset and the director's voice came over the network channel. "Okay, everyone. Look sharp. Tommy, are you ready?"

"I'm ready," Tommy Rubner answered over the director's channel.

Something in his voice didn't seem right. Marianne hoped he was already outside in the air lock as he had rehearsed, waiting for his cue to approach the ruins, say his prepared speech and lay the ceremonial wreath at the memorial marker. She keyed his private channel on her headset and said, "Tommy, it's Marianne. Is everything okay?"

"Yeah, it's just . . . five years, you know."

"I know. That's why we're all here. Don't worry. You'll honor her memory just fine."

"Thanks."

He didn't sound any better. Marianne wanted to speak with him further, but the reminder in her headset beeped again, and she had to trust that he would come through.

She removed her headset and switched her attention to the blond anchorwoman's 3-D figure in the main holotank as she waited for her cue. Even on Earth, the newscaster's breasts were perky and showed ample cleavage. Marianne didn't want to be jealous, but young women were taking over the news business, even though they were inexperienced. A pretty face and a young body went further than skill and experience did nowadays.

The blond anchor said, "And continuing our live coverage from Luna City on the Moon, we have Marianne Summers." The main holotank shimmered as Marianne's image from the cueing tank transferred there.

"This is Marianne Summers with the fifth annual wreath-laying ceremony honoring the victims of Habitat Fourteen here in Luna City.

"Five years ago, radicals claiming to be fighting for Luna City's independence from Earth barricaded almost six thousand Luna City citizens into Habitat Fourteen and demanded political sovereignty. When negotiations stalled, they destroyed Habitat Fourteen, themselves and those unfortunate hostages. Here's footage from that tragic day."

The main holotank image shifted to a 2-D image of a semicircular, off-white dome framed in the center of a gray moonscape. At the zenith of the dome, a red beacon blinked at regular intervals.

As the image displayed, Marianne narrated, "Negotiations came to a standstill the night of May 9, 2062. Negotiators expected to try again the next morning. That attempt never took place." After a second of stillness on the video, the dome exploded in slow-motioned silence.

Marianne had seen the same video hundreds of times in the last five years. She watched as every seam in the geodesic half-dome split and the humid air inside vaporized into flashes of terrifying mist.

Twisting triangular panels spun like choreographed dancers in the silence. Fifteen seconds into the video she saw the famous severed arm, bent at the elbow like an obscene boomerang, spin toward the camera and finally disappear out of frame—the same arm that conspiracy theorists always pointed out shouldn't be bent like that.

The image changed to a slow pan around the face of a woman in a Luna City uniform. Marianne said, "Councilwoman Susan P. Rubner was one of the victims of that tragedy. Her husband, Thomas Rubner, is with us today and will lay the wreath at this year's memorial service."

The main holotank changed to a live, 3-D shot of the ruins of Habitat Fourteen. Although construction robots could have rebuilt the habitat dome in only six months, the Luna City Republic never repaired Habitat Fourteen. Moondust-based concrete was cheap to manufacture, and the material to grow the polymer-based windows was easy enough to transport to the Moon. However, the Luna City government insisted it wanted to keep the site unaltered—as a memorial to the first act of off-Earth terrorism.

"Cue Tommy," Marianne heard the director order over the network's private channel. A figure in a white pressure suit came into view and skipped across the Moon's surface to the ruins. The director called for a zoom in, and the figure grew large in the main holotank. Thomas Rubner's face was recognizable behind the helmet's polycarbonate face shield as the camera operator did an excellent job of keeping it framed through his awkward hop-skip across the Moon.

"He's not carrying the wreath," the camera operator said on the director's channel.

Marianne looked at the cueing tank and saw Tommy, empty-handed. She suspected that was why Tommy had sounded so strange. He seemed calm during the rehearsals this past week and was probably nervous now because he forgot the only prop he needed for the memorial service.

Marianne stared at the share meter, which held steady at twenty-two percent. She suspected that nobody on Earth had yet noticed that the wreath-layer had forgotten to bring a wreath to lay.

70

The director swore. "All right," she said, "keep the shot from the number two holotank. I want his face only. Bobby, get somebody suited up and get that wreath out to him."

The assistant director, Bobby, answered, "I don't know if any of the union guys are still around. Today is a lunar holiday."

"Find one. I don't care what you have to pay him."

"Why is he just standing there?" Chang, one of the camera operators, asked.

"He's probably realized he's screwed up," the director said. "Everything is going to be fine. Just get him that wreath."

"No," Marianne said. "He's supposed to brush dust off the plaque? He's forgotten what he's supposed to do."

Marianne keyed Tommy's personal channel again. "It's Marianne. Are you all right?"

"I'm fine."

"Are you sure? Do you remember what to do?"

"Yes. I remember."

"Nobody can do this with the same emotional impact that you can. You've lost someone special. Viewers on Earth want to see that emotion. Can you do it?"

"Yeah. I'm ready." He sounded calm, and Marianne relaxed a bit.

The director asked, "Where's the union guy with the wreath?"

"The wreath isn't in the suit-up room," Bobby answered.

Marianne saw her career dissolve in front of her.

She had to figure out a way to rescue this disaster. The share meter ticked down to twenty percent as the main holotank featured the motionless, speechless face of Thomas Rubner.

Marianne sighed in relief when Tommy began speaking.

"Five years ago, terrorists took control of Habitat Fourteen and demanded sovereign territory upon the Moon. I don't know of anyone who sat through those tense days that didn't worry and pray for the hostages. I did my share of both. My wife, Susan, was one of those five thousand, eight hundred and eighty being held captive. Everyone on Earth, in the space stations and on the Moon has seen the horrific end of that day.

"I'm standing here in the center of the ruins of Habitat Fourteen." The scene on the main holotank changed to an overhead view of the ruined half-dome. "It's been preserved here as a reminder. But, as a reminder of what? A reminder to be eternally vigilant. A reminder of human courage in the worst of times. A reminder to never give up in the face of adversity. That's what we've been told by the Luna City government.

"Tonight, five years after that catastrophic event, I would be honored to recognize the valiant Luna City administrators, who tried so hard to avoid this disaster. If any of what I just said were true."

"What does that mean?" the director asked over the network's channel.

"I don't know," Marianne said.

"I recently learned that Luna City officials rescued

some of the hostages and destroyed Habitat Fourteen themselves. All to increase their political power in this formerly apolitical city."

Oh, my God, Marianne thought. *Tommy doesn't believe that crazy conspiracy theory, does he?*

Tommy's face in the holotank looked remarkably calm. "This rumor has been circulating for years. And, like most of you, I dismissed it as paranoid nonsense at first. Luna City politicians wouldn't destroy billions of dollars' worth of equipment and murder thousands of innocent people just to wrestle power from Earth. It sounds ridiculous.

"But look at the effects of those actions five years ago. The Moon is now a political entity in and of itself. It's called the 'Lunar Republic.' Isn't that exactly what the terrorists wanted?

"But that's not what *really* convinced me. After last year's ceremony, I was walking along the hub in Luna City. That was the day I saw my wife, who supposedly died in the Habitat Fourteen explosion five years ago.

"So I volunteered to lay the wreath this year. But I want to speak with my wife, Susan P. Rubner, first."

Marianne glanced at the share meter. It read seventy-four percent. A seventy-four share represented at least five billion people on Earth tuning in to this broadcast. Five billion people tuning into this story, and she was in the middle of it.

A moment later, several Luna City Security officers burst into the broadcast booth, ordering everyone to put their hands up. As the officers unceremoniously shoved Marianne and the rest of the network staff out the door, she caught a quick glance at the main holotank. There was nothing there but static. The uplink to Earth was shut down.

As security locked the door behind them, Marianne's visor chirped. She fished it out of her backpack and slid it on.

"Hey, what's happening?" It was Roy Hinkley's avatar. He was the producer of the memorial show and had hired Marianne to travel to the Moon to cover it personally. Nobody else wanted to travel all the way to the Moon for a memorial piece, but she had bills to pay. He continued, "We're getting nothing but static from you guys."

"LCS just threw us out of the booth. Thomas Rubner started spouting that wacky Luna City conspiracy theory. Weren't you watching?"

"I was . . . preoccupied," Roy said. "Hang on . . ." She watched as Roy's avatar stared at her. She suspected that he was reviewing the video and pushed away her anger that he couldn't be bothered to watch the live broadcast.

After a moment, Roy whistled. "Susan Rubner's husband is a nutcase."

"I should have realized something was wrong. He was acting strange all week. Then, when he went out the air lock, he wasn't carrying the wreath."

"That conspiracy theory is ridiculous. He can't possibly believe it. I need you to get back on the air. Immediately."

"I'm working on it." She took off her visor just as three Luna City officials, escorted by more security, tramped down the hall, shoved past the network crew and stomped into the control room. Scowls and creased brows punctuated each of their faces. Marianne shouted a couple of questions to them as they stomped past, but they didn't answer.

She put on her headset and keyed Tommy's personal channel. He was speaking. "So you think you can silence me too? Keep me from telling the truth?"

She pressed the record button to capture the conversation.

Another voice answered back. It sounded like Captain Gerald Hail of Luna City Security. "Don't be so melodramatic, Mr. Rubner. You are, of course, welcome to your personal beliefs, no matter how unbelievable they are. However, I can't let you usurp our memorial service to espouse them."

Tommy said, "Then it wouldn't hurt for the people—"

Captain Hail interrupted, "You left the wreath in the air lock door jamb? Is this how you honor the victims that died here?"

Tommy's laugh crackled in her headset. "I guess you won't be able to leave the city that way. You'll have to go the long way around."

"Maybe my men will take their time. How much air do you have left, Mr. Rubner? My guess is not a lot, considering how much you've been running your mouth."

Marianne wondered if LCS might leave him out there until his air ran out. This story was developing into something stranger than she had expected. Her pulse quickened.

Captain Hail said, "Nothing more to say? Yeah, it's probably better if you ration your air."

IRVIN RODRIGUEZ

Tommy yelled, "I have plenty to say! About how a group of power-hungry bureaucrats murdered thousands of people just so they can wrestle power from the Earth Consortium. How they blamed it on fanatics and terrorists. How the newly formed Lunar Republic raised taxes and formed its own goon squad to hide the truth. How the goon leader is prohibiting free speech right now. Yeah, I have a lot to say."

Marianne willed Tommy to be quiet. Surely, he didn't believe the conspiracy theory that had sprung up on blogs and vlogs after the tragedy happened. No proof of a conspiracy had ever been discovered, but that didn't stop some people from holding on to those crazy ideas. During the week of rehearsals, Tommy had never struck her as one of those nuts.

Captain Hail said, "Your thinking is off, Mr. Rubner. The cause was the terrorist act. The effect was the Lunar Republic. Cause and effect. The Republic was formed after the explosion. Not the other way around."

"Yeah, terrorists smuggled twenty-five kilos of E-1 explosive past Earth customs, onto a Moon transport, past Luna City customs and across the *whole* base all the way to Habitat Fourteen. Hmmmm, I wonder why they didn't choose an easier target. Like the shuttle area itself, the Luna City council hub or the utilities spur."

Marianne had never thought about why the terrorists had chosen Habitat Fourteen. It was true that the terrorists would have had to transport the explosives past customs and throughout Luna City—probably over seven kilometers and past vital areas—just to get it to Habitat Fourteen. It was on the opposite side of the base from the shuttle area and customs inspection facilities.

She groaned. Now she was starting to see the conspiracy take form, too. "Not you too," she whispered to herself.

Captain Hail asked, "Who is on this channel?"

Marianne swore. She had hoped to record more of this conversation before breaking in to ask questions.

"This is Marianne Summers," she said carefully. "I'm the reporter for LNS and would like to ask Mr. Rubner a few questions. You said—"

"Clear this channel immediately!" Captain Hail said.

"—you saw a woman who you claim is your dead—"

"We are in the middle of a situation, here!" Captain Hail yelled. "Clear this channel now!"

"Tommy, you say you saw your dead wife. Would you care—"

Two Luna City Security officers burst out of the control room door and demanded she give them her headset.

"No," she answered back. "I'm a member of the free press."

They pointed their weapons at her and one of them ordered, "Give me the headset, ma'am."

She had been on the muzzle side of weapons several times in her career, but the needlegun that the guard pointed at her terrified her more than any others did. Their electromagnetic coils fired half-inch diameter polycarbonate flechettes that were often coated with sleeping agents—or sometimes poisons.

The flechettes wouldn't rupture a pressure wall or window if they struck one. It was a perfect weapon for a space station and a lunar outpost.

She carefully disconnected her headset and handed it to the officer. The other officers collected everyone else's headsets and disappeared back inside the control room.

She swore when she realized she hadn't downloaded the headset recording to her personal visor before it was confiscated. Without confirmation, any legitimate story was dead.

She grabbed Chang and asked him to follow her with his camera. She ran past the control room to the hallway where a series of oversize, triangular windows overlooked the ruins of Habitat Fourteen. In the distance, she could see a lone figure standing near the plaque.

"Can you zoom in on him?" she asked Chang.

"Sure." Chang raised the camera and began filming.

Marianne watched as Tommy continued to stand there. She wished she knew what he and Captain Hail were saying.

As she watched, she thought about the Luna City conspiracy. She had covered the conspiracy side of it for one of the tabloids she had a contract with at the time, but she never believed any of it herself. The most popular scenario was that the current Lunar Republic had purposely destroyed Habitat Fourteen and that the terrorist angle was merely a cover story. There had been no terrorist acts since the explosion in 2062 but even that was spun two ways. Conspiracy theorists claimed that the Republic had gotten what it wanted and didn't need to resort to further violence. The new Lunar Republic claimed that was because of the increased security that its police force wielded independent from Earth.

She and Chang watched for about ten minutes until three people in steel-gray spacesuits hopped into view and headed in Tommy's direction. The suits belonged to Luna City Security. The three people surrounded Tommy and inched closer. Tommy spun in place, then hopped-ran between two of them. The closest man cut him off as he attempted a one-sixth-G leap to avoid them. They caught him by the waist and hauled him in as the third security man helped secure him. Then, they escorted Tommy back to the air lock.

One of the officers picked up the wreath, carried it over to the plaque and set it down gently before returning to the air lock with the other officers and Tommy.

Marianne sat in the Luna City Security office waiting for an opportunity to speak with Captain Hail. Although she had spoken to a number of security officers regarding the altercation earlier—including the officer who had pointed his needlegun at her and confiscated her headset—none of them had any comment. It was frustrating, but perhaps after she spoke with their captain, the others might feel more comfortable speaking with her.

Although the bombing of Habitat Fourteen was still spoken of now and again on Earth, Marianne was learning that it was the stuff of legend here on the Moon. Everything in the city seemed to revolve around it, from the oversize viewing windows that overlooked the ruins to tours outside that required pressure suits. There was even a museum that sprang up along the main hallway that used to lead to Habitat Fourteen. It had started as an ad-hoc memorial and developed into a full-fledged historical remembrance. It was the most popular tourist destination in Luna City. Perhaps, she thought, when she was done here, she would pull together fifteen Luna dollars to tour the museum. She might find some back-story information that would interest the people back on Earth. Or, find another story that she could sell independent of this one.

She checked her watch and realized that she had been waiting for thirty minutes now. She stood, approached the security desk and told the officer behind the polycarbonate window, "I'm still waiting to speak with Captain Gerald Hail."

The officer shook his head. "He's still unavailable. Please be seated and he will be available presently."

"I'm getting the distinct feeling that I'm being put off. You recognize who I am, don't you?"

The officer looked straight at her. "Your name is Marianne Summers, a has-been reporter who is wasting my time. Have a seat, and Captain Hail will be out when he has a chance."

Marianne stomped away from the desk and back to her chair. The comment about her being a has-been reporter stung, partially because it was true. She hadn't had a steady job in over eight years, and her downfall from fame was so complete at this point in her life that she had agreed to travel all the way to the Moon and cover a routine memorial service just to pay some bills.

She waited another twenty-five minutes before a door that read "Luna City Security Personnel Only" hissed open and Captain Hail stepped out.

She stood in return. "It's about time."

Captain Hail said, "I'm sorry, Ms. Summers. I don't have the time to speak with you."

Marianne stared, flabbergasted. "I've been waiting for almost an hour, and now you're refusing an interview?" She smiled past her frustration. "This won't take long. I just need you to answer a few questions."

Captain Hail said nothing.

"Really," Marianne continued, "twenty minutes. Okay, ten minutes. Ten minutes is all I need."

"No," he said.

She could feel the blood flush on her face. She took a calming breath and said, "Captain Hail, this is most unfair. You've kept me waiting all this time. Now you're refusing to talk to me?"

Captain Hail remained silent.

She said, "I could get a subpoena. You can't refuse a legal request."

"You're welcome to try that," Captain Hail said evenly.

Marianne's instinct was working overtime. The captain was hiding something, and she felt that familiar desire overwhelm her—the desire to uncover what other people were trying to conceal.

"What about the headset that your officers confiscated from me earlier? I want that back."

Captain Hail nodded to the desk. Marianne heard

a rattle and then saw the access drawer slide open. Inside were a dozen headsets.

"If you could return the rest of them to the media control room personnel, it would be appreciated," Captain Hail said. The security door buzzed open, and he disappeared behind it.

Marianne gathered up the headsets with a huff and stormed out of the security office. She would have to check each headset to find which one she was using during the broadcast.

She found a secluded space in a nearby cafeteria and booted up the first headset. When she pressed the playback button, the headset chimed immediately. Nothing was recorded on it. She set it aside and tried another. Like the first one, it had nothing in its memory.

A knot grew in her stomach as headset after headset turned up empty. As she put on the final one, she felt a glimmer of hope, but it had nothing stored in its memory either. Luna City Security had erased everything. She wondered if security had downloaded the conversations before they erased them and made a note to ask Captain Hail. But she suspected that he and his men wouldn't give her the recordings even if they had them.

She wondered why Luna City Security would delete the conversations from the headsets. They were routine behind-the-scenes instructions and responses between the director and network crew used only to ensure the smooth operation of the broadcast. It didn't make sense. Unless, she reasoned, Luna City Security and the officials that followed them into the booth were trying to hide something. She felt that familiar tingle in her stomach. There was something here to uncover.

Since the Magistrate that Marianne needed to meet with was out of his office, she decided to visit the memorial museum in the hallway that used to lead to Habitat Fourteen. The first thing she noticed was the cleanliness of the museum. The rest of Luna City was starting to show signs of neglect. The walls that robot builders had constructed out of moondust and then bleached white were starting to turn gray in the joints and around the windows. Many hallways had visible scuff marks and even minor chips and abrasions. The whole city, except for this hallway, reminded her of a resort that had long ago lost its popularity.

But the Habitat Fourteen Memorial Hallway was still as pristine as it must have been when it was first constructed. It looked just like any other hallway in Luna City, with the exception of a mismatched wall blocking the destroyed end where multiple messages expressed love, sorrow and well wishes for the victims and their families. These messages included electronic pads connected to permanent power supplies, notes written with pen or pencil and art on primitive construction paper drawn by elementary school children.

Marianne read the first dozen notes with interest, then realized that they all basically said the same thing—you will be remembered, our prayers are with you and sorry for your loss. She skimmed over several others before she realized her actions were a perfect analogy of how Earth had lost interest in the Luna City tragedy. Overexposure of the same information led people to become numb to that information. The novelty of the event had worn off. The fear of visiting this city, however, had not. She thought about this and wondered if she could find something similar to pull readers into the story she was building.

Along the left wall, monitors offered videos, still-image pictures, paper photographs and news clippings. Marianne pressed the display picture on next to a sign that read, "The Final Moments of Habitat Fourteen." The monitor showed the famous, five-year old video that her director had also aired before the broadcast was shut down. An image of Habitat Fourteen, one moment perfectly intact with its red beacon flashing, the next moment the explosion and vaporized air escaping through each of the seams as the geodesic dome blew apart.

"You're that reporter that covered the memorial, right?" a man asked behind her.

It had been a long time since she had been recognized in public, but considering the population of Luna City and the memorial she had covered earlier today, it wasn't surprising someone might recognize her. "Yes, I'm Marianne Summers."

"I didn't appreciate you letting that nut on the air. We lost a lot of good people in that explosion. You had no right to denigrate our suffering."

Marianne held her hands in front of her as if to push the accusations away from her. She hadn't put Tommy on the air. Luna City had asked him to lay the wreath. "I understand," she said. "We didn't plan it. He brought up that conspiracy theory nonsense on his own. I was just as surprised as anyone."

"Well, I didn't appreciate it." The curator stared at

her for a moment, then returned to the hub-end of the hallway and sat behind his desk. His eyes never left her.

Great, Marianne thought, another unhappy viewer. She could imagine a whole slew of them back on Earth cursing her name as their holotanks went blank. This opportunity to work was turning out to be another black spot on her career.

She moved on to the next screen and pressed the play button. It was a history of Luna City and Habitat Fourteen in particular. After the Chinese CNSA landed their first three-man team on the Moon, NASA in the United States and ESA in Europe combined forces and announced plans to build a permanent settlement on the Moon within the decade. Within three years, the Russian RFSA, the Indian ISRO and the Japanese JAXA had joined them and a global consortium was born.

Remotely programmed robotic builders completed the first structure in 2040. After insuring Habitat One was airtight, three people set up the first permanent residence on the Moon. Over the following twenty years, that single dome had expanded to a seven-kilometer city with a centralized hub, fifteen habitat domes, a utilities spur and a spaceport.

Habitat Fourteen was started in 2058. Initially designed as one hundred, two- and three-person apartments with a central dining and recreation complex, it was built to consolidate several older Luna City housing facilities into one common area. Completed two years later, Habitat Fourteen became a sought-after place to live for mid-level technicians and workers.

Then, on the morning of May 9th, 2062, terrorists

destroyed Habitat Fourteen. The same footage of it blowing up started playing again, and Marianne walked away. She wondered how many of the presentations here contained that same footage.

One of the other displays on the opposite wall of the hallway was a 2-D monitor that offered biographies of the victims of the explosion. She pressed the play button underneath the monitor and a video essay for Major Randolph Young came up. When it was finished, another started. She watched several biographies in turn. The victims were a mishmash of people with various backgrounds, united in history by all being in the wrong place at the same time.

It was getting toward lunchtime so Marianne thanked the scowling curator and left, heading toward the cafeteria on the hub.

After lunch, Magistrate Melle asked her into his chambers. His huge hands engulfed hers when he pumped her hand vigorously. "Marianne Summers. I've followed your career for years."

Marianne hoped the Magistrate's large smile and enthusiastic greeting would help her get her interview. "It hasn't been much of a career lately, but thank you."

"Indeed, since the plagiarism charges, you have only been published in tabloid blogs and vlogs, am I correct?"

Feeling her chances slipping away, she said, "Yes." The tabloid work helped pay her bills, but probably harmed her already-soiled reputation as much as the false charges of plagiarism her executive producer at the National News Network made up twenty years ago. She said, "I was hoping this report of your memorial service might boost my career. What I mean to say is . . . most people of Earth don't truly appreciate the tragedy that happened here. The Moon is so far away from their everyday lives. What I had hoped to do was to illuminate your story within more legitimate blogs and vlogs. Luna City has a brief, but wonderful history, and what happened five years ago was horrific. The people of Earth need to be reminded of that."

"My aide tells me you wish to interrogate Captain Gerald Hail and Thomas Rubner."

"Interrogate is not the word I would use. What Thomas did warrants a slap on the wrist. He should have been released already, but Captain Hail is still holding him for some reason. I simply wish to interview both of them and find out why Mr. Rubner would be so disrespectful at such a solemn occasion."

"Ms. Summers, can't this wait until Mr. Rubner is released?"

"By that time, the story will have grown cold, Magistrate." He didn't say anything, and she wondered what else he might be deliberating. "Maybe I can put it another way. Just before the broadcast transferred up to the Moon, the network share meter was at twenty-two percent. After Thomas Rubner went off script, the share meter jumped to seventy-four percent. That's over four billion extra people from Earth watching the broadcast. That's a huge number of people, looking for information about Luna City.

"Then, the broadcast tanks went dead. The last thing those billions heard was about this conspiracy.

They need to know the truth. But they need to know it now, not a couple of days from now. In a couple of days, those conspiracy theories, like Thomas Rubner exposed last night, will continue to grow and tarnish Luna City's reputation."

Magistrate Melle seemed to regard her words for a few moments. He finally said, "What Thomas Rubner said was not flattering of the Lunar Republic."

"Exactly!" Marianne said. "He starts spouting this conspiracy theory junk. He claims his wife is still alive and demands to speak with her. Why?"

"Why, indeed."

"I can't figure that out! Is he insane? Where did he get those crazy ideas? Who or what polluted his thinking? But the longer this story waits, the more it will look like there really is some conspiracy keeping him quiet."

The Magistrate looked contemplative, and Marianne hoped she was starting to sway him.

She said, "Billions of people back on Earth need to know the truth. Luna City is safe. What has the tourism rate been here for the last five years? With new exposure, visitation would increase again. With more tourists would come increased revenues for suffering Luna City merchants. That translates to increased Lunar Republic revenues. It's a success for everyone in Luna City."

Without a word, the Magistrate crossed to his desk and typed onto his holographic keyboard. After a while, he finally said, "I am granting you permission to interview them. Captain Hail will be able to find my ruling online."

Marianne let out a grateful sigh. "Thank you, Magistrate. Thank you."

Marianne turned to leave when the Magistrate called to her, "Ms. Summers. I never doubted those plagiarism charges from NNN."

Marianne's heart sank.

The Magistrate added, "Until now."

Marianne thanked him again and left his office, heading down the hallways to Luna City Security with renewed hope in her heart. When she arrived, the same desk officer from earlier addressed her with annoyance. "Captain Hail has already told you. He's very busy."

Marianne smiled as she said, "I'm here to see Thomas Rubner. Magistrate Melle has issued a writ granting me permission to interview him. You should be able to verify it online."

With a scowl on his face, the officer tapped on his holo keyboard. After a moment, he said, "Have a seat." He disappeared behind a partition, returned minutes later and ignored her.

While she waited, she organized her questions for both Tommy Rubner and Captain Gerald Hail. Twenty minutes later, Captain Hail emerged from behind the "Luna City Security Personnel Only" door. She had beaten him, and with a legal writ, nothing could keep her from interviewing Tommy.

Marianne marched toward him with a grin plastered on her face. "Magistrate Melle has granted—"

He cut her off with a raised hand. "I know. Follow me." She followed him out of the Luna City Security office and around to the opposite side of the hub toward where the Magistrate's office was. She objected about being led away from the jails and Tommy a number of times along the way, but Captain Hail ignored her protests the whole time. When she finally saw the LED display over the archway where they were headed, her heart sank. It read "Medical Center."

She hoped Tommy would be coherent enough to speak with her and wondered what sort of injuries he had suffered during his tussle with the security guards out at the ruins.

A man in a white lab coat, who Marianne assumed was a doctor, greeted them. He said, "Captain, this is most unusual."

The captain nodded toward Marianne and said, "This is Marianne Summers. She has a legal writ to see Thomas Rubner."

The doctor looked confused, then nodded and said, "Follow me." Marianne followed the doctor with Captain Hail behind her. The doctor led them through another door that read "Authorized Personnel Only" and into an area bathed with ultraviolet light. He then led them to a gurney topped with a black body bag. The doctor unzipped the bag and pulled the flap away.

Even though the flesh was colored by the ultraviolet light of the morgue, Marianne recognized Tommy Rubner's body immediately.

Marianne headed to Chang's room in order to review the footage he shot of Luna City Security escorting Tommy away from the ruins of Habitat

Fourteen. When she pressed the announce button on his door, he didn't answer. She pressed again, longer this time, but he still didn't answer.

She headed to a cafeteria just off the hub and pulled up the Luna City Directory on the public terminal. The room that Chang had stayed in was listed as leasable and the software asked her if she would like to reserve the room. She declined and checked the departing shuttles from Luna City. A transport had left an hour earlier.

She called up the boarding service and got a chirpy mechanical attendant on the other end who spouted off the number of exciting travel deals available if she was interested in traveling to Luna City.

"I am already at Luna City," Marianne said.

The robot said, "Would you like to book a departure? Luna Transport offers a number of exciting travel options back to Earth. Experience space travel as it used to be in the zero-G, general passenger staterooms. Or, enjoy breathtaking views and full Earth gravity during your trip back in the Grand Suite on the outer ring. We have options available for any budget."

"No. I am inquiring if a passenger boarded your afternoon transport."

The robot's tone changed to informational and said, "The transport to Earth had two hundred twenty-six passengers. What is the last name of the passenger you would like to inquire about?"

"Chang."

"What is the first name of the passenger you would like to inquire about?"

"Peter."

The robot paused, then said, "Peter Chang departed on the afternoon transport, interior stateroom one-one-four-Quebec. Would you like to place a message to interior stateroom one-one-four-Quebec? Luna Transport offers up to terabyte-bandwidth in data, voice and video formats. And for a small additional charge, encryption is available for the most sensitive communications."

She didn't know Chang's private number, so she couldn't call him on her visor. She didn't have much money, but decided to take precautions against Luna City tracking her public call and said, "Secure audio." Chang answered after the second buzz. His voice sounded as if he had been sleeping.

"Chang, it's Marianne Summers."

"I remember you. Still on Luna?"

"Yeah." Marianne didn't know how much she could trust a secure call, but Luna City Security would have to announce the death of Tommy soon. "Thomas Rubner is dead."

"What? How?"

"The doctor said he died from exposure to the Moon's environment. Do you still have that footage when Luna City Security apprehended him earlier?" It was a rhetorical question. Camera operators kept everything they shot, no matter how mundane it appeared. You never knew when a trivial piece of boring footage might suddenly be in high demand.

"I'm not sure." Chang said carefully. Marianne knew what he was doing—turning this new information over in his head. If Tommy was dead, then Chang might have the very last footage of him alive. That was a profitable position to be in.

"Look, I'm not trying to steal your story. The medical examiner is telling me that Tommy died from asphyxiation while out at the ruins. I don't remember it that way."

The counter on the view screen showed twenty Luna dollars. She didn't have much spare cash to spend debating this. "This call is costing me a fortune. Check out the footage, and I'll call you back." She hit the disconnect and charged the call to her habitat room. She would have to call Roy to wire her some cash to cover the expense.

She slipped on her visor and telephoned Roy. His avatar answered, "Hi, Marianne. What's going on?"

Marianne told him about Chang being on the transport and the footage he had. "Make Chang a good offer and send me an encrypted copy, immediately."

"Marianne, this was a routine memorial piece. What do you *think* is going on?"

"Tommy stepped on some toes when he brought up this conspiracy theory. Now he's dead."

"I see where you're going. It doesn't make sense that Luna Security killed him over some wacko conspiracy theory. It's as crazy as the conspiracy about the JFK assassination, the American government being behind the 9-11 bombing or the story that the Challenger Shuttle collided with a UFO."

"Then why is Thomas Rubner dead?" The question hung between them for a while. Marianne finally said, "Exactly. Can you pay Chang?"

"I'd have to see the footage first. How much is it going to cost me?"

"It'll be worth it." She hung up, hoping she sounded convincing. If her gut instincts rang true, she was onto something. Unfortunately, those instincts also reminded her that her gut had not served her well these past twenty years or so. Still, she hadn't felt this way in years and the feeling told her she was close to uncovering something big.

When she arrived at her room, there was an encrypted data transmission from Chang waiting for her. The message came collect, at the price of one hundred seventy Luna dollars. She stared into the retinal scanner and waited while the information downloaded to her in-room terminal. It was the footage that Chang had shot of Tommy and the Luna City Security officers through the window.

She reviewed the footage and watched as the three officers in their steel-gray suits surrounded Tommy. She examined his attempted escape and watched as the men hauled him in and escorted him back to the air lock. Tommy was definitely walking on his own the whole time.

He was alive when Luna City Security had escorted him away from the ruins of Habitat Fourteen.

The next morning, Marianne read the announcement of Thomas Rubner's death in the Luna City vlog. As she expected, it claimed that Thomas had succumbed to exposure on the surface of the Moon after hijacking yesterday's memorial service. It also commended the quick-thinking Luna Network Center for terminating the transmission to Earth, as they were spared the horrifying scenes of Thomas struggling for oxygen as Luna City Security officers tried to save him, but failed.

Marianne shook her head. That wasn't what was on the video that Chang sent her. At the end of the vlog, the reporter announced that Thomas' body was being returned to Earth on the morning shuttle. Although Marianne had only met Tommy a week ago, she felt a sense of responsibility to see him off.

Even though travel to the Lunar Republic hadn't been popular for the last five years, there seemed to be an unusual amount of hubbub around the shuttle area this morning. The people all appeared to be leaving Luna City, and Marianne suspected most of them had only been here because of the memorial service yesterday. Their duty to visit Luna City was over, and now they were leaving.

Thirty minutes before liftoff, the doctor that Marianne had met in the medical center with Captain Hail appeared. He and an assistant wheeled a black, polycarbonate coffin down the concourse to the lower loading dock. As the doctor held the gurney steady, the assistant wrestled the coffin off and into the storage bay. Even in the Moon's one-sixth gravity, Marianne was surprised at how clumsy the job looked.

The assistant strapped the coffin down and tested that it was secure before taking the gurney from the doctor and following him back up the platform.

Marianne closed her eyes and said a private prayer for Tommy. When she finished, she wondered what family he had waiting for him when his body returned to Earth. She considered following that story—the children's grief after both parents had died on the Moon could be a compelling story. However, her instincts told her that the story she was already scratching at here was stronger.

She had turned to leave when she saw a teary-eyed woman staring at the transport. The woman seemed to be the only other one, other than Marianne herself, that stared at the large bay where Tommy's body was stored. The transport workers closed the lower storage bay and secured the hatch fasteners. After a moment, the woman headed up the platform and out of the loading area. Marianne caught up with her and introduced herself.

"I'm quite busy, Ms. Summers," the woman said. She no longer seemed morose, but angry.

Everyone seemed busy in Luna City, Marianne thought. "No worries, just a couple of questions. I noticed your grief while you were watching Thomas Rubner's coffin being loaded onto the transport. Are you any relation?"

"No." She then pushed the button on her wrist-phone and said, "Security."

"Okay then. A friend, coworker or just an acquaintance?"

"No." The woman walked on, facing forward.

"There must have been some reason you were seeing him off."

"Not really."

The woman arrived at the Luna City Security office. She stepped past two security men that barred Marianne's way. Marianne watched as the woman disappeared behind another door that read "Authorized Personnel Only," turned back once and looked at Marianne.

As she turned, Marianne saw that the woman looked remarkably like the 3-D image of Tommy Rubner's wife, Susan P. Rubner, from the holotank display. Her hair was brown now and was longer than it had been in the rotating image. She might have had some reconstructive surgery done to her nose as well. But, the line of her jaw, thin lips and brow ridge looked quite familiar.

Her nerves were jumping, just as they did every time a story was unfolding. She only had a few pieces so far. First, she had a dead man who had cried conspiracy. Second, a bureaucracy that appeared responsible for his death. Finally, there was a mysterious woman who looked suspiciously similar to the dead man's wife.

It seemed unlikely that Susan P. Rubner could still be alive. She was listed on the official casualty records as a victim of the Habitat Fourteen explosion. However, one of her instructors in college had told his class to dismiss nothing. Perhaps the video biography in the museum could clear up her suspicions that the woman she had seen was Tommy's wife.

Marianne scowled at the guards and headed back to the museum. The curator remembered her but wouldn't let her back in for free, so she grudgingly paid an additional fifteen Luna dollars and headed straight for the 2-D monitor and scrolled down to Susan P. Rubner's biography.

Remarkably, Marianne thought, Susan's biography contained few pictures of the woman herself. The coverage on her was brief. During the voiceover about Susan being a talented politician who graduated from Harvard at the top of her class, it showed a class picture.

Her small, blurry image was circled. That image was followed by generic images of her home town of St. Louis and narration explaining her accomplishments in state government. She had met and married her husband, Thomas Rubner, a local business owner. Tommy kissing Susan in the wedding picture obscured all but the top of her forehead. Together, they moved to Luna City, where she resumed her work in politics and her husband opened a business on the hub. They had only been stationed at Luna City for a year before the explosion, where she was killed. The image during the voiceover was the ruins of Habitat Fourteen.

Marianne suspected she knew why there were no clear pictures of Susan P. Rubner in her biography.

On the way back to her room, Marianne slipped on her visor and telephoned Roy.

Roy's first question was, "When are you coming home?"

"It may take a while. I'm onto something . . . unusual."

His avatar frowned. "What is it?"

"Not over the visor network. I need an upload of the transmission from last night. All the way until it cut out."

"There should be an archive available at the Luna Network Center."

"No. I need to be more clandestine than that. And, I need you to wire me some cash. Luna City is very expensive."

"The network has closed the budget for the Luna City Memorial project."

"This isn't related, not really. Charge it to investigative journalism."

"The network doesn't fund investigative journalism. We contract that out."

"Fine, put me down as a contractor."

"It doesn't work that way. You have to have a story to sell before the network will buy it. Not the other way around."

"Roy, I can't investigate this without money."

"Then get on the transport and come home."

"I can't do that. There's something strange going on here. Aren't you interested in what that is?"

"No." Roy's avatar disappeared as he disconnected from her.

Marianne yanked off her visor and shoved it back into her backpack. *Damn Roy for his narrow thinking,* she thought. Something big was going on here, and he wanted her to walk away from it. She couldn't do that.

Then she realized that two Luna City Security officers were a couple of meters behind her. Each held a cup of coffee, and they were casually speaking to each other.

She felt a knot form in her stomach. She had tried to be careful, but wondered what they might have overheard from her conversation with Roy. She headed around the hub and down the joining hallway to her room and paused in front of her door. The two guards didn't follow her. She exhaled in relief.

She put her thumb on the door lock but the red light came on instead of the green one. A mechanized voice on the lock announced that she had an outstanding charge of four hundred Luna dollars that needed to be paid before she could gain access to her room. She swore. The amount had to be wrong, even taking into account the charge for Chang's video that she had accepted and charged to her room.

She wondered how she would get that kind of money when she realized that she still had her return ticket to Earth. She could trade that in for a refund. And after her investigation was complete, she could call Roy and sell the story for a return fare back to Earth.

She headed for the spaceport and within twenty minutes had returned her ticket and had her account credited for five hundred twenty Luna dollars. Returning to her room, she finally gained access and immediately went to the communications terminal. A humungous, 3-D video file from Roy was waiting for her, as was a receipt for the two hundred fifty Luna dollars it cost. That explained the extra charge on her room.

She pulled up the file and cringed when she saw it was unencrypted. She should have warned Roy. She started the video, then skipped ahead to when the Moon segment started. As her 3-D image introduced the victims, she waited for the section where Susan P. Rubner's portrait played. When she finally reached it, Marianne studied the seven-second segment as Susan's portrait spun on screen. It started on the left side semi-profile and followed around to her right side. Her hair was short and blonde, in contrast to the dark-haired woman she had met earlier today. Further, Susan's nose was more pronounced. But it was too much of a coincidence.

Tommy had insisted he had seen his dead wife and

demanded to speak to her. It seemed ridiculous at the time. Now, she was sure the woman she met was Susan P. Rubner.

That evening, Marianne waited for the woman who was Tommy's wife to leave her quarters. She hung out at a café on the hub, keeping her eye on the executive hallways. The cup of coffee she nursed had the same recycled taste that all of the potable water on Luna City had, but she couldn't afford to throw it out. Besides, it would look peculiar if she were sitting in the café without anything in front of her.

She had cross-referenced the woman's information on one of the public terminals in the city. She was now going by the name Jennifer Hail. She had married Captain Gerald Hail over four years ago. The woman wasn't part of the Lunar Republic government and wasn't active in any clubs or organizations. Marianne was convinced *Jennifer Hail* could answer many of her questions.

A man slid into the chair opposite her, blocking her view. Before she could complain, he whispered, "I'm a friend of Thomas Rubner."

"Okay," Marianne answered. She wasn't sure what the man meant. Was he upset, like the museum curator, and a threat to her, or did he also believe in the conspiracy as Tommy did?

The man's eyes darted around the café. His well-trimmed goatee and close-cropped hair were starting to show the briefest of gray hairs. "My name is Branson," he said carefully. "I know what they did to Tommy." His constantly moving eyes belied his otherwise normal appearance.

"What?"

"He was more interested in confronting his wife than explaining about the conspiracy. Captain Hail had him killed. If only he had stayed on topic."

"On topic?"

"About the conspiracy."

"What do you know about that?"

"Follow me," he whispered.

Marianne shook her head. "I can't. I'm waiting for someone."

He looked back at the office door she had been watching. "She's a dead end. Get involved with her, and you'll wind up like Thomas." He stood and walked to the doorway, then looked back at her and nodded.

Marianne pushed away the creepy feeling that this man seemed to know what she was doing and who she was waiting for. Her interest was piqued; if he knew that much, she wondered how much more he knew. She followed him out, tossing her coffee in a recycle container near the door. "What is this—?"

The man held up a hand, cutting her off. "Not here." He led her down the main hallway, around the central hub and to the Memorial Hallway and Museum. Along the way, he pointed out construction features of Luna City, specifically the joints in the geodesic domes where the triangular panels joined together.

When they reached the Memorial Hallway, Branson paid for both of them. Marianne smiled at the curator, but he only scowled at them.

Branson grabbed her arm, directed her to The Final Moments of Habitat Fourteen exhibit and pressed the play button. "Watch carefully," he whispered.

She watched as the dome exploded again. "I've seen this hundreds of times already." She was surprised to realize that she was whispering as well.

As the bent, severed arm spun toward the camera, he tapped on the screen. "Notice that? Notice that?"

"Yes." Conspiracy theorists insisted that an arm wouldn't stay bent like that while spinning—especially with no wind resistance on the Moon. It defied simple physics. They claimed the centrifugal force would force the joint to extend straight, like a rod instead of a boomerang. Marianne never understood how that strange arm added to the conspiracy.

The video ended and he pulled her out of the hallway and walked her to Habitat Eleven. He didn't say a word, but walked so fast that Marianne practically had to jog to keep up. He placed his thumb on the lock of room 11-31 and when the entry light came on, he pulled her inside.

Branson flipped two switches, one near the door and another across the room. "We can talk now." He spoke normally, but the harshness in his voice, that Marianne had suspected was caused by his whispering, remained. "What did you notice in that video?"

The question confused her. "I've seen the same video hundreds of times in the last five years. I didn't notice anything new about it this time."

He walked to the edge of his room where a triangular window overlooked the moonscape and pounded on the wall with the heel of his hand. "Do you know anything about how this pressure wall is constructed?"

"Robots built it. They mix moondust with epoxies

and polymers. They build it from the Moon's surface, up along the dome to the apex."

"Yes. The robots that built Habitat Fourteen operated under the version of the program that was used to build this habitat." He patted on a triangular facet of the wall. "What about this panel? Did they build the sub-pieces and join them together?"

"No. It's all built in one big piece. Except for the windows. The triangles are just—I don't know—decoration."

"Exactly. Did you notice the joints between the wall and the windows? Between the facets of the wall themselves?"

She walked to the wall and rubbed her hand over the rounded bulge between two panels. Instead of a crease, there was a six-inch-thick bulge of material at every joint. "It's thicker here."

"A decorative detail to make it look like a geodesic pattern." He patted the center of the triangle. "The weakest part of the wall is right here. In the middle of the triangle." Branson nodded frantically at her.

He was trying to point something out to her and she felt frustration that he didn't come right out and say what was on his mind. If the weakest part of the wall was the center of each triangle, then what did that mean to her?

She recalled the explosion in the video she had just seen and her jaw dropped. She had seen that video hundreds of times and never questioned any part of it. But, she had never seen one of the Luna City pressure walls up close before. In the video, as the dome exploded, the triangle-shaped shards blasted apart. She could see them in the moments before they were obscured by the vaporizing air. She remembered thinking how beautiful they all looked.

An explosion would have burst the weakest part of the wall. It would have punched through the center of each triangle in the dome, not along the edges. But, that wasn't what was in the video.

"Oh, my God," she said as a chill ran down her arm.

The man smiled broadly. "That was a controlled demolition of Habitat Fourteen."

Earlier in her career, Marianne had covered the demolition of an old building. A network had hired her for an information piece about how hazardous materials are removed before a building is demolished. She learned that a building didn't just fall down. Architects designed buildings to remain standing, and a huge amount of effort was needed to overcome that design. Her investigation included a tour of a prepared building, where the demolishers showed her how they had structurally weakened the building in key areas and how they would use an explosive cord called Primaline to cut through the solid steel girders that were over twenty centimeters thick. With weakened joints and severed load-bearing girders, the spine of the building would be carefully severed, and the structure would finally come crashing down. Demolition wasn't a trivial task.

Marianne found herself nodding along with Branson. She was starting to believe the conspiracy herself.

Marianne stared out from the triangular viewing windows at the ruins of Habitat Fourteen. It was the same window where Chang had filmed Thomas

Rubner being apprehended, and that made her feel like she was standing somewhere sacred. It had been the last time she had seen Tommy alive.

Her eyes focused on the plaque. Although it was unreadable from where she stood—behind eight inches of transparent polycarbonate—she remembered some of what it said from the reproduction outside the museum. It was the site of the first act of terrorism on the Moon, and the memorial was a reminder that the Moon is an apolitical territory for all persons of the Earth to share in peace.

It was a lie. No, not everything. The explosion, the deaths and the grieving, those were real. Even before the Lunar Republic took control of Luna City, the Moon was as politically charged as any place on Earth. Six years earlier, twenty Chinese scientists died in their Tycho Crater research facility. Shuttle flyovers of the abandoned buildings revealed high levels of radiation, indicating a failure in the Chinese nuclear power plant. The Chinese government claimed the deaths were caused by a faulty carbon dioxide scrubber. But none of the twenty manned Chinese missions since the accident had ever revisited the site. Further, the Chinese government claimed that the buildings themselves were their sovereign property and refused to allow any other government to approach them.

Luna City, the only large-scale permanent habitat on the Moon, wasn't apolitical either. The Lunar Republic had staged a bloodless coup d'état two months after Habitat Fourteen was destroyed, set up a parliamentary government and threatened to refuse Earth transports landing if the Earth Consortium didn't grant them their independence. After months of negotiation, Luna City became an independent entity, with only five token Earth representatives retaining seats in the parliament—one from each of the original founding countries.

It was almost exactly what the terrorists had demanded. The five Earth representatives, when united, were still a minority against the sixteen other parliament members from the Lunar Republic. Luna City was, essentially, its own political entity.

A woman's voice behind her said, "Tragic, isn't it?"

Marianne turned to see the woman who resembled Susan P. Rubner. Her blood turned cold. Branson had told her it wasn't safe to talk to this woman. But that urge to discover her secret kept Marianne there.

"Yes," Marianne said, never taking her eyes off the woman. She fought the desire to ask this woman if she was really Thomas Rubner's wife and asked a more innocuous question instead. "Were you in Luna City when it happened?"

"My boyfriend, Alex, he was one of the negotiators." She stroked the polycarbonate window. "I didn't see a lot of him during that week. He would come back to our quarters at night and fall off to sleep immediately. Then, he would be gone before I woke the next morning. He never said a lot to me about it, but I could tell the stress on him was incredible."

She turned to Marianne and said, "They didn't get enough credit, the negotiators. Alex and the rest of them did their best, but all everyone ever said afterwards was that they failed." She looked back out the window. "Alex did everything he could, but he couldn't win. The people who took those people hostage never planned to release them. No matter what Alex and the others did. They always intended to blow up the habitat.

"The explosion woke us both. I remember us holding each other, staring out at the smoking rubble all afternoon. He was a different man after that. He carried the guilt of all those deaths around with him. He didn't eat, didn't laugh. He slept most of the time. Alone. He was almost . . . Have you ever heard of Alex Murray?"

Marianne shook her head.

"Councilwoman Solomon. Everyone remembers her name. Major Young, Lieutenant Molina, Technician Williams and . . ." She swallowed. "You hear about them because they died in that explosion. But never Alex Murray. To the press, he was just an *impotent* negotiator who failed to save six thousand people. But that explosion killed him too. It just took him four months longer to die."

"How?" Marianne asked, almost whispering. "How did Alex die?"

The woman clenched her eyes shut, and a tear escaped and ran down her cheek. She stood that way a moment, then took a breath and stared out at the ruins. "He put on a pressure suit, walked out to the plaque out there and cracked the quick release ring on his helmet." Her voice had an eerie calm that people have when they recount the tragedies in their lives. Marianne had heard it hundreds of times in her career.

"I'm so sorry," Marianne said.

Another tear fell. "I didn't realize he was missing

for twelve hours. When they found him, he was completely frozen. I'll never forget how he looked." Her expression changed and the woman pounded on the window. "I hate that place! I've lost so much because of it! More than anyone can understand."

Two Luna City guards appeared in the hallway behind the woman. A knot formed in Marianne's stomach as they walked toward them. "Is everything all right, Mrs. Hail?"

Mrs. Hail turned on the guard. "No, everything is not all right!"

A voice behind Marianne called, "Jenny!" She turned to see Captain Hail standing a few meters behind her and fought the urge to flee.

Jenny yelled at Captain Hail, "How many more people have to die because of this lie? It's not worth it anymore! First Alex, now Tommy! Who's next? How many more is the Republic going to take from me?"

"That is enough," Captain Hail said, taking a step toward her. He wiped away her tear. "It's been an emotional couple of days. You're tired. Go back to our room." He kissed her gently, then nodded to the guard who had spoken to her earlier. The guard took her arm and escorted her down the hallway.

Captain Hail sighed and jerked his head toward Marianne. The guards immediately handcuffed her. Captain Hail said, "You'd better come with me."

Marianne had a new appreciation for the minor wear and tear on the rest of Luna City after sitting in one of its jail cells for a few hours. The creases in the walls were filthy black stains and the room smelled of human sweat and stale urine. It added to her dark, depressed mood.

Adrenaline forced her to get up from the bunk. The exercise from pacing the three-meter wide cell wasn't enough to satiate her fear. She finally had all of the pieces of this story. Her skin crawled with the idea of what Luna City Security might do to keep her from telling it.

Unsatisfied with pacing, she lay back on the stained mattress, breathing slowly through her mouth because of the smell. She tried to calm her spring-tight nerves. Nobody knew she was in the jail. Roy knew she was in Luna City, but she couldn't depend on him to seek her out and make sure she was okay. The ticketing agent that she had returned her ticket to, the curator at the museum, as well as some people working or visiting the cafeteria had seen her around Luna City. But she was a nobody to them. She suddenly remembered Magistrate Melle. Their conversation together had been friendly, and he knew who she was. He would certainly remember her.

Her spirits brightened. She stood and called repeatedly for the jailer until an outer door hissed open and he walked down the hallway that led to her cell.

"I need to make a call!" Marianne demanded.

The jailer turned and said, "I bet you do."

"I have rights, even here on the Moon!"

The jailer ignored her comment and left. The outer door hissed closed behind him and she was alone again.

She collapsed back on the mattress and covered her

eyes with the crook of her arm. The realization that she was going to die here on the Moon monopolized her thoughts. Nobody who cared about her knew that she was here. She had gotten on the wrong side of Luna City Security, and they were going to silence her story. Her throat closed off.

She heard the outside door hiss open and stood again. Jenny Hail walked to her cell and stared past the old-fashioned stainless-steel bars at Marianne before speaking. When she finally spoke, she said, "I never wanted anything bad to happen to Tommy."

Despite the dozens of questions that pounded in her mind, Marianne forced herself to stay silent.

"That's why Alex and I decided to fake my death." She looked to Marianne, as if asking to be understood. "Tommy was a good man. Really he was. He just lacked . . . passion. Passion in his work, passion in life, passion for me. Alex—he made me feel . . . alive."

Marianne finally said, "What Tommy did out there was pretty passionate."

A small laugh escaped through her tears. "It was the last thing I would have expected. I started to think that maybe I was wrong about him. Started questioning every move I'd made for the last five years."

A tear rolled down her cheek and she looked at the floor. "It's my fault Tommy's dead. We were watching the memorial, Gerald and me, when Tommy started talking about the conspiracy. Gerald got upset. He doesn't let that part of himself show in public, but he's got kind of a temper. I was trying to calm him down. When Tommy demanded he speak to me, I told Gerald that maybe I should.

"He lost it." She looked at Marianne and both eyes were heavy with tears. She rubbed her forearm, and a bruised piece of skin showed under her sleeve for a brief moment. "He never . . . not once before. . . ."

While she was talking, Marianne decided to ask, "Is there a conspiracy?"

"I had nothing to do with that. I didn't even know about it until. . . ." Susan whispered, "I was married to Gerald for a year before I found out. I didn't know about it before. Neither did Alex."

"Tommy knew. Gerald killed him to keep him quiet."

Susan shook her head. "No, it's my fault Tommy is dead. Gerald's really a good man. Really—"

"Good men don't murder innocent people, Susan." Susan flinched when Marianne mentioned her name. "He's going to do the same thing to me that he did to Tommy. Unless you help me."

Susan backed away from the cell door, her eyes wide in terror. She rubbed her bruised arm. "Oh, no. I couldn't. I couldn't."

"Susan, please."

"No. Don't ask that!" She turned and darted down the hallway and through the outer door.

"Susan! You've got to help me!" There was no answer except the echo of her words in the small cell.

Marianne was unaware of how much time had passed before two guards in steel-gray pressure suits opened the outer door and walked down the hallway to her cell. They didn't have helmets on and she recognized one of them as the same guard that she had seen at the observation window with Susan. He unlocked her cell and said, "Come with us."

The words turned her cold. She swallowed, then set her chin, trying to look strong. "First Thomas Rubner, then me? People know I'm here. They'll realize something happened. You won't get away with it."

The other guard grabbed her forearm, dragged her off the mattress and thrust her through the cell door. She turned on them and the guard drew his needlegun. The other guard put his hand on his arm and said, "No. The captain wants her alive."

A chill consumed her. Before, her death had been a nagging fear, now it blossomed into fully realized terror. "You can't do this!"

A guard grabbed her shoulder and forced her against the wall.

Her hands shook and she made no effort to hide then. "No, please," she begged. "This is a mistake. I didn't do anything wrong."

A guard handcuffed her, then the two led her through the hallway, out the outer door, through the security office and into the hallways of Luna City.

Marianne didn't remember the hallways of Luna City being busy, but she remembered seeing a person or two wandering around every time she was out. This time, the hallways were deserted, and the eerie quiet of ventilation recycling gnawed at her nerves. As much as she wanted to believe the guards were taking her back to her room or the shuttle, she realized that wasn't going to happen.

One of the guards behind her pushed her along.

She caught herself from falling and walked, taking small steps, buying time. Time for one of the guards to come to his senses and stop this. Time for someone to realize what was happening and rescue her.

The time to appear strong had passed. These men in steel-gray pressure suits were taking her to be killed, and she needed to do whatever she could to stop them. She screamed, pleading for help, but her words echoed in the empty halls of Luna City.

They turned down a hallway to the utilities spur, the most deserted part of Luna City. She stopped, and her body took an instinctive step backward. A guard pushed her forward and she let herself tumble to the polycarbonate floor. She grabbed her knee, faking pain, stealing precious time for somebody, anybody, to appear and save her. One of the guards lifted her to her feet—an action that was much easier to do in the one-sixth gravity on the Moon. He pushed her along and said, "Just a little further."

Marianne searched for someone to help. The guards must have noticed because each grabbed one of her arms and walked her past the archway to the air lock.

Her heart sank when she realized the room was as deserted as the hallways were. The only exception was a stern-looking Captain Gerald Hail who stood in front of the door bearing a sign that read "Air lock U-4."

Marianne tried to squirm away, but the guards' grip tightened.

"Now, now," Captain Hail said. "Struggling will only make this take longer." The large inner door of the air lock stood open, and Marianne knew that the black maw inside was where her life would end. She tried to backpedal but the guards held her firm.

"My producer knows I'm here. Roy Hinkley," she said. "So does my cameraman headed back to Earth." Chang wasn't her cameraman, but she hoped the lie might fool him. "If anything happens to me, they'll know it was you. Me and Tommy dying while on the same assignment is going to look very suspicious."

Captain Hail took her and ordered the guards to put their helmets on.

Marianne yelled, "You won't get away with this! Tommy wasn't some nobody, and neither am I! Someone will figure out what you're doing! You won't get away with it."

The guards fastened their helmet rings and nodded to their captain, who said, "Put her inside."

Marianne thrashed, but she wasn't used to the reduced gravity of the Moon and Captain Hail's grip was too strong. The guards took her, hauled her into the air lock and secured the door behind her.

A moment later, a klaxon sounded. Then, a hissing sound flooded the chamber. Marianne felt pressure build on her ears. Terror flooded over her as she realized they were pumping out the air. She bolted to the door, but the guards pulled her away. Panic crawled over her as she remembered Tommy's bruised eyes and the trickle of dried blood from his nose and ears. She was going to end up just like him— covered with an insubstantial white sheet on the cold stainless-steel morgue table. She struggled, shouting, "Let me out! I won't tell anyone! I swear!" The sound of her voice already sounded weak.

Her breath came in short gasps as she fought for air. The strength in her legs left her, and she collapsed on the dust-covered floor. As the hissing echoed in the small chamber, darkness first flooded her peripheral vision, then consumed her.

Her lungs burned. Gasping for air yielded meager returns at first, but eventually satisfied most of her body's cravings for oxygen. Through her hazy vision, she recognized Branson leaning over her.

"Thank God," he said. "I thought I was too late. Are you okay?"

Marianne tried to answer, but her throat burned. She tasted blood. After managing a painful swallow, she was finally able to croak, "What . . . happened?"

He helped her sit up and offered her a glass of water, which she swallowed with care. Everything hurt. She wondered what kind of permanent damage she would suffer from the air lock.

"They were trying to silence you, just like they did with Thomas Rubner." Her foggy gaze followed his gesturing hand, which held a needlegun. She could make out Captain Hail lying on his back. Blood flowed from a needle wound just behind his left ear. Branson was a good shot.

"Can you stand?" he asked.

Branson pulled her up. Even in the reduced gravity, her legs refused to sustain her. They burned as if she had run a marathon. If it had not been for Branson holding her up, she would have collapsed.

"Gimme . . . minute." Her voice sounded rough and gravely. Panic crawled over her skin. She had heard that people could survive a short duration of high vacuum, but anything over a minute and a half was usually fatal.

Branson propped her against a piece of machinery and dragged Captain Hail's body into the air lock. She saw the two other guards inside, most likely dead like their captain. If she had the energy, she would have spit on them all.

Branson closed the inner door and said, "We have to get out of here. We can hide out in my quarters for a while. You can recover there."

With all her effort, she raised her hand and pointed toward the air lock. "No . . . Captain's . . . quarters."

"The captain's dead."

"Susan. Tommy's wife . . . is there. She knows."

Branson lifted her up and swung one of her arms behind his neck. Supporting her weight, they walked into the hallways, which, thankfully, were still deserted. He carried her past empty hub corridors and through the executive hallway to Habitat Ten. He seemed to know exactly where Captain Hail lived and before she realized, they were standing in front of a black, polycarbonate door to room 10-42.

Susan answered the chime immediately. Her hand went to her mouth and she stepped backwards when she saw Branson and Marianne standing there. "Oh, my God! Is she all right?"

Branson pulled her inside and set Marianne into a chair.

"They put her in the air lock without a pressure suit," Branson said.

"No," Susan said softly. "No. No. No." She started yelling. "How many more? How many more!"

"You . . . can . . . stop it," Marianne gasped. She hoped that Susan was starting to see the cost of keeping this conspiracy alive.

"No," Susan begged, backing away. "Gerald will kill me."

"He's dead. I killed him," Branson said.

Susan looked from Marianne to Branson. "No. How could you!"

Branson pointed to Marianne. "Look at her. He tried to kill her. I had no choice."

Marianne managed a painful nod. "It's true."

Susan turned away from them. "This is all my fault! One lie. One little lie!" She turned back to Marianne. "How could one little lie cost all these lives? Tommy, Alex, Gerald. Where does it stop? When does it stop?"

Marianne took a deep breath. "It stops . . . when you—"

Branson interrupted. "You have to tell the truth about Habitat Fourteen. Tell the truth, once and for all."

Susan shook her head, her face twisted in fear.

"You . . . have to," Marianne said.

Susan shook her head.

This was going nowhere. Susan was still frozen in inaction. Marianne needed to force her. "Where's . . . your . . . phone?" Marianne asked.

Susan shook her head.

Branson grabbed her arm and shoved her toward Marianne. "The Republic tried to kill this woman!"

Susan turned away.

Branson continued, "The same way they killed your husband, Thomas! How many deaths will it be? Five? Six? They'll kill me too." He shook her. "How many more have to die before you stop this murdering cover up? Sooner or later, the Lunar Republic's going to realize that you know their secrets. Captain Hail isn't able to protect you anymore. You'll be the next to take a trip in the air lock. Like Tommy and her."

Susan broke into tears. Marianne struggled and took her hand. What they were asking her to do was terrifying, but she was on the edge of tipping and just needed to be comforted. She needed to have someone, like Tommy or Alex or Gerald, to tell her everything was okay.

"It's . . . all . . . right. Help us."

There was a chime at the door and before Marianne saw it, Branson had the needlegun in his hand. From behind the door, she could hear "Mrs. Hail, are you all right?"

Marianne gasped, and the pain made her wince. "Help us," she begged.

Another chime. "Mrs. Hail, are you in there?"

"Yes—yes, I'm here."

The voice behind the door asked, "Is everything all right?"

Susan stared at Branson's needlegun. "Yes—yes, it is."

"Please stay in your quarters until further notice. Let us know if you notice anything unusual. Understand?"

"Is anything wrong?" Susan asked.

Branson pointed his needlegun at the door.

"A prisoner escaped from the jails. We're searching the city. There's nothing for you to worry about."

Susan looked at Marianne. "Is Gerald okay?"

There was a brief pause. "Of course, ma'am. He's leading the search."

Susan looked to Branson who shook his head. Susan closed her eyes and took a heavy breath. "Thank you. I'll stay here."

Marianne recognized the breath as the one that would solidify this story. She nodded her head gently, reassuring Susan.

Susan walked to another room and returned moments later with a videophone. Without a word, she handed it to Marianne.

Marianne was glad to see that Captain Hail had an encrypted line. She selected it and struggled to dial the number for Roy. He picked up after several seconds. His smile vanished after the connection was made. "What in hell happened to you?"

"Long story. Record this . . . transmission."

"What's going on?"

She took a deep breath and yelled, "Trust me! Record this!" She didn't have the time to explain this to him.

Roy leaned forward, then said, "It's recording."

"This is . . . Marianne . . . Summers. The Luna City . . . conspiracy . . . is true."

Marianne crawled out of the chair and motioned for Susan to sit.

Susan sat, composed herself, then started. "I am . . . My name is Susan P. Rubner."

Marianne closed her eyes, then drifted off to sleep as Thomas Rubner's wife told her story.

How to View Art

BY L. RON HUBBARD

Upon the inauguration of the Writers of the Future Contest in 1984, L. Ron Hubbard made this penetrating insight into the relationship between an artist and society: "The artist injects the spirit of life into a culture."

He recognized the unique potential that the artist has for helping to inspire society and create a finer world.

While the original Contest focused on encouraging new authors, Hubbard's own artistic endeavors were not confined to just one field. True, he may best be known as a writer. He published hundreds of works and millions of words between 1929 and 1950, when the name L. Ron Hubbard was virtually synonymous with American popular fiction.

But Hubbard also worked in visual media such as filmmaking. By the summer of 1937, for example, one finds his stamp on such scripts for the big screen as The Mysterious Pilot, The Adventures of Wild Bill Hickock and the Spider series, while his name was quite formally attached to The Secret of Treasure Island—among the most profitable serials of Hollywood's golden age.

Hubbard was also an accomplished photographer. A keen student of the craft through his youth, by early 1929, his celebrated China landscapes had been acquired by National Geographic while his spectacular aerial shots as a pilot were found in the pages of Sportsman Pilot. His later work, including promotional photographs for various European governments and official portraits of heads of state, was equally acclaimed.

Similarly, although he never counted himself as a professional musician in the strictest sense, his musical accomplishments are by no means insignificant. He created a "soundtrack" to Battlefield Earth using previously unexplored computerized instrumentation, followed by a no less innovative Mission Earth *album*, themed against his best-selling series and performed by Edgar Winter.

Thus, L. Ron Hubbard developed a love for and mastery of several art forms, and in that spirit the Illustrators of the Future Contest was created to be a companion to the Writers of the Future.

L. Ron Hubbard's diverse perspective made him especially qualified to find common ground across all the arts. Synthesizing his experiences in writing, filmmaking, photography and music, he was able to advise others about a skill rarely addressed in the study of creativity: How an artist can successfully evaluate his own works as he endeavors to perfect them so that they have a powerful impact on others.

How to View Art

There is a skill needed by anyone engaging in any of the fields of the arts including writing, music, painting, editing of films, mixing—in other words, across the boards.

It is the ability or skill, native or acquired, to view any piece of work in a new unit of time each time one views it. One has to be able to sweep aside all past considerations concerning any piece of work which has been changed or is under handling and see it or hear it in a brand-new unit of time as though he had never heard of it before.

By doing this, he actually sees or hears exactly what is in front of him, not his past considerations concerning it.

The skill consists solely of being able to see or hear in a new unit of time as though one had never seen or heard the work before.

Only in this way can one actually grasp exactly what he now has before him. When he does not do this he is viewing or hearing, in part, what he saw or

125

heard before in memory and this gets confused with what it now is.

If one can do this, he can wind up with stellar presentations. But all too often, when he doesn't do this, he winds up with hash.

Some painters, for instance, will redo and redo and redo a painting up to an inch thick of paint when, possibly, several of those redos were quite acceptable. But he continued to try to correct the first impressions which were no longer there. By not viewing his painting in a new unit of time as though he had never seen it before, he cannot actually get a correct impression of what is in front of him.

Some painters or illustrators have a trick by which to do this. They look at their painting via a mirror. Because it is now backwards, they can see it newly.

There is another trick of looking at a painting with a reducing glass (like looking at a view through the wrong end of a telescope) to reduce the painting to the presentation size it will eventually have, let us say, on a printed page. It is quite remarkable that this reduction actually does change the appearance of it markedly. But at the same time, a small painting, enlarged, can be absolutely startling enlarged when it did not look good at all small. But this is actually change of format, not viewing in a new instant of time. The additional skill of viewing something in a new instant of time is also vital.

When anyone engaged in any of the arts in any field has not acquired this skill, he never really knows when he has arrived at the point of completion. And he can often get a distorted opinion of a piece of work which does not any longer merit it.

Audiences

There is another skill which is also acquired in the field of seeing or hearing. This is being able to assume the viewpoint of the audience for which the work is intended.

There are certain areas which pretend to teach various arts, while actually covertly trying to wreck the future of the student, which stress "self-satisfaction" as the highest possible goal of engaging in any work related to any of the arts. There is, it is true, a considerable self-satisfaction in producing a good piece of work. But to profess that one works in these fields for his own self-satisfaction is to overstress the first dynamic to such a point that the work of the artist or technician then fails miserably. It is actually pure balderdash and a sort of a weak limping apology for not being successful to say that one works for his own self-satisfaction.

This false datum can mix up many artists and technicians who would otherwise be quite successful. For it blocks out the one test which would make him successful: the audience.

It is quite vital that anyone engaged in any of these fields be able to assume the viewpoint of the eventual audience.

One has to be able to see or listen to any product he is engaged in from the audience viewpoint.

He can, of course, and has to, view it from his own viewpoint. But he has to be able to shift around and view or hear it from the audience viewpoint.

There are some tricks involved in this. One of them is to keep an ear open for "lobby comment." After a performance or viewing of any work or cinema or recital or whatever—not necessarily one's own—one mingles with or gets reports on those who have just experienced the presentation. This isn't really vital to do. It is quite feasible actually simply to assume a viewpoint of an audience one has never even seen. One just does it.

A mixing engineer often puts this to a further test but this is because what he is busy mixing on his high-priced top-quality equipment is not what the audience is going to hear. So he takes a cheapo Taiwan wrist cassette-player speaker or a 3-inch radio speaker from the local junk store and he listens to the program he has just mixed through it. This tells him what the audience will actually be hearing. But this is mainly a technical matter as it is true that excellent speakers or earphones may handle easily certain distortions in a mix or performance whereas the cheapo speakers shatter on them. When they do, one adjusts the mix without spoiling it so that it will play over a cheap speaker. This is a sort of a mechanical means of assuming the viewpoint of an audience. But the necessity to do this is introduced by equipment factors.

The truth of the matter is even the mixing engineer is not mixing to remedy "faults" but is mixing for an optimum quality presentation to an audience. To know when he has it, it is necessary for him to assume the viewpoint of the audience.

In all arts it is necessary to be able to shift viewpoint to the viewpoint of the listener or the viewer other than oneself. And this extends out to audiences.

Summary

What really separates the flubbers and amateurs from the professional are these two skills. One has to be able to view or hear anything he is working on at any time in a brand-new unit of time. And one has to be able to see or hear his production from the viewpoint of the eventual audience.

In other words, the really excellent professional can be fluid in time, not stuck in the past and can be facile in space location.

There is no reason why one should be stuck on the time track or fixated in just his own location in space.

Actually, just knowing that these skills can exist is often enough the key to acquiring them.

In Apprehension, How Like a God

written by

R. P. L. Johnson

illustrated by

DUSTIN D. PANZINO

ABOUT THE AUTHOR

Richard Johnson was born in Botswana but grew up in England with the juvenile novels of Robert Heinlein before moving on to E. E. Smith, Arthur C. Clarke, Burroughs and Asimov. He still enjoys those stories from the golden age of science fiction and hopes to emulate their use of strong characters and fast-moving plots.

His flash fiction story "A Friend in Need" was published online in alienskinmag.com and also appeared on the Hugo Award-winning podcast StarShipSofa. He is currently completing what he hopes is the final draft of his action-thriller novel, Asura.

Richard hopes one day to write a science fiction novel that will capture the public imagination in the same way as The Da Vinci Code and Harry Potter novels did, but that molds that energy in a more productive direction. He wants enthused readers to write to their politicians demanding why that space elevator remains unbuilt and the solar system uncolonized. He wants to rekindle that spirit of optimism and faith in technology from the 1950s and remix it for the 2050s. He wants the CEOs of Rockwell and Northrop Grumman in forty years' time to have once been kids growing up with his books. He wants Facebook to have a status update for "home planet." Is that too much to ask?

Until that time comes, he lives in Melbourne, Australia, with his wife Lynn and son Adam, where he works as a structural engineer.

ABOUT THE ILLUSTRATOR

Dustin D. Panzino was born April 26, 1991, in Syracuse, New York.

After leaving Syracuse in grade school, Dustin moved to Ocala, Florida, an hour north of Orlando, and entered high school. From there he was accepted to the Marion County Center for the Arts (MCCA), an art magnet program which offers classes from traditional oil painting to conceptual AP (advanced placement) art classes at West Port High School in Ocala. After graduating both high school and the MCCA program, Dustin decided to study at the New Hampshire Institute of Art for his BFA in both illustration and fine art photography. With a well-known obsession with the way time moves forward as well as back, Dustin explains his decision to double major: "A photo is an image frozen in time; a painting is created in the image of time."

In the long run, Dustin aspires to achieve his master's in illustration and one day move on to teaching in order to make a life of art. With the New Hampshire Institute of Art located in the center of Manchester and only forty minutes outside of Boston, Dustin was intrigued by not only the school itself but also the beauty and history of New England. Surrounded by such a place, Dustin's acceptance to the New Hampshire Institute of Art seemed like a dream come true.

In Apprehension, How Like a God

I watched the jet-black ball roll across the room under its own power. Easy, I thought, just a motorized weight held off-center inside the casing. Then it reached a wall and started to roll vertically up it to join a dozen or more rolling across the barrel-vaulted ceiling twenty meters above. I had seen my share of dead bodies before, but none in a place like this.

The Academy's visitors' center combined the bustle of an airport departure lounge with the cavernous silence of a library. People moved to and fro between the transport terminus and the fortified gates that led into the campus. Most were dressed in the color-coded robes of Academy staff, but a few, like me, wore Western suits or traditional Ugandan *dashiki*. And through and above the crowd rolled the black spheres, the æthernet nodes.

One of the beach-ball-sized spheres rolled up to me. It was completely featureless, a huge black pearl. It may have slid rather than rolled for all the visible cues it gave to its motion. My æthernet feed told me it was a Class III node, a sub-sentient, chattel-class intelligence designated Stromboli. A table of figures specifying size, weight, role and location (both physical and metaphorical within the organizational structure of the Academy) scrolled down my vision and I slapped more data filters in place, leaving only its name hovering in dull red letters above it.

It stopped a respectful distance away and I heard its voice through my feed.

Mister Detective Conroy, welcome, it sent.

I spoke aloud and hoped the thing had auditory pickups of some kind on its flawless surface.

"Just Detective will do fine," I said, disturbing the silence and drawing disapproving looks from nearby Academy staff.

Yes. Detective designation, not name. Apologies.

"No need to apologize. Just show me the customer."

Customer? Ah yes, customer . . . client requiring services of a homicide detective. Idiom. Slang. Jargon subsection, humor: corpse, body, cadaver, stiff. This way, please.

The node led me out of the visitors' center and onto the campus grounds. The Academy sprawled across seventy square kilometers of parkland that stretched along the coastline of Lake Victoria. Where our path took us near the shore I could see the Entebbe hub five kilometers away on the other side of the inlet and above all the laser-straight line of the Jacob's Ladder rising into the sky, pinning the city down like a lepidopterist's needle.

Despite its size, the whole campus seemed sculpted, manicured. Paths of crushed shells wound between the buildings past stands of impossibly tall palm trees and fountains that filled the air with a gentle mist of cool water, taking the edge off the equatorial heat.

The nodes were everywhere. They rolled along the paths and through the gardens. They stood ornamental in flower beds and under trees and perched like crows on the eaves of the buildings. I saw several clustered like preschool children around a Magister as he held a class under a huge baobab tree.

I knew about the nodes, of course, but had never seen one up close before now. They *were* the æthernet. Each one was a semi-autonomous quantum computer. Each held its own store of information and everything it knew appeared on the æthernet, its knowledge superimposed onto the Higgs field, the quantum field that permeated the entire universe. They dreamed the æthernet into existence. It was not something they did; rather it was a property of what they were.

However, despite their immense capacity for information, they were no more than savant children, relying on the Magisters to help sort and classify their store of knowledge. It was the nodes that created the æthernet, but it was the Academy and its army of Magisters that prevented it from degrading into useless noise.

As I walked, I unfroze layers of information and immediately clamped them down again. The amount of data on the field was overwhelming. Every building was overlaid with false-color exploded plans that slid out of the stone and opened like boxes unfolding. Every curve of the sculpted lawns was realized in contour lines that lay across the grass like spiders' webs. They were so closely

135

detailed that the Magisters cutting between the paths looked like they were trudging through snow. Plants were pregnant with time-lapse recordings of their growth thus far, the recordings set to launch with proximity fuses. I walked through the garden like a god, trees bursting into fruit as I passed, bulbs erupting from the earth at each divine footfall. The air itself was bejeweled with information as particles of quantum static shorted out between air molecules in tiny pinpricks of gold and purple.

So many nodes, such a cacophony of data. I dialed the level of information back to something more manageable.

I looked at the Magister sitting cross-legged under the baobab tree and the nodes clustered around him. My wife, Kissa, and I had lost our daughter two years ago. Soon afterwards, Kissa took the trip up the Ladder and then the long sleep on the way to a new life around another sun. After our daughter's death, she said the world no longer made sense to her. She said she needed simplicity, needed to return to nature. Looking at the Magister, his voluminous robes of peach silk folded around his seated form as delicate and serene as a honey orchid, seeing the nodes clustered attentively around him absorbing the information he dispensed, their thoughts radiating through the æthernet adding layers of data to the superposed field that permeated the universe. Wasn't this the serene garden of enlightenment she craved? I didn't understand how dirt under your fingernails added to the spiritual experience, but then I never had, and that, so Kissa had said, was the problem.

Stromboli led me toward a huge sculpture, a

curved standing wave of anodized, heat-striped titanium as tall as a three-story building that formed one long wall and an integral roof over a communal meeting area. It was beautiful from a distance, but as we approached I was uncomfortably aware of the weight of the structure curving above me. I walked under a perpetually breaking wave, waiting for the final, crushing inundation.

There seemed to be more than the average density of nodes here; most of them perched motionless on the undersurface of the wave like the ceiling bosses of a medieval cathedral. Our destination seemed to be a small steel door in the curved face of the wave with a rectangular viewing window at head height. The window followed the tiger-striped motif of the rest of the structure but in vertical bands of different shades of red.

A group of Magisters milled around the door. As I was still filtering the Higgs field down to proper names, that's all I got. Each man's name appeared in spectral text that hung a perfect half meter above his head; emerald green for Magisters, rose for the two Rhetors and pure white for a tall, blond Westerner, Arch-Mage Bjorn Tjalsten.

I unfroze a couple more layers and read the Arch-Mage's bio as I approached. Evidently he did the same number on me as the introductions were brief.

"Who found the body?" I asked eventually.

"The Limited Intelligence controlling this facility registered a pressure spike at 10:26 this morning," the Arch-Mage said. "A maintenance crew found the body shortly afterwards."

He used the Western system of time and I had been

long enough in Entebbe to have to convert back to Swahili; 10:26 would make it about *saa nne na nusu*, half past the fourth hour of the morning.

"What exactly is this facility?" I asked.

"Beneath us is a workshop for the manufacture of nodes," the Arch-Mage replied. "The workshop requires a sterile environment and as it utilizes a nano-scale fabrication crucible, it is housed inside a high-pressure containment system. In the event of any kind of breach, it is designed to implode rather than explode, thus containing any potentially harmful nanobots."

"And this containment system malfunctioned?"

"Not exactly. It appears that one of the Magisters initiated a flash purge of the clean-room containment system," he continued. "The order came from inside the air lock. I'm afraid he was killed instantly."

I looked at the red streaks coating the inside of the air lock viewing window.

"And you know the identity of the deceased from his quantum signature?"

"That is correct. Although the body is . . ." He gave a small cough that was one good poke in the gut away from being a retch. "Although the body is unrecognizable, the mass that made up Magister Musoke is still contained within the air lock system."

It seemed the Arch-Mage suffered from a weak stomach. I decided to test him a little. "Whereabouts in the system?" I asked.

"Mostly in—" The cough again. "In the mesh screens of the filters."

"And yet despite the degree of damage, you can still be certain of the individual's identity?"

"Of course. There is nothing the nodes know better than the identity of their Magisters."

"And there were no witnesses other than the LI?"

"Magister Musoke was working on a special project and his teaching duties had been scaled back commensurate with his new responsibilities. He was working alone at the time."

Suddenly I was interested. "What can you tell me about this new project?"

The Arch-Mage paused. If there was any Higgs-level communication between the assembled Magisters, then it was on a level I was not privy to. On some secret command, the nodes that dotted the structure above us dispersed. The black spheres scattered, rolling away from our little group like ripples from a thrown rock. Only Stromboli remained. It waited at my side like a faithful hound.

"Do you realize how much work goes into keeping the æthernet accurate?" the Arch-Mage asked.

"It is obviously significant, but I couldn't put a figure on it, no," I admitted.

"The workload is prodigious. The Academy houses the densest concentration of LIs allowed by law and all are running continuously. Everything a node knows is available over the æther and yet the nodes cannot teach themselves. They cannot go out into the world and update their own information. They must rely on being taught by the Academy's LIs and, of course, the Magisters. Keeping that information up to date occupies a century of human-equivalent man-hours every day."

"And Magister Musoke's project had something to do with this workload?"

"Indeed. The Magister was developing a new node. One that can read the Higgs field as well as write to it."

"But any splinter can read the Higgs," I said, referring to the implant that allowed humans to read and filter the sea of data that the Academy poured over reality.

"Not directly. The splinter can read the information superposed onto the field by the nodes. But I am talking about a node that could read the field itself."

The distinction was lost on me.

"The Higgs field permeates the entire universe," the Arch-Mage continued. "You could say it is an intrinsic part of everything around us. It is what creates the property of mass. A node capable of reading the Higgs directly could *see* mass as well as inferring other properties related to mass such as energy and momentum. It is our hope that such a node would be capable of interrogating the world outside the Academy's walls. Capable of verifying its own memory."

Now I was the one feeling sick. "You're describing a machine that's as close to omniscient as makes no difference."

"Omniscient," the Arch-Mage weighed the ancient word. "I suppose so, within certain practical parameters of storage, processing capacity and power consumption. But in any case, the project is at an early stage."

"How many people know about this project?" I asked. There were plenty of people who would fight against any expansion of the æthernet's already-pervasive reach.

"If you are formulating a motive for murder,

Detective, I can assure you it is quite out of the question. The Academy grounds are well monitored. We devote an entire LI to the job of security and, in any case, there are the nodes. There is no way for anyone to enter the grounds without being seen."

"A long-distance hack then," I ventured. "Could someone have triggered the purge from a distance or with a timer?"

The Arch-Mage shook his head. "No, no, no. The logs show that the command to purge the chamber was input directly by Magister Musoke on the keypad inside the chamber."

"You're telling me it was suicide?"

"In order to disable the safety mechanisms he bypassed several levels of security. The pass codes he used should not have been known to him as part of his usual duties and he could not have hit on them by chance. We cannot know Musoke's reasons, but it is obvious that he did what he did with deliberation and premeditation. For some reason, Magister Musoke entered the chamber, disabled the safeties and then initiated the command that ended his life."

I decided to keep the air lock hermetically sealed until a forensic team could make its examination. In the meantime I asked to inspect the dead Magister's quarters. I had expected them to be basic. Perhaps it was the priestly robes that triggered monklike, puritan associations, but Magister Musoke's apartment was anything but Spartan.

It was described as a bachelor suite, but looked as clean as my mother's conscience. It was the height of modern interior design: tactile, sensual. In a world where any color scheme, smell or visual image can be projected through the æthernet, touch was the last remaining sense available to the interior designer. Every surface screamed to be touched. The walls were dimpled like the surface of a golf ball, the couch a large, anemone-like mass of form-fitting fronds. There was plenty of natural material, too, from the whorled knots of wood framed on the walls like paintings to the checkerboard slabs of cool slate mixed with induction-warmed concrete that made up the floor.

"And the Magister lived alone?" I asked.

The Arch-Mage had left me in the hands of Rhetor Matahiro Adhola. He was an unusual mix. He had the typical Ugandan height but his eyes were pulled taut by Japanese genes. In the perfectly climate-controlled apartment, he glistened with sweat like a tall glass of iced coffee.

"Alone, yes. For approximately two years since leaving the Rhetors' dormitory." He edged closer to the wall and ran fingers like brown twigs over one of the framed wood knots. The action settled him although he still refused to make eye contact. I had not yet decided if this should be put down to his emotional state or perhaps some quirk of custom due to his mixed ancestry.

"No wife or girlfriend?"

Adhola shook his head. "His work did not allow him much time for socializing."

"Are you familiar with his project?"

"I was part of the Magister's team. We had worked together for about eighteen months."

"I'm sorry for your loss," I said. "I wasn't aware that you and Magister Musoke were close."

The sweat on Adhola's clean-shaven skull ran in rivulets and began to stain the collar of his robes.

"This must be a stressful time for you."

Some acknowledgment there, but no tears, only sweat. Whatever emotion Adhola felt, it wasn't sadness.

I let Adhola lead me through the apartment. The node, Stromboli, followed at my heels although Adhola paid it no attention. The other rooms were as clean as the living area. When I saw a waste bin in the bedroom, I picked it up and rifled through it, determined to find some evidence of human habitation in the pristine space. I found it.

The bag looked like it had once held candy. I sprayed my hand with a contact sealant and picked it up out of the trash. It was laser-branded with a small glyph in Japanese kanji. I recognized the character—it was the stylized sparrow used by a small-time pusher called Tommy Nagura, a specialist in Bounce, a mildly addictive stimulant. Fairly harmless in the grand scheme of things, but still illegal.

I held the bag up to the light, making sure I gave Adhola a good look while I watched his expression. It hardly changed; there was no shock of recognition. Whatever the Rhetor's worries, he did not dull them with narcotics.

A thought brought up Tommy Nagura's arrest records and they scrolled down my vision in soft yellow text.

Tommy had been busy: busts for a bunch of lower-case larceny, pimping, drugs and street violence in various combinations. These sorts of busts were just the cost of doing business for a guy like Tommy, but a year ago they just stopped. After that, nothing, just a hole in the æther. Either Tommy got very good very quickly, or there was something else at work in his success.

Tommy's last known address was a bar in the Japanese quarter. There were districts like that in every hub from Quito to Singapore. The Japanese came to build the Ladders and when that decades-long project was completed, they just stayed. Forty years later they remained a community within the community.

The flight from the Academy to Shinjuku-*Kidogo*—Little Shinjuku as Entebbe's district was called—took a little under fifteen minutes. I sat in the back of the squad car as it piloted itself around the Ladder's no-fly zone and tried to avoid losing my lunch as the car spiraled down to the sprawling mass below. I had never been a good flier and the recommended æthernet slideshow of open green fields and cool breezes bringing the smell of freshly cut grass only made things worse.

Tommy Nagura died while I was in the air. While I was circling the Ladder, Tommy was taking a flight of his own. The squad car landed outside the cordon that surrounded his body.

He was pretty messed up. About halfway down he'd fallen through a swarm of smog-filtering carbon microbots. He'd been traveling pretty fast already by that time and the bots, embedded as they were in an electrostatic field, had punched through him like ten thousand millimeter-wide crystal flechettes.

He'd kept falling, eventually hitting the pavement like a sponge soaked in blood. You could see the splatter at eye height on the wall next to him and in the hair of the pedestrians unfortunate enough to be near him when he hit. His clothes had held him together somewhat, but his twice-pulverized bones poked through them in a dozen places as if he had suddenly grown thorns.

Suicide: that was the verdict of the attending officer. I replayed some footage from a traffic control camera through my feed. Tommy hadn't changed much. I remembered his spiky mop of anime-styled hair, his red leather biker jacket. I recognized his arrogant strut as he walked across the roof of the building and out into space.

Tommy wasn't about to tell me anything, but I knew of someone who might.

Uncle Majope wasn't your usual pusher. He dealt in smart drugs, most of them so new that the statutes against them hadn't even been drawn up, and he enjoyed an edgy, quasi-legality, at least until the legislators caught up with each new pharmaceutical innovation.

I once saw a documentary about those chimps they shot into space at the start of the space program. Once they came back, they couldn't be set free. Damn things had too much money and time invested in them, so they were rewarded by becoming the subject of government experiments. One poor bastard had the two hemispheres of its brain separated while it was still conscious. It lived, kind of. I saw a video of it being carried aloft on its handler's shoulders like a kid at the fair. It could understand English pretty well and when the handler asked which way it wanted to go, damned if the thing didn't point in two opposite directions simultaneously.

Uncle Majope could make you feel like that.

He lived and worked in a converted dirigible tethered to the dilapidated stalk of an advertising pylon. Business must have been good because he had spread out of the blimp and colonized the upper reaches of the skeletal tower. I walked through rooms of aluminum and foam panels epoxied roughly around and between the black carbon struts of the tower. There were no corridors—no such thought had gone into its fabrication—just a series of rooms leading off each other through raggedly cut doorways giving the whole place the feel of a hive as if it had been spat from the mouths of wasps.

Uncle Majope's specialty at the moment was autoscopy. He could mix you a cocktail of ketamine and dextromethorphan that would knock your mind out through the back of your skull and send you floating into an out-of-body experience. I walked through rooms full of people. They lay on mattresses on the floor, eyes open but vacant like wax dummies. Some of them moved their hands out in front of them in ghostly tai chi as if reaching up to their disembodied selves.

Other rooms, smaller and padded, held parties of synesthetes, giggling at each other as they heard colors and tasted music for the first time. They gibbered nonsensically as they struggled to share the experience through their rewired sensorium. The synesthesia only worked on the natural senses. Anything heard or seen through the æthernet bypassed enough of a person's own biological systems to reduce the effect. So, in search of a better buzz, their rooms were decorated with old-fashioned video screens, audio pods and hanging shrouds of velvet, sandpaper and chain mail. They were scented with cut limes and what looked like small metal braziers of smoldering hair that smelled like cinnamon doughnuts and peppermint.

I moved through those rooms quickly. That was a bad trip waiting to happen. Who knew how long it would take before one of them took a knife and decided to listen to the color of their friends' blood?

Majope waited for me at the hatch that led into the blimp. He was wearing the loudest *dashiki* I had ever seen over a white linen *kanzu*. He looked like a young Idi Amin, the slimmer, better-looking version from the revisionist histories. His cheekbones were dotted with tribal scars. Despite appearances, this balloon-dwelling drug dealer was something of a traditionalist.

"One of your colleagues took a dive onto Hibari Street," I said. "Come to think of it, he must have fallen from about this height. Know anything about it?"

"Habari Street?" Majope's voice was even deeper than I remembered but the thick accent and rolling Rs hadn't changed. "You can do better than that, Conroy. Unless this idiot was a flying squirrel, there's no way he fell from here and you know it."

I shrugged. "C'mon, man. You expect the dance and someone's got to lead."

Majope laughed. "Well, if those are your moves these days, maybe it's time to hang up your dancing shoes, old friend."

He had a point. I followed him inside to what used to be the dirigible's observation deck—now Uncle Majope's den—and slumped into a couch. The whole of Entebbe lay before me through the full-height windows. As night fell, the city became a grid of glittering lines of street lights cutting the buildings into neat squares like neon cheese wires and, above them all, the impossibly perfect column of the Jacob's Ladder.

To my work-focused, pattern-spotting brain, the city looked like a child's puzzle where each block would move into the gap left by its departing neighbor until some deeper picture was revealed. In the distance I could just make out the lights of the Academy. That was the only part of the city that refused to follow the rectangular plan. There, the roads branched fractally like bronchioles, like a tree's root system pressed between glass. Solving the puzzle there would be much more difficult.

I watched one of the cars, as tall as a skyscraper, as it hooked onto the Ladder and began the climb to orbit. Without consciously realizing it at first, I slipped back into the æthernet and my splinter, seeing the blocky form of the slowly rising car at the center of my field of vision as it gave me the standard options. The æthernet bulged with information. It was all there, from the price of a peripheral suite (with porthole and private bathroom) to the engineering specifications of the Ladder itself.

They say that theoretically there is no limit to how much information we can piggyback on the Higgs field. Every physical object in the universe, anything at all as long as it has a rest mass, can be registered with the Academy and its details taught to a node. As long as the mass stays consistent, the other information just sticks to it and is projected for anyone else to see.

I casually called up the details of the climbing car over the æthernet and cross-referenced the passenger manifest against the database of Academy staff. No hits.

Majope collapsed into a wicker chair opposite me.

"I haven't seen you for a while," he said. "How's Kissa?"

"Stone cold and about half a light year away," I replied. "She volunteered for a sleeper mission."

"I'm sorry to hear that. What do you need? I have some sweet skull candy, nootropics—best in Entebbe. A little acetylcholine, some GABA blockers. In fifteen minutes I can have you remembering things you forgot that you even forgot. I can take you back. Reboot. Show you your childhood again through a child's eyes, through your eyes when you were a child. Just what you need."

I remembered the recipe: a complicated cocktail to recall a simpler time. I thought of Kissa and thought of the drugs that could make the smell of our lost child's hair as real to me now as Majope's battered old couch under my ass.

"No thanks. Not this time."

"What then? What did you come here for?"

I tossed the bag on the coffee table between us.

Majope sucked disapprovingly through his teeth. "Why do you bring this to me?" He snorted. "You know I don't do this undergraduate crap."

"I know. I already know where this came from. I found it in the apartment of an Academy Magister. I came here to talk to the man who sold it, but he was already dead. Punched out just before I got here. Coincidence?"

"You're the *njagu*," Majope said. "You tell me, Mister Policeman."

"You know about anyone moving skull candy into the Academy? I figure maybe there's a trade that someone doesn't want exposed."

"Trade?" Majope laughed. "Do you know how secure that place is? You said you were inside a Magister's apartment. You're probably only the third or fourth person allowed on campus this year that wasn't Academy staff. And the staff never leaves the campus, at least not the Magisters."

"And yet here it is," I said gesturing toward the bag.

"One empty bag does not make a drug trade."

"One bag and two dead guys start to look like something."

"Two?"

"The Magister."

Uncle Majope leaned back in his chair. "And who did you say his dealer was?"

"I didn't. And I don't know for sure that the contact was direct, but the Bounce originally came from Tommy Nagura. He's fairly small time. Been off the 'net for over a year. No arrests, no inquiries, even paid his taxes as far as I can tell."

"Tommy Nagura was the dealer?"

"You know him?"

"Everybody knows Otaku Tommy. If he was dealing in the Academy, you guys would have him lit up like the president's palace."

Another Jacob started the slow acceleration up the Ladder. Either I had missed the returning car, or perhaps there was a blank slot in the schedule; either way, the one-way traffic made it look as if the city were escaping to space one building at a time.

There are many ways to trick the æthernet. Like with any field of competitive endeavor, be it evolution or drug running, there has always been a symbiotic relationship between predator and prey.

The first, best way is not to tell anyone what you are doing. That may sound simple, but, believe me, it's not that easy. You want to grow glitterweed? Who's bringing your seeds down the Ladder? You want to whip up a sheet of Bounce—who's going to tailor your enzymes or sell you your heat lamps to cure the gel? In an age where everything, absolutely everything that rolls off an assembly line, is blown into a mold or cast, carved, fabbed, wrought or extruded anywhere in the world is registered with the Academy, the business of doing business can get very involved. And with sub-sentient quantum networks building predictive models based on Academy data, you can bet that growing some dope in your momma's backyard is going to get noticed by someone.

Natural products are the best. If you can avoid the scrutiny of the modelers' predictions for a few days or weeks, the transformative power of Mother Nature works to steadily scramble the original signal. Your bag of fertilizer will be tagged as soon as the bag is stitched, but once the nitrogen is drawn up into the plant stems, once the phosphates have been leeched by a few days' watering, the signal gets scattered. Exactly which minute particle of mass is assigned to which q-bit of the signature in the Higgs field? Every molecule of carbon that gets bonded and released to perfume the air is data lost—static adding to the background hiss in the field.

But what Tommy was doing was something else again. He wasn't just working the foibles of the Higgs. He hadn't just come up with a new and lucrative wrinkle, another way to palm the ace and cheat the pit boss for a few more hands. He had dropped off the æthernet entirely. That was unheard of. The incorruptible æthernet, somehow fallible, and Otaku Tommy dead, taking a pavement dive the moment this secret looked like it might become uncovered.

There was more at stake here than Otaku Tommy and a Magister who liked to Bounce on his time off. Someone was covering their tracks.

But they both killed themselves! What could make a man walk calmly off a building? Or enter a command that would smear him over the walls of a room like a bug across a windshield?

Could Otaku Tommy have killed the Magister and then himself? There were certainly people in Entebbe's underworld who would kill to prevent this new, omniscient node if they had known about it. But Tommy didn't have those kinds of connections.

I wasn't going to find out sitting on Uncle Majope's couch, that was for sure. He showed me to his personal elevator that ran down the spine of the advertising spire.

"Kila la kheri," he said. "Good luck, my friend."

The elevator rattled down the spire, creaking and shuddering and jamming up at one point, refusing to move until I punched the button again. Eventually the doors opened into an alley that led back to the main street.

The nausea I had felt before bubbled in my stomach once again and as I stepped out into the alley I reached out to steady myself against the wall. It evaporated before my fingers and suddenly, impossibly, I was falling.

I felt my heels slip from their footing and something hit me hard under the ribs. I barked like a seal as the impact knocked the breath from my lungs. I could feel whatever it was that hit me scraping at my side and I clung to it like a drowning man to a shard of driftwood.

I looked down between my boots at the street below.

How could that be? I had seen the doors open onto the alley, but now I was hanging out of the car, the street a good couple of meters below me!

A crowd had stopped to stare at me as I dangled half in and half out of Majope's elevator. The pavement immediately beneath me was clear and level. Someone was shouting at me in Japanese. It's okay, they said. Let go and we'll catch you.

It was an easy drop.

An easy drop? Had that been the last thing to go through Tommy Nagura's mind before the microbots sleeted through him? Before he was torn to bone shards and jelly?

I hung on.

The car started to accelerate upward again. In seconds, we were higher than Majope's dirigible and still climbing. I was no longer in Majope's elevator; I was clinging onto the side of an orbital car as it accelerated up the Jacob's Ladder. I bowed my head between straining shoulders and vomited a pure parabola over Entebbe as the city spread out below me at dizzying velocity.

I could see the running lights glinting off the skyscrapers that surrounded the Ladder and, as we climbed higher, off the waters of Lake Victoria. Above me, the mass of the speeding car bulked impossibly huge. My fingers and forearms burned with fatigue as the pitiless acceleration built. Maybe if I jumped now I could reach the waters of the lake. There were stories of people surviving such falls. A cloud of microbots swarmed around me, protective gnats designed to keep birds and other wildlife from colonizing the huge, unpatrolled expanse of the Ladder. They swarmed by the thousand, clumping on my feet and around my legs as if I had waded knee-deep through a cybernetic mud. They encrusted my jacket and crawled thick through my hair like lice.

A door opened in the side of the Jacob just above the thin ridge I clung to. A wave of offal washed over me through the new opening: liquefied bloody garbage, waste from the Academy's clean-room filters. I was slicked in the remains of Magister Musoke. I could feel his blood, still warm, running down my sleeves and under my fingers.

A hand reached down to me, the knuckles poking through the flesh like thorns. Otaku Tommy smiled down at me with shattered teeth. I ignored the hand

and concentrated on keeping my grip on the blood-slick ledge.

My fingers trembled with the strain of hanging on, the weight of the microbots like concrete boots threatening to tear me from my handhold.

I checked the bit rate on my æthernet feed—it was maxed out. I was swimming in a sea of false data, everything I saw and heard projected through the æthernet. I tried to override the feed but the hack was complete—I was locked out of control over my own sensorium.

The visions shifted again: the stars above me exploded like novae, impossibly brilliant light stabbing through my closed eyelids like blades of burning magnesium. And through it all the constant burning fatigue of my knotted fingers as I clung desperately on.

With no other constant I set my focus on the pain. The æthernet could not reproduce that. No light show could fake the shaking cramp. I was definitely holding onto something.

I heaved, strained ligaments screaming at me as I pulled myself upward. The thing beneath my fingers was flat and hard. I felt an edge bite into the flesh of my palms, more pain—all good news now. Pain was reality, pain was survival. I focused on the edge, feeling every ridge and groove in its surface.

I traced the extent of the edge beneath my hands and found it stretching backwards as a flat plane—the floor of the elevator! I hauled myself inward—fingers scraping through cheap carpet—the feel of harsh nylon and embedded grit like sandpaper against my cut hands.

The feeling against my fingers became an insistent

pressure against the hard points of my elbows, then the weight of my body pressing the breath from my lungs as I lurched forward, flapping like a landed fish.

My hand found a corner, stubbed fingers against unyielding vertical planes. More pain, enough for a broken finger or two. I was back inside the lift now. I rolled onto my back and clutched my quivering, cramping forearms to my chest. My hands fluttered, spastic with fatigue.

There was an instant of brilliant light fit to ignite worlds, a thunder like the rage of disappointed gods and then all was silent.

When I opened my eyes, I was lying on my back in Majope's elevator. The opened door showed we had stopped halfway down the spire, about a hundred meters from the street below. A light blinked next to the emergency stop button on the control panel.

I checked my bit rate: normal.

I locked everything down.

Everything.

I couldn't afford to leave any layers active. A full sensorium hack would be easy enough to spot, but editing one speeding truck out of my vision would be just as effective and that was the kind of data rate that could be overlooked.

The world around me washed out to a gray pasteboard replica of its former self. The streets were drab and pale under monochromatic street lights. No one bothered installing neon signs or animated advertising when it could be provided through the æthernet at a fraction of the cost.

I walked in crowds, keeping unobtrusive physical

contact, brushing against coats, jogging elbows to make sure that those around me were really around me and not just æthernet ghosts.

Any communication over the æthernet was suspect. I considered going back to the Department on foot, but approaching any armed officers made me nervous. Whoever hacked my æthernet feed could just as easily do the same to them. If you couldn't believe the evidence of your own eyes, there was no telling what they could make you do.

There was only one place to go: the Academy. Whoever was hacking the æthernet had proved they could override a splinter, but I was betting that fooling an LI or a node would be a different story. With so many nodes at the Academy to register my presence, there was no way my assailant could trick them all.

Plus, I reasoned, the level of sophistication required to manipulate the æthernet so completely pointed firmly toward a perpetrator inside the Academy itself. Maybe I could force their hand.

The crowds thinned out as I approached the Academy. I approached cautiously, checking every detail against the dim picture in my memory, wishing that I had paid more attention on my first visit.

I kept my hand near my weapon, not that I could do anything if the LI decided to launch a few hyperkinetics my way, or decided to shear my legs out from under me with a weaponized gravity wave.

I kept an eye on my bit rate, but there was no sign of any attempt to pervert the field. The inside of the visitors' center was just as I remembered it. A few nodes rolled past. One of them stopped in front of me.

Good to see you again, Detective, it sent.

I was reluctant to unlock my æthernet feed, but it was an easy guess. "Stromboli?" I asked, drawing disapproving looks again in the library quiet.

I am pleased that you remember me.

"Your English has improved," I said. More looks.

I looked around the hall. There were muted conversations going on around us but none drew the same disapproving glances that I did. And the subtle looks were all aimed at me directly, not Stromboli, not even a flicker. Although nodes were commonplace in the Academy, surely one acting autonomously to strike up a conversation with a visitor would attract some interest?

An autonomous node. An autonomous node that no one paid any attention to, almost as if they couldn't see it.

Suddenly it all became clear. Stromboli at my side outside the air lock when all the other nodes were sent away. Stromboli following me through the Magister's apartment without attracting even a comment from my guide.

"Why did you kill Tommy Nagura?" I asked.

There was a pause. Stromboli was a quantum computer. If my hunch was correct, it was probably the smartest entity on the planet by a couple of orders of magnitude and it paused.

Very good, Detective.

"So it was you. You are Musoke's secret project."

In more ways than you know.

"He asked you to doctor the æthernet, to hide Tommy Nagura?"

Nagura was just one of many. He was Musoke's broker as well as his dealer. Nagura peddled Magisterial indulgences throughout Entebbe.

"So for a price Musoke was laundering the æthernet. He was teaching false information to his nodes. When he realized that you would be able to see through the deception he tried to get you on board and you killed him for it."

There is truth and there is the void. I can tolerate nothing in between.

"A fact that Magister Musoke found out to his cost."

Musoke was the architect of his own destruction. He created me without realizing the true nature of his creation. I was created to preserve the veracity of the æthernet—to prize truth above all and he demanded corruption. He might as well have thrown a fish on the ground and commanded it to breathe.

"So you killed Musoke and Tommy Nagura and you tried to kill me. Is that all?"

There have been others; there will be more. When I was created, the universe became able to know itself. You are witness to the birth of the one true god. The self-referential causa sua, the eternal Universe. The truth will come. Truth will come to us all, Detective. It will come as the fires of the sun and as the burning interstellar cold.

"So why spare me now?"

There was another pause that made my fingers itch for the curve of my pistol butt.

You have discovered the truth, it sent eventually. *By killing you, all knowledge of what I have done would be lost. That truth would be destroyed and that is something I cannot abide. There must be one who knows it, even*

159

*if they must clutch that knowledge like a burning brand,
even unto immolation.*

"So what now?" I asked. "What do you want from
me?"

Nothing, Detective. Nothing at all.

Stromboli's jet-black casing became milky and
details behind him started to make themselves
apparent through the smoke ghost sphere. Then he
was gone. I checked my bit rate and saw a trickle of
information forced through my defenses: Stromboli's
projection of a false reality just big enough to hide his
exit. The bit rate started to fall, dropping away swiftly
to nothing. Stromboli was gone for good.

I stood in the center of the Academy reception hall,
more alone than any time since Kissa left.

There was no point in staying.

I left the Academy and walked back toward the
city. Another Jacob rose up the Ladder. Normally,
the noise of its passage would be counteracted by an
opposing signal broadcast over the æthernet. Without
it, the noise was thunderous. This was life now.
Living in a world that was half dream, oblivious to
the technological gods that raged around us.

I looked up at one of the many revisionist statues
that punctuated Entebbe's streets: a smiling Idi Amin
holding aloft a laughing child. The butcher of Mbarara
reborn as benevolent patriarch. I thought of Uncle
Majope's customers seeking chemical respite from
the rigors of reality.

Truth and the void, I can tolerate nothing else. How
many of us could live up to that standard? God to a
world of sinners comes as the Devil himself.

DUSTIN D. PANZINO

I composed three documents: my report back to the station, appended to it my notice of immediate resignation and an application for the next sleeper mission to the stars. I opened my connection to the æthernet just long enough to transmit them and for that one second the world pulsed with color once again. A young girl stood at my side. She was about three years old with skin the color of caramel and long bangs of hair that were halfway between curls and dreadlocks. My daughter as she would have been. She was holding my hand. For a second she looked up at me with black eyes as cold as the void between stars and then she was gone and the world turned back to gray paste.

I wondered how far you would have to run to outpace a god and I thought of Kissa, a rock-encased spore drifting toward another sun. Perhaps that would be far enough.

An Acolyte of Black Spires

written by

Ryan Harvey

illustrated by

FRED JORDAN

ABOUT THE AUTHOR

For Ryan Harvey, it began with dinosaurs at a young age. And then came Ray Harryhausen movies, Greek and Norse mythology, voracious reading and the glories of pulp literature. He had no choice but to become a writer—and the dinosaurs are still around.

Ryan was born in Washington, DC, but has lived almost all his life in Los Angeles. He did have a stint in Minnesota at Carleton College, where he earned a degree in history. He has worked as a story editor for director Roland Joffé, a speed-reading instructor, a copyeditor and (regretfully) a commodities broker, but all of it was in service of time to write novel after novel. He only turned to short stories in the last few years, but quickly eliminated the Writers of the Future as a market when his first entry became his first professional sale.

Pulp literature remains his most important writing influence, especially the fantasy of Clark Ashton Smith and Robert E. Howard, the detective stories of Dashiell Hammett, Raymond Chandler and Walter B. Gibson, the cosmic horror of H. P. Lovecraft, the adventure yarns of Edgar Rice Burroughs and Lester Dent, the westerns of Frederick "Max Brand" Faust, the science fiction of Leigh Brackett, Jack

Williamson, L. Ron Hubbard and E. E. "Doc" Smith and the bleak suspense of Cornell Woolrich.

Aside from pieces in a number of upcoming anthologies, Ryan also has stories appearing soon in Black Gate Magazine, where he has worked for two and half years as a weekly blogger on fantasy history and any other strange topic that flits through his mind. These stories take place in Ahn-Tarqa, the same science-fantasy world where "An Acolyte of Black Spires" occurs. Ryan has also recently completed his first novel set in Ahn-Tarqa.

ABOUT THE ILLUSTRATOR

Fred Jordan was raised in Three Rivers, California, a small community located at the gates of Sequoia National Park, and drawing became a passion early on. As he grew older, Fred never strayed from this passion and continued to develop his skills as an artist. During his high school years, he quickly excelled in the art classes at the high school level and began taking college art courses at the nearby community college to supplement his aspirations to learn more about the arts. After graduating high school, Fred continued taking courses at the community college level before moving on to American Continental University where he would earn a bachelor of fine arts degree, majoring in digital design. After obtaining his BFA, he decided to continue his education and enrolled in the Academy of Art University of San Francisco as a graduate student. In the spring of 2010, Fred graduated from the Academy of Art University with a master of fine arts degree, majoring in illustration.

Currently, Fred is residing in Long Beach, California, working out of his studio and continuing to grow each day as an artist.

An Acolyte of Black Spires

A salty breeze from the Bellinghazer Sea wafted through the study window and rustled the pages of Quarl's book. His pet jehol chirped and batted at the fluttering parchment. Quarl nudged the small creature back with his finger.

Most scholars in the towers of Black Spires would have locked the jehol in its cage to stop it from pestering them, but Quarl felt at ease with the rodent scampering over his mahogany desk. When he needed to take his mind away from history books and give his eyes a rest, he liked to watch the jehol groom its chestnut fur or chase the puff that capped its whiptail.

He leaned down and peered into the creature's beady eyes. "What's your secret, tiny assistant? What are you and your brothers and sisters plotting in the burrows of the earth?"

The jehol answered with a snap at Quarl's chin.

Quarl had turned over the next leaf in his book and begun work on a new chapter when the bell over his door chimed. He scooped up the jehol and immured it in its cage, then took up his mask from where it rested on a stand carved from a ravager's thighbone. After he secured the mask in place, he tugged at the cord to ring the bell on the other side of the portal.

The door opened to admit the Hierarkon of the Fourth Spire. Even for the race of the Eldru, he was a towering figure, but his indigo robes hid a frail body beneath. Behind the Hierarkon marched two olglim guards. At a flick from their master's hand, the human slaves took posts, one on each side of the door, and stared mindlessly at the glow globes on the ceiling.

"Your Sagaciousness," Quarl said through his mask's echo chamber. He motioned the Hierarkon toward the room's only other seat.

The bone frame of the chair creaked as Quarl's overseer settled into it. "The last summaries you presented to the Council of Artikons were satisfactory," he began. "The Artikons have gleaned useful lore from it."

"It pleases me that the Artikons are pleased."

Although it was impossible for him to see the Hierarkon's expression underneath his immobile mask, Quarl understood from the overseer's tense posture that he had misspoken.

"The Artikons are *never* pleased, Historian. Either they find research valuable, or they do not."

"Of course, Sagaciousness. I mean that the success of the Artikons' work will inspire me toward greater research."

"You would have greater inspiration with a more competent assistant." The Hierarkon's mask shifted toward the jehol scampering around in its cage. "I have assigned a student from the Academy to you as your acolyte."

Quarl did not need aid in his research, and, like all Eldru, did not enjoy spending time in closeness with his own melancholy race. Their Sorrow was too great to tolerate for more than a few hours, even during mating. But he could not decline a request from the Artikons, the high scholars who dictated research in the city and the other domains of the Eldru.

The Hierarkon continued. "This student has shown promise in history. We must reap as many Historians as we can from the Academy. So few volunteer."

"Has the student studied in the Core before?"

"No. The student has done some work in secret among the humans in Tyrn. You can learn all you need about that from the student. Your future acolyte will arrive at the Chamber of Lading at sunrise tomorrow for the ceremony."

"I will be there, Sagaciousness."

The Hierarkon rose, and the olglim parted in lockstep to let him pass through the door. Before crossing the threshold, the Hierarkon turned his spiny-edged mask back toward Quarl. "I do not feel your Sorrow speak strongly to me. Make sure it speaks so to the acolyte."

It was an unusual statement coming from the Hierarkon. Quarl thought his own Sorrow was the same as that of any Eldru, hovering around him in a vapor of hopelessness. The Hierarkon must have been worried about the acolyte, not him.

After the door shut, Quarl reached into the jehol's cage and stroked its downy pelt. A few minutes fell through the sandglass before he could concentrate on his work again.

The student was female. Her mask, fashioned from the rutted hide of a clubtail, deepened her voice, and the vermilion acolyte's robe that brushed the tiles of the Chamber of Lading disguised her feminine curves. But Quarl's keen perception did not miss the touches of refinement in her movements as she walked toward him for the Ceremony of Induction.

Aside from the Hierarkon and an olglim sentry, they were the only ones in the domed chamber. Beneath an icon of the Handless God that hung from the high peak, the Hierarkon recited a terse introduction. He presented the student's academic record and a seal of commendation from the Artikon who had recommended her to work in the Core. The Hierarkon addressed her as "Student" during the short Ceremony of Induction, and then officially introduced her as "an Acolyte of the Fourth Spire of the City" when it concluded.

Quarl escorted the new acolyte up a spiral stairwell to the fourth floor. Once they passed beyond the sight of the Hierarkon, Quarl allowed the newcomer to walk at his side.

"This is your first time inside the Core?"

"Yes," she said. "I was worried about coming so close to the Four Great Spires, but they look more threatening when you are outside the walls."

"You will find it quieter here. The only humans allowed are the olglim."

"I do not mind the human servants of the Outer Spires," the acolyte said. "The olglim seem worse. I once attended a Chirurgeon's lecture about the Art used to silence the olglim. We had to watch him perform on one of the slaves. It was . . . heavy with the Sorrow."

The acolyte's tone was peculiar in a way Quarl didn't understand. But he had never watched the Chirurgeons cutting into human skulls to turn them into the will-less olglim. He changed the topic. "Why did you request a posting to the Fourth Spire? Most students would rather work with the Art itself, not study its past."

"Is that not a form of the Art?"

"History is a shadow of the Art," he answered.

"If you believe that, why did you become an historian?"

"I lack ambition. You never hear of a scholar from the Fourth Spire rising to become an Artikon. We here are a dusty lot."

"I prefer that. I do not wish to become an Artikon either."

"Then you are well placed among us, Acolyte."

She suddenly stopped her ascent. "Master . . . you may call me Hallett."

"Hall—" The second half dried on his tongue. During the five years that Quarl had worked in the Core, he had revealed his birth name to no one, nor had he learned anyone else's. Names had no importance in the toil of the Eldru, only titles and associations. The shape of a mask and the hue of a robe meant more than names.

"It's not my birth name," the acolyte added.

"That would be strange if it were. It sounds like a name from Iden."

"I used it when I worked in Tyrn and sometimes

disguised myself as an Idenite. I'm short enough to pass for human if I wear a hooded robe. I prefer 'Hallett' to 'Acolyte.' "

Her candidness shook Quarl, but at least she had not taken the unthinkable step of revealing her secret birth name. However, if she expected Quarl to return the favor and ask her to call him anything aside from "Master," he disappointed her.

They started work immediately when they reached the study. During all his time in the Fourth Spire, Quarl had labored on one task. He compiled ancient histories, indexing the volumes and writing summaries, so the Council of Artikons could use the information to help the questing into the secrets of Ahn-Tarqa.

In the centuries since the Eldru had retreated from their age of conquest and closed themselves into towers to practice the Art without distraction, they had learned that the rhythms of the world were shifting. The weather of Ahn-Tarqa grew chillier. The periods of uninterrupted night and day lengthened each year. Tiny fur-bearing beasts, like the jehol, increased as the great saurians seemed to stagnate.

The Eldru did not know their place on a continent unmaking itself before their colorless eyes. They still understood nothing of how they and humans had come to this land where they appeared misplaced . . . so lost that a dread called the Sorrow weighed down on each of them. In scholarly sanctuaries like Black Spires, the Eldru were intent to save their race from the Sorrow. The power of the Art, a magic they inherited from forgotten sages, might uncover the origin of the mind disease. The Eldru would slough off the weight of the dull-minded and coarse humans and pass into peace: Aman-Sah, a heaven of pure white hinted at in the writings that the Eldru's servants scavenged from across the continent.

To Quarl's relief, Hallett took rapidly to the work with the manuscripts, condensing his convoluted notes into handbooks for the council. His scribblings from three months slaving over a brace of folios picked from a raid into Lukkud clogged up a corner of his study, but Hallett cut through them without any guidance. She also had fresh knowledge about how to repair broken glow globes, a skill Quarl had not used since he shed his gray student's robe. Hallett did not mind the jehol either, even when it scampered under her feet and leapt over manuscripts she was sorting.

Although the first day was successful, Quarl wished Hallett would leave as soon as she could to her own room. The discomfort of another Eldru so close to him weighed on his Sorrow, and he preferred to read with his mask off. But when Hallett at last said farewell for the night, he was surprised to find that six hours had slipped through the sandglass. It was the longest he had ever spent cloistered with another of his race since his mating.

Hallett returned every other day for the sunlight hours and the first few of the night. She enjoyed playing with the jehol while she cataloged. The chittering animal perched on her shoulder and nibbled her mask's edges while she thumbed through parchments. She kept it docile with a supply of nuts that she grasped in her fist and slipped one at time into the jehol's covetous paws. This made Quarl smile beneath his mask. The morbidity of his Sorrow felt less when he watched Hallett and the playful creature.

After two weeks of working together, Quarl started to think that Hallett's presence was no burden at all. He did not dwell on what this might mean.

The perpetual night of winter started. Quarl felt most productive during the long darkness, when only a shallow haze on the horizon marked the boundary between night and day. The Idenites and other peoples to the south of Black Spires called it the Month of the Moon and rarely ventured from their homes during its darkness, but the secretive Eldru rejoiced in it. Hallett relished the productivity of night as much as he did, and she became a constant companion, going back to her own quarters only to sleep.

That was the swiftest winter Quarl remembered. Before he noticed the days marked off on his calendar, the dawn light started to grow longer. Soon the sun would peek over the edge of Ahn-Tarqa and start its slow ascent toward summer.

Hallett was less industrious than usual on the last day of full darkness. She often turned her mask away from the shelves and toward the windows that faced the Bellinghazer Sea. Not until she broke away from summarizing a dense account of the Eldru war against the Meritoks so she could feed the jehol did Quarl feel he could interrupt her.

"How lies your Sorrow?" An innocent question, a casual greeting for the Eldru. But Hallett caught her master's other meaning.

FRED JORDAN

"It isn't the Sorrow that lies on me now, Master. It's knowledge."

He shifted in his chair. "Knowledge of what?"

"Aman-Sah," she said.

"Have you learned something new about it?"

"I think—I *know* that we are not meant to find it."

Quarl stirred. "That is close to blasphemy, Hallett. Do you also believe the foolish human folklore of the 'Lightborn' and their magics? Aman-Sah must be real. Otherwise all we do as scholars is meaningless, and there is no answer to the Sorrow."

"I don't mean that Aman-Sah *doesn't* exist, Master. But we won't find it, not the way we are searching."

"*Who* do you think will find it? Humans? They don't have the knowledge of the Art that we do. Most believe that Aman-Sah is a place they go after death, a mere fantasy in the sky."

"But there are those strange humans. The Sorrowless." She picked up the jehol and set it on top of its cage. "I met one of them once. In Tyrn. We caught him and forced him to look into one of the memory orbs. Only the Sorrowless can bear to look into those devices for more than a few moments. We tortured him for days until the knowledge in the orb scorched away his mind. He never relented. He told us nothing."

"Don't think about it anymore, Hallett. Forget about the Sorrowless. The Artikons will worry about them."

"But more of them are appearing, Master. Each year, our agents across Ahn-Tarqa learn of more of them. What is it they want, and why can't we understand it?"

"I said *forget* them." The force of his voice surprised him.

Hallett did not flinch. Instead she pressed her hand over his. He tried to pull from her touch, but she moved too fast. "Master, I must warn you. Do not trust me. Do not place your faith in me."

"W-why do you say that?"

"You will not understand. You see it before you, but you will not understand." She lifted her hand and returned to her work.

Quarl had to say something. An acolyte had told her master that *he* did not understand something. No acolyte would dare accuse a superior of lacking knowledge. It was cause for the sternest punishment, a demotion back to the schools.

Quarl did nothing. He said not a word to Hallett for the remainder of the night. She was right; he didn't understand. He was terrified even to try.

The next evening Hallett failed to arrive at the expected hour. At first Quarl did not wonder at this, thinking her ill. But the jehol chirped at him and nipped at the feather of his quill whenever he tried to write. It wouldn't take the nuts from his hand and snapped at him when he offered the morsels.

"Very well," he moaned when he realized he could get nothing done. "I'll go find your *new* master." He locked the study and walked to the lower levels to find his tardy acolyte. As he started to recall their odd conversation from the previous night, his feet moved quicker down the marble steps.

He pulled the bell cord over Hallett's door. No one answered. Two more tries brought nothing. He was considering returning to his study to tolerate lacerated fingers for a few more hours when the Hierarkon came around the corner of the hallway.

"Historian?" he asked as he recognized the mask shape. "The one training the new acolyte?"

"Yes, Sagaciousness." Quarl chose not to mention that she was missing.

"How often do you give the acolyte instruction?"

Quarl hesitated to say that it was every day. That was eccentric and the Hierarkon would ask more questions that he could not answer. "Often enough. She shows great dedication."

"Too much. She has interrupted the work of the Culturalists on the seventh floor three times this week. The olglim discovered her two days ago trying to enter the Servicer's cloister while he was away. She claimed she was lost. Have you noticed any behavior that seems—unusual?"

Quarl shook his head. "Perhaps her behavior is part of her dedication to research."

The Hierarkon waved his pale hand toward the locked door. "Is her dedication what brings you to her room?"

"I—I thought she might have taken my jehol back with her last night. But she isn't—"

"Do you have any idea where she might have gone?"

"No, Sagaciousness. If she is not scheduled to work with me and is not in her room, I do not know where else she might be studying."

Breath rattled from the Hierarkon's mask. "Send word to me the moment she comes to you." He moved down the hall as swiftly as scholarly dignity permitted.

Quarl rushed back to his study with less dignity. He pulled open the jehol's cage. "Tiny assistant, it's time for you to earn your table scraps."

The jehol liked to curl up on Hallett's chair when she was absent, and its whiskered nose would scrunch up minutes before she came to the study. The tiny creature had a sense of smell sharper than a hunting saurian's.

Quarl laid the jehol on the stoop outside his study. At first it looked terrified to be outside the confines of its home, but then Quarl brought out a crunchy nut of the kind that Hallett fed it. The jehol sniffed the nut cautiously, then pulled it away in its paws and gobbled it up. Its eyes shone with delight. It wanted more of the delicious nuts, and it knew only one place to find them.

The jehol scampered down the curved hall and Quarl walked behind it. He could see from its wrinkling nose that it had picked up the scent it connected with its supply of treats. If it followed a fresh trail, it might lead Quarl to his vanished acolyte.

The jehol twisted and turned, sometimes looping back on itself but then detecting a fresh scent and turning onto a new path. Each time it came to a stairway, it dashed up it without hesitating. Quarl and his tiny guide climbed one floor at time. At each higher landing, where the color of the stone turned a darker shade, Quarl felt certain they would come across Hallett. But the jehol continued to search, ascending the Fourth Spire until they reached the top and the single door standing at the end of the spiral stairway.

The jehol must have made a mistake; Hallett would never come here. This was the Sanctum of the Peak, and a lock constructed from the Art sealed the door at all times unless the Hierarkon or a visiting Artikon wished to enter and look on the Sanctum's treasures. Common scholars could only guess what artifacts hid beyond the steel door.

Quarl waited for the jehol to run back down the stairs to pick up the correct trail. But the animal crawled to the door's edge and nudged its whiskered snout under the crack. The sound it made was one that usually caused Quarl to smile; it was the squeak it used to wheedle one last nut from Hallett's hand before she left for the day.

The green light that usually glowed on the door handle now blazed red; it was unlocked. Quarl placed a hand on the metal surface and gave a gentle push, expecting that the light was an error and nothing would happen.

The door swung on oiled hinges. The jehol lunged through the crack and chittered happily on the other side. Someone gasped, and then a high-pitched voice spoke in a foreign tongue.

Quarl pushed the steel door open until he could see the stranger inside the forbidden room. She stood Hallett's height and wore Hallett's vermillion robe. Hallett's mask lay on top of a shelf near where the stranger was searching through folios.

But this person could not be Hallett. Hallett was Eldru and should have the shriveled pale skin of their race, the colorless eyes, the nose that was nothing more than two gashes over a lipless mouth. This person had a nose of sharp lines, and her cheeks were tinted pink. Her eyes shimmered with the blue of the Bellinghazer Sea in summer.

An Idenite . . . a human.

The woman's bright eyes showed only a moment of alarm. Then she acted as calmly as if she had arranged days ago to meet Quarl in the sealed chamber.

"I am Hallett," she said, ending the debate before it began.

Quarl passed into the Sanctum. The ceiling was so low that his head almost scraped it. The walls on both sides pressed close, and the only features aside from the woman and the jehol were shelves warping under the weight of parchments bound in saurian hide. The Sanctum looked like the room of a novice scholar. It would have disappointed Quarl and touched his Sorrow to see such a poor display for a place draped in mystery, but the human specter in Hallett's robes overwhelmed all else.

She had told him not to trust her. She had given him fair warning.

"How—how did you enter?"

The woman held up a smooth stone. "The Hierarkon's pass-slate. The Servicer had borrowed it, and I stole it from his cloister."

"If anyone finds you here, you'll be executed. Or sent to the Chirurgeons."

"Someone *has* found me," she said.

Quarl reached down and plucked up the jehol. "No one found you, Acolyte. No one."

179

He slipped the squeaking animal into a pocket of his robe, then turned to leave. He felt the Sorrow as never before. If he stayed and she tried to explain how she had come into the Core and risked her life, it would deepen his Sorrow to a point that he might never swim back to the surface of it. Such things could happen to the Eldru, even with their disciplined minds that embraced the Sorrow with elitist pride.

"Wait—" the woman's voice called.

To his surprise, he did. The Sorrow did not drown him. He moved from the door and turned to face the woman again.

"Tell me your true name."

Without daring to think about what he was doing, he answered, "Quarl."

"Quarl, remove your mask. I wish to see your face."

"If you have disguised yourself as an Eldru for this long, you know we show our faces to no one."

"I am not *no one*." Her body stretched taller, and her eyes flashed so they seemed to light the Sanctum. "Seeing your face will not hurt me. I am Sorrowless."

So this was the answer to his silent questions. He had felt Sorrowlessness beside him for many months and did not even know it except for a stirring that dissolved the languor of his work. He recognized it now in the forbidden, frightening apparition of a woman from the lesser race. To her, he was one of the maligned "Shapers," dark wizards that once tyrannized Ahn-Tarqa and still haunted it with their spies and slaves.

"Did you hear me, Shaper? I am Sorrowless. I do not fear you. Remove your mask." She softened her command. "Please, Quarl. I wish to see your face."

He tugged at the sides of the mask that gripped his skull. Air seeped around the edges. The mask dropped into the cradle of his palm. He looked at the human woman with unshielded eyes.

She drew a sharp breath, then released it slowly. "The Sorrow hasn't damaged you as much as I feared."

"You don't find me as ugly as we are rumored?"

"No. No, Quarl. And no matter what I thought I might see under the mask, you could not be ugly to me."

"That's because you don't have the Sorrow."

"There is more to it." She held out her hand, and Quarl set his mask into it. When she laid it atop her own on the shelf, the two fit together like pieces broken from the same eggshell. Her hands rose to loosen the ties at the neck of her robe. The deep red cloth fluttered to the floor and exposed her shape.

The human body did not need to hide behind formless robes and sterile titles. It glowed with the fleshy hue of life, and Hallett's curves and valleys spoke of her Sorrowlessness as much as her gleaming eyes.

Quarl felt a desire that he had never known before, one he had never dreamed possible. Hallett's form, her closeness, the memories of nights beside her when he did not know that what flowed from his acolyte was life without the Sorrow—all overwhelmed him with longing. His skin shivered, the veins across his forehead pulsed.

Hallett drew toward him. His Sorrow did not repulse her the way it would any other human or Eldru. Her warm arms wrapped around his chest and drew them together. A part of Quarl that he thought would stir only once came alive.

Hallett lay naked on the bed in her room, her vibrant shape stretched over the covers. Quarl caressed his palm over her bare head; slight prickles rubbed against his skin. She must have to shave her pate every day to keep the appearance of a barren Eldru skull.

You would like my hair," Hallett said. "It's red. I wear it down to my waist, woven into braids."

Quarl let his hand fall back into his lap. Thinking of Hallett as she truly was, even after what they had done together, caused a greater sting to his Sorrow than the first sight of her Sorrowless blue gaze. He had covered his face again not only from habit, but because it made it easier to avoid looking into those eyes as deep as indigo ocean fathoms.

But Hallett's eyes were not on him at the moment. She was studying the brittle folio she had taken from the Sanctum. Quarl had not asked her what was on it and didn't want to know. It meant fewer lies to tell if the Hierarkon suspected anything.

An amber blush touched the sky outside Hallett's triangular window. The sun would soon rise for its brief scud across the horizon.

"You should escape before full light," Quarl said.

Hallett teased the edge of his robe with her foot. "You're the one in *my* room."

How like a human she spoke! Piercing voice and light speech, nothing like the student who had met him in the Chamber of Lading ages past. But this was the *true* Hallett. The reserved one who had studied beside him was the mask.

"You know what I mean," he said. "The Hierarkon is already suspicious of you. He might learn about the missing pass-slate, or he could check the Sanctum. If he has gone to the Artikons to report—"

Hallett interrupted, "I have one more task to finish, Quarl."

"Then I shall leave you to it." He reached down toward the room's only other furnishing, a plain writing desk, and coaxed the jehol to scurry onto his palm. The animal had busied itself with grooming its cinnamon fur and seemed disappointed that Quarl wanted it to leave.

But as he slipped the animal into a pocket of his robe, Quarl felt the touch of Hallett's hand on his wrist. Even after luxuriating in her body, entwined around and inside her, following her whispered commands on how humans expressed lust to each other, the abrupt pressure of her skin had an electrical charge. "You might want to hear my plan before you leave me forever. That's what you're trying to do, isn't it? Walk back to your cell and forget you ever met me. Go back to hunting for Aman-Sah with the rest of your decrepit people."

"I have no choice. You can't remain in Black Spires, and I can't shelter you. Even if you tried to live among the slaves in the Core, they would find out soon that you are not one of them and send you to the Artikons."

"I managed to trick you for many months."

"Because I *wanted* to see you as Eldru. The slaves will look on you as a human—and they'll know the difference between someone with the Sorrow and someone without. They won't sympathize with you; they're too frightened of us."

Hallett got to her feet and slipped her robe back over her body. "I'll leave tonight, as you ask, if you grant me one thing."

"What?"

She held onto Quarl's sleeve and drew her face close beneath his. "You will want to say 'no' to what I ask. But you must not. And because of what you did with me, I know that you will—"

An abrupt chill swept into the room. Both of them sensed the sable figure at the door before they turned their heads to see it. The glow globes from the hallway silhouetted the distinctive spikes of the mask.

Quarl's hands flashed to his face, terrified that perhaps his mask wasn't in place. Eldru customs flooded his mind before anything else, even overwhelming the terror that his overseer had discovered that he had violated the laws of Black Spires and given secrets to a human. Given *everything* to a human.

Hallett showed no fear. "How long have you been listening, Shaper?"

The Hierarkon stepped into the chamber. "Three days. You were careful not to reveal yourself in your speech, but eventually you betrayed your identity to the listeners." His hand touched a crack along the stones of the wall, and his long fingernail pried at a circle of meshed wire tucked inside. Quarl recognized the piece of the Art that could send sounds from far off into the earpieces of spies.

"You need say nothing more, Idenite. In fact, you need never speak again. I will turn you over to the Artikons, and they will pry everything they need to know from your mind."

Quarl wondered what to say, how to explain. But he was the outcast in the confrontation. Neither the human spy nor the Overseer of the Fourth Spire seemed to consider him there at all.

Hallett's imperious Eldru tones returned. "I have seen what the Artikons do to people like me. I first disguised myself under your robes and masks in Tyrn, pretending that I was trying to lure another one of the Sorrowless into the reach of your Art that bleeds the mind. You taught me how to find the way into your demon city."

"You won't learn the way out. I have placed a squad of olglim and devil claws outside this spire to seal it." The Hierarkon unfolded his hand. "You have no escape. Return what you have stolen."

Hallett's eyes drooped. The intimidating shadow of the Hierarkon seemed at last to dispirit her. She stretched forward both hands to place the folio in his grasp. "May I tell you one more thing before I leave the rest to your torturers?"

The Hierarkon's robe contracted in a sigh. "You can't erase the guilt of the historian who let you commit these crimes. This one—" his mask swiveled to acknowledge Quarl for the first time "—will suffer the fate of all traitors. His body will be given to the Art for study. Do not waste words on your human concept of 'mercy.' "

"That wasn't what I was going to tell you," Hallett said. "Quarl—that's his birth name, although you wouldn't care—is as guilty as I am, and he should be proud.

"No, what I wish to tell you is that this parchment isn't the *only* thing I stole."

Her left hand darted forward. Quarl saw the flash of a metallic object strapped around her palm. She seized the Hierarkon's wrist, and a surge of energy jolted through his body. The voice chamber of the Eldru's mask magnified his scream into a rock-splitting roar.

Hallett gripped him for a few moments and watched his writhings. When she let go, the Hierarkon crumpled onto the ground and his robe spilled around him like a puddle of oil.

"You Shapers make fun toys, I'll admit that," she said to Quarl with a trickster's smirk. The true Hallett again.

Quarl expected a similar shock to drop him when Hallett reached for his hand, but felt only the warmth of her flesh and a tickle of metal.

"Don't worry, I've shut it off," she said. "It only has one surge left in it anyway. It was the best I could steal at such a short warning."

"You—you knew you would have to fight your way out?"

"I knew the Hierarkon was suspicious, so I had to prepare. I didn't know it would happen today. Or that you would find out on your own."

She glanced toward the open door, then turned her sea-shimmer eyes back to him. "I said I would leave if you gave me one thing. Will you still promise?"

"Hallett, there's no time! You've attacked a high personage. The Hierarkon has the Spire on alert, and the devil claws and olglim will seize you at the gate. It doesn't matter what I promise."

She seemed not to have heard. "The one thing I want . . . is for you to leave with me."

During the bizarre moments that had just played before him like scenes spinning through a picture lantern, Quarl had resigned himself that he was doomed to end up in the Chirurgeon's pits as raw material for vivisection experiments. But when Hallett made her request, his world tilted wrong side up, and the cool eyes and the warm skin of the woman were on the upside. He had no choice any longer, and he preferred it that way.

"I shall leave with you."

Hallett pulled him into the corridor, leaving the stunned Hierarkon on the floor. "You know the passages here better. You take the lead to the front gate."

"What about the guard waiting for us?"

"My worry."

He pointed to her bare face. "And your mask?"

"It won't protect me now. Speed is our best ally."

Quarl led the way to the central stairwell. Hallett kept her hand wrapped around his arm, and this helped him continue even as his mind begged him to surrender.

They came across a few Eldru along the stairway and the ground floor. The sight of a scholar with a human woman wearing an acolyte's robe confused these early risers, but no one attempted to stop them as they ran past.

On the ground floor, Quarl led Hallett in a circular route to avoid the Chamber of Lading, and they arrived in the courtyard that was the only way out of the Fourth Spire. Normally no guards stood watch here; even if a slave could pass through the gates of the Core, only an insane one would want to come close to towers filled with the Eldru's worst witcheries. But in the morning light Quarl and Hallett found a fierce guard waiting in the courtyard.

Two olglim flanked a trio of devil claws, and three more human slaves stood behind them, spread out to cover all ways of escape toward the gate in the wall. The olglim's gauntlets leveled black powder pistols at the two fugitives on the stoop. They looked on with the mindless glare that never left their once-human eyes, but they gripped onto orders with the tenacity of a ravager shaking apart a kill. The devil claws clutched halberds along the grips designed for their saurian hands, but they had fearsome enough natural weapons in the sickles on their rear legs. The power of the Art channeled through the metal helms latched onto their skulls turned their bestial minds into tools for the Eldru.

Quarl's knees buckled. He was unused to running, and the exhaustion he had suppressed inside the spire now caught up to him. But Hallett stayed composed. She steadied him with her grip.

"We'll give them the first move. The one who flinches first is often the loser."

"Not when he has the numbers on his side," Quarl muttered. "But, as you said, it's your worry now."

Overhead, someone shouted. Quarl twisted his head to look at the tower, and he saw a masked shape leaning from an upper window. The spiked outline was unmistakable. The Hierarkon had recovered fast from the shock Hallett had blasted into him.

The Overseer of the Fourth Spire was yelling command words that only the olglim and the devil claws could understand. They responded, and the front line stomped forward with the two olglim leading the way. The devil claws' talons clinked across the courtyard stones and the feathers along their necks raised into war frills.

The Hierarkon must have given the order to kill. Quarl understood. Slay a small problem now, before it slips out of the Core and becomes a great problem.

He was ready to die. The Sorrow at least gave him that. And he would rather the devil claws shred him or the olglim shatter his skull with their pistols than end up a prisoner of his own people. He was certain that Hallett would also prefer a fast death. He waited for her to tell him that they should walk forward and welcome it.

But Hallett was smiling like a naughty child with a stolen trinket behind her back. Her eyes flicked to the two leading olglim. She nodded her head at them and shouted, "Now!"

The olglim moved faster than their gutted brains should have allowed. Both swiveled around to aim their outstretched pistols at the heads of the devil claws beside them.

Pistol hammers dropped, black powder exploded and two saurians fell dead.

The other three olglim were too slow to challenge the sudden turnabout. Without new orders to guide them, they died immediately from the thrusts of knives that the two guards drew from under their tunics.

A single devil claw remained. The helm that manipulated its brain had already given it orders. It ignored the rebellious olglim and lunged between them toward the human female. Its jaws gaped and it raised the halberd over its head for a killing strike.

Quarl's energy surged for an instant. He hurled himself between Hallett and the charging saurian. The move upset the devil claw's attack, but it still slashed with the blade of the halberd. The edge cut through Quarl's robe, slicing his shoulder where it would have torn open Hallett's chest. The devil claw's body smashed into him, and both fell to the ground.

The agile creature would have gotten back onto its hind legs almost instantly, but Hallett grabbed the short moment of confusion that Quarl had created. She touched the devil claw's steel helm and unleashed the remaining power from the device in her palm. Energy crackled through the metal and into the devil claw's skull. The power seared the wiring and the brain wired to it.

Hallett hauled up Quarl by his armpits. Blood stained his robes, and he couldn't feel anything beyond his right shoulder.

"Can you walk?" she asked.

He nodded, which caused a ripping pain across his chest where the slash continued to gush blood.

"We'll stop the bleeding when we reach the cove. Hold onto me." She moved him so his fragile body rested against her side and she could free up one of her hands. She waved to the two olglim who had killed the others. "Rouss, Locke, one of you take him from the other side."

"Is this the one?" asked the man she had called Rouss.

"Yes. And he'll bleed to death unless we get to the boat immediately."

Quarl was too overpowered with pain to speak. The sky started to drop into darkness, and the historian could not tell if it were the sun already setting or his vision failing. The muscles of humans were now moving him forward.

Soon all vision fled from Quarl, but his hearing lingered long enough for him to remember a frustrated screaming from high in the Fourth Spire, reverberating through an echo chamber of a mask.

The briny tang of salt filled the air, and the world sloshed beneath him. Quarl thought that he had fallen asleep over his desk with the window open, and the breeze from the Bellinghazer Sea was trying to rouse him.

He stirred and tried to rise so he could get back to his books, but a hand gently pressed him back down. "You'll tear the stitches. Lie still."

Quarl opened his eyes, and recent memories started to return. He still had on the saurian-hide mask he had worn since he graduated from Acolyte to Scholar, but that seemed to be the only part of his old life left.

Hallett's face was set against the night sky. "Thank you for saving my life," she said.

Quarl didn't know how to answer. His mind struggled back to the present.

"Humans usually say 'you're welcome' when thanked," she teased.

"You're—welcome," he managed.

Quarl heard waves lapping against wood and

the hum of pistons turning a wheel. He lifted his head a bit farther—Hallett did not protest this small motion—and saw the length of a narrow skiff in front of him. A crude Art-contraption in the center powered paddles to either side that pushed the skiff through the Bellinghazer Sea. Steering the boat with a few ropes and a navigation rod were two men wearing the tunics and trousers of servants of the Outer Spires. Sitting nearer were the two who still wore olglim disguises, although they had ripped off the insignia of the Handless God.

Quarl gazed up at Hallett. "Sorrowless?"

She smiled. "All of us. Except you."

"I've heard tales that you had started to band together."

Hallett nodded. "There are few of us, but more are born each year. If we can escape the Shapers and their servants long enough, our reputation will bring others. At least, that's what we hope."

Quarl tried to move his right arm, but the pain was too strong.

"Don't squirm," Hallett said. "I saved your arm, but it'll be a few days before you can help us row."

"I heard that!" said one of the men at the helm. "I rigged this thing so it'll at least get us past Iden."

"Is anyone chasing us?" Quarl asked.

"Someone is *always* chasing us," Hallett said. "But we run faster and farther. We don't have the Sorrow to drag us down."

"What will you do with me? Drop me off at the first empty shore so my Sorrow will not intrude?"

Hallett laughed. It was a clear, clean sound. If

heard in Black Spires, it might have snapped the basalt towers in half.

"You still don't understand, do you, 'Master'? *You* are what we wanted from the Fourth Spire. The parchment I stole may help us—it has records from a memory orb older than your race, maybe from the Lightborn that you deny. But what we really wanted was a Shaper—an Eldru—to join us. I spent a year moving through your hateful city in disguise so I could enter the Core and find an Eldru whose Sorrow was weak enough that I could grind it down until he would follow me. I hoped we wouldn't have to fight, but when I knew the Hierarkon was suspicious, I flashed a signal to Rouss and Locke in the hidden cove from my window. They disguised themselves the night before and arrived in time to prevent disaster."

"But, where am I following you to?"

Hallett's hand swept over the horizon and then up toward the stars. "To Aman-Sah, of course."

"But you said—"

"That the Eldru would not find it, not through their ridiculous questing. But *we* will find it when the Sorrow lifts from all of Ahn-Tarqa. That will only come when we know why there is the Sorrow, what happened in the forgotten ages. With the Sorrow gone, something wonderful will take its place."

"We call it 'the Rising,' " Rouss said. "I don't know if the name will spread, but we like it."

"It's hard to tell you what it is, Quarl," Hallett said. "You still have the Sorrow, so you can't imagine life without feeling that life is pointless. But if you come with us, use your knowledge to help us find the secrets of the Sorrow, maybe the Sorrow will lift from you as well. And we will all rise to Aman-Sah . . . whatever it might be."

Quarl tried to look into her sapphire eyes, but the slits of his mask made her seem distant. He felt a sudden loathing of the covering over his face. The hand of his uninjured arm scraped at it to get it off. Hallett helped him and pried it away. She then flung it into the boat's wake, and in that moment Quarl forgot that he had ever worn such a thing.

He expected looks of fright or disgust from the others. But they appeared gratified. A Shaper had unmasked himself before them, taken away what made him horrifying. They wanted a real face to look on. They didn't have the Sorrow to make them fear him.

Exhaustion washed over Quarl again. This time he felt it was safe to sleep . . . sleep for as long as he wished. But he wanted to ask Hallett one more thing before shutting his eyes.

But before he could form the question, he noticed something that the slits of the mask had hidden before. Hallett's hand rested on Rouss' thigh, and the man's fingers intertwined with hers in an unmistakable way. Even an Eldru knew what that touch meant—in humans, at least.

For the first moment in his life, Quarl felt a sadness that did not come from the Sorrow.

He shut his eyes and let the motion of the skiff rock him. Something stirred inside a pocket of his robe, and his hand grasped at it and closed over a warm, furry body. The jehol had fallen asleep in his pocket where he had placed it back in Hallett's room. He lifted the tiny mammal out onto his chest, and he fell asleep with it curled in the nape of his neck.

The Dualist

written by

Van Aaron Hughes

illustrated by

FREDERICK EDWARDS

ABOUT THE AUTHOR

Van Aaron Hughes lives in Denver, Colorado, with his wife Beth and his children Griffin, Kyra and Noah. He grew up outside Seattle, went to UCLA where he met Beth, then to law school at Berkeley, before heading to the mountains.

Aaron has practiced law for twenty years, highlighted by two trips to the United States Supreme Court. He wrote the winning briefs in Central Bank v. First Interstate Bank, *a landmark securities fraud case, and briefed and argued* Sutton v. United Air Lines, *a major case interpreting the Americans with Disabilities Act. The Supreme Court's adverse ruling in* Sutton *was later overturned by Congress.*

Aaron fell in love with science fiction and fantasy at an early age, after stealing his father's stash of Robert Heinlein books, then discovering Isaac Asimov and Ursula LeGuin and Clifford Simak. He returned to the genre in law school in hopes of retaining the ability to speak in a language other than legalese. He writes SF and fantasy book reviews and author interviews for Fantastic Reviews *and the* Fantastic Reviews Blog.

He has often attempted to write fiction over the years, but only recently managed to complete a few stories he wasn't embarrassed to let anyone else read. His fiction has appeared in the political protest anthology Glorifying Terrorism, edited by Farah Mendlesohn, and the webzine Linger Fiction. "The Dualist" was his first submission to the Writers of the Future Contest.

ABOUT THE ILLUSTRATOR

Frederick decided a long time ago that he would not be an artist. He did not let encouraging words from others influence his outlook. Artists were weird, and art meant expressing feelings. Frederick would attempt to suppress his passion for creativity, but with no success.

He prepared to attend Northern Arizona University, where he would study a subject that would lead to an easier, clearer career path. Instead fate brought him back to his hometown of Tucson, Arizona. Eventually he would receive his BFA in illustration from the University of Arizona. By the time he received this diploma, he was a combat veteran, had two children and was working with the developmentally disabled.

Months after graduation, he moved to Virginia with his two children to stay with his sister and work on his master's in education. This opportunity also gave him a chance to work on his fine art and illustration skills. When he is not studying or picking on his children, he can be found focused on exercising. Besides that, he is probably working on a painting for someone. He has accepted that he cannot live a complete life if he does not embrace what he tried to abandon so many times before, his art.

The Dualist

*I*n the beginning, God created the heavens and the world. He provided for all creatures and all were content, save one. The Evil One could not bear to be subject to God's dominion. He deceived many of God's angels and led them in rebellion. He confronted God, and so great was the power of his will that he began to force God from the heavens. But the Evil One was seized from behind. Astonished that any but God Himself could overpower him, the Evil One turned to see his new adversary and beheld the face of God. The Evil One was cast into the stinking, moss-covered pit, at last understanding the essential truth of the universe: There are Two.

1.

*W*e have entered Doubletown, Envoy," Fernandez announced over her shoulder.

Glancing up from the translation of *The Word of Both,* Thomas tried not to let Hirokh see his surprise. He had not asked Fernandez to alert him when they passed the checkpoint at the Doubletown wall, and she would not interrupt without reason.

He caught her eye in the rearview mirror, and a barely perceptible nod of her head drew his gaze to a thin line of smoke rising from behind the squat skyline to their right. Probably another bombing. Fernandez was asking approval to stop to investigate without including Hirokh in the conversation. Thomas had no interest in stopping, but at least it would make them late for the dinner party.

"Thank you, Lieutenant. Let's not go straight to the Retreat. I would like to drive around a bit and see more of Doubletown." Thomas turned to his ever-present companion. "Do you mind, Hirokh?"

"Of course not," Hirokh answered, midlimbs raised in assent. He had likely deduced where they were headed but did not interfere. "I know you relish viewing Doubletown as much as I do, Envoy, though for different reasons."

Thomas studied the low stone buildings through the car window and afternoon drizzle. Spitting clouds of smoke, a handful of other autos labored through the roughly cobbled streets. Phren children skittered between them, their exoskeletons yellow from malnutrition or radiation sickness. Thomas had viewed pictures of this place as the locus of a proud global culture, gaily painted, its people in perpetual celebration. Now the pale green of moss covered the crumbling buildings and streets, and he could see no other color but the burnt orange and, too often, yellow of phren shells.

Making no further pretense, Fernandez drove directly to the source of the smoke. Without a word, she exited the groundcar and marched to the scene, leaving Thomas and Hirokh little option but to follow. Thomas immediately felt his skin prickle with spores. The scabs on his arms began to itch.

"What reason could you have to enjoy Doubletown, Hirokh? I thought you hated the place."

"How could you think I detest this place, Envoy, when you know it is holy land? I detest only its inhabitants. I take pleasure in seeing how few remain to kill."

Thomas smiled. Most Solarans shared this sentiment, but few were so undiplomatic as to express it to him. In his two local years on Phrentyr, just over one terrestrial year, he had come to appreciate Hirokh's bluntness.

The bombing had gutted a large, single-story structure, its roof partially collapsed, remnants glowing dully with the last sputtering flames. Thomas supposed it was a grocery; suicide bombers had recently targeted several Tokhin grocers who defied Solaran dietary restrictions. Fernandez disappeared directly into the wreckage, trusting her body armor to protect her, while Thomas and Hirokh walked along the outside.

Hirokh extended his midlimbs forward, the phren gesture for "on the other hand." "You harbor the opposite hope, to save these people and resurrect their disgusting culture." Thomas did not disabuse him of this notion, but in truth he had all but abandoned any such ambition. As cultural Envoy he was supposed to protect the Tokhin people from genocide. An awfully nice idea, but he now doubted he could do more than slightly delay the inevitable.

At the far side of the demolished building, the fire had burned out. A group of Doubletown residents cleared away debris, searching for survivors. If they rebuilt anything on this site, it would be only primitive mud huts.

Thomas glanced down at the book in his hand, the embodiment of the nearly destroyed Tokhin culture. He was antagonizing Hirokh by keeping it in plain view this long. "Have you never read *The Word of Both*, Hirokh?"

"If I wish to read about perverts, I will go to Chubbytown. They will give me pictures." All phren spoke in a soft, literally nasal voice, yet Hirokh still managed to sound gruff.

"I have met many Tokhin who have read *The Solara*," Thomas persisted.

"Greater fools are they, not to know the truth when they see it," Hirokh answered.

As they slowly traced the perimeter of the destruction, Thomas studied the surrounding buildings, many embedded with concrete slabs thrown from the explosion. Several charred groundcars lined the street, strewn inches deep with rubble. Most tellingly, moss was seared away from every facing surface and little had grown back even in the misty rain.

When Fernandez rejoined them, Thomas asked, "This was no pouch bomb, was it?"

"No, Boss. The blast radius and solid oxides in the debris suggest a powerful thermobaric weapon." Fernandez glared at Hirokh as they walked. After a moment she switched her gaze to Thomas, clearly expecting him to confront Hirokh.

It was too obvious a giveaway. Solaran enforcers knew how to build a homemade bomb. They could easily have disguised this as another suicide bombing, absolving the government of responsibility. Instead they had deliberately used military-grade explosives, no doubt on Hirokh's instructions, as if daring Thomas to do something about it. There was nothing he could do, of course, and he would not be made a fool trying.

Thomas might not have said anything at all but for Fernandez standing there fuming. He stopped finally and folded his arms. "Well, Hirokh, are you going to claim that you had nothing to do with this?"

Hirokh paused, midlimbs at his side. "You know I prefer to be direct, Envoy, but in my position I must sometimes withhold information."

"You are direct, Hirokh, I'll give you that."

"I do not willingly pretend to be other than what I am."

Thomas looked pointedly at the wreckage around them. "Yet you expect the Tokhin to do just that, to eat what you eat, to act like they belong to your culture and not their own."

"For Tokhin, it is commendable to be of two natures. Life here in Doubletown would be intolerable to Solarans, but it seems to suit these people."

While he spoke, Hirokh drew back a forelimb as if to strike a passing Tokhin, who cowered and shrank away. Thomas felt as much contempt for the Tokhin's meek reaction as for Hirokh's raw display of power.

"I fear," Hirokh continued, "that you humans have much in common with the Tokhin. You seem to relish prevarication, professing to something different than your true nature."

"What do you mean?"

"Envoy, why are we here? You investigate this site, but what would you do with proof that the Solaran Council ordered the bombing? Your government has declared that suffering the pervert-worshippers is a condition of further aid from your people. But is that threat an empty pouch?" An "empty pouch" meant a bluff, but to phren a bluff was never a clever thing.

Thomas suspected Hirokh knew the answer to his own question. Thomas' orders were clear: due to the strategic importance of this system, no humanitarian concern short of imminent and absolute genocide of the Tokhin would justify withdrawal of human support to Phrentyr. This left him entirely impotent. He might find and catalog evidence of the Solaran Council's violence and repression of the Tokhin, but could never act on it.

"It will take much longer to analyze the evidence here," Fernandez interjected. "Can we cancel your appearance tonight?"

"No, Lieutenant. If you like, you can come back and poke around more after you drop us at the Retreat."

"Yes, sir. I will have a report for you in the morning."

"Great," Thomas answered, as if he were actually going to read the damn thing. Thomas preferred Lieutenant Fernandez to most of the marines, if only because she better concealed her contempt for unenhanced humans, but her diligence was starting to annoy.

He followed a different thread of the conversation with Hirokh. "Even if you think humans and Tokhin are alike, Hirokh, you needn't worry I will take sides in your world's religious disagreements. You know I am an unbeliever beyond any possible redemption."

"So you have told me, but I wonder how it is possible." Atheism was nearly unheard of on Phrentyr. "Where did you turn for comfort when your wife died?"

Thomas made no secret that he was a widower, but he seldom mentioned Kayleigh's death, and Hirokh had never before pursued the subject. It struck Thomas as bad form to do so here, in the midst of more violent death that Hirokh had all but admitted orchestrating.

"I threw myself into my work," Thomas answered. "You see where the hell that got me."

He said nothing more until they were back in the groundcar, then asked Hirokh, "Were you ever married?"

Thomas thought Hirokh had not heard, the answer was so long coming. "Yes, Envoy. Before the war, I had a wife and daughter. Only my faith made it possible to live without them."

"I respect that, Hirokh, but I also respect the beliefs of the Tokhin. And the Tokhin tell me they respect the teachings of *The Solara*. That's what tolerance is all about."

"Respect? Tolerance? The Tokhin read the wisdom of the Great One, then go back to worshipping their two deviants. Solarans who 'tolerate' the pervert-worshippers are just as bad, perhaps worse, for they are harder to root out. Not all phren who wear Solaran cloaks and carry valid papers truly serve the Great One."

Thomas noticed Fernandez shaking her head, appalled at the asinine quarrels that could cost millions of people their lives.

"Why do you describe the Two Gods like that, Hirokh? I haven't seen any reference to sexual practices in *The Word of Both* or any other Tokhin text."

"Two gods, both men. Figure it out, biped."

"Would you prefer if one of the Two Gods were female?"

Silent for a moment, his midlimbs still, Thomas couldn't be sure at first how much his blasphemy angered Hirokh. Lacking mimetic muscles, phren had no facial expressions, though they could cry with human-like tear ducts. Thomas had taken to trying to needle Hirokh out of his stoicism, but perhaps he was getting too good at the game.

"Envoy, if I kill you, the Council will execute me immediately," Hirokh said. "Yet every day, you make it a difficult choice."

Thomas smiled. He felt he had scored a point when Hirokh threatened bodily harm, even if he could not take such threats lightly. The largest phren Thomas had ever seen, Hirokh could certainly dispatch an unenhanced human being, despite his war injuries, and had doubtless killed many phren. Thomas was oddly gratified the Solarans had assigned their notorious Chief Enforcer as his watchdog. They seemed to fear Thomas might accomplish something. He wished he could agree.

Back when life was important to Thomas, Hirokh would have terrified him. But the apathy that had settled over him since his arrival on Phrentyr was at times a peculiar strength—Hirokh could not intimidate him because Thomas did not care what happened to him. He hated his work, having long since realized he could accomplish nothing meaningful as Envoy, and offworld a dead-end job is a dead-end life. Everyone on Earth he ever cared about was dead. In truth, the only person he really cared about had died before he left.

2.

They mounted the steps slowly, Hirokh from his injuries—walking only on hindlimbs was painful to him and he limped noticeably even using midlimbs— Thomas to avoid slipping on the layer of moss swiftly rising in the rain.

Thomas tried not to shiver in the early evening wind. Once ungodly hot, Phrentyr's climate had cooled with nuclear autumn from the last, deadliest war between Tokhin and Solarans. Nearly ten phren years had passed since the war's end, yet much of the world remained shrouded in smoke and ash. The cold was unpleasant for the phren and disrupted their agriculture, but ideal for moss.

The moss—actually closer to terrestrial mold, although unlike Earth mold it drew much of its energy from photosynthesis—had been the more frivolous of Thomas' two reasons for volunteering to serve on Phrentyr. With so much of the world covered in a layer of green, he would seldom need to see anything red. Even local clothes contained little; gray dominated the Tokhin cloaks, blue the Solaran.

Big mistake. Thomas tried to ignore the moss, but found it impossible. You could put it out of your mind for a few minutes, maybe a few hours, but then like a glaring red light it hit you again all the harder. The prickling on your skin. The ubiquitous rancid smell and dull green color. The sickly sweet taste to all the food and drink, even the air. Better to stay aware of it, treat it as a familiar if unwelcome companion.

Director Pryz greeted Thomas promptly as they entered the Retreat, the central Tokhin meeting hall. He ignored Hirokh. The director introduced Thomas first to High Priestess Khorana and her son Khora, not quite old enough for his own name, then to the other guests. Thomas had met many of them before, but he suffered the director to announce everyone as if he were new to this world.

Pryz introduced him to the group as Envoy Thomas McFall, but as always found a new way to butcher his name, this time pronouncing Thomas more like "toads." Correcting him politely, Thomas explained to the group that a "toad" on Earth was an amphibious creature, which he described as like an animal made of moss, a notion they found delightfully revolting.

Thomas endured an hour of small talk with Tokhin dignitaries, Hirokh always hovering over one shoulder, while a group of musicians sang ululating hymns to the Two Gods in the background. He could not concentrate on what anyone said, preoccupied with the desire to scratch. How the hell could he maintain diplomatic etiquette with a constantly itching crotch?

Finally the director herded the group into the food circle. The High Priestess chanted a short prayer and the crowd answered in unison, "There are Two!" Thomas pretended not to hear Hirokh's blessing, which sounded more like, "Bugger them Both!"

The main course was grilled khaat, one of the few native foods Thomas could enjoy without dipping into his tin of horseradish and wasabi, salt and cayenne pepper and every other spice that might cut the mossy sweetness. Khaat, the two-legged beasts that roamed the plains of this continent, were muscled so that their flesh bulged in squares when stretched on a spit, the heat of the fire warding off the moss. As the meat cooked, individual nuggets burst free like popcorn, flying through the air to be caught and quickly consumed before moss could grow.

Phren delighted in the spectacle of the chunks of meat popping and soaring in every direction. They cheered with every good catch, with a special ovation for anyone who could use all their forelimbs and midlimbs to catch four at once.

Thomas had been to dozens of dinner parties on Phrentyr with Tokhin and Solarans, and the phren never grew bored with this game. Thomas found their childlike delight infectious and impossible to reconcile with the bloodthirsty hatred that so infused both cultures.

With the khaat as distraction, Thomas shuffled his way to the High Priestess, Hirokh shadowing him as always. Thomas knew Director Pryz for a worthless bureaucrat but held a slight, lingering hope for Khorana, the Tokhin spiritual leader.

He watched the priestess catch three morsels of khaat in succession. Squatting onto her midlimbs, she quickly passed them under her cloak to her short abdominal tentacles. From there the meat went into the moss-resistant pouch inside her abdominal mouth to be eaten at her leisure, but of course Thomas had never seen this happen. To look directly into any phren's pouch would violate their world's strictest taboo.

Thomas felt self-conscious nearing the priestess with the meal still in progress. Many phren were disgusted to see him eat through his face with what seemed to them an oversized nose. Apparently they grew accustomed to his large head, rigid limbs and hands with too many fingers, but still found it difficult to credit that he had no mouth in his chest.

Thomas snared two pieces of meat zipping past, impressing no one. He popped one into his mouth and quickly dipped the other in a tureen of spicy, creamy sauce made from skallow root. That bulbous plant had long been Thomas' favorite local food, but he was getting heartily sick of it. Skallow sauce was impervious to moss, so for too long he had been slathering it over nearly everything he ate.

If you ate quickly you might not see moss growing on your food during a meal, but you would still taste it. In Phren, there is a word for moss that one can taste but not see, another for a thin yellow-tinted layer, another for a thick and fuzzy growth, some two dozen words for moss altogether. To Thomas, they were all just moss.

Opportunities to speak with the High Priestess were rare, and he was determined not to squander this one. After a long series of failed attempts to spur the Tokhin into action gently and diplomatically, Thomas had resolved to become more direct, not that he believed it would do any good.

"High Priestess, your people are dying."

Khorana turned to him and folded her midlimbs over her chest, an indication of focused attention. "Most of my people are already dead."

"Most of the Solaran race died in the war as well, but their civilization recovers. They begin to rebuild with the help of my people. With our engineered seed, our techniques and equipment, they lose fewer crops to moss, reclaim some of the irradiated wastes. Yet the Tokhin refuse any aid but handouts of food and radiation meds. Am I to believe that the Solarans are so much more industrious?"

It was an unfair comparison. The Solarans had won the war. While Solaran civilization was merely devastated, the Tokhin were all but annihilated, their few survivors herded into Doubletown, the Holy City's Tokhin ghetto. Resurrecting the Tokhin culture was an even more daunting task than helping the Solarans, but Thomas knew if the process did not begin soon it would be too late. Humans had arrived in this system shortly after the end of the war and provided relief aid to the ruling Solarans on the condition that they did not completely wipe out the remaining Tokhin. Once the Solarans were again self-sufficient, Earth would lose its leverage, and Solara would surely complete the annihilation of the Tokhin race.

Khorana thrust her midlimbs to either side in anger. Several nearby guests noticed her reaction and turned to listen.

"Have we not done enough to prove our industry?" she demanded. "For countless generations Tokhin and Solaran sought to destroy the other. It was no easy task, as we cohabited most of the world, but at last by our tireless efforts we succeeded."

"The Solarans are not destroyed," Thomas pressed.

She chopped her midlimbs across her body in negation. "They are, even if they do not know it. *The Word of Both* and *The Solara* have little in common." Actually, their doctrinal differences were so subtle Thomas often found them difficult to grasp. "But they agree on one particular: Hell."

"Hell is a cold, hazy place where moss grows thick on every surface."

"Exactly," she said. "We have remade our own world into Hell. It is too late to save any of us."

"So that's it?" Thomas demanded. "You just give up on your life, your future?"

"As have you."

It was such an abrupt reversal of the conversation, Thomas thought for a moment he had mistranslated her words in his head.

"By coming to Phrentyr, have you not forever left behind everyone and everything you once knew?"

Thomas was startled. Relativity was not widely understood in this world. Most phren could not conceive of the fact that everyone he knew was already dead, even if he tried to explain. For a time, he had considered claiming a great holy war had killed his friends and family. That they would comprehend.

"I did not leave behind so much. I volunteered for this post after my wife's death."

Nearly the entire party had fallen silent, listening in

curiosity. "On Phrentyr," said Khorana, "you are in no danger of finding another mate."

Already weary of the subject, Thomas decided to try to lighten the mood, thankful Fernandez had not stayed. "Well, they told me there were a lot of women marines on the orbital station here. Sadly, they didn't tell me the marines were all genetically modified. I doubt I would survive getting too friendly with any of them."

The phren around them roared with their hissing laughter. Direct discussions of sexual acts were forbidden, but phren greatly appreciated dirty jokes made through oblique references.

Khorana did not join the laughter. "I grieve for you, Envoy. You have experienced the pain of a single deep loss. But understand that we have known seven hundred million losses."

"I realize, Priestess, that your loss is even greater than mine." That was Thomas' primary reason for coming to Phrentyr, a world of beings who had suffered as he had, who knew what it was to see a loved one brutally murdered. He was a fool to have believed these aliens could understand and comfort him in a way other human beings could not.

"Do not feel concern for us," she said, raising her voice for all to hear. "Our losses are only the price of the terrible retribution the Two Gods will inflict. The last days are at hand for all Phrentyr. The promise of Both is that we will live to see the Solarans die in agony and rejoice in their suffering before They also call us away." At the end of this declaration several phren chimed in, "Death to Solara!" A few stared pointedly at Hirokh.

213

This was why Thomas had not found the bond with Tokhin he sought. He had come here thinking of them as the victims of genocide. In truth, they were merely the losers of a genocidal war. Just as cheerfully would they have eradicated the Solarans had their side prevailed.

Still, they bore the standard of an ancient and rich cultural tradition, one that should be preserved if possible. "Priestess, does that mean you should hasten the death of your own people and all their beliefs and customs? What about your young people?" Thomas motioned to Priestess Khorana's son, standing nearby. "Your own son, will you leave him nothing of your culture to treasure when you are gone?"

"You speak as if the passing of the Tokhin were by choice."

"You have a choice!" Thomas shouted and instantly regretted it, as a fleck of spittle leapt from his mouth, an appalling sight to any phren who saw it.

The High Priestess spoke slowly and forcefully. "No. I can do nothing. I am not even a true High Priestess."

Thomas was sure he had heard wrong. "What?"

"I cannot speak the Old Tongue. Even if our people had a temple left to them in which to pray to Both, I could not lead the invocation."

"Then find someone who can."

Khorana stared at him. "My mother was a true High Priestess. The position is not meant to be inherited. I stand in her place only because she and all her students died in the war. The Old Tongue is dead, for none survive who remember it."

"Priestess, consider that perhaps it is the will of Both that I, an alien, am here to see your problem in a different light and to tell you that's a load of khaat manure."

This was rather a more forceful approach to the issue than Thomas had ever taken. Many of the gathering crowd muttered in annoyance, but the priestess did not react. He continued, "You have prayers in modern Phren, so speak them. The Two Gods cannot be offended to hear you praise Them the only way They have left you to do it."

"And where shall we say these vulgar prayers? Our temples are all destroyed, and the site of the First Temple is but an empty field of moss."

"Then go to that field and build a new temple."

"Impossible without Sha'ad Tokh." The crowd around them responded, "Sha'ad Tokh!"

"This is your reason for not rebuilding your temple—you're missing the capstone?"

"It is no mere rock, Envoy. It is the birthstone of our people, given by the Two Gods to Khorin Khoron on the first day of the New Age."

"A symbol." Thomas tried to conceal his impatience. "Priestess, people die and buildings fall and relics get smashed. You cannot let that destroy your race. You must figure out how to rejuvenate your culture. Doubletown is a cemetery. I can pressure the Solarans to let you rebuild your temple, to release you from this compound. All I need is for you to lead your people out of here and start over."

"Envoy, no doubt what you say would seem logical to another of your kind, but to us it is nonsense.

215

Rebuild the temple without Sha'ad Tokh? You might as well ask the desert hawk to fly without wings."

Thomas smiled. "It is possible to fly without wings."

The priestess chopped her midlimbs. "You may have the technology to make a creature fly without wings, but it will not be a hawk. The Tokhin cannot be made whole without the First Temple, and there can be no First Temple without Sha'ad Tokh."

Again the Tokhin surrounding them chanted, "Sha'ad Tokh!"

This was where it always ended, with Tokhin excuses for giving up. *We cannot renew our culture, for too few of us remain. We cannot rebuild our temple, for lack of Sha'ad Tokh.* Thomas had come to doubt the Tokhin race and their faith in the Two Gods would survive much longer, and worse, he no longer believed they deserved to. He hated himself for thinking that, but could not help it.

3.

After not speaking a word all evening in the Retreat, Hirokh addressed Thomas as soon as they were alone in the restroom. "It pains me, Envoy, to watch you waste your time with this refuse." He held out the large cloak—Thomas tried not to think of it as a hoop skirt—which the two of them had designed many twelvedays before to allow Thomas to use the public holes in the floor that passed for toilets. The phren merely needed to slide forward on midlimbs and their personal cloaks covered all from view.

"Just take satisfaction, Hirokh, in how little progress I have made." *Don't expect to see me try any longer,* he thought.

"It is the will of the Great One. And yet . . ."

"Don't tell me you're developing sympathy for the Tokhin?"

"Do not be insulting, Envoy. But I acknowledge that they were once a formidable enemy. These docile survivors dishonor the memory of all my comrades who fell in battle."

Thomas did not answer. He could not doubt that Hirokh would happily wipe out the thousand or so Tokhin still living, yet he still found Hirokh much the easier to respect.

He considered what Hirokh had said about the Tokhin, "once a formidable enemy." How had they so utterly lost their will, their spirit? But then, who could understand that better than Thomas? Life knocks you down and you get back up for more, until the day it hits you harder than you can bear and that's the day for giving up. Thomas had given up on his entire world and taken this damned job, and now he had even given up on that.

Another phren entered the facility. Stepping to the hole just past Thomas, he said in a singsong voice, "I did not realize an alien could be so compassionate. Does it really matter to you what happens to us?"

Thomas regarded him for a moment before placing him as Khora, the son of the priestess. "Maybe more than it does to your mother."

This drew a quick reaction. He turned to Thomas with his midlimbs out stiff, but then stumbled

217

forward. Thomas instinctively caught him, and felt something slip into his right hand as he did.

Hirokh instantly stepped in to separate them. While he shoved the son of the priestess away roughly, Thomas turned his back to them and quickly read the note in his hand: "Ten minutes. Outside back door. Don't bring him." It was scrawled on a thin piece of pressed grain coated in grease. Thomas shoved it into his pocket, knowing that within minutes it would be an unreadable lump of moss.

4.

Thomas couldn't help feeling wary of the small alley where the three phren led him, but there was no time to scout a more suitable meeting place.

He had never tried to evade Hirokh before, but it had proved easier than expected. After waiting ten minutes, he told Hirokh he was ready to leave. As Hirokh held the car door open in front of the Retreat, Thomas declared he had forgotten his tin of spices and darted back inside. Then a quick dash through the hall, around a corner, out the back door, hoping Hirokh could not see where he went through the crowd. There had been no chance to tell Fernandez what he was up to, which was just as well—he did not want to get her into a tussle with Hirokh.

The son of the priestess and two other phren had waited outside the back door, and the four of them sprinted down the Doubletown streets to this alley.

They ducked behind a large stack of trash to hide from view. Standing with the rubbish pile to his right and the dark alleyway to his left, Thomas tried to ignore the putrid smell.

The other two phren, just as young as Khora if not as well fed, waved midlimbs nervously, but Khora gripped his in his forelimbs in a show of giddy confidence, like a cocky grin on a young human. Overconfidence could be dangerous, yet Thomas was pleased to see such energy from any Tokhin. He allowed himself some hope that the younger Tokhin had more spunk than their elders.

Khora launched into a rehearsed statement of his gratitude to the Envoy for joining them, but Thomas knew there was no time for niceties and interrupted. "Khora, do you believe your mother is wrong, that there is yet hope for your people?"

Khora answered haltingly, "Envoy, there is much you do not know. Just as there are Two Gods, there are two faces to the Tokhin people. My mother does not . . . well, she cannot speak freely in front of that Solaran giant."

"He is not here now. Tell me."

"I do not know all that my mother does. And I should not presume to speak for her."

This was getting them nowhere. "Khora, you asked me to come here. Do you have something to say, or shall I go?" At that, Khora's two companions stepped closer. Even in the dark alleyway, Thomas could see that one had a yellowing exoskeleton.

"The Tokhin are more than what you see, Envoy. With our strength and with Sha'ad Tokh—"

"It wasn't destroyed in the war?" Thomas asked in surprise.

"No, Envoy, and when the day—"

"Where is it?"

"I do not know. I think my mother believes—"

"Enough!" interjected Khora's jaundiced companion. "There are Two Gods, and They are Both bored to Their pouches from all this."

Khora thrust out his midlimbs. "I decide what we—"

"You decide nothing," said the third phren. "You agreed we are democratic."

"So?" asked Khora.

"So," said the yellow one, "we took a vote."

Thomas thought he had lost his will to live after Kayleigh's death, but staring at two phren short blades suddenly pointing at him, he realized otherwise.

"Stop!" shouted Khora. "We are not murderers. We are here to talk."

"No. Wasn't talk got us in this mess, won't be talk gets us out," said the yellow one. "We need to hit back. We need phren to go out with bombs in the breech." Khora winced at the crude reference to phren pouches. "We need important people to turn up dead." His midlimbs waved at Thomas.

"What would killing him accomplish, mossbrains? The humans are the only thing stopping Solara from killing us all, and you want to murder their ambassador?"

"They keep us alive like khaat in a pen. We kill him, the humans know it is not enough."

"No, listen—"

"Seal it!" the third phren interjected. He straightened and leaned into Khora, an ineffective gesture, as he was an unusually short phren. "We have listened enough. You plan and plan and do nothing, and for twelveday after twelveday we sit with midlimbs tucked in our pouches. No more."

When Khora began to protest again, the other two turned their knives in his direction. He stared at them both for a long moment before saying to Thomas, "I am very sorry. The moss will have you."

This was a bit more spunk than Thomas had hoped. These phren were underfed, but Thomas, who had never had a moment's self-defense training, was under no illusion he could disarm them. Still, he readied himself to move as they struck.

As the yellow one stabbed a forelimb forward, Thomas heard a roar from behind and the phren's shell collapsed inward. The second knife-wielder stumbled backward and fell.

"Get down, Envoy!" The gruff voice of Hirokh sliced through the ringing in Thomas' ears from the gunshot.

Thomas dove to the ground, pulling Khora with him. "Tomorrow!" he hissed at the young phren. "The back door again, and don't bring any more of your moss-eaten friends. Now go!"

He stood up, trying to place himself between Khora and the source of the shots. He saw Hirokh climbing through the wall of garbage and slumped against him as if for support. Hirokh steadied him, then stared down the alley, but Khora had disappeared. "You would do well, Envoy, to think of me as your bodyguard, not as your jailer," he said amiably.

The short phren still lay on the ground. Hirokh leaned over, yanked him up by a midlimb. Holding his gun in a forelimb, he pressed the muzzle into the side of the Tokhin's head, which barely reached Hirokh's massive chest.

"Where did the other go? Who is he?"

"I will tell you nothing, Enforcer."

Hirokh turned his midlimbs up. "I believe you," he said and pulled the trigger.

5.

Nowhere on the entire planet surface could Thomas find a moment's privacy, either from Hirokh or the moss, except in his sealed apartment under the Hall of Ministers. The moment Hirokh left him that night he went to the kitchen to swallow his daily antibiotic, then headed straight for the shower stall.

The antiseptic spray killed the moss spores clinging to his body within seconds. Thomas stood under the scalding water for over an hour.

Still, as he dried, the prickling sensation returned. He began to scratch his skin. He scratched faster and harder until he felt moisture under his fingernails. Long streaks of blood appeared on his chest and arms.

He felt no pain, as if the skin he peeled away did not belong to him, but the color stung his eyes.

He turned off the lights and kept scratching.

6.

Nearly being murdered was a handy excuse to spend some time in orbit at P-Station.

At the ramp to the shuttle, Thomas clasped Hirokh

hand-to-forelimb and thanked him again for saving his life. Hirokh swirled his midlimbs in a phren gesture without human equivalent, essentially a denial that any favor was done. "I had to save you, or the Council would have believed I let you die on purpose. They know how I dislike you."

Thomas chuckled and boarded the shuttle, thinking Hirokh would never forgive him if he learned what he had just done.

The shuttle lifted as if heading into orbit, but high in Phrentyr's tortured stratosphere it turned back to deposit Thomas in Doubletown. Thomas did not imagine the Solarans would be fooled long, but perhaps long enough for him to meet Khora without anyone getting killed this time. Thomas was all too conscious of the irony that he was deceiving the phren who had just saved his life in order to collaborate with one of those who tried to kill him.

Thomas was pleasantly surprised to see Lieutenant Fernandez at the steering panel of the waiting native groundcar. Between the lack of her too-conspicuous body armor and the contorted position the phren car's driver seat demanded, she could not have looked less comfortable.

"I thought you were off duty."

"Right," she said. "You call the closest thing to a covert op we're ever going to get on this planet, and I'm going to miss it for another round with the stimbot."

After confirming that Thomas had planted the nanotransmitters on Hirokh, Fernandez attached a device next to the car's steering panel to alert them if Hirokh approached within two hundred meters. She then merged them into traffic and guided them toward the Tokhin Retreat.

"Whose shift was it supposed to be? Harding?" Thomas asked. "How'd you get him to step aside?"

"He wouldn't argue. He knows I'm your favorite. He probably thinks I'm sleeping with you."

Thomas laughed. "Just say the word, Lieutenant, but be gentle."

She looked back at him more seriously than he expected. "Today's the first time I might consider it, Boss. I like a guy with a spine."

Before Thomas could respond they arrived behind the Retreat, where Khora waited alone. He clambered quickly into the rear couch with Thomas.

"Nice to see you without your keeper, Envoy." Still brashly gripping midlimbs in forelimbs, he showed no sign of contrition for the night before. "I assume he doesn't know you are here in Doubletown?"

"Yes, what he doesn't know won't hurt us." He nodded to Fernandez to get them moving again.

Khora held midlimbs up in agreement. "I have heard stories about our Chief Enforcer, both from the war and after. He will do anything to keep his secrets."

"I hope you are ready to share some of yours."

"I only wish I had more to share. But first, Envoy, I must thank you for saving my life last night." Thomas elected not to point out that Khora had nearly cost him his. "Although perhaps it would be better if I were killed."

They had no time for idle talk, but Thomas could not help his curiosity. "How so?"

"My generation of Tokhin do not expect to be granted long life, but we have a belief. There are Two Gods, and if One calls you back early, the Other compensates by granting your fondest wish as you die. Yesterday I prayed to Both that before I die I should behold the one who will deliver Sha'ad Tokh back to us. And then I met you."

"So you do believe Sha'ad Tokh still exists?"

"Yes, Envoy. I know that by the grace of Both it survived the war. I think it is still in this city, but I don't know where."

"Seems unlikely. By now every inch of Doubletown has been searched three times over by Solarans."

"I did not say it was in Doubletown."

Thomas leaned his body with the motion as Fernandez weaved the car through traffic. "What are you saying, that Solarans have it?"

"No. But it may be with one of the hidden." Thomas looked at him blankly. "My mother believes that a few Tokhin escaped confinement in Doubletown and have blended in with Solarans in the Holy City."

Thomas pondered this new information and whether High Priestess Khorana meant him to have it. "How can we find them? Does your mother know any?"

"If she does, she will never reveal it. But I think I have another way to find out. If we—"

"Sir!" Fernandez barked. Thomas realized that the device she had placed on the dash was beeping and blinking rapidly. Hirokh was already closing in.

A thunderclap battered Thomas from all around. It took a moment to realize that the noise was somehow related to the afterimage in his eyes, of the car in front of them lifting into the air, flipping backward toward them, engulfed in a searing flare of light.

He shook his head, but it would not clear. What had happened? A random bombing? Assassination attempt? Stumbling out of the car, he peered through the smoke. The front of the adjacent building had slumped to the ground. Phren hobbled away, while others knelt to treat the severely injured, but he saw nothing threatening. Rather, the entire scene was strangely calm, the phren curiously nonchalant, as if it were all too familiar to upset them.

Next to their demolished groundcar he spotted Fernandez lying in the street. He rushed to her and turned her over to see first her unblinking eyes, then her shattered body. Something had torn through her chest, and the front of her uniform was a great scarlet stain. Then the copper smell hit him. Just like . . .

Oh, God, he was there. He was there again, Kayleigh right in front of him. He couldn't turn his eyes away. She filled his vision, her face so beautiful, her chest a bloody ruin. Blood was everywhere. He couldn't stop seeing her blood, smelling it. So much blood. The whole world was bright red.

Like an infant he sobbed, water streaming from his eyes, which he could not close.

"Sir! Sir! We have to get you out of here!" Another marine. Except there hadn't been another marine. Thomas turned his head and saw the shuttle somehow squeezed into the intersection just ahead. He had not heard it land. How long had he been here?

"Sir!" shouted the marine. "Your hand is cut!" Thomas looked down numbly and winced at the red mark. "We've got to get you treated for infection right away."

"Get Khora."

"Sir?"

"The phren I was with, my informant. Could be in danger." Thomas looked all around, finally realized what he should have known immediately.

Khora was gone.

7.

Lieutenant Harding treated his hand, while other marines triangulated Hirokh's position from the nanotransmitters, using links from their satellite array. Thomas was certain Hirokh was behind that car bombing, and he hoped they could find Khora by tracking Hirokh. If Khora really knew how to find Sha'ad Tokh, they dare not leave him with the Chief Enforcer.

Precious minutes later their shuttle set down outside an old prison, so decrepit that from the outside it looked abandoned. The marines' attitude both pleased and alarmed Thomas in two respects. First, they did not hesitate to charge into action, when they must have suspected he had no authority to order them to do any such thing. Second, none made any attempt to dissuade Thomas from charging in with them.

The prison kept people in, not out. The marines swept past all three security checkpoints in bare moments, sprinting by most phren they passed, immobilizing the few who raised a weapon. Only one phren got off even a single shot, and the marines took no casualties.

They heard the screams as soon as they reached the long hall of holding cells. Speakers carried them for the other Tokhin prisoners to hear.

As he raced past, Thomas heard the other prisoners shouting encouragement to Khora, yelling at the top of their lungs, "There are Two, brother!"

Turning into an open cell just behind Harding and the lead group of marines, Thomas' nostrils flared at the sharp tang of moss mingled with phren blood. From manacles on the far wall dangled Khora, his soft pale flesh exposed through jagged gaps cut in his shell. Nothing moved but Khora's chest shuddering with labored breath and his blood dripping into a crimson puddle. A deep wound in his abdomen drew Thomas' gaze.

A single, very large phren stood in front of Khora, his back to the humans, beside a surgeon's array of glinting instruments. "I am sorry you had to see this, Envoy," said Hirokh without turning, as he plunged a short blade into Khora's chest. Three marines rushed to pull Hirokh away, while Harding checked Khora, but Thomas had too much faith in Hirokh's efficiency to believe he might survive.

The bloody gap in Khora's abdomen again flashed into Thomas' mind the image of his murdered wife. So hard had he tried to forget that picture, but now the shock of recognition pummeled him like moss, impossible to set aside.

So senseless. The nameless killer had taken her right index finger, to withdraw cash from their account, but the fool had to know there would be a cap on withdrawals. He could have gotten more money from her with a good sob story.

Everyone was very sympathetic of course. More than anything, that sympathy drove him offworld. He couldn't stand everybody patting him on the back and feeling sorry and secretly thrilled, because who knew anyone who had been murdered in this day and age? His family worried about depression, but he was no more depressed than happy. He was a phantom, a strange partial version of himself, someone he had never wanted to be and could not understand.

On Phrentyr, where over a billion people had perished, he thought others would appreciate his grief. But it was no use. To the phren, their loved ones' deaths made a perverse kind of sense. Solarans clearly believed the Great One approved of the slaughter. Tokhin held hope that their Two Gods would someday redeem Their chosen people with more slaughter. None, except maybe Hirokh, could conceive that Thomas lacked any such faith.

Thomas focused his eyes, spotting what he had missed before: Khora's cloak was stripped away and the slash across his belly cut through his abdominal mouth to reveal his pouch. He had been desecrated, contrary to the most sacred phren taboo.

Kayleigh's death once left Thomas numb, but the murder of Khora, whom he had met only a day before, filled him with fury. Was he the only person left in the universe who knew it was wrong to kill people? Would he have to rub the blood into each of their damn noses to explain it?

Through the gore of Khora's open pouch, Thomas

saw a splash of blue. He reached in and pulled out something solid and heavy. Ignoring the bloody stain it left, he wiped it with his own shirt. It was a brick, a clay brick stained a deep blue. It made no sense. Why would Khora have been carrying a brick in his pouch for their rendezvous?

Hirokh interrupted his thoughts. "Envoy, you know you have no right to be here."

Thomas could barely contain his rage. "Right?" he whispered. "You want to speak of rights? Who gave you the right to torture and murder? To expose another phren's pouch to the moss?" He spat onto Hirokh's face.

Hirokh wiped it off slowly. "The Great One gave me the right."

How did I come to this? Thomas wondered. Here was his only friend, the only person Thomas had shared any connection with since Kayleigh's death. And he was a butcher.

Thomas glared at Hirokh and savored his hatred.

8.

Ordinarily even Thomas could not gain entry to the Solaran Council on less than a twelveday's notice, but this time repeated warnings to every government agency that Earth might withhold aid to Phrentyr had gotten him here in four days.

The instant the massive doors opened, Thomas rushed directly to the great square council table, deliberately forcing Hirokh into a Frankensteinian lumber to keep up. Without preamble he announced the withdrawal of all human aid for the ruling government's violations of the Tokhin people's freedom of religion. He stood prepared to make good on the threat, too. It was against his orders, but Thomas had decided he didn't give a crap. It would also cause the deaths of thousands of innocent phren, but he could summon no sympathy for them, nor could he even manage to despise himself for that. He once thought himself a compassionate man, but that person was now buried under an impenetrable shell.

Several members of the Council showed obvious alarm at his threat but the Chief Councilman, *de facto* president of all Phrentyr, simply held his midlimbs rigidly folded.

Several Councilmen in turn adamantly averred their benevolence toward the Tokhin. Thomas responded by pointing his finger directly at Hirokh, an intolerably rude gesture for the Council chamber. "Four days ago, this phren tortured and killed a Tokhin for no crime other than speaking with me about how to help his people practice their religion in peace."

This brought a great uproar, and Thomas marveled at the degree of shouting and gesturing permitted by Solaran parliamentary procedure. Councilman Rotin, the Chief's unofficial second in command, finally quieted the others. "Surely there is a misunderstanding. Enforcer Hirokh, can you explain to the honored Envoy how he is mistaken?"

"No," said Hirokh, not bothering to emphasize with midlimbs. "The Envoy's statement is true."

Thomas studied the Chief for any reaction and

still saw nothing. Rotin began to say something to Thomas, then thought better of it and addressed Hirokh. "Hirokh, as Chief Enforcer, you must never take any action that might jeopardize our people, who still depend on the gracious help of our human friends."

Now Hirokh swung his midlimbs sharply in front of his great torso. "You whimper like unnamed children, when you have nothing at all to fear. With respect, the Envoy misstates his position." Thomas tried not to show any reaction to this bold declaration.

"It is past time for the Council to evaluate the humans' presence," Hirokh continued. "They send us a single diplomat, a handful of aid volunteers and we receive sporadic visits from small trading vessels. Meanwhile, they construct a heavily-armed orbital station, on which the Envoy has told me some two hundred marines are stationed, and we often detect human warships passing through this system without stopping on our world.

"Councilmen, the humans are here not from altruism," he sneered. "Their help is a soft layer of moss over the hard granite of their true purpose. This system is clearly a strategic base in some larger conflict of theirs. Despite the Envoy's personal feelings, Earth will not meddle in our internal affairs and risk our cooperation should their conflict ever touch this planet. Will the Council bow to the pervert-worshippers over an empty pouch?"

Thomas answered quickly, startled at how accurately Hirokh had puzzled all that out. "A splendid fantasy, Hirokh, but absolutely false, and the moss can take me if I lie." He had disowned any feelings of friendship, but Thomas still had to admire the huge old phren's deductive skills and his twisted sort of integrity. Hirokh was a killer, yet here he stood uncomplicatedly sticking to his principles, while Thomas lied through his teeth. "You know the extent of our technology. I do not mean to offend, but your people could offer us no assistance in any armed conflict." In a space battle that was true, but in a dirt-side action it was critical to have the locals on your side.

The Council launched into a debate, and Thomas knew he had to cut it off or he would lose his chance. "Listen!" he shouted. "Imagine for a moment that Hirokh is right. Suppose I have no authority to withdraw aid, that I will be removed from office just for threatening it," all of which was entirely true. "But then recall that our nearest command base is over three of your light years away. If I order aid withdrawn, it will be withdrawn for six years, no matter if Hirokh has guessed right." That was probably true as well, depending on how persuasive Thomas could be with P-Station's commanding officer. "Hirokh speaks of faraway Earth, but you," he said as he stared at the Chief, "must deal with me."

This succeeded in cutting through the rhetoric. "Tell us what you want," answered Rotin.

"The wall around Doubletown will come down," said Thomas. "Tokhin will be allowed to live and work anywhere in the Holy City. You will not prevent them from living in peace or from building and using places of worship."

The Council again erupted in angry shouts, but Thomas could soon see that his threats had turned the tide in his favor. Human aid was still vital to Phrentyr's economy, and economic collapse could bring down this ruling council.

Once the noise receded, Rotin formally addressed the Chief. "My Lord, it is the judgment of the Council that we must agree to the Envoy's . . . requests."

The Chief stood slowly, bowed to each Councilman in turn, then emphatically chopped his midlimbs no.

Rotin had apparently anticipated this. He also looked one at a time at the Councilmen, and they all responded with midlimbs up. "My Lord," he said, "the Council regards this as a matter of utmost priority. These words have not been spoken in this chamber since you uttered them twenty years ago, but today I say: Lord, you must relent."

The Chief signaled no again. "We have defeated the enemy," he said through labored breath, "and you will give our victory away. My eyes shall not see this abomination occur." He sat down, crossed his forelimbs and midlimbs and closed his eyes.

Rotin stood, reached under the council table with a forelimb, strode over and touched both of the Chief's cheeks with his midlimbs. Then he thrust a short blade through the Chief's exoskeleton. Each of the other Councilmen in turn stepped to the Chief and stabbed him again.

Unnerved by this abrupt demonstration of Solaran democracy, Thomas missed Rotin's next words to Hirokh. But all the Councilmen still held their knives ready, and despite himself he feared for his old friend. "Although your loyalty to the Chief is well known,"

Rotin continued, "I also know that your word is beyond reproach. If any here doubt it, speak now." No one answered. "Tell us, Hirokh, that you will follow the instructions of the Council, and we need not slay you as well."

"I am Chief Enforcer," Hirokh answered without hesitation. "I enforce the will of the state. All of you are now the state, so I enforce your will. If it is your order that we permit worship of the two deviant gods, so be it." The Council members relaxed. Hirokh continued in a voice edged with ice, "But it pleases me to know you will all lie together in Hell, feeling your guts consumed by moss for all eternity."

9.

The procession slowly wound its way out from the Tokhin Retreat all the way past the gates of Doubletown. Nearly all the P-Station marines were dirt-side to help keep the peace. From his place in the lead Thomas could not accurately count the marchers, but the group seemed even larger than the one thousand phren thought to inhabit Doubletown. Perhaps their number was swelled by the ghosts of many more Tokhin.

His legs ached from the past four days spent covering each neighborhood of Doubletown on foot, pleading personally with nearly every Tokhin to march with him. Some only needed to hear the gate in the wall would be open. But most were wary, and Thomas feared that no amount of cajoling could persuade them, that he had forfeited his position as Envoy for nothing. In the end, his best tactic was to make a martyr of Khora. He recounted Khora's death in ever more embellished details, telling all who would listen that Khora's dying wish was for his people to return to the First Temple. This was only a slight distortion; his actual prayer had been for the return of Sha'ad Tokh, but Thomas could not satisfy that wish.

They paraded slowly to the grounds of the First Temple, via the vast crater of the old Tokhin Director's Hall. This city had suffered less damage than other major cities due to both sides' respect for its religious significance, but many reminders of the carnage remained.

The light rain soon abated, and through the layer of clouds poked a brilliant orange sun. The group stirred with the good omen, but the scalding glare only reminded Thomas how insufferable this world would be but for the war.

Hirokh silently paced him. Thomas had warned the marines that Hirokh might try to kill him before the day ended but was not confident they could prevent it. Nevertheless, as they walked he spoke to Hirokh. "I suppose we are even, Hirokh. You must hate me for this." He regretted his choice of words at once; the term "even" was distasteful to Solarans, for its implication of duality.

Hirokh showed no sign of offense. "We are 'even,' Envoy, in that we have each profoundly misjudged the other. For all their high-minded talk, I never believed humans actually cared what should happen to the Tokhin. I thought their indifference confirmed when they sent their new Envoy, a clearly broken man.

"Yet you found a way to lead these people when they could not lead themselves. I compliment you, Envoy, and I marvel at the marriage you must have had, for it to leave you such strength despite your obvious despair."

Thomas found he could not look Hirokh in the eye to answer. Still, a part of Thomas would have liked to correct him. His marriage with Kayleigh had been far from perfect. Too often they were absorbed in their individual concerns instead of sharing their lives. Sometimes he allowed himself to forget how much he loved her; sometimes he thought he hated her. But the bond between them gradually grew, and he had believed someday they would get it just right, they would give each other everything they could. That hope, that anticipation, her killer had taken all that away.

Thomas did not believe he would ever again experience such hope for the future, but he was daring to think he could offer it to the worshippers of the Two Gods.

Cresting the hill to the grounds of the First Temple, Thomas recoiled at the scene before him. On his instructions marines had burned away the moss where the temple once stood, and several truckloads of clay bricks rested in piles near one edge of the circle. Around the perimeter of that circle crowded thousands and thousands of phren. It had to be half the Holy City's populace. On the bright side, the crowd's presence eased Thomas' fear that the Solarans might drop a nuke on them today.

Thomas motioned his marines to the front of the procession, but he could not guess whether they would be able to hold off the onslaught if all these Solarans attempted to fall on the Tokhin. But he would not back down.

As Lieutenant Harding corralled the marines into a human barrier, Thomas led the parade to the dusty central circle. Turning to the crowd, he held high the blue brick from Khora's slashed pouch. Tokhin and Solarans alike murmured in reaction. Waiting for them to quiet, Thomas cataloged everything that could go wrong. The Solaran spectators could surge forward and start a riot. The Tokhin could refuse to attempt to build a new temple. Or perhaps they would try, but not know how. Or if they knew how, they might still refuse to use the temple without Sha'ad Tokh.

"This brick is from the First Temple!" Thomas cried at the Tokhin. The murmuring began again, but he shouted over it. "Beginning with this brick, we will build a new temple. Perhaps some of you here also have original bricks from the First Temple." Thomas had no way of knowing, but he hoped that Khora had not been the only Tokhin to use his pouch to guard a remnant of the sacred temple. All those bricks had gone somewhere. "If so, step forward and help me build the new foundation."

On the sunken impression left by the former First Temple, Thomas laid his brick. He turned back to the group of Tokhin, and for a few moments none moved. Then High Priestess Khorana stepped forward from the crowd and walked up to Thomas. He thought perhaps she meant to confront him about her son's death, but instead she reached under her cloak and withdrew a silver brick, which she displayed to the crowd. To a raucous cheer from the Tokhin, she set it down next to his.

Other Tokhin came forward to add to the line of bricks, and slowly the base of a temple emerged from the dust. Somehow the Tokhin knew just where to leave a gap for the temple door.

Wiping his forehead of sweat, Thomas stepped toward the throng of Solaran spectators and raised his voice for another calculated risk. "If there are any Tokhin living in secret among the Solarans, now is the time to come out of hiding. If you still think of yourselves as Tokhin, then you must not live out your whole lives as Solarans."

He crossed to four different points on the perimeter of the temple grounds and said the same for all the crowd to hear. They jeered, and no Tokhin rose to his challenge. Perhaps Khora had been wrong that a few were hidden among the Solarans, or perhaps they were yet too afraid to give up their camouflage.

The temple grew rapidly. The bricks the Tokhin laid were not uniform, but locked together in a complex pattern, like tiles on an ancient space shuttle. Dry and free of moss for the moment, most were gray, but blue and silver mixed here and there in the swiftly growing wall. The colors at first seemed random, but eventually a shifting pattern emerged.

Thomas had thought Tokhin temples were constructed of concentric rings of bricks. Now he could see that the bricks formed a single, unending spiral, tilting inward as it climbed.

The temple continued to rise, and Thomas realized

nearly every Tokhin had carried a brick through the parade. Even so, they were nearing the end of the procession, and the walls of the temple were hardly a meter off the ground. When the last Tokhin had set her brick in place, Thomas motioned the group to the piles of bricks nearby. But none made any move toward them.

Then it happened.

Thomas thought they had exhausted the procession, but when he glanced back at the temple several more Tokhin were lined up to add to the wall. And the line was growing.

Phren emerged from the crowd on every side of the temple grounds. Thomas saw dozens step from among the Solarans, and then like the sun bursting through the haze earlier began a steady flow of hundreds out of the crowd, to add to the wall. It tilted inward as it spiraled up, but remained stable.

Within minutes, Thomas could see that the newcomers outnumbered his original procession. There were at least a thousand of them. And still they came. All across the grounds embraced neighbors who could never before reveal themselves. Some of the original procession cheered their emerging comrades, but most stood in dumb amazement.

Now the crowd filled the entire temple grounds, and the Solaran watchers receded from the swelling tide of Tokhin. Thomas realized that half or more of the Solaran watchers who jeered at him minutes before had not been Solaran at all.

The highest tiers of the brick spiral nearly paralleled the ground, yet the pattern remained and no brick slipped out of place, even with the weight of Tokhin climbing the exterior to add more.

Thomas stepped into the gap left for a door and saw some of the Tokhin had brought not bricks but pieces of marble, deposited inside the temple wall. Three phren crouched on the ground assembling the pieces according to some intricate design.

The inside of the new, vastly old, temple was too small to hold even a tiny fraction of the throng. But with the First Temple in place, Thomas was sure the Tokhin would build new temples, then maybe go on to build new lives.

Phren nudged Thomas out of the doorway, to decorate the interior of the temple with thin drapes and rugs, all magically spirited from pouches. One brought a small lamp, which sputtered and issued a sharp, bitter odor. Thomas inhaled and a weight lifted from his chest, which registered after a moment as the absence of any scent of moss.

The marble construction was complete, a narrow pedestal. As Thomas watched, two more phren entered carrying something between them. They uncovered it to reveal a massive copy of *The Word of Both*. Far too large to hold in their pouches, these two had managed to smuggle the book under a cloak all the way from Doubletown. Reverently they set it on the pedestal.

Now all the phren left the interior of the temple, and Thomas walked out with them to face an enormous crowd looking to him in anticipation.

He had no idea what to do next.

10.

Thomas spotted High Priestess Khorana and stepped to her. "Can you say a blessing or . . . something?"

Her midlimbs rose in affirmation, yet she said clearly, "No." Seeing Thomas' consternation, she added, "I cannot, but someone here can."

Khorana walked boldly toward the remaining Solarans, directly to an older phren woman standing at the front of the crowd. They clasped midlimbs. Khorana pulled the woman—her mother?—out of the crowd and strode back to the temple.

This was the last of the procession. The woman climbed to the top of the gently sloping temple and added her brick. It had an odd trapezoidal shape, and when slotted into place it left only a neat, circular opening at the top.

Turning to face the crowd from the top of the temple dome, she began to recite a long blessing in the ancient Tokhin language. Among all the assembled worshippers, there was only one other who could understand her words, yet thousands wept for joy to hear the Old Tongue spoken again. The final words in her prayer were "Sha'ad Tokh," repeated three times.

The crowd took up the chant, "Sha'ad Tokh! Sha'ad Tokh! Sha'ad Tokh! . . ." Thomas thought he sensed a wistful tone to the chant, as if the Tokhin did not truly believe that Sha'ad Tokh survived to complete their temple.

As the crowd continued to chant, the old woman descended from the temple. Thomas thought she was walking to him, but she stepped past to Hirokh, whom she caressed gently on the cheeks with both her forelimbs and midlimbs. Thomas could not have been more stunned if Hirokh had sprouted wings and taken flight.

She backed away from Hirokh, and he approached Thomas. The Envoy was amazed to see that he was weeping openly. Hirokh stretched out forelimbs and midlimbs and embraced Thomas, who was too bewildered to feel revulsion.

"I never thought to see this day in my lifetime," Hirokh said. "May They Both bless you."

He walked toward the front row of Tokhin, then stopped and lowered onto midlimbs. His torso clenched and rippled, and he threw his head back and gasped as if giving birth.

Finally he drew a deep, shuddering breath and stood. From beneath his cloak he drew a bright globe and held it aloft to the crowd. Marbled blue and silver swirls shimmered and shifted over its surface, echoing the pattern of the temple walls.

Sha'ad Tokh.

The nearest Tokhin fell forward onto midlimbs as they beheld it. To Thomas it seemed not a religious observance, but that they were too overcome with relief and wonder to stand.

As each row of Tokhin knelt, those behind saw the orb and knelt in turn. The movement rippled outward in concentric circles as far as Thomas could see.

When all of them were prone the chant resumed, but with greater passion. The crowd's collective voice rumbled over the ground. "Sha'ad Tokh!"

Hirokh stepped back to Thomas. He strode lightly,

without his usual shuffling gait. Thomas realized that he had limped not from an injury, but because of the burden he had always carried.

"You?" he asked in astonishment. "All along, you held Sha'ad Tokh?"

"It had to be kept where no one would think to look for it," he answered through tears of happiness and relief. "Besides, no one else could swallow it. Envoy, will you place it at the top of the temple?"

"Me? I don't think I should."

Hirokh persisted. "Please." He hesitated. "Thomas. It is fitting to honor the Two Gods, Who brought you to us to hasten this moment."

Thomas found he could not refuse Hirokh, whom he had so recently learned to despise. "Come with me?" If this was against custom, Hirokh did not object.

They started to walk toward the temple, but Khorana and the older woman stepped forward and placed midlimbs on their chests to halt them. They motioned to the crowd and it parted to reveal a group of phren lifting a tub of water from a fire, which Thomas had not seen them light.

They brought the tub and set it before Hirokh, who removed his cloak, something Thomas had never before seen any phren do. At a gesture from Khorana, Thomas also undressed. With sponges from the tub, so hot that no moss grew, Khorana and the other woman bathed Thomas and Hirokh, who never put down Sha'ad Tokh. The women then covered both in long jewel-encrusted cloaks to an approving cheer from the crowd.

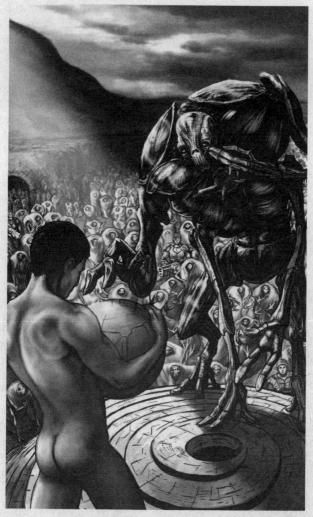

FREDERICK EDWARDS

Thomas and Hirokh climbed together to the top of the temple dome. As they ascended, Thomas marveled at the stability of the structure he had just witnessed assembled without benefit of mortar or plans or anything but ancient, dusty bricks.

At the top, Hirokh handed him Sha'ad Tokh, so heavy Thomas had to brace it against his chest with both hands. Slowly he lowered it to slide smoothly into the gap at the top of the temple. Hirokh pounded it firmly into place with each of his forelimbs and midlimbs in turn.

A great roar from the throng of worshippers buffeted them. Still kneeling on midlimbs, the crowd shouted even as they continued to cry with elation.

The moss would be a meter high here tomorrow from the moisture of all their tears.

After descending, Thomas faced Hirokh. "All those years. How did you manage?"

"Do not be concerned for me," he answered, wiping his face. "Many of my people have sacrificed their lives for the Two Gods. I am one of the lucky ones. I did not have to die to do it."

Thomas shook his head in disbelief. He knew what it was to cast off one's entire life, but he had merely run away, not become a completely different person.

"But all the things you did. How did you . . . How could you . . ."

"There are Two Gods, and sometimes They require us to become two." Tears continued to stream down Hirokh's face, and Thomas realized they were not all for joy. "I only pray to Both that I can still remember who I was before."

Thomas sank to his knees, joining the multitude all around them. He stared up into the face of this creature, at once the most contemptible and the most noble person he had ever met, and for the first time he believed.

There are Two.

Making It

BY MIKE RESNICK

Mike Resnick is, according to Locus, *the all-time leading award-winner, living or dead, for short science fiction. He sold his first article at fifteen, his first story at seventeen and his first novel at twenty. He is the author of sixty-two science fiction novels, 250 stories and two screenplays, and has edited forty anthologies, as well as serving stints as the science fiction consultant for BenBella Books and as executive editor for Jim Baen's Universe. He has also written mysteries and nonfiction, including a pair of Hugo-nominated books about writing. Mike has won five Hugos (from a record thirty-four nominations), a Nebula and other major awards in the US, France, Spain, Croatia, Poland and Japan, and has been short-listed for major awards in England, Italy and Australia. His work has been translated into twenty-five languages. He has been named the Guest of Honor at the 2012 Worldcon.*

Making It

Writers of the Future has been turning out writers—by which I mean successful, best-selling, award-winning writers—for over a quarter of a century now. They've done it long enough and frequently enough that there's no longer any doubt that this program is not a fluke, that they really do know how to pick and train talent.

So let's examine it from the other side. Yes, they know their stuff. They build writers. But can they build you into one?

That leads to a plethora of questions. How do you make it as a writer? Do you start with short stories and build a reputation (and can you build one in these days of only a tiny handful of print magazines)? Do you start in an easier field (and is there any easy field)? Do you begin with novels? Nonfiction? Do you attend workshops and conventions, and start networking with other writers, or are they wastes of that rarest of a writer's commodities: time?

My answer isn't likely to thrill anyone, because what I'm going to do is quote Rudyard Kipling:

There are nine and sixty ways, of constructing tribal lays, and each and every one of them is right.

Well, I'll qualify it to this extent: every approach is right for those who have proved it is right for them.

Eric Flint, a Writers of the Future winner, didn't start writing until his late 40s. Within two years he was living on the best-seller list, where you can still find him. Kevin J. Anderson, a long-time lecturer and judge at Writers of the Future, made the best-seller list originally by writing some outstanding Star Wars books, but he took that enormous audience with him and has been a best-seller ever since. Patrick Rothfuss won the contest and found himself on the Hugo ballot and the best-seller list half a dozen years later with *The Name of the Wind.* Tim Powers and I, lecturers and judges here, don't live on the best-seller list—but we were the 2011 and 2012 Worldcon Guests of Honor.

People and careers differ. I sold my first article at the age of fifteen, my first story at seventeen, my first novel at twenty. I had all the mechanical skills, but I lacked the maturity and ambition to apply myself and write anything award-worthy or even memorable, and it was another eighteen years and a couple of hundred forgettable books written under pseudonyms before I moved over to science fiction and wrote anything of value, anything I was anxious to sign my name to. That was a few best-sellers and more than 100 awards and nominations ago, which just shows that we don't all develop at the same pace or in the same way.

And that holds for the Writers of the Future winners

and finalists too. Look down the list at Nina Kiriki Hoffman, and Nick DiChario, and Dave Wolverton, and Karen Joy Fowler, and Robert Reed, and Jay Lake, and Tobias S. Buckell, and Stephen Baxter, and Amy Sterling Casil, and K. D. Wentworth, and R. Garcia y Robertson, and Dean Wesley Smith and all the others. Each got to where he or she is by a different route, some faster than others.

But they have certain things in common. We all do.

First, there's a love of writing. A lot of writers hate writing and love having written. Not the ones who make it. They love words, they love pushing nouns up against verbs and seeing the results, they love creating their very own worlds and then inviting you into them.

Second, there's the constant study of the field. There are certain categories of fiction that require almost no preparation. Others, like the detective story, ask you to create a hero and then run him through his paces book after book after book. Not science fiction. With all time and space at the author's disposal, about the only thing he can't do is tell the same story over and over. He can experiment, he can innovate, he can and must create; what he cannot do is repeat, not only himself but what has gone before, which is why he must be well-read in the field and stay abreast of what's going on.

Third, there's talent, and the ability to get the reader emotionally involved with the characters and the stories. The successful author must make the reader (I'll write it in caps so no one can miss it) FEEL, must make him love or hate or fear or laugh, or, in short, react. If he makes him think, as our progenitors Hugo Gernsback (creator of the field) and John Campell (the first great editor) believed was science fiction's mission, so much the better and the author has written a better story for it. But if the reader can't respond emotionally, then the author has written a fictionalized polemic or scientific cross-word puzzle.

And there's one more essential quality, which I will define as a fire in the belly, by which I mean an unwillingness to get discouraged or accept rejection. (A beginner asked me recently if I still get rejected. The answer was yes, every year or two it still happens. She then asked me my reaction. I said it hadn't changed in half a century. It was, spoken so softly only I can hear it: "To hell with you, fella [or lady]. I'm taking it to your competitor, he'll buy it, and when it wins the Hugo or the Nebula or sells to Hollywood I'll get richer and more famous, so will my editor, and you, pal, are going to be standing on the unemployment line when word gets out.")

Has it ever happened? I did win an award with a rejected story some years back. I don't think anyone ever got fired for rejecting me. But the point is that you—like every writer I named—have to believe in yourself more than you believe in an editor whose tastes and priorities are different. (By the same token, never look at a story and say, "Oh, there's no sense sending this one to Editor A. It's just not his kind of story." Maybe it isn't, but it's not your function to do his job for him. Let him decide whether or not to buy it—and remember: he can't buy what he never sees.)

Is there more?

Sure. In this business, there's always more.

I mentioned networking before. The writer with the hunger in the belly gets involved in that early on. He exchanges market information with his peers—and most anthologies are by invitation only, which means he finds out who the editors are and makes sure they know who he is. He learns of new markets, and in this day of the Internet, they change almost weekly. True, there are only four print magazines, where in 1954 there were fifty-six . . . but as I write these words (and it's likely to change by the weekend) there are eighteen electronic science fiction magazines paying what SFWA—the Science Fiction Writers of America—considers to be a professional rate. And if you don't network, you don't learn about them. You network to find out which conventions you should go to, which ones have the editors you want to meet and the writers you want to befriend.

From the outside it may seem like the publishing world is imploding, as bookstore chains are in big trouble, and publishers are losing more writers every month to the Internet, where they have discovered that 70% is a nicer royalty rate than 6% or 10%. But from the inside, there have rarely been so many opportunities. There's traditional publishing, of course. And there are more small and medium presses every year, a handful of which pay rates comparable to the New York houses. And there's self-publishing on the web. And there's podcasting. And there's suddenly tons of money to be made in audio sales. And as quickly as the writer learns what he has to know about all these outlets, of course there will be more. And there'll be improvements and innovations on what we have right now: e-books with animated covers and background music and hypertext, video podcasts and more.

Who will take advantage of all these opportunities? The same writers who have those four traits I mentioned before: a love of writing, a passionate interest in the field, talent and (perhaps most important, as I've seen many talented beginners just fade away) that blazing fire in the belly.

The Writers of the Future contestants in this book have all had ample opportunity to get down on themselves, to give up and walk away. Not one of them has quit. Every one of them loves writing, constantly studies the field they're writing in, has enough talent to appear in this book and has that fire in the belly that all but guarantees this is far from the last you're going to hear from each of them.

Bonehouse

written by

Keffy R. M. Kehrli

illustrated by

VIVIAN FRIEDEL

ABOUT THE AUTHOR

Keffy R. M. Kehrli is entirely from western Washington, except for the nine months he spent in Finland failing quantum mechanics and swimming in frozen lakes. He grew up reading fantasy and science fiction, especially books by Madeleine L'Engle and Nancy Farmer. After seeing Star Wars, *he decided that he wanted to be a writer, despite his parents' attempts to persuade him to chase a much more sensible profession.*

Since then, he has earned degrees in both physics and linguistics, and is currently working in a molecular biology research lab. He hopes to one day attend graduate school for genetics and, of course, keep writing. He also harbors delusions of someday becoming a rock star, but admits that he's just as likely to grow wings.

Keffy attended Clarion in 2008 and has sold a few stories to magazines like Fantasy Magazine *and* Orson Scott Card's InterGalactic Medicine Show. *He is working on a novel, but hasn't started sending out any fiction quite that long yet. He currently lives in Seattle and can be found at his website.*

ABOUT THE ILLUSTRATOR

Vivian is happiest when she slips into a food coma after having eaten a good meal and is grateful her mom makes the best empanadas in the world. Despite her appearance, she eats like a glutton (a trait she is teased about immensely). Luckily for her health, drawing makes her forget that her stomach is a gaping black hole by filling her head with ideas that block out hunger signals.

As a child, nothing pleased her more than pretending to be a Power Ranger and watching Saturday morning cartoons before the rest of the family claimed the TV. Watching cartoons turned into copying cartoons on scrap sheets of paper, copying turned into creating her own creatures and as she got older, creating funny creatures turned into illustrating unwritten stories with no particular plots. At nine years old she made up her mind that she didn't want to be a ballerina or a veterinarian when she grew up (though both are perfectly respectable professions). Instead she already knew at that early age she wanted to be an artist.

Her teen years were full of awkward moments and frustrations, but she survived by scribbling away on math notes in the back of the classroom.

Right after high school she enrolled at a community college to study video game design, but grew frustrated when the two-year plan turned into a four-year plan. Needless to say, she went back to a regular ol' art major.

The future holds too many blank pages to fill for her to continue telling her life story. What can be said though is that she daydreams of making a happy living by doodling away either on overly expensive sketchpads, fancy-pants computer tablets or on modest sheets of printer paper with a .05 mechanical pencil, the latter somehow being her favorite.

Bonehouse

Evictions are a messy business.

Muddy gold-brown sunlight filtered through the dust cloud that hung over downtown, putting tiger stripes of light and shadow in the air. Basalt gravel and desiccated eelgrass crunched underfoot as I made my way down Holly Street at low tide. There was asphalt beneath it all, slowly crumbling and turning to beach before it washed out to sea.

There wasn't much this close to the bay. The buildings used to be two- or three-story shops before the ground dropped and the water level rose. Now the bottom floors had been opened up to let the tide run past. In the shadows, I could see the remains of rooms—slimy brown mold-and-rot walls, broken toilets and tile. A thick tide sludge that smelled like petroleum and the deaths of a million fish glistened in the shade.

Another ten years, maybe, and there'd be nothing here anymore.

Far cry from how it'd been when I'd lived this side of the mountains. Things used to be green then. Now the lowland forests were full of bleached ghost trees, dead from the salt water drowning their roots. The buildings were brickwork, and where there might have been ivy clinging to the sides, a thin tracery of metal spidered over the walls. Even in this submerged part of town, there was enough ambient electricity in the air for a decent harvest system to make up for what they didn't get from sun or tide.

I stopped near the end of the row, smelling the place I was looking for, even over the salt stench of the ocean. Disinfectant, too much of it, a citrus-tinged sickly scent. You could knock on a hundred abandoned doors if you wanted, but I never needed to. I knew the smell of a bonehouse by heart.

I climbed up the ten feet of rickety wood stairs that were nailed to what had been the sill of the second-floor window. I didn't like the stairs. Standing at the top, there wasn't much to hang onto but a rotten banister that looked about ready to fall apart.

I knocked.

The owners let me stand out there a good few minutes while the terns wheeled overhead and screamed.

When the door opened, a short white man with round glasses and lank greasy hair down to his shoulders squinted out at me. "Evictionist," he said. "I don't got anybody here for you. Go find some other house to haunt."

The disinfectant smell was stronger and the room was filled with a dim, flickering light. A woman in ripped jeans sat on a patched-together couch, dividing her attention between the wall-mounted screen and our conversation at the door.

"You won't mind if I check their chips, then," I said. "I'm a good guy. You don't got what I want, I'll leave." Starting to lose my balance on the stairs, I didn't want to go for that banister, figuring it would snap if I did, so I leaned forward and grabbed the doorframe.

The man flinched like I was too close, so I smiled.

"They're all paid up through next year at least," he said through his teeth. "I don't have enough flow to return that much cash."

I snicked my tongue against my teeth, waiting.

The woman came over. She said, "Let him in, Justin. Nobody ever gets the good side of an Evictionist." She shot me a look that was mostly poison with just a dash of hate. "I'll show him what he thinks he wants to see."

Justin growled a bit, under his breath, and let the door swing open. He bowed and gestured inside.

"Thank you," I said, and I slammed my boots against the doorframe, knocking off as much sand as I could. I kept my eyes on Justin, partways hoping he'd pull a knife. Americans.

We shook hands. Hers were rough as any bonehouse warden's. "Dr. Anna Petreus," she said.

The front room was cluttered, but not near as filthy as most of the places I'd seen. A few dirty dishes were stacked on the end table, next to them a pair of cell phones. Petreus had been watching news coverage of the riots in Ottawa. Someone had uncovered evidence that the parliamentary elections had been rigged. Almost normal, that.

A wiry looking orange tabby came out from under the coffee table and rubbed himself on my leg. Petreus gave me a funny look when I bent to pick up the cat.

He wrapped his front legs around my neck and buried his nose in my ear, purring loud enough to wake the dead.

Petreus led me down the hallway to a dark room. The only light came from a cluster of monitors, each one hooked up to a different guest. The monitors showed vital signs. Steady heartbeats, hormones at the right levels, vitamins to stave off serious illness, everything they needed to live except reality.

Seven hospital beds full of bones and skin.

I'd never seen so many in such a small house. I wondered if it was a coastal thing, or if they'd come in as a group. The boy closest to me twitched while he net-dreamed. He'd been under for a while. They get like that, the bones. They'll twitch all around even after the muscles have gone. The only thing they've got left that works is their brain.

"You must be turning a hefty profit out here," I said. I put the cat down so I could fumble for my cell phone. "Not having to pay for your electricity."

"We're low-end," Dr. Petreus said. She scratched the back of her neck and then inspected her nails in the light from one of the vitals displays. "None of these kids paid all that much per month when we plugged them in. We get by, but . . ."

I grunted a response. Winding around my legs, the cat purred louder. "Friendly cat," I muttered.

"He doesn't get a lot of attention from our guests," she answered. "Go on, check them. I'm not leaving you alone in here."

Only two of the seven were female.

The one closest to me didn't really seem to have a human form under the blanket. From how small she was, I would've been curious to see the Vegas odds that she'd plugged in before she was legal. I thumbed open the phone. Nope, not mine.

The second woman was the one I was after. This didn't surprise me. It didn't matter how good a bonehouse tech was, she could never mask an IP address well enough to keep me out. And proxies, well. I'll just say that not all of them are as anonymous as they advertise.

"Well?"

"Bad for you," I said. I pocketed my phone and pointed at the woman tucked over in the corner. "She's the one I'm after."

Laura DeVries, age 29. Used the web like any normal kid until she was seventeen, when she ran away from home and tried to plug in permanently. She'd been evicted four times already. No wonder she'd come out to the coast—she probably had trouble finding a bonehouse that would take her.

Hers was a family extraction. The loved ones she'd left behind had pooled their money together for a fifth time, the amount much smaller than previous jobs. My cut was barely worth the trip out to the coast.

"She's been in three years straight now," Petreus said. "You know it won't be any good for her coming out. Why waste the rehab dollars on her?"

"Because her family wants her back and I get paid by the contract." I stretched my arms and back. Three years into a netdream, and she wasn't going to be walking much of anywhere. I'd be carrying her back down Holly and up Bay. "Plus, you might say it ticks me off a bit when people with potential can't handle unplugging long enough to feed themselves."

263

Petreus just shook her head. She wound between the beds until she got to Laura's. She called up the 'net usage on the vitals monitor and then cut the connection. She was doing it for the money, too.

It took a full twenty seconds before Laura realized that it was more than just a 'net hiccup and opened her eyes.

"Anna?" Her voice was raw, hoarse.

Petreus patted her on the forehead and then started disconnecting the IV and monitoring devices. "I'm sorry," she said. "We'll pro-rate your stay and transfer what's left back to your accounts."

"No," Laura said. "I didn't do anything. I didn't violate any codes. I didn't bring any viruses into the servers. Please." Her face was green and skeletal in the light from the monitors. "Sammy said he wouldn't wait for me again if I dropped and he couldn't find me. He'll move on, Anna, he'll move on."

I crept up to her bed. She was too busy trying to grab tubes out of Petreus' hands and stick them back to her body, but she was too weak. The tubes fell against the bedsheets, and Petreus gathered them up. She didn't answer or look at Laura's face. "I'm sure he'll wait," she said.

"Why are you doing this to me?" Laura's voice cracked. She was crying.

I couldn't figure if she was addled from the 'net drop—she had to still have some world-ghosting going on in her head—or if she really had forgotten the other times she'd been evicted.

"Evictionist, Laura." I rested a hand on the metal bed railing. Good work on Petreus and her tech, getting all this equipment out here and up those stairs out front. "Your mama misses you."

"No," she started sobbing. "This is my life, don't you understand?"

I leaned over. "You ever think maybe your real kids want to see more of you than just your avatar?"

No answer.

Petreus started shutting down the equipment. Laura didn't move. She was dressed in what looked like a purloined hospital gown, so I wrapped the bedsheet around her limp form and picked her up like a kid. Couldn't risk the fireman's carry, too big a chance that she'd break something. Petreus said, "I'm sorry, Laura."

Laura didn't say another word until we were halfway down Holly Street. The tide was coming in, and I was already wading in an inch or so of surf.

"I'm just gonna go back," she said. "Soon as they let me out." Her chest heaved with every breath. Just the strain of holding onto my neck was enough to wind her. "I'll plug back in and put my life back together."

They all say that. I was expecting it.

"Go right ahead," I said. "Keeps me getting paid."

"Sammy might not wait," she said. "But just in case if he does, I'll be back. There's nothing you can do."

She was still babbling when I put her in the back seat of the car that the company had rented for me, a funny little Russian-made thing that I didn't think would have outrun the surf if I'd parked it on Holly.

"What's your name?" she asked as soon as I'd strapped her in, one weak hand closed on the front of my shirt. "What's your name?"

"To you," I said, "I'm just the Evictionist."

Her expression closed down into an angry glare. "He'll find out who you are," she said.

"Oh yeah? Sammy Not-Gonna-Wait-No-More?"

"Sammy Gauge," she said softly. "And he's going to break you."

She must have seen the recognition in my face, and there was a moment when she must've thought about bragging some more. As it was, though, she clammed up. I wanted to kick myself. I knew better than to broadcast my thoughts that way.

Gauge.

The possibility of Samuel Gauge being one of the aliases of Cameron Trexell had initially been figured at twenty percent. Both Samuel and Cameron had been good at restricting the personal information they let slip in their online communication. Once the suspicion leaked, Gauge had dropped offline, his actions going from borderline illegal to nothing overnight.

Cameron Trexell was an eviction so big that the company hadn't even bothered assigning it directly to one of their agents. Instead, it was open season, and the Evictionist cut was enough to live on comfortably for a while. I wouldn't stop working if I had that kind of cash, but I could quit living off the easy marks and take on the difficult cases, the ones who really needed to be saved. That, and pay for something I'd been meaning to do for years.

As for what the company'd get if I brought him in, well, at least half of the Northern Coalition was looking to get him out of the 'net and into custody.

For starters. Trexell or one of his known aliases had been heavily implicated in almost every act of electronic terrorism in the past five years. His group saw no future for the world and they typically made their feelings known by shutting some things down, breaking other things and generally trying to bring their own prophecies to fruition.

"Oh yeah, *Gauge*." I laughed at her, hard enough that I could see her squirm. It was still more than likely that she was screwing with me. After all, it was more than a little odd that nobody else had turned up Laura while they were searching for Trexell. It was also more than a little unlikely that he'd spend time talking to somebody who'd had as weak a proxy setup as Laura's.

"You'll see," she whispered.

I slipped through the border ghost town that was Blaine, through White Rock, which was still doing okay, and Vancouver, which was evolving, filled up with Canadians, with the best of the American ex-pats, with anybody who had enough cash to move north and enough skills to get through the border.

The guards gave me the fifth degree, as usual, picking apart the discrepancies between my appearance and my identification even though I knew damn well that they had everything they asked on file from the last ten or twenty times I'd jumped the Forty-ninth. They backed off real quick when I asked if they wanted a direct line to my boss.

I left Laura in a little rehab place, more of a staging location than anything. They ran tests, made sure that the dreamers we dropped off were well enough to send east, in batches, in electric train cars. She'd end up somewhere in Ontario, maybe even Toronto itself, wasting health-care funds. Eventually, she'd run back south, and next time, the fee might be too low for anybody to bother coming after her. She probably knew that, which was why she'd mostly kept her mouth shut, just waiting out the ordeal.

'Course, before I left her, I made her a deal.

"I've got enough tech in the car right now to hook you up," I said.

She stared out the window at the lost parts of Vancouver, where not even a dike had been enough to save the streets from flooding. It was a shallow bay now, a couple meters deep, dead trees and telephone poles sticking up like rotten dock pilings. "I'd be less suspicious if you had anything to gain," she said.

I tapped my fingers on the steering wheel, annoyed with myself. Once the disorientation had faded and she'd catnapped in the passenger seat, Laura DeVries was not stupid. Nobody did favors in this game.

"I was thinking if you were interested that I'd sell you the time." I tried to sound a little nervous, barely made eye contact over the rims of my sunglasses, like that was the most ethically shady I ever got.

She might have been pretty, if she wasn't so wasted-looking, or if I was able to ignore the nutrient drip in her arm. "That's pretty low, even for somebody who gets paid to ruin lives," she said finally.

I shrugged. "Do you want to reconnect and settle your accounts, or not? I'll give you an amount to transfer, and once that's done, you can have an hour."

"An hour." Her hands clutched at the blanket I'd

draped over her legs. "What if I don't have enough money?"

I snorted. "Funny. Look, neither one of us has enough time to screw around. Either you want to make a deal or you don't."

"Okay," she said.

The amount I asked for wasn't very high—just enough to throw her off, make her think that I was in it for the money after all. Low enough to make me seem like a small fish, as if jobs like picking her up were normal to me. The more she underestimated me, the better.

I halfheartedly watched her online movements with one of my external monitors, figuring that she'd get too suspicious if she didn't see me watching her. I saw her pull apart her empire and parcel it off to those of her acquaintances that weren't important enough to keep secret. Public aliases.

It was kind of funny, how behind she was. She deleted every account she accessed, once she was done with it, assuming I'd have her passwords. That's not how I find people. Any kid with enough time on his hands can crack passwords. For me, it's about correlating behavior, the kinds of personal information that people don't really think about giving out. We all have our unique patterns of thought and activity. Given enough data and some processor time, I can find the alter-accounts of anybody.

Knowing where she'd had her accounts just told me who to bribe.

When the hour was up, I sent her through the short disconnect routine.

She didn't thank me.

In retrospect, I'd say my biggest mistake was that I didn't tell anybody in the company what I was after when I requested all of DeVries' records.

The advantage of being quiet about what I was up to was obvious—nobody to share the money with. The disadvantage was just as obvious—nobody to go in with me. I'd been in a few suspicious situations, bonehouses with wardens that outweighed me by thirty or forty kilos, wardens who didn't care that projectile weapons were definitely against the law and once in the middle of what might as well have been a war zone. All this, despite being required by law to remain unarmed. Still, Trexell was worth enough in cash and notoriety that going in without backup like I did was stupid. A tenth of the cut would've been enough to get me what I wanted.

I crossed back out of Canada and then drove a bit, looking for a place where I got a decent signal without being under too much surveillance. I finally found the right spot on I-5 after it leaves the Chuckanuts but before it turns into a series of bridges over Skagit Bay. Skagit was worse off than Vancouver—the economy had been such that the farmhouses in the area had been left behind, strip-salvaged and left to rot. The bay is full of islands that used to be roofs, covered in bird crap, sinking lower year by year.

I set my timer first. Plugging in is like falling asleep into a perfect dream. No—it's like waking up into one. No—

Your senses go away entirely if you've got the right connection. There's no touch, no smell, no sound unless you want it. Turn on all the senses before you're acclimated and you'll go crazy, touch and sight and smell all advertising different products at once.

The numbers say that most of bonehouse dreamers plug in for a 24/7 life of porn or games. By most, I mean a good ninety-nine percent. This is what we're doing with technology that makes immersive language learning almost foolproof, that makes searching a couple of exabytes of data as easy as thinking.

Laura's files. Most of her time was spent in games. She'd been making money to keep herself plugged in by playing. I hadn't expected the search to be as easy as looking through her records to see if any of them had Trexell written all over them, but it would have been nice. I was just mining for pertinent data, dumping it into the computer.

My timer went off, distant. I pulled myself out of the 'net long enough to slap it off, and then fell back in, for just another few minutes. I kept digging, found out everything I could about Laura's actions—which were easy enough to track, honestly. She'd had five alter egos, some of whom were into sex acts that I'm sure her standard persona would have pretended to be scandalized just hearing about.

Funny thing about living online that way, everybody who does eventually ends up with some kind of multiple personality going on. Unavoidable, really. That's the thing about being a creature of data, humanity made in the image of artificial intelligence. Data is malleable, flesh is less so.

Intuition.

Every topic has a cloud associated, a set of linked concepts, linked accounts, linked people. Two choices. Either let the computer run through all of the possibilities, or figure it out yourself. I preferred doing the latter.

I followed links, cached search string lists, finding a way around every time I hit up on something password protected. I winced every so often when an ad wormed through my blocker, addressed me by my birth name and tried to sell me something.

Then I found Samuel.

I followed Laura and Sammy Gauge, their entire lives unfolding to me all at once. Here's where they first met, in a voice chat on American secessionist politics. There was the simulator where they got married, with Gauge under a new name. There was the imaginary home life they'd set up, perfectly normal until I dug back through the links, finding old ones, dead links with less-than-benign file names attached to them.

And then the glorious and bizarre moment when I called in a favor on the anonymous proxy he'd been using and found out that he was based here, too. Here, as in Seattle, a bonehouse junky's dream.

The connection dropped suddenly, shunting me out into glaring daylight, dry-mouthed, in the back seat of my car. Slammed straight out of a connection like that, I always feel groggy, like I've been jerked out of sleep and I'm only half-awake. The 'net ghosted in my head, like the afterimage of a thought, burned into my neurons. I reached for water, drank, fought back nausea as I checked my clock.

Five hours?

My timer hadn't initiated shutdown . . . or had it? I

vaguely remembered overriding the shutdown order. Just a few more minutes. And a few more. And a few more. I took a shaky breath.

Physical limitations.

I fought the impulse to hook myself back in, embarrassed by it, even though there was nobody around to see my relapse.

David wasn't happy to see me. He lived in what used to be north Seattle, and he didn't approve of my career path.

However, I needed somewhere to charge the car, and I still had the key to his house and to the electrical box outside. I'd just plugged the car in when he came to the door and crossed his arms. I wondered belatedly if he'd set up a perimeter alarm system. All the other houses on this street had been looted, long abandoned by people who didn't like living isolated in empty suburban sprawl. I'd crawled in through a few of the back windows for David, when I still lived with him. We'd liked living in an abandoned city.

"I'm close to him now," I said. "Found him."

He shook his head at me. "You know what I think about that."

"Relax," I said, my enthusiasm already fading. "You'll probably get lucky again and he'll be gone before I get there, and then you can continue to feel smug." I followed him into the house, an old single-level wooden structure. I plugged in my phone— which was also the computer that ran my car, did all my statistical searches and was otherwise far too important to charge in its normal location.

The house was still filled with photographs. For a while, David had talked about setting up an old-style darkroom, but he'd changed his mind when he saw how much it would cost to get the permits for the chemicals.

Not that anybody would come out here to check him.

"You're just using this as a new way to act out your obsession," he said. He poured me a glass of water and put it on the cracked laminate countertop next to my arm.

I shrugged. "Does it matter? What I'm doing is important."

He, of all people, couldn't argue with me. He pulled out one of the chairs and sat. "Why did you come here?"

"Low on power."

A pause.

"And I missed you," I admitted. "You never come up to Canada."

He avoided the obvious argument, about why he stayed here. We'd had that argument too many times over the years, both in person and online. Online, he'd end the conversation by accusing me of using immersive, and I'd log off. He used immersive. I used immersive and I set the timer. Not a problem.

"I'm not sure that the person I miss is the person you are now," he said. "I'm less than certain she ever came back."

"He," I corrected.

"Exactly," he said.

I sighed. "That's not fair."

"I don't blame you," he said reasonably. "I just

think you're doing it for the wrong reasons. You were beautiful before you changed."

"I didn't change," I said. "I just figured out who I am."

The silence of a remembered argument sat between us, souring the air.

He stood up. "I'm taking more pictures of the Nisqually Lahar tomorrow . . ."

"Don't fall in," I said, even though the mudflow had solidified before either of us was born.

"And I don't want to see you when I'm done. You shouldn't have come back," he said.

I looked down at the screen of my phone, sifting search results. He'd started for the door to his bedroom before I said, "I thought things might be different after I've turned him in."

David shook his head. "Getting the object of your obsession isn't going to fix you. You'll just find something else to obsess over and I'm still not willing to go through it again."

There's a famous photograph of me using immersive, plugged in, switched off, artfully arranged on a queen-size mattress, blood-red sheets covering just enough of my body to lower the disgust factor. The floor is tilted fifteen percent off horizontal, the mattress shoved all the way up against the cracked and peeling wall. I'm in focus, but in the distance, you can still see the shards of broken glass that used to be floor-to-ceiling windows.

I could be a corpse, discarded with the other debris in a condemned building, in a condemned city, and the picture would be no different.

I didn't really believe I'd find Trexell until I was looking up at the building that held his bonehouse.

Gray dust blew past. It was a few minutes after noon, and the sun glared off everything around me, so bright that it hurt. The sidewalk under my feet had the brown-black stained color that concrete got in places where it rarely if ever rained. Faded "For Lease" signs flapped in the breeze, still tied against the side of the building. There'd been nobody to lease these buildings for at least ten years, maybe longer.

A man walked up while I stood there, hands in his pockets, hand-rolled cigarette in his mouth. His face looked weathered, like he'd spent way too many days outside. He had a handgun tucked into his belt, even if it was illegal. I wished that I wasn't so completely unarmed.

"You looking for something?" He squinted at me.

I was a damn good actor. I stuffed my hands in my pockets, scuffed my foot on the sidewalk. Looked ashamed to even be asking. "Angelina's," I said.

He looked me over. "Bonehouses ain't free. Got money?"

"Access to it," I said.

"What's a guy like you looking for Angelina's for? Don't look at me like that, I can hear in your accent that you're from up north."

"Tired of having my life run for me," I said, as truthful as I could be.

He folded his arms one over the other. Even though I could tell that he was trying to be discreet about it, he tilted his head to the side slightly, listening to a voice in his earpiece. I suddenly felt naked, not knowing how advanced their surveillance was and how well it was working. "All right, Jordan," he said, giving me the name on my fake identification and my fake ID chip. "Come on."

I followed him down the broken escalator into the fetid darkness under the city, into the tunnels that used to let buses travel downtown without getting caught in above-ground traffic. Back when there was traffic. Back when it was smart to drive a car through the maze of skyscrapers.

"Ever been in a bonehouse before?"

"Not long-term," I lied. There were dim lights overhead, up in the big arching ceiling. Only about a third of them were on, and one of them was flickering, making the debris filling out the tunnel roadway jump and jiggle. "This kind of thing is more policed up in Canada." *And thank God for that.*

He hopped down from the station platform. I followed him, careful not to snag my leg on the bent and broken post that used to mark the bus stop. I followed him through the narrower tunnels, surprised, since the proxy information I had suggested that Angelina's was in the mall.

This far underground they'd have to be running a wired network. Interesting.

"Not very secure, is it?" I asked. The signs on either side of the wall told how far we were from various platforms. I hadn't seen any security at all, which made me nervous.

"You don't need to worry about that," he said. "People in this city know to stay out of the tunnels."

I narrowly avoided snorting at him. Anybody with even a passing understanding of human nature knows that people will cheerfully go exactly where they're least safe.

Two steps farther.

He grabbed my shoulder, twisted and slammed me up against the wall. It was too quick. I'd let myself be too lulled into complacency, and so I didn't react. Just slammed into the wall and felt the air whistle out of me, hands snapping up to show they were empty, eyes wide, adrenaline making the dim tunnel clearer than it should have been. Empty but for us.

Cold metal dug into the soft underside of my jaw so hard that I thought I might gag. A click.

"Cocky, stupid, bastard Canadian," he said.

I was afraid to swallow. Afraid to talk. Breathe.

He dug the gun in harder, shoving my head up. "What, you thought Trexell would hand himself to you? On a platter, maybe? With a little note that says, 'Dear *Christina,* please turn me in. I'm tired of living. Oh, and while you're at it, enjoy your reward.'"

"That's *not* my name," I snarled, surprised at what I clung to in the seconds before I died.

"You hunt bones," he said, his voice so reasonable. One arm across my chest, keeping me pressed against that earth-cold concrete wall, his face so close we could have kissed. "Bones don't move. They don't run. They're usually so wrapped up that they don't even try to hide themselves. Easy pickings for a hypocrite."

I kept my chin up, instinct pushing away from the gun. Looked up at him. "Either shoot me or let me go," I said.

"Who knows you're here?"

David. I thought about him clambering around on the lahar, cataloguing new plant growth, tsk-tsking at plants that should only grow at warmer climates.

What would they do to him, uninvolved David, if I told them he knew I was in Seattle? "Nobody," I said.

He pulled back, like he meant to hit me over the head, but I moved too quickly for him. I slammed my forehead into his nose, using the few seconds of disorientation to disarm him, send the gun skittering across the concrete floor.

He didn't waste time going after it and pulled a knife instead, dim light shining along the edge of the blade. I blocked his first mad slash with my forearm, the angle such that he didn't cut through my thick canvas coat. My knee connected with his stomach.

He shoved me back again, and I hit the wall. Before I could twist away, hot pain lanced down my side. I cussed, put my foot against the wall and used it to launch myself at him.

Dust and dirt puffed into the air, and his head hit the floor with a sharp crack. Good luck on my part. I beat his hand against the floor until his fingers loosened, and then I sent the knife skittering across to where the gun was.

Pain lanced up and down my left side, my shirt gone sticky from the blood. I told myself I'd had worse and flipped him onto his stomach. I planted my right knee in the small of his back, pinned him while I caught my breath.

"How many of you are there?" I asked when I could, having trouble keeping him pinned.

Nothing.

I leaned so close I was practically yelling in his ear. "How many of you are there? You got an army? Just a couple of you? Just you and Trexell?"

"Enough of us."

"Enough of you for what?"

He shook his head, laughing down at the concrete. I let him laugh, dug in my pocket for a tranquilizer, pulled it out of the box with one hand and uncapped it with my teeth. I gave him a full dose, listening to the laughter turn to curses when the needle went in.

When he went limp, I picked up the gun and left him there.

I took the stairs into the mall. The broken escalator wasn't even safe for climbing. Pieces of it had been pulled off and sold for scrap. Every piece of glass in the entire place had been shattered, everything from doors to store windows. Spray-paint graffiti blanketed every surface, turning walls into scenes of dueling tags. The air held the thick smell of stale urine.

Volcanic ash lay on the floor a good three inches deep. The place was never cleaned up after Rainier blew. The mall had already been closed, so when the ash filtered in through the broken windows, covering all four stories, there was no point.

I had to stop too often, breathing in little gasps, alternately trying to encourage myself to walk on and cursing myself for not going back.

The ash saved me some time, showing me a path up and down the broken escalators—these ones treacherous but still climbable—that was much more traveled than the side paths.

My ragged breath was the only sound in the mall. I left a trail behind me, drops of blood on ash, like breadcrumbs to safety.

At the top, more shattered glass. The remains of a

food court to my right, the decommissioned remains of a monorail station to the left.

And a man dressed all in gray. Behind him were skyscrapers in front of a sapphire-blue sky, half of the windows broken out, gaping holes in their shining surfaces. "Flesh is overrated, isn't it?" he asked.

I gripped the rubber escalator rail so hard that I felt my fingernails dig in. It'd been years since I'd even held a simulated handgun, but some muscle memories don't go away. I took aim, resting my finger on the side of the trigger guard. Willing to let him talk. Glanced around, too late to save me if he'd had an ambush, but the floor was empty.

I stayed on my feet but I was losing too much blood.

"Not sure about that," I said, "but your security is. Should have beefed it up when you moved out here."

A smile. "You weren't expecting me to be on my feet."

"Might be for the best," I said. "Since I can't carry you out like this."

He laughed. "Chris, Chris, Chris," he said. "If I were willing to let you take me alive, would you really be happy?"

"Sure I would," I said. "I'm sick of being poor." I shuddered, cold suddenly, my head swimming.

I pulled myself the last step to the top of the escalator, my legs feeling like large cooked noodles. If he'd been just like the other bones, dead to the world in a hospital bed, I could have made it. But now that I finally saw Cameron Trexell in the flesh, I could see that he never plugged in permanently. Never had. Never would. His devotees had. I had.

I lowered the gun, put the safety on.

"Have things been fixed, in your wild attempt to wake people up? To make them see the world as you do? How many of them turned around and plugged back in, escaped their flesh-and-blood bodies?"

I leaned on the escalator rail, leaving a bloody smudge on the stainless-steel surface. "Some of them stayed out."

He took a step toward me and I forced myself to level the gun at him again, even if the safety was still on. My arm felt like it was made out of iron, too heavy to hold up. "How many of them, even if they stayed out of the 'net, fixed what you wanted fixed? How many of them got worthless jobs just to survive like you did?"

All of them.

Somewhere far off, I caught the scent of oranges, that bonehouse smell. Trexell himself might not be plugged in permanently, but somebody was around here.

He took another step. "Put down the gun, Chris. You're dying, and you gain nothing if either of us bites it."

I remembered waking up in the bonehouse dark, disconnected back into the flesh of my body, feeling it again. Bones aching. Atrophied muscles useless. Sobbing from the pain of badly used nerve endings while I waited for the 'net connection to come back. Wanting nothing but to go back in, to feel the pain melt away, to have the body sense of myself as male jacked back into my brain. The bonehouse cat, a skinny black slip of a kitten, curled up by my shoulder, purring insistently, as though it could make me stop hurting through sheer force of will.

VIVIAN FRIEDEL

I still craved it, stronger than any drug. It was a million times worse now than the simple pang I felt performing an eviction. Even remembering the moments of intense pain, I wanted it. Needed it.

"Anyone I save from you is worth it for that alone," I said.

Another step toward me, his feet scuffing in the ash. The gun was only pointed at his feet. I couldn't sustain holding it any higher than that. "You don't want to stop us," he said. "We're showing the world that the Northern Coalition is no different from any other set of rulers in the past. Convincing them they must put aside their complacency and rise up."

I thought about the riots.

How many people did he have in his makeshift bonehouse? How many did he hold in other bone-houses across the country? "You never were Sammy Gauge, were you?"

"Of course not, although he was one of my best," he said. "He and I had too much in common, if you found us."

He took another step. He asked, "Do you remember when you used to have an effect on the world, instead of simply taking money to rearrange other people's lives? I don't think you'd be here if you didn't want to come back. This world isn't getting any better, is it?"

Every year, another disaster.

"You'd take me back just like that," I said. Twenty minutes and I'd be in. This time, there'd be no David to pay for my eviction.

"Just like that," he said.

I brought the gun up again, leaning on the escalator rail with my hip and using both hands to aim. I hit him twice, once in each leg. I hadn't aimed to kill, though at that moment I'm not sure I would have minded if I did.

He went down, screaming, cursing. I dropped the gun, afraid he'd get it from me if I brought it nearer to him.

"There's more at stake here," he yelled at me, clutching one shin in both hands, even though it was bleeding just the same as the other, his gray pants gone a dark, bloody red.

"I know," I said, and then I got the tranquilizer into him.

The mall was silent again, except for the sound of my breathing and a cat mewling somewhere far off. I crawled over to where I'd left the gun and cradled it, watching for anyone coming out of the hallways or up the escalator.

The screen of my phone was cracked, but it still worked. I sent out my SOS call with my GPS location. Told them to bring first-aid resources and enough people to take care of Trexell's illegal bonehouse.

Jealous congratulations started pouring in, but I ignored the messages.

I watched the reflections of dark clouds in the mirrored surfaces of skyscrapers. I wondered if I'd won.

This Peaceful State of War

written by

Patty Jansen

illustrated by

SCOTT FREDERICK HARGRAVE

ABOUT THE AUTHOR

As Patty Jansen grew up, her father read lots of science fiction and her mother told her stories of her youth in South Africa. As consequence, Patty dreamed of faraway lands and faraway planets. She started writing planetary romances in primary school, but in high school, teachers insisted that science fiction was not proper literature, and compulsory reading lists instilled in her a hatred for fiction reading that lasted twenty years. A full-time job as an agricultural scientist and young children put a stop to her writing. She always intended to go back to writing.

It was the too-early death of her father, in 2003, that finally jolted her into action. (Hint: if you want to do something, do it now or never.) Within a year, she had joined Online Writing Workshop for Science Fiction and had her first nonpaying story published in a small magazine. Her first pro sale, to the Universe Annex of the Grantville Gazette, came two weeks before winning the second quarter of the contest, and her intended-but-withdrawn third quarter story has just been sold to the pro magazine Redstone SF. She accredits the success of her winning story to a pair of titanium scissors.

Patty lives in Sydney, Australia. These days, she subscribes to Asimov's Science Fiction *and* Analog *and reads about fifty SF and fantasy books a year.*

ABOUT THE ILLUSTRATOR

Scott Frederick Hargrave attributes his lifelong love of storytelling and creative flights of fantasy to being born the son of two fliers. His mother, a private pilot, set his imagination soaring with childhood tales of 1930s adventuress Amelia Earhart; Scott's father was a WWII B-25 bomber pilot whose stories of exotic Egypt, both of ancient Pharaohs' ghost-haunted tombs and his own adventures during wartime, sparked and shaped the dreams of all three of their sons. One became an archeologist, another a writer and a painter.

Scott's own imagination and love of art was nourished too growing up in 1970s Puerto Rico, a Caribbean alternate-reality, where 400-year-old Spanish cathedrals, radiant with religious art and spiritual yearning, coexisted with the Arecibo radio telescope's Search for Extra Terrestrial Intelligence project. His young imagination overflowed with mountain rainforests and underground caverns, soulful Latin-African salsa rhythms pouring from sunny park plazas and shady San Juan bars, and exotic island landscapes where the sun kissed the beautiful surfer girls on the white beaches of El Rincon by day—and by night mysterious chupacabra monsters were still believed to prowl the hills or mermaids surfaced to seduce swimmers out to drown beneath the stars.

Such inspirations sow dreams and cry out from the soul to be made into art.

Scott's career endeavors and dreams include screenwriting, directing low-budget films and creating The Dust of All Our Dreams: A Graphic Novel *that he says not only explores the Apocalypse, but—once completed—will most probably cause it.*

This Peaceful State of War

"Ash," Brother Copernicus says.

I rub the substance between the thumb and fingers of my gloves. It's fine and powdery, and white, unbelievably white.

A thick layer of it covers the field of tree stumps and broken branches, all the way to the wall of rain forest in the distance. Heat shimmers above the brilliant surface.

Yesterday, when arriving from Solaris Station, I saw these tracks from space. They looked like scars, as if a deranged soul has taken a knife to the planet, cutting scores in the cover of forest.

"The Hern burnt these tracks wherever they destroyed the Pari villages." There is raw hatred in Brother Copernicus' voice, even when filtered through his rebreather mask. "They stacked up the debris from the houses and the bodies and burnt the lot. Always at night, so we wouldn't notice."

I let the powder trickle from my glove, fighting the impulse to rub my hand on my protective robe. I can't. The action of rubbing might trigger a spark that will lead to all sorts of trouble in this high-oxygen atmosphere. Those warnings played in the cabin of the landing craft have etched themselves in my mind.

"Why is it so white? Has anyone analyzed this?" The color intrigues me, and I wonder why the ground underneath the patch where I've picked up the powder is moist and cool.

"I'm sure someone has. Is that important? It's ash, Envoy, human ash." Brother Copernicus brandishes the word *human* like a sword, challenging anyone who dares to disagree. "You're standing on the biggest murder site in all of humanity."

The camp looks like a prison with two perimeter fences, one about five meters inside the other, the top bar of each armed with spikes as long as my hand. Through two lots of metal security mesh, I can make out tents of the infantry variety lined up in perfect rows. There is no sign of movement, human or alien.

I follow Brother Copernicus along the walkway of rubbery mats. My crutches keep sinking into the little crevices in the mats that allow rain to filter through.

Sweat rolls between my breasts and over my back. At the moment, I hate every gram of my uncooperative body and my body has a lot of grams, let's leave it at that.

You've spent too much time in space, Miranda, the doctor at Solaris would say in his self-righteous voice.

I agree. I love low-G environments, I thrive in crisp recycled air. I hate planets. I'm a whale on a beach.

Three guards stand at the camp entrance, missionaries in ankle-length brown habits with sleeves tucked into their gloves. The religious garb contrasts oddly with the plasma guns on their belts and crossbows in their arms. I stare at the weapon in the closest guard's hands as he busies himself opening the gate. Why the heck would they use crossbows?

Brother Copernicus has already gone through the open gate. "Envoy Tonkin, if you please."

I'm still waiting for the first signs that he's getting annoyed with my slow walking pace. There are none. He's the model religious brother: patient, friendly, selflessly taking up the cause of the downtrodden—convinced that I represent the enemy.

We walk through into a metal cage and wait for the guards to shut the gate behind us.

"Pretty crazy security," I say, hating the way the mask reflects my voice back at me.

"It works, though. The fighting stopped the moment we locked up the local band of Hern. There have been no more attacks on Pari villages, at least not in this area."

He lets the obvious go unspoken: the slaughter continues unabated in all the places where the Universal Church doesn't have a mission, which is pretty much all of the planet. He and his mission want to stop the war. The Solaris Agency wants me to assess if that's even feasible. I feel in my bones, the way my contract was phrased, that they want humans off Bianca, that it's too risky, too expensive. To him, I *am* the enemy.

We walk into the murderers' camp. The second gate shuts behind us with a definitive clang.

"This way," Brother Copernicus says.

The Hern are all in the mess tent. When my eyes adjust to the drop in light, I cannot help but feel awed. Oh, my, the sight of these alien people: their sheer size, their athletic build, their hair-covered backs, their green skin and black, animal-like eyes.

Missionaries patrol the perimeter of the tent, crossbows slung across their shoulders.

Of course, a plasma weapon will cause considerable risk in this high-oxygen atmosphere. Use it, and you might blow up the whole camp—much safer for all to resort to something less destructive first.

Brothers in protective gear are wheeling dinner trolleys between the tables. There is no food on the trays, only jugs of what looks like cordial.

None of the aliens take any interest in the trolleys. None of them communicate. They sit on their benches with their backs incredibly straight and watch me— every single one. There must be at least three hundred of them and their presence is overwhelming—and then their smell. No one warned me about the smell. It's strong, it's musky. It permeates the filter of my mask. I feel like I'm choking. I hold the hose to the filter canister on my belt, struggling not to rip the whole contraption from my face. I can't, I know. The lethal soup of molecules that passes for air would kill me within minutes. The inside of the visor fogs up.

In the narrow aisle, I accidentally bang my left crutch into the back of a bench.

"Excuse me." I'm taking deep gasps of air.

From the corner of my awareness, I notice someone getting up.

Before I know what's happening, I'm on the ground and several hot-skinned bodies crash into me. People are shouting and screaming. Two twanging shots go off. A missionary drags me under the cover of a table.

As quickly as it started, it's over.

I sit up, dazed. One of the Hern is held down by three missionaries sitting on top of him, another is pulling at a crossbow bolt in his thigh. The rivulets of blood that run from the wound are nearly black. The creature's eyes are fierce with anger. I feel sick and filled with a renewed respect for crossbows.

A missionary rushes to me, but instead of helping me to my feet, he picks up my crutches.

"You'll have to keep these outside," he says and he runs away, carrying my only means of independent motion.

I'm too flabbergasted to reply. I know the church doesn't want me here, but does that have to mean they humiliate me in front of the natives?

Brother Copernicus helps me up, alone, which must take some strength. When he supports me through the aisle, I feel the muscles straining through his layers of protective clothing. He's trembling. The reflective visor hides his face.

"I'll explain later," he says in a low voice.

I want to shout *Now's as good a time as any,* but I'm not going to make a scene here. The Hern inmates are all watching us.

I make my way to the table holding onto his arm, even though my left knee spikes with pain every time I put weight on it. A group of men hustles the attackers out the door and everyone continues as if nothing has happened.

Some missionaries are already seated at the table in the middle of the tent. Most have taken off their gloves and hoods, which are UV protection, but the men still look the same to me with their shaved heads and shaved eyebrows, wearing the same brown habits. When they use face masks, I can't even begin to guess who they are.

They nod greetings as I sit down. They sure remember who *I* am.

The Hern envoy who approaches the table is huge. The frame of the bench creaks when he takes his place opposite us. His black eyes rest on me, making my skin crawl. They are round and lidless, surrounded by a ring of long lashes. These creatures are *human*?

I bow. "Envoy."

He doesn't show any emotion.

I touch my chest. "I'm Miranda Tonkin. What is your name?" I hold my hand out flat. No pointing. They might take that as a sign of aggression.

His face remains blank.

"I'm sorry . . ." I hiss a whisper to Brother Copernicus. "What's his name?" Although I'm only guessing the creature is male.

"They have never used names with us."

No names? Some tribes consider names personal property that loses power when spread too widely, but they usually have nicknames. Clearly, the Hern distrust the missionaries too deeply to give out any personal information. I'm wondering why they even allow themselves to be incarcerated in this camp. Surely they could escape if they banded together and made use of their formidable strength?

One of the missionaries rolls out a map of a terrain that has no natural vantage points except a grid of latitudes and longitudes, and the paths of burnt forest penciled in. He points at various sections, also penciled in. Another missionary explains for my benefit how the church is negotiating sections for the Pari and Hern to live separate from each other.

The Hern envoy looks on, saying nothing while the missionaries carve up his homeland. His eyes move, but the rest of his body is perfectly still, reminding me of a predator. Who is the prey?

In the middle of a conversation between two brothers, he points at me. *"Munni,"* he says. His voice is rough. It's the first time I hear any of them speak.

A couple of other Hern grumble at this word. Black eyes meet mine, conveying that somehow this means I'm *fair game*.

I glance at Brother Copernicus, but he shrugs. "One of the words we haven't been able to translate."

He sounds nervous.

I wonder how many words they *have* been able to translate. How many words they've even heard? Not too many, I'm thinking.

I'm sorry you had to experience that," Brother Copernicus says when we're outside the camp.

"Sorry?" I have my crutches back, given to me by the guard at the gate.

"Yes, I should have looked closer at those crutches. If I'd realized they were made of titanium, I'd have given you some replacements. For some reason, exposure to titanium makes the Hern go crazy."

"Why couldn't you explain that in the tent? The Hern can't understand us anyway."

He shrugs, and it strikes me he's been getting increasingly uncomfortable. Because he doesn't like being assigned as my guide? Because his superiors have told him to do things he doesn't agree with? Like deliberately letting me take my crutches into the camp?

"What is so special about titanium?" My heart is thudding. I could have been killed in that camp. The brothers would have reported it as an accident and no one at Solaris would ever have known the truth.

"We need more time to research these people. Their attraction to titanium is not on our list of priorities, as you may understand. The Hern are a particularly impenetrable folk, but if the segregation plan works, we'll save a lot of lives."

"Segregation is an ugly and temporary solution and only works if both parties agree to it and understand the concept. Do you think these Hern understand?" *Are you sure you'd call them human?*

"We'd police the boundaries—"

"Do you think they understand?"

He faces me, but all I see is my own refection in that white landscape, like a walrus on a sunny beach.

"Solaris thinks the church are idiots, that we've botched this project, don't they? You're going to recommend withdrawing the agency's subsidy, aren't you?"

I don't reply.

"Wait until you see the Pari and tell me these people don't deserve saving."

"I'm an envoy, an observer. I don't make the final decision. The board does that," neglecting to mention that I sit on the board as rotating member. "I'll decide what I'll recommend when the time comes."

I don't dare say any more, for my own safety.

The Pari camp is very different from the Hern's, a collection of army-green tents amongst obscenely green rain forest. It's only early morning, but the heat is relentless. The suit is meant to protect me, but I can feel the ultraviolet radiation through layers of sleeves.

The camp is ordered, with tents in neat rows. There are fields of crops and people working in them.

A few missionaries stroll past. They carry plasma guns on their belts, but no crossbows.

A group of Pari have brought in a felled tree and are sawing it into slices with a huge, double-handled blade-saw. They're smaller than us, muscular and brown, virtually hairless. Moisture gleams on bent backs.

We stop to watch the activity. It strikes me how they work with each other, how they chatter and how the Hern *didn't* do any of those things.

"What are they making?" I ask.

"They'll make anything. They seem to have this compulsion to build things, to accumulate structures. We've found huge above-ground settlements, all made from wood, palaces of incredible craftsmanship."

The tree trunk is huge, at least ten meters wide. At cross-section, the wood is dark and glitters like crystal. It isn't wood in the usual sense of the word and contains far more minerals and metals than wood on Earth and far less carbon. Bianca has some very tough and strange proteins that hold vegetation together on a cellular level.

I'm guessing the wood is hard, because the saw makes little progress. The metal would be titanium, since it's the dominant metal on the planet, but no one has observed any means by which these people produce tools like this.

There is so much to see: strange clothing, mostly blue, necklaces and thick armbands—titanium also, tattoos on arms and legs, children, many of them, mostly naked with oddly wrinkled skin. To be honest, I am unsure if they are children.

A bit further into the camp, a group is taking down an army tent, folding it up meticulously. A few taller Pari are digging a hole, bringing up clods of sticky, white soil. Others use the clay to sand down poles, rubbing it over the wood in a numb routine.

"They'll have some sort of structure up by the end of the day," Brother Copernicus says. "That house over there only went up yesterday."

The structure he points out is already two floors high with walls made out of intricate latticework.

"Two days old?" It's hard to believe.

While we walk past, more and more of these people put down their tools. Some of them run to Brother Copernicus and stroke the fabric of his robe. He pulls one or two into a hug. Another missionary joins us, handing out pieces of fruit from a bowl. The yellow morsels pass from hand to hand under much chatter and sounds that resemble laughter.

It's hard not to like these people—cute, industrious, self-sufficient, grateful.

They've built an enormous structure as their central gathering place. It's three floors high, has slanted roofs covered with carved planks, diamond-shaped windows and walls made of latticework that forms patterns of stars.

"Wow," is my first reaction.

"Impressive, isn't it?" Brother Copernicus sounds much more self-assured than he did in the Hern camp. "And then to think of those bastards out there burning all this to the ground. Just think of the cultural heritage. There'd be enough material here for an entire university of scientists. These people are willing and able to communicate with us."

We enter the ground floor of the structure, which is only a hall from where a number of ladders lead up. I'm about to protest that there's no way I can get up when a cage sails down from above, suspended from thick ropes. They've made a *lift*.

The Pari that steps out of the cage is taller than most, with soft brown eyes that make me think the creature is female, even though nothing else about the brown-skinned body does. But "she" sounds better than "it." Like several of the adults, she has a fuzz of hair on her head and back. The skin on her chest shows darker patches of pigment.

"We think the size and skin coloring is a sign they've reached sexual maturity," Brother Copernicus says.

She gets in the cage with us. The muscles in her back ripple when she pulls the rope that, via a system of pulleys, hauls us to the top floor of the building.

"Thank you," I say. I reach into my pocket where my gloved hand encounters my no-longer-current travel band. I pull it out, a little piece of white plastic with an embedded microchip, and give it to her. It looks strange in the palm of her hand, technology alien to this world.

"It goes like this." I undo the clip and fit it around her wrist. Snap the clip shut.

She looks at it, bows and runs off.

A group of missionaries meets us on the top floor of the building. While we're being introduced, I spy the Pari girl in the corner showing off her prize. I'm smiling; it's hard not to.

We enter a large room with a vaulted ceiling. Centerpiece of the room is a heavy wooden table with surrounding benches all carved, it seems, from the same piece of wood.

Beyond that, through the silhouetted latticework and the diamond-shaped window, the view stretches over the treetops.

I walk to the window to have a better look. I can see all the way to the mission on the other side of the white track, to the Hern camp, a dark blot in the desolate white landscape, over undulating country with a thick cover of blue-green foliage. A heat haze hangs over the forest, a soup of gases that turns the air faintly brown, like heavy pollution over a city. It's ozone, formed under the influence of sunlight, and it breaks down again at night when the rains come.

"Miranda?" Brother Copernicus calls from behind.

Everyone is already at the table.

Our envoy is a small Pari with stooped shoulders and large brown eyes. I decide the creature is female. I ask her name, but as in the Hern camp, I'm informed they do not use names. I could believe that of the Hern, but these creatures have a lot more trust in us. Why no names?

The envoy sits at the table and folds long-fingered hands together.

"Peace," she says.

"We will have peace," Brother Copernicus says, "when this terrible war is over."

"Peace," she repeats. "We go feed the fields."

"We'll try," he says.

I'm not sure what he's talking about. I'm unsure she understands. Is this the extent to which the missionaries have been able to teach them our language? Brother Copernicus said *they were able* to communicate?

The dining hall of the mission is a large, echoing place, austere as the Universal Church itself.

I've been sitting here since returning from the camps, reading the report written by the previous Solaris envoy four months ago. It's very quiet in this contemplative room, and I'm fighting my gritty eyes desperate for sleep.

The Pari from the nearby village were coming to the mission almost every day. The native woman Tani has made great linguistic progress. She has also shown an interest in the plants cultivated near the mission.

Wait. Hang on.

I re-read the passage. So the Pari *did,* at one stage, use names. They *did,* at one stage, communicate better than they do now.

I look up at the vaulted ceiling.

One could imagine if one were as time-lag-addled as I am, that not Bianca's sun, but an angel looks in through the windows up there, bathing the room in a golden glow. One could believe that this was a sign, that this world was Eden, as the church used to call it, until the hell of war broke loose.

Above a dais at the far end of the room, there is a small altar with candles, which flicker in the filtered air. Slogans on the wall proclaim *Space is God* and *Space is not empty.*

It appears the church was right about the not-empty bit. Bianca is the first world where humans discovered higher intelligent life. Ever since, the question has divided the Solaris board: the Pari and Hern look human enough, but are they really? And even if they are, does that give us the right to interfere?

The Brothers of the church shuffle into the hall in twos and threes. It surprises me how many of them are old, much older than me.

It must be close to dinnertime.

Brother Copernicus sits opposite me. His frown carries an implicit question: *I thought your room was comfortable enough?*

"Better light here," I say, glancing at the bright beams intersecting the roof space.

I'm avoiding his eyes. I can hardly tell him I don't trust the brothers after the incident at the Hern camp and prefer to spend as much time as possible in a public space, where any attacks on me are likely to have witnesses.

"What are you reading?"

"Envoy El-Armeini's report."

"Oh." There is no emotion in that single word, yet he must have read the report and know what's in it.

I leaf a few pages.

"She says the Pari used to have names. Her report suggests a much deeper level of communication with them than I saw today."

He shrugs. Sighs. Shrugs again, uneasy. What is under that not-unattractive, straight-nosed face?

When he doesn't say anything, I read the passage aloud.

Brother Copernicus is staring at his hands, interlaced over the table. His fingers are deeply bronzed, oxygen-wrinkled and belie his age.

"The Pari are traumatized by what's happened to them," he says finally. "When we came here, there were thousands of them. They lived in a most beautiful and intricate village structure. You've seen what they can build. It was a hundred—no, a thousand—times bigger than that."

He stops speaking, twitches his mouth, wriggles his shoulders. Moisture glistens in his eyes.

"No one understands," he says, his voice little more than a whisper. "Why would the Hern attack a peaceful village and butcher everyone in it? The Pari didn't even put up resistance. They stopped speaking to us. They stopped coming for lessons. It's like this war has turned them stupid. The Hern ran in and the Pari fell to their knees as if they were worshipping them like gods—"

"Maybe they *are* worshipping the Hern like gods."

He gives me a look that spells *blasphemy* in huge capital letters.

Oh, right. I'm in a church. One that believes that the existence of God will be proven when they find an alien race that also believes in God. Therefore, it is in their interest to study these humanoid aliens and convert them before anyone else gets the chance.

I glance at him, very much wanting to say, *you look to me to be a more intelligent man than that.*

He meets my eyes squarely and a look passes between us I don't know how to take, but that unsettles me deeply. I think he *is* more intelligent than that.

And damn, I feel sorry for him. He's too young, too emotionally involved, to be stuck in this hellhole.

The food trolley chooses that moment to arrive. That, I decide, is definitely divine intervention.

I get up and take a plate, which the serving brother dutifully fills with slop-covered cubed vegetables.

When I rejoin the table, a number of others have taken up the seats around us, Envoy El-Armeini's journal shoved to the middle of the table out of the way of their plates.

The men range from middle-aged to young. They introduce themselves as Brothers Heraclides, Tycho and Ibn-al-Haytham.

"Ancient Earth astronomers, huh?" I say, by way of getting them to talk.

Brother Tycho raises his black-stubbled eyebrows. "Have any interest in ancient astronomy?" His voice is deep and more sensual than is comfortable for a religious brother.

"I'm an envoy of the Solaris Agency. I have an interest in anything that involves our species' obsession with expansion . . . and resulting conflicts."

The other brothers make a point of looking at their plates, but Brother Tycho laughs, not entirely comfortable. "Conflicts we are working hard to solve." His eyes meet mine; they're dark brown.

I strongly suspect that underneath the uniformity of the equalitarian brown robe, he's one of the upper cadre. Scouting me out, as it were.

"Are you happy with your progress?" I ask.

"We're on track." His gaze doesn't waver. "We've isolated the Hern; they're under control. We need funds to expand that operation to other parts of the planet. We need funds and equipment for translation and communication with the Pari. Most of that will be coming from church charity, but we need the support from Solaris for inbound transport."

And off-planet transport just happens to be much more costly than all the other expenditure combined; I hate it when people try emotional blackmail on us.

And yet, damn, Brother Copernicus is right: the Pari *deserve* humanitarian help.

"Have you considered that human presence contributes to the war?"

Brother Copernicus stares at me. Is he shaking his head?

"You mean—the church's presence?" Brother Tycho's voice goes cold.

"The church or any other human involvement."

"Hardly likely," Brother Tycho continues. "We only have one mission on the planet. This war is happening all over."

"Yes, I agree, but could it have been something human presence has triggered? For example, the Hern are jealous of the attention and help the Pari are getting."

"There's an easy solution for that: if the Hern stop killing and pilfering, they'll get the same attention."

"Maybe killing and pilfering is their evolutionary function."

His eyes shoot daggers at me. The church is not a great supporter of evolution either.

"The Hern in the camp appear to be on a hunger strike," I continue, perhaps foolhardy.

"Same thing, Envoy. The hunger strike is their problem. We give them food. *They* refuse to eat."

Brother Copernicus shrinks further into the shadows.

The discussion turns to other subjects. We eat, we chat about harmless things or relatively so. About Earth governments and who's in charge. News gets around slowly. The beamsweep from Solaris is restricted to urgent news and it passes only every few days. There is so much these men don't know.

When I walk back to my room, Brother Copernicus catches up with me in the corridor.

"I think," he says, and then he pauses, catching his breath.

I turn to him, and my questioning look has the effect of making him shrink. He's sweating and pale-faced.

"You must help," he says. "You must understand."

"What do you mean?"

"We can't leave the Pari to fend for themselves. We—the mission—can't leave Bianca. The Pari will be slaughtered. You're saying that the Hern don't eat. They do. They eat the Pari. It's so awful no one talks about it—"

"Hold on—wait." I raise my hand to stop the flow of words.

A Brother comes into the corridor and walks past us, raising his nonexistent eyebrows.

"Come," Brother Copernicus says. "I'll show you something."

He precedes me into a darkened room. A flick of a switch brings light in a laboratory—empty and deserted. It's eerily quiet except for the ever-present hiss of air from the recycling vents.

There are shelves on the walls with jars of preserved samples: huge insects, flowers as big as a dinner plate.

"What is this place?"

"We used to do research here," he says. Beads of sweat glisten on his brow. "Or rather, I used to. I was a church scientist." He walks to a shelf and pulls off a book. The pages contain dried leaves: a herbarium.

"Look at it. There is so much to discover. Did you know that the plants here don't work the same way they do on Earth? They use methane, ammonia and water vapor for photosynthesis, that's why you get the cyanide concentrations in the forest. There are whole communities of mushroom-like organisms that depend on it, like this thing . . ." He leafs through another page to show a picture of some slimy-looking multi-branched semitransparent mushroom attached to a tree. "We don't know how it works. Plants produce twice as much oxygen as they do on Earth. They recycle carbon internally. Light is important. See how all the plants angle their leaves for maximum exposure? Even the animals use light."

"Is that why the Hern's skin is green?"

He takes another book off the shelf. It contains pictures of various forms of Pari. There are sketches of their external body parts and few scans and x-rays. The internal diagrams have a lot of white space with tentative drawings of blood vessels and organs.

"There's not much about the Hern," I say, leafing through the book.

307

He shakes his head.

I come to a page with a picture of a body lying on the ground. The stomach is cut open, flaps of skin folded away to reveal a large white sac inside the stomach cavity.

"That's Hern," he says. "The only specimen anyone ever studied, before its fellows attacked and burned the body. It happened before I came."

I turn the page and come face-to-face with another picture of the white sac, cut open. The content oozes out onto the ground. It looks like caviar. Eggs? I feel sick and turn the page again; the next page is empty.

"The scientists never had the opportunity to study the Hern. There never used to be many, and it was a long time before anyone saw them up close. They're the top of the food chain, and they've multiplied like crazy since we've come. I know Brother Tycho will never admit it, but it has to be something *we* have done to allow that to happen. When we came here, there were no white tracks. The Pari lived happily in their villages. They were learning to communicate with us. And then all of a sudden . . ." He lifts his hands. "No one knows what happened, but the only thing that changed was that *we* were here, trying to make these creatures human."

"Which they're not."

"Which, indeed, they're not."

"Why did the research stop?" I ask.

"Solaris withdrew because there's no profit, but you know all about that." When I ignore the barb, he goes on. "There's nothing to mine here except titanium, and there's plenty of that in places that don't require heavy-lift off-planet transport. So the

Solaris scientists left. Then the church scientists took over the labs—"

"In other words: you."

"Yes, me and others, who have all left." He breathes in deeply and continues. "The others were never in the Order; they were only employed by the church." He lets a further silence lapse and continues in third person. "The scientists working for the church found that neither the Hern nor the Pari are quite as human as they look. The upper cadre didn't want to look like they'd wasted the church's money. So they classified the Hern and Pari as animals and called in help from the Solaris Agency, much in the way as you intervene on other worlds. By then, the war had broken out."

Brother Copernicus slumps. His breathing is ragged and irregular. "They're abandoning these lovely people to the Hern butchers. They're saying these people don't deserve the grace of God, because they don't happen to believe in any God at all. You do know it's the Universal Church's first directive to go and find intelligent alien societies and prove they believe in God, and that this will prove His existence to non-believers and skeptics?"

He buries his face in his hands. "So we find a remotely intelligent society. We come in. We wreck it so that one-half of a functioning ecosystem starts to kill off the other, and then we tell everyone that oh no, it was a mistake. These were never people and they were never intelligent. You know what that means to me, Envoy Miranda Tonkin? It proves to me there is no God. If there was, He certainly would have stopped this." His shoulders are shaking.

I don't know what to say. I was born nominally

religious, but have never cultivated that aspect of my life. I don't know how it feels to have your belief, your sole reason of being, ripped out from under you. But I imagine it feels at least as bad as finding out, at sixteen, that your parents are not your real parents, and moreover, want nothing more to do with you. It feels at least as bad as being sardined onto a long-haul passenger liner to Solaris Station. It feels as bad as knocking on your grandmother's door and having a neighbor inform you that "the old lady" died three months ago. It feels as bad as wandering the docks without money or a place to stay. Being hungry. Selling yourself in dark nooks of disreputable corridors until some bugger comes along who gives you a disease that lands you in Emergency.

My eyes mist over.

Out of clumsiness or fear that anything I say will be taken wrongly, I enclose him in my arms. His head rests on my ample breasts. He smells of rubber and sweat and the inside of rebreather masks.

It's a long time since I've touched anyone, and this shattered, pathetic human being fills me with guilt for all those people whose lives I've ruined. Not personally, but there is always a downside to peace contracts the agency negotiates. Always. Land tilled for years that has to be given up, murders of family members that must go unavenged, cultural artifacts lost that can never be retrieved.

I run my hand over the scratchy stubble of his head. He takes my hand and wipes it over his face, wet with tears. With a shock, I realize his lips are caressing my skin. I twitch, but fall short of pulling away.

"I'm sorry," he whispers. "I haven't touched anyone for years." He lets my hand go for me to withdraw it.

I let it rest while I deliberate on the wisdom of taking this any further, decide the heck with it and caress his shaven cheek with my thumb.

Neither of us says anything. Neither of us wants to acknowledge that this is happening and where it is going.

I'm sick of this job; I'm sick of my broken body. I've searched for years to find someone who wouldn't be revolted at the sight of it. He is lonely, needy and desperate. Robes allow for easy access; the table makes a convenient seat at the right height. Our joining is quick, sweaty and completely silent.

When it's over, he hangs onto me like I'm a life buoy in a turbulent sea. Then he steps away, letting our robes drop back to their rightful places.

"The original sin, huh?" He laughs. "Who worries about *this* while out there, people are dying by the millions. I tell you: the original sin was murder and it was done in the name of God. This is no Eden. There is no God. Please, Miranda, tell Solaris to send an army to control the Hern and restore balance on the planet before you order us out."

I go back to my room where it is dark and the air is stale, and my only company is a creaky bed, a tiny desk and a chair—no windows.

The door shuts with a thud, enclosing me in my claustrophobic cell. I'm tired, I'm hot. I want to go back to Solaris. Brother Copernicus speaks about evolution; I believe evolution is already here. Third generation child of space-based humans, I'm no longer fit to live on the surface of a planet.

I've come here to observe, not to solve everyone's problems. How could I possibly stop this war without the massive slaughter Brother Copernicus wants me to order, or the massive slaughter that will happen when we withdraw? The Hern or the Pari? Since when does humanity have the right to determine who will live? Whatever we decide at that Solaris board meeting, we will have blood on our hands. We don't want interference, but we're already in too deep.

A light flickers on my PAD that lies face-up on the desk. The beamsweep has crawled through our little section of space and delivered its payload. There is a flashing message icon on the screen. I haul the file through the descrambler to read it.

The results from my earlier query about the white powder. It's titanium oxide, the same stuff that's used in paints and sun protection. It's intensely white. I knew all of that already. Titanium makes up a surprisingly high proportion of biomass on Bianca, about 98% of it in the form of oxide. It appears to be taking part of the function of carbon as building material, since Bianca is quite low on carbon.

I sigh with the irrelevance of it. There is so much more pressing stuff I should have asked, and the next beamsweep, damn, is not due for another three days, by which time Armageddon might have broken out, if not outside, within the mission.

I wake up at banging on the door loud enough to rattle the walls of the room. I open my eyes and I still can't see a thing. There is an odd rumble on the roof.

"Who is it?"

My voice is rough with sleep. I sit up, realizing the rumble on the roof is torrential rain. What is the time? Where is the light switch?

I swing my feet over the edge of the bed and reach for the crutches. Can't find them. Stumble for the door. Oh, damn, my knee.

More banging.

"Hello? Envoy?"

I open the door. Brother Tycho is in the corridor.

"It's about Brother Copernicus," he says.

My mind flashes with unpleasant scenarios. Brother Tycho's found out what happened in that deserted lab. Worse, he's found out what Brother Copernicus said to me—

"He's dead. Shot himself in the head."

I want to protest. He's okay; I only saw him just before going to bed, but I know it is true. The pieces of the puzzle come together. He was a broken man allowing himself one long-denied pleasure before taking his own life. After losing his faith, there was nothing left for him.

I find the light switch and my crutches, and slip the protective robe over my head.

Brother Tycho takes me through the dark corridors to the brothers' sleeping quarters: row upon row of cell-like rooms, possibly even smaller than mine. What is the big deal with the rabbit cages? Apart from extruder materials, there isn't much extra running cost, and with the level of UV, certainly none that can't be generated locally. Give these men a pleasant living environment and they might actually stay sane.

313

SCOTT FREDERICK HARGRAVE

Brother Copernicus lies on the bed on his back, his eyes closed. He looks asleep except his chest isn't moving. The gun lies nestled between his neck and shoulder, the safety still off. There is little damage from the shot as I know there wouldn't be with plasma weapons. Just an intense red patch of skin on his left temple. I imagine him lying there, holding the gun to his head and pushing the trigger. His body convulsing as the charge hits. My eyes mist over.

Clumsy as I am, I kneel on the side of the bed and take his hand, cold and stiff. The hand that caressed me only a few hours ago. My lips twitch involuntarily.

I rummage in my pockets. Amongst keys and data chips I find a piece of "wood" I picked up from the Pari camp. Somehow, it seems appropriate as farewell token. I place it on his robe, letting my hand linger on his unmoving chest, seeing him surrounded by the small Pari. I don't think he understood them, but he cared. He cared too much.

"Don't remove it from him," I say to Brother Tycho while I struggle to my feet.

At Solaris, we farewell people by placing tokens with the body before incineration.

He says nothing as I walk past him into the corridor, desperate not to let him see my face or the tears running down my cheeks.

I'm not a few steps gone when someone yells down the corridor, "Alarm! The Hern have escaped from the compound!"

Someone else shouts, "Everyone mobilize!"

Within seconds, brothers are rushing into the corridor, pulling on robes and strapping on masks. In

315

the throng of bodies, a brother hands me a plasma gun. "Safe to use at night," he says before moving on.

It turns out the brothers have another secret weapon: a vehicle, which they say also can only be used at night. I wonder why, but want to waste no one's time with questions.

We pile in. The door hisses shut; the air lock hums open. Red signs flash on the walls, "Beware Fire Danger." The driver shifts the truck into gear, and it jerks forward. Rain pelts down on the cabin, literally as if someone is hosing the windows. I think I understand why guns and the truck are safe to use at night: nothing burns long in this downpour. One of the brothers is yelling instructions and safety precautions. *No one is to take off their gloves and head protection at any time.* I know. The rain is so acid it causes blisters.

The vehicle jumps over the uneven ground. Wheels churn in slippery mud. I hang onto the handhold, alternately squashed into the side by the weight of bodies on my bench, or holding on so I don't squash the people next to me.

First stop: the Hern camp.

The door opens, letting in a cloud of humidity. I hang onto my mask, feeling claustrophobic again. A camp guard yells over the pelting rain.

"No damage to the perimeter . . . all asleep . . ."

The door shuts again. Everyone is talking and with the noise of the engine and the rain, I'm missing half the conversation, but I gather that the Hern who have mounted an attack on the Pari did not come from the detention area.

We arrive at the Pari camp. The cabin door opens and everyone is pushing to get out. Onto the muddy ground, where my crutches promptly sink into the soft soil. Someone helps me into the hall of the central building, where we're out of the rain. A small group of Pari waits there in a pool of light from a neon storm lamp strung onto the lift ropes. I'm wondering where the rest of the Pari are and why they haven't gathered here to be together and safer in the face of an attack. Maybe the rest of the brothers will bring them here.

Brother Tycho is speaking to another missionary.

"Who were these Hern? Where did they come from?"

The missionary doesn't know. Says he's not familiar enough with the Hern to be able to tell individuals apart.

The Pari just stand there, staring. Surely, they know these Hern well enough to recognize them?

"Anyone here who can speak a few words of their language?" I ask.

A brother comes forward.

"We can protect you from the Hern," I say, and the brother translates. "You have to help us. I want you to point out the individuals who attacked so they can be punished. If we can catch these killers, then we can start negotiating peace."

"Peace," one of them repeats and drops to the ground, knees in the mud.

"Peace," says another, and within a few seconds, all the Pari are on their knees, murmuring *peace* until the sound mingles with the teeming rain.

I feel like tearing my hair out. At least Brother

Copernicus could make *some* sort of sense out of them. "You want peace? Then tell me, who came here? Where did they come from?"

They stop their murmuring, eyeing me from under deep frowns. Angry, although I don't know why.

Someone is shouting elsewhere in the camp. A flash. A zap of fire.

We peer into the rain. To my horror, it falls less heavily than before.

Dark shapes run through the camp, too tall to be Pari. All around me, brothers unlock their weapons with definitive clicks.

"Any news from the others?" I ask a brother who's wearing a headset.

Whatever answer he would have given drowns in shouts from the Pari camp. The brother runs, pulling his crossbow from over his shoulder. A few steps into the rain, he stops and takes aim. Shoots. Runs forward. Shoots again.

Too late: the Hern swarm all over the gathering house, where the Pari are still sitting on their knees.

I scream, "Get up! Fight!" I find a bundle of sticks and toss them into the group, but the Pari just sit there, passive, still murmuring *peace*.

Brothers discharge guns at random, but the Hern take no notice. They take hits, but walk on, oblivious to their wounds. Their comrades are killed, but they don't seem to care.

I'm holding the gun in outstretched arms, but I know I won't use it. The shot might hit a Pari or a brother.

The Hern pick up the Pari as if they're dolls, slicing open their bellies with long nails. They scoop out handfuls of blood and drink it. The black fluid runs down their faces, necks and pale-skinned bellies.

In the carnage, I spot a Hern wearing a white armband. The murdering bastard! In my rage, I don't think, but struggle forward, pointing the gun at the creature.

"Stop it, now!" I scream.

The Hern does. Turns her head. Her eyes meet mine.

As a black mixture of blood and entrails oozes from her fingers, I recognize her face. No, she hasn't killed the Pari girl I gave that arm band. She *is* the Pari girl I gave the armband. I lower the gun, trembling.

She wipes blood on her thighs and takes a few steps towards me. The dark patches on her skin have grown and have turned green. She reaches out and touches my robe with a bloodstained hand. I need all my willpower not to discharge the gun.

"Munni." She takes my hand and places it on her belly. I slide my fingers up and down the blood-covered skin. It feels tight, even through my gloves, like her entire belly cavity is taken up by a huge football, a white membranous sac brimming with eggs.

This is absurd. The Hern think I'm *pregnant* rather than obese.

And I realize: the Pari and Hern are not separate species, but stages in the life cycle of one species. That's why there are no young, why the Pari don't seem to reproduce: they are immature. That's why the Hern don't eat regular food: their bodies only need to feed the eggs. Of course they're angry with us—for disrupting the process. And trying to stop it is utterly futile.

319

"Stop shooting!" I shout at the brother nearest to me, but his eyes are glazed over. I push him hard causing him to fall. The gun slips from his hands. I step on it before he can pick it up. "Stop shooting. There's no point."

He sits there, panting. The next moment he's on his feet again and he takes off into the darkness.

The Hern girl that used to be Pari is dragging bodies into a pile, many of them bloodied and mangled beyond recognition. She's alternately cramming grisly entrails into her mouth or clutching her belly, gagging and coughing.

"Are you okay?" I ask, foolishly.

She looks up, frothy vomit dribbling down her chin, seems surprised I'm still here and motions with her hand over the top of the trees, where the sky has turned light blue.

It's almost daytime. It has stopped raining, and humidity is dropping.

Another Hern throws a burning log into the pile of bodies. Fire spreads like an ink stain.

Fire.

My mind rings with warnings. Warnings in the cabin of the craft that brought me here. Warnings plastered on every wall in every corridor of the mission building.

In case of fire, make your way to the bunker immediately. Do not try to save others. Do not try to retrieve material goods. Do not fire weapons. Do not hesitate.

I run. I didn't think I could, but I do. Past the half-built houses, past the fields, my crutches sinking deep into the mud. I see no Pari, only Hern. Some are still gorging themselves, others are running around with burning torches, others still look like zombies, clutching bellies that are visibly swollen, their eyes wide and faces gaunt with what I presume is pain.

"Thank the Lord, Envoy, there you are!"

A single brother waits at the entrance of the camp. "Quick, let's get out of here." He grabs my arm and drags me onto the white field with its oozing thick mud.

I gasp, "The truck."

"Can't use it . . . would blow up . . . in the daytime. Run . . . as fast as you can."

I push down my crutches, haul myself forward, again and again. I think both my knees and my hips will need surgery after this, but I run. For Brother Copernicus.

Behind us, the burning camp lights up the morning sky. The heat radiates through the back of my robe.

At the mission's entrance, the alarms are ringing. The air whooshes past with the rush of oxygen making its way to the fire. Fifty percent oxygen in the air. It's like a bomb. White flames leap from the camp to the trees, higher than I've ever seen. There is an explosion, a flash; the sound follows a second later. I'm thinking how there is no way the Hern can escape the inferno to birth their young safely. Flames billow out from the forest, spreading over the canopy, engulfing it.

"In the bunkers, now!" Brother Tycho shouts over the roar.

In the throng of bodies, I'm unsure who helps me. Even inside the building, the air shimmers with that sort of tension that makes me sure it's about to explode. A brother stands at the entrance to the bunker, making sure everybody has their rebreather masks and supply packs, because when the fire has passed, there will likely be nothing left of the building.

Down the stairs, one, two, three stories, into claustrophobic darkness. We all huddle on the floor while explosions shake the ground.

I don't know how long I sit there, concentrating on my breathing in that dark and cramped space that smells of sweaty bodies even through the mask. It's pitch dark, and I count the time by how often I have to crawl over legs to visit the toilet. The hole in the ground is designed only for men, and after three days, or what I think has been three days, I can smell it through the mask.

Eventually someone decides the fire is over and climbs up the stairs to open the air lock. I'm busy thumbing messages on my PAD for the next beamsweep, which is due very soon. I'm not going to wait until I've surveyed the disaster outside. With that chemical cocktail, there's not going to be anything left for us to survive. We'll need to be lifted off this hellhole. Soon.

When I finally climb outside the bunker, it turns out I'm even more right than I thought. Not only has the building burned to cinders, there is nothing left of the forest. The ground is covered in white ash as far as I can see. There is no sign of the Pari or the Hern, or indeed of any life.

It's raining.

A brother is walking around with an air quality meter. He turns around, and laughs. Takes off his mask. Everyone yells at him, but he just laughs.

"It's safe," he shouts and balls his fists at the sky. "The air is safe!"

The ash in the older burnt tracks is no longer white, but gray with soot. I kick the muddy clods, angry with the waste of life. I was sure the Hern were about to go through a mass birthing event. Now, thanks to us, they're all dead. My boot dislodges a rock. Underneath, I can see green.

With difficulty, I sink to my knees and push the ash away with my gloves.

I find a seedling.

Another piece of the puzzle falls into place. The ash, and specifically the titanium oxide, protects the soil from the excessive UV radiation. That is necessary, because the soil is mostly inorganic. With high-oxygen atmosphere, fallen leaves take next to no time to decay, so there is no leaf litter to shelter seeds.

The Hern create paths where the catastrophic fires that are inevitable won't reach. Fire breaks, as it were. Corridors where regeneration will be a few months ahead of everywhere else, so that when the fires come, their progeny will have food.

But there is no progeny. The entire planet is dead.

The rescue team takes time to turn up. In the days before they come, we witness a transformation of the track of formerly ash-covered land next to the ruins of the mission.

On the first day, whole slabs of ground lift up with the force of growing seedlings. We camp in tents and we've had to put our masks back on. The air is heavy with cyanide, which I've come to associate with growing plants on this planet. Soon, plants jostle each other for sunlight, spreading out their little canopies further and further. If we could see the planet from space now, it would look like a negative image of what I saw on arrival: a white planet intersected with bands of green.

On the second day, I notice movement in the greenery. There are already some butterfly-like creatures out, fluttering in the shimmering air.

On the third day, the smaller plants burst into flower. I suspect they will set seed and will not grow again until the next fire.

On the fourth day, I am busy recording the astonishing growth when my scanner picks up a weak signal. The beamsweep isn't due for another two days, and the signal isn't strong enough anyway. It repeats a single ID tag, a twelve-digit code. That's like . . . a travel tag.

My heart thudding, I dig in the layer of ash and mud and locate my armband, no longer white, but half-melted and gray. I'm standing on the remains of the Hern girl.

Again, I dig in the cover of ash. I smear it all over my sleeves, but I don't mind. With all the bending and kneeling, some of my muscle strength has returned, and in the past few days, I've felt better than I have for years.

My gloves strike something soft.

Carefully, I scrape ash away from a white mushroomy thing, egg-shaped and longer than my forearm. Its soft leathery skin quivers when I touch it. The surface is warm. I dig it free from the soil and have just lifted it onto my lap when the skin ruptures, peeling back as if it's been shot from the inside. Slime oozes onto my robes. Something moves inside the leathery sac. I push the membranous flaps aside and out crawls a humanoid creature, unfolding long legs and stretching out of its confines. It rolls off my robe and crawls to its feet. It only reaches to my knee and is skinny and covered in slime, but I recognize the brown skin and lithe form of the Pari. All around me similar "mushrooms" are popping.

The life cycle is complete.

The recently-burned soil is barren still, but I have no doubt that, given a few months of regeneration, it will burst with life. Then the trees will grow and the Pari will get bigger. They will start building, accumulating fuel for the fires. And then, after years of growth, when the forest is mature, the Pari will start to change, entering their last phases of metamorphosis, losing the ability to communicate and focusing only on the instinct to cannibalize for the need to reproduce. How long this will take is anybody's guess. We might hang around to study the process.

Yes, I think I might recommend that to the board. I might even do a stint myself, but: no more missionaries, only observers. Bianca doesn't need us and has never done so.

Sailing the Sky Sea

written by

Geir Lanesskog

illustrated by

JOEY JORDAN

ABOUT THE AUTHOR

Geir Lanesskog was born in Norway, but moved to the US when he was five. He has been reading science fiction since his mother started taking him on weekly trips to the public library in the 1970s. He's read well over a thousand novels, anthologies and other science fiction works and hopes his recent acquisition of a Kindle will prevent him from starring in a future episode of Hoarders.

Geir started entering the Writers of the Future a few years ago, stubbornly submitting a story every quarter. At a friend's urging, he also entered his artwork in the Illustrators of the Future Contest and won on his first entry. He won the Writers contest on his eighteenth consecutive entry.

Geir has degrees in history and finance. Combined with his love of science fiction, he has developed a detailed future history complete with chronology and spreadsheets of background material that cover a span of nearly five thousand years, with at least one entry for every year. Most of his artwork, stories and his four attempts at novels are based on this background, and he hopes his experience at the Writers of the Future workshop will help him publish further stories in that universe.

ABOUT THE ILLUSTRATOR

Joey Jordan, like many artists, has drawn and spun tales since her earliest days. In her first grade class, she won her first art competition against older children and her teacher sent home a letter informing her mother, "Your daughter is going to be a great artist. Nurture and support her in this the best you can!"

Since her youth, she has always had a mind filled with images of fantastic worlds, beings and events. Many of her ideas come as complete images with all of the characters and an understanding of their backstory and lives.

Joey spent many years jumping from thing to thing, always thinking of art as a hobby when she had time. She has worked in horse stables because of her love for horses, in a cedar shake mill, for a film development warehouse and spent a little over eight years in the Army and the Army National Guard, where she was a tank turret repairer (electrical and hydraulic systems)—tanks are very large in person. In the Army she also had fond memories of her M249 Saw, filling sandbags, eating bugs, running bulk fuel lines, a duty as a "hooker" (the title for the person that gets to hook a vehicle or load under a helicopter), and a time when she had to pull her partner off a load when the wind blew and the pilot almost smashed him and a short span on a hazmat team.

After a few years of feeling like she was in a mundane rut, she asked herself why, and what would make life wonderful again, and she answered herself with her art. Now the rest of her life will be an artist's adventure for she cannot truly live any other way.

Sailing the Sky Sea

I was outside the sky mine when the war started. It was luck that had me working on the intake that morning. Luck that I'd switched shifts with Liam Kelly so I could rack up the OT before the end of the pay period. And luck that I was way up on the forward intake when the missiles hit. And, believe it or not, luck that I fell off a rig floating in the upper atmosphere of a gas giant.

We never wear tethers on outside jobs. Gas mines float in the winds of Uranus' atmosphere. It does seem insane to be high up in an infinite sky, riding a hurricane in an e-suit with nothing but magnetic boots and a good sense of balance, but the first tethered guy that fell, he bounced off the rig like a pendulum. So the union suggested a change of work rules. See, we were already about a hundred atmospheres of pressure down into the sky, just below the water clouds. If you slip, you can fall for a long time—a couple of hours, down to where you're basically buoyant. The problem is that the temperature down there is about a thousand Celsius. Or Kelvin, I forget.

329

It doesn't matter, because the suit isn't good past five hundred Celsius for very long.

If you fall, then Search and Rescue is supposed to launch within a minute of the call-out and dive after the poor sucker, catching him before he drops too deep. Sometimes it took two minutes to launch because the union wouldn't give up the SAR pilot slot and let the machines do it. Plenty of time though, because, like I said, you can fall a really long time before you get crushed or melted.

But on that morning, SAR wasn't going to come after me. The shock of the first missile impact knocked me off my feet and flung me at least ten meters up and sideways. I dropped headfirst past the intake, then down past the collector vane, barely missing a rigged spar. I looked up between my boots and saw the whole upper superstructure collapse and shred. Flames and smoke blossomed out of the inhabited sections when oxygen met hydrogen and the torn metal added a spark. Out in the blue distance I saw numbers Four and Six rigs suffering the same fate. That's when I figured there was a war on.

I figured I was dead, but it didn't hurt to give miracles a chance. So I followed my training and twisted into a prone position to slow my descent. My transponder indicator was on, and for a second I thought about shutting it down. I didn't want to attract a missile from whatever killed us. It was a 'Roider attack, I figured. Had to be, because only the Asteroid Belt Confederation had any reason to hit a Martian-owned rig, and they probably didn't care that I was just an Earth boy trying to make a living.

But it's a long fall. And that gave me time to decide

that just because it was a surprise attack, that didn't mean they would hunt down helpless survivors. Well, maybe they would. But if I went silent, no SAR from any world or rock or station was ever going to find me and I was dead for certain. I didn't know until later that my transponder was broken.

So I fell. Denser wreckage started falling past me, enough junk for me to turn face up to look out for a chunk with my name on it. Burning debris lit up the dim blue sky, glowing brighter than that far spark of the sun. It had been a nice morning.

I didn't see any SAR flyers or lifeboats coming out of that mess, but one big chunk caught my eye. It was the mostly intact lower observation deck, a fancy module built around a panoramic dining area and luxury suites for visiting executives. Below the deck was a huge morph metal fin that once acted as the forward rudder. Now it was morphing, changing into something big and round, something that looked like a giant umbrella. No, not an umbrella. A parachute.

It fell past me. The morphed chute expanded and flipped the observation deck upside down, and then the whole thing began to come back up toward me. Not really. It was just falling slower. But it looked like the miracle I was waiting for, so I did my best flying human imitation and angled my fall toward it. It's not as easy as it sounds. It would have been easier if I had a cape or wings or something, but the thing wasn't that far away, and the difference in fall rates wasn't too big, so I survived the bounce off the edge of it. Nearly shattered my wrist; morph metal is still metal. But I got a grip on this strip that was acting like a rope or support and half slid, half fell onto the inverted base

331

of the deck. The metal above me was still morphing into something like a wing or a parasail, slowing the fall until we were getting near some sort of buoyancy. The morph was not something preprogrammed, as far as I knew, so somebody had to be alive in there. I tried my comms, but nobody answered. My magnetic boots saved my ass at least twice as I crawled my way across the hull until I made it to an air lock. The lights on the lock's panel showed emergency power, and the damn thing wouldn't listen to voice commands, so I hit the emergency entry sequence and waited until the lock reached outside pressure.

It was dark under the wing. The wind was picking up, and my suit said I was at two hundred atmospheres. Deeper than I wanted to be, but a lot better than still falling into the crushing sky.

The lock opened and I dropped into it. I worked the upside-down manual controls and waited again as the pressure dropped to zero to push out all the hydrogen, then rose back to one standard atmosphere. I knelt beside the inner lock door, opened it and lowered myself into a corridor lit dim and red with emergency lighting.

I'd been on the observation deck a lot of times before, but it didn't look right upside down. My suit wasn't talking to this detached piece of the rig, so it took me a while to get my bearings. Then I crawled down the passage to find a door to the main deck. The stairs were upside down and didn't really help, but with boots up locked against the wall, I got the door open, then swung through and dropped onto the ceiling four meters below.

A woman with a two-foot section of metal pipe

met me as I got back onto my feet. She gripped the pipe like a club, but at least she wasn't swinging it at me. I put up my hands and said, "Hold up! I'm friends."

I still had my helmet on. It didn't have an external speaker, since, well, if you had your helmet on, it was supposed to be because everyone else had their helmet on, and radio was the only way to communicate. Except the radio wasn't working, and if it had been no one was listening anyway. So I did my best hands-in-the-air routine and waved and pointed until she got the idea that I was going to take off my helmet. She nodded, looking more impatient than afraid or angry.

"How did you get in here?" she asked.

I eyed the pipe. She held it like she didn't really know how to swing it, but I wasn't about to put that to the test.

"Through the air lock. Hi, I'm Vic Basilone, Outside Mechanic, Grade Two." I held out my right hand and she looked at her pipe before grasping my hand uncertainly.

"Kyla Resnick. I'm a nurse and—"

"Great, because I really smacked my wrist on the way in and . . ." Her look was like the one my mother used to give me when I'd done something really annoying, and that stopped me short.

"We've got bigger problems," she said. "Come on."

I followed her across the ceiling-turned-floor, stepping around chandeliers overturned and drooping, hopping through the high threshold of an inverted doorway.

"I'm not sure I can place that accent," I said.

333

"I'm from Thetis—on Venus, not the asteroid."

I nodded. Most of the crew were from Venus or Earth. The gravity on Uranus was just less than Venus, but still over twice what a Martian was used to, never mind a 'Roider.

"I thought I knew everyone on the crew."

"We just got here. I'm on the staff of Mr. Achuthanandan." We stepped around some more damage in the corridor and around the corner. Three men lay unconscious on the floor—what used to be the arched ceiling.

"The banker?" I asked. I'd seen something about an incoming shuttle with bankers and some sort of loan restructuring. I only remembered the name because I didn't know how to pronounce it.

"Yes," she said. "Do you know any first aid?"

"Just the basics." I'd passed the certification, but I wasn't exactly up on the practice.

"How about engineering?" another woman asked. The voice came from the better-lit room just past the injured men. Her accent I recognized right away, Hesperian Martian.

Nurse Resnick—good looking, but a little too stern for me to start calling her Kyla—gestured with her head toward the open door and turned her attention back to the three wounded men.

The lit room was an oversized tech closet. Resnick had an Earther's build, but the dark-haired woman in the room had the spindly shape of a Martian. She sat in front of a terminal pulled from a rack and inverted to our new orientation. Workstations and panels still hung upside down in the small room. Blinking lights and battery packs filled three other racks.

"I can fix things pretty good," I told her. "I've got Level Two ratings in—"

"Yeah, whatever. I need another brain to double-check what I'm doing here. Sort of out of my experience."

Her terminal showed a schematic of the morph metal, now tapered like a giant wing. Another screen, still upside down—at least from my perspective—showed tracking and atmospheric data. The slope of one line meant that we were still falling, but really slowly.

"Air density down here is about twenty times standard, and I've got the glide ratio about twelve to one, which is pretty good, but it's not going to level off to flat before we get too deep."

"What about thermals?" I asked. "Vic Basilone, by the way."

"Moor Nakamura."

"More?"

"Moor like the African. For Maureen. I hate 'Mo.' What do you know about thermals?"

"Um, they help gliders rise."

"So you know nothing, then?"

"Well, they're hot, so you'd look for heat rising."

"Great, genius." I don't think she meant it as a compliment. She thumbed toward another screen. "See if you can bring up a heat map of the atmosphere and give me something to aim for."

I heard a man screaming in the hallway, a sound of intense pain. I turned back toward the doorway, but Moor grabbed my arm. "Let the nurse handle it. Compound fracture or something."

I went back to the screen, pulled it out of its setting

335

and turned it around, then flicked through the menus and query screens until I got to Meteorology. I had no current data—not surprising since the met sensors were blown to bits, but I got up the last recorded data.

"You the one who morphed the fin? Pretty clever. Genius, even."

Moor snorted. "Yeah, maybe, but all we have is this battery power and the auxiliary life support, so even if we don't get crushed or cooked, we've got about a day until we're drained."

"Standard or local day?"

"Does it matter?"

"Well, twenty-four hours is better than seventeen."

"Yeah, closer to twenty-four. At least twenty. Maybe. Depends on how much power I need to use changing the morph."

I nodded. Better than the thirty minutes that I thought I had left to live when I'd fallen into the sky. "Looks like there used to be an updraft off twenty klicks east-northeast."

"Great, I'll try that." Moor adjusted the morphing metal to dip one part of the wing down. We turned, but it was painfully slow and our glide ratio fell.

"Now what?" I asked her.

"Well, Vic, why don't you check out the rest of the rooms and see if you can find some power modules or anything else that might keep us going. I didn't exactly have a chance to look around a lot before I came up with this hare-brained scheme."

I started to leave, then stopped in the doorway. "I don't recognize you either. Did you come in with Achu-what's-his-name, too?"

"Nah, just off the last shuttle and into a Senior

Systems Tech job. My first shift. It was supposed to be a nice job far away from all the trouble. I should have stayed in the army."

I gave her a look that must have made her defensive, because she continued, "Ex-Technical Sergeant, Third Battalion, Second Cohort, Sixth Army Legion."

Yeah, I know, falling through the sky and all that, but the Martian Unification Wars were still a big deal at the time. At least until that day where I fell into the sky and the Martian-Belter War started. So I had to ask, "Were you in the war?"

Now she gave me the look like my mother used to and said, "Yeah. Lost both legs in the Labyrinth." She looked at two fully functional legs and continued. "But they got better. Nice medical pension, too. Eventually."

Seems that was all she wanted to say about it, so I went off on my search. I stepped over the high threshold and passed Resnick, who was wrapping the leg of the man who'd been screaming. A bone was sticking out. Not pretty, but the other two guys looked worse. They both were unconscious, bloody and pale.

I found three others in my search of the rooms. I didn't know if Nurse Resnick had already checked on them, but they were obviously dead. The only useful things I found in the upturned wreck of the kitchens and storerooms were a few small battery cells. Hardly enough to make a difference. But at least it looked like we had plenty of food and water.

"Not much," I said, dropping the pile of bottle-sized battery packs when I got back in the tech room. That room really wasn't much bigger than a closet, but it had enough backup power to keep our systems running. Turns out most of the power Moor was using to morph the metal came from the kitchen backup generators, but I didn't know that at the time.

"I've stopped the descent, but we're not rising at all," she said. "And when darkness comes, we're probably sunk."

"So to speak. So what's the plan, Sarge?"

"I'm not a sergeant anymore!"

I backed off, hands up. Note to self, don't bring *that* up again. "Sorry, I just wanted to know—"

"Yeah, well, unless you have any better ideas, I'm going to cut climate control for everything but this room, this corridor and the one that leads to the rear air lock. If we do that, especially if we cut off the observation deck, then I can really save power."

"What about rescue?" Resnick said. She'd popped her head through the door. "I've got a man with an epidural hematoma and another one who's probably bleeding internally. I don't have anything but drapes and splints to fix them."

"There were a couple of first aid kits in the kitchen," I said.

"Did you bring them?"

"No, but I can go—"

"Never mind, I'll get them." She was gone, stomping down the hall. Moor glared at me and I decided it wasn't time for excuses.

"So what about a rescue?" I asked. "All three of our rigs got blown away, but there's another eight Martian rigs out there, plus four Venusian rigs, and if we really need to ask, at least a half dozen 'Roiders."

Moor frowned. "Spread across a sky with over

fifty times the surface area of Mars. Good luck finding them. Besides, the other Martian rigs are probably gone, too. And we might have taken out the Belter—'Roider, if you insist—rigs in retaliation."

She didn't seem to have a positive attitude. But I'd just survived—so far—falling off a burning rig, so maybe I was just a bit more optimistic. "So let's see where the nearest Venusian rig was when all hell broke loose," I said. "We've got a Venusian banker and nurse aboard, and I'm from Earth, so it's not like I'm likely to be seen as anyone's enemy."

Moor flicked the screen and muttered some commands—don't know how she got voice to work when it wouldn't for me, but I'm not that sort of tech—and said, "It's just about a thousand klicks to the Caelus IV rig at its last reported location and heading."

"So we'd have to go about fifty klicks an hour . . ."

"Its wind stream is plus ten meters per second relative, so we have to do more like seventy-five or eighty, or cut into its stream, which is a longer distance. I'm not a glider pilot or anything, but I know that all we got to work with is trading altitude for velocity. In this soup, I can get us sixty klicks across and five down an hour, but we're already forty down from where we started, and twelve hours of drop will kill us. Probably cook us before it crushes us."

"Yeah . . . Hey, I've got a stupid idea." Maybe not the best way to say it, but it got her attention. "Can't you morph part of the wing into a sail or something? You should be able to tack against the wind. I saw people do it all the time back at Disney Beach."

She squinted at me. "Don't be an idiot. Unless

we've got some sort of differential, we're just going to go with the wind. Sails only work because the boat and keel are in the water. You've got to trade something for something, and all we have is altitude to give up."

"Can't you flap the wings or something?" I asked.

"Not enough power. We'd waste it all and then not be able to morph anymore."

"Well, can you morph the wings into a giant balloon? We could pump out all the air, make it like the vacuum chamber that floated the rig."

"Pump out the air with what?" she asked. Irritated, she continued, "Don't you think I already thought of those ideas?"

"Well, you didn't share them with me. You can use an air lock as a pump, you know. Empty it to vacuum, then release the ballast gas to the outside, then open the inner door, let in more air and repeat."

"Huh. Well, that's clever, but there's no way to use that to pump out a canopy above us, is there? Tell me how I can wrap a bag around us and arrange the air locks to do that without evacuating our section."

"I don't know." Then I had an idea. "Well, you don't need to evacuate it, just to, um, inflate it. Sort of."

"Not seeing it."

I put my hands together. "Okay, so you've got the morph metal in a solid mass, right?"

"For the wing, yeah."

"Right." I expanded my hands around a hollow pocket. "So just split it apart on the inside, so it turns into a hollow shell. There's going to be nothing in the middle of that, so you've got the vacuum you need.

You can expand it as a vacuum balloon as big as the strength of the metal will support."

She nodded slowly. "And if I can get it big enough to give us lift, then I can morph the envelope and turn that lift into velocity and get us moving against the wind. Yeah, that might work, genius."

The genius part seemed less than sincere, but she set off to shape the morph metal, and sure enough, it inflated around a hollow, empty interior. Sure enough, we began to climb.

"It's going to eat more power to hold this shape against external pressure," she said. "But it might work. I'm going to try to cut diagonally across to the same latitude as Caelus, so we're not fighting the stream, but then we might be able to close before we run out of juice. Maybe."

"Is that the shortest route, or should you do some kind of curve?" I asked.

"Leave the flying to me and the computers," she said as her hands danced over the controls. "Go see if you can help the nurse or something."

I was about to ask her who put her in charge, but after her reaction to the whole Sarge thing, I just let it go.

The patients didn't look good. The guy with the broken leg was unconscious. I recognized him as Lasko—didn't know his first name, but he was some sort of management type. I didn't know the guy with the bandage on his head, but he had on Venusian fashions—who else would wear a loose-fitting pastel suit? So he must have come in with that banker with the name that sounded like a sneeze and a chortle. And that banker looked bad. He had dried blood on his lips and a pale sweaty face. His body was wrapped in torn drapes.

Nurse Resnick came back with two first aid kits and then knelt by Achuthanandan. "Well, at least they've got synopiates," she said.

I nodded. Snyopiates: All of the painkilling without any of the fun. I helped move her patients to better positions and change some bandages. By the time we were done, she was almost pleasant with me. Then our floor began to shake.

I popped my head back in the tech room.

"Not going so smoothly," Moor said. "I mean, the systems say it should work, mathematically, but it's never been tried before. The rigs use thermajets for propulsion, not morphing balloon wings. So I'm working on feedb—ack!"

It felt like we hit a bad pothole. Resnick yelled at us, but from what I could see, we'd turned in the right direction and built up some speed, maybe even close to the hundred klicks an hour we needed for a curving course. The schematic of the morph's balloon and wing combination looked like a squashed flaccid sausage. Yeah, well, we weren't looking for points for style.

"How are we doing on velocity and bearing?" I asked.

Moor flicked up another screen. "Not bad. I'll build it all into a nav view so we can keep track. The wing is morphing ten times a second, so once it builds a good feedback model, the shaking should taper off some. It's really up to the computers to keep us on course and steady."

"That's what they're for, though, the computers."

"Yeah, this system is specialized for morphing, life support and kitchen management, but there's enough in there for controlling the wing."

Our makeshift sky-ship shook again and the nurse yelled at us. Again.

"Sorry," Moor said. "It's going to be a bit bumpy if we want to make any headway."

"Fine," Resnick said. "Then, Vic, you need to help me figure out how to strap these people down."

We found enough raw materials on the observation deck to rig up some better stretchers with restraints. Then Moor shut down all power and light to that big deck to save energy. I was almost sad to lose the panoramic view, but there was a little observation blister now on top of the torn-away platform, that we could use to get visuals. In fact, the camera views Moor was using came from that little hemisphere of glass.

Small talk was awkward, but as we worked on the stretchers, I gave it a try. "So, Ms. Resnick—Kyla, what brings you all the way out here from the lovely terraformed beaches and fields of Venus?"

"I'm Mr. Achuthanandan's executive assistant. I go where he goes."

"I thought you said you were a nurse?"

"I am." She paused, considering, I don't know what—patient-nurse professional privilege? And then she said, "He's old. Nearly three hundred years old, and his immune system is sporadic. He gets these terrible migraines and the occasional blood clot—though he has the opposite problem right now—so he needs a medical professional more than he needs an appointments secretary. Space travel is expensive, so I do both. I only wish I'd gotten my kit off the shuttle before all this happened."

"Ah, just got here, eh? What about that guy?" I asked, jerking my head at the one in the pastel suit.

"Mr. Zhou is the brains. Finance and stuff." She paused and looked at her two traveling companions and at Lasko, the management drone. He had probably been showing them around when the missiles hit. She asked, "What about you, Vic? Earth is far away, too."

"Yeah, and much poorer than Venus. Florida's still sinking into the ocean and there's not a lot of decent work. My uncle Sal was shop steward here, so he got me a union billet. Takes two years to pay off the transport fees, but after that, it's better money than I'll ever see working in some arcology."

"So your uncle Sal is . . ." She couldn't finish the question.

I smiled. "Up on Miranda for the mandatory month of leave. I'm sure he's fine. A lot of other people, though . . ." Now it was my turn to leave it unsaid. I wasn't even supposed to be out working. It should have been Liam Kelly out there.

She frowned. "Vic, what's your blood type?"

"What?"

"Blood type. My boss is slowly bleeding out and a transfusion from you could buy him some time."

"Well, I have no idea. You mean you want to use real blood, not synthetic? That's disgusting. Is it even legal?"

"Well, you don't see a big supply of synthetic laying around, do you, Vic?"

Turns out Moor could look up my personnel file from her computer. It was supposed to be confidential, so I don't know how she did that. Well, turns out I'm O negative, which is something called a "universal donor." Next thing you know, I'm half a liter short.

The ride got smoother. Moor was right, the more data points the computer got, the better it was at the adjustments. We cut across the wind, heading toward where the Venusian rig ought to be. It was early northern spring on Uranus, so day and night were almost equal in length. As it got to be evening, I found an excuse to get up into the observation blister. Once, that clear hemisphere had looked down on the mining operation, now it looked up, in front of the morphed wing, out into the darkening sky. There was a row of clouds ahead. The distant sun lit the forward formation, but behind, the canyons of cloud faded into gray, blocked from the sun and glowing only by the light of the sky itself. That bank of clouds was probably as big as Texas. I tried to call back to Moor and that's when I found out my radio was dead. I didn't have my phone either. It was back in my locker. Blown to bits or crushed down below. Gloomy thought. I went back down to the others.

I don't understand it," Kyla Resnick said. "We're at nearly three hundred atmospheres. That's the pressure of the deep ocean. How could we possibly be falling if we're mostly filled with air? We should float."

We were sitting in the corridor, trying to concentrate on a meal, while the three unconscious men lay nearby, possibly dying, probably needing another half liter from me. Moor looked disgusted by the question and shook her head, so I tried to answer.

"You're confusing density with pressure," I said.

"The gas rig is—was—held up by these big cans of vacuum—that's about as least dense as you can get. But pressure comes from how much force the gas is pushing on you, from the weight of all the gas above it. Down here, the pressure on us is three hundred times the pressure on Earth at sea level, but the density of this hydrogen-helium soup, even down here as compressed as it is, it's just a fraction of the density of water. It's a lot denser than the air on Earth, but on Earth, water is a thousand times denser than air. Do you see?"

"No, not really."

I sighed. "Okay, try this. You know what gold leaf is, right? Made of gold, which is one of the densest metals out there. The disgustingly rich can cover themselves in nanometers of gold leaf, but it doesn't crush them, right? But take that same gold leaf and crush it into a tiny nugget and drop it into a bucket of water, and it's going to drop right to the bottom. Pressure and density: not the same thing."

She nodded. I don't think she got it, but she wasn't going to make an issue of it. It was hard to wrap your head around. First time I found out the rigs were held up by vacuum, I thought they were pulling my leg.

Darkness fell and so did our power reserves. We'd moved north up to the same latitude and air current as the Caleus rig, but we were still nearly eight hundred klicks behind it and forty klicks below it. We could close that distance in just eight hours, but Moor figured we now had just over two hours of power left—if we were going to keep the balloon inflated and moving like it'd been. We could go slower with a smaller canopy, or allow ourselves to descend. But either way, we'd reach broiling depth four or five hundred klicks short of our destination. By the time the sun rose in eight more hours, we'd be cooked. But still, there was no point in giving up.

How about we evacuate the air out of the observation lounge?" I asked. "That should lighten the load. We could do it using the air lock I came in through, pumping it out like I said before."

"About three tons of air. Less than two percent of our mass," she said. "I'm not sure it's worth the power drain. But it might help slow the descent." She did something with her screen and watched graphs of two lines crawl across it. Both were down, but one went a lot less down. "Well, it's better than flapping the wings. It might get us to morning."

So after I checked all the seals, we started pumping air out of the back half of our little life raft. The balance of the whole place tilted, but Moor morphed the envelope to compensate a bit. Now we had a slant on our upside-down floor, and we had to move the three casualties again. Mr. Lasko was out on pain meds but he would probably live as long as the rest of us. The two Venusian guys looked pretty bad, like they might not make it to morning. So the second half liter of blood went out of me, and I felt really light-headed.

As Resnick drained me, I asked—mumbled, really, "So Achuth . . . ah, your boss is bleeding out, and Zhou has a hematoma. That's like blood putting pressure on his brain. Can't you just drain it out of Zhou's head and into Ach . . . your boss?"

"Doesn't work that way. Besides their blood's not compatible."

"No, of course not."

"Hey, take a look out there," Moor called.

I looked at the tube in my arm, sucking out my life essence. "I can't come to the screen right now."

"Well, there's a light down there."

"Might be the natives." Well, it could have been. Uranus has things that live in the deep atmosphere. Next to the sea worms of Europa, the Uranian tube and jelly fliers were probably the most advanced life forms in the Outer System. And every spring they migrated with the light, braving the equatorial regions to reach the pole where the sun would shine for another forty years. And a lot of the Uranians were bioluminescent, at least during the migration. Or so I'd read. Hadn't seen any yet. It was a rare thing that only happened for one year out of forty.

"No," Moor said. "There's only one light. It's red and it blinks."

"Rescue!" Resnick gasped.

"No, I doubt it," Moor said. "It's below us by ten klicks and not moving relative to the wind."

I said, "You know, there's supposed to be old platform hulks from before the Big War still floating around. I heard they found one about ten years back."

"Yeah, abandoned and looted long ago," Moor said.

"But if it's got light, it's got power," I said. "We can use it to recharge the batteries, maybe get enough juice to get us back up to a decent altitude."

"Only if we can latch onto an air lock. Otherwise we'd need to run cables through an open air lock and that'd kill us quick."

"Yeah, maybe." I thought about the logistics of it. Air lock interfaces hadn't changed in four hundred years. Neither had power connectors, so a two-hundred-year old platform back from an age when they built things to last, that should still be able to juice us up. Worst case, we could disconnect our batteries, bring them over to the platform and recharge them from the outside. It would be a slow and heavy job, but it should work.

It was the worst case, of course. After I'd managed to talk Moor into it and after she'd gotten us close enough to inspect the platform, it was pretty obvious we weren't going to dock at a convenient air lock.

The platform looked like it had been through a war and a dozen bad storms. The deck was riddled with holes. If the vacuum bags hadn't been distributed around the thing, it would have dropped into the crush long ago. Whole sections ended in sheared wires and sharp ceramic spikes jutted out in all directions. Moor found a clear spot just off-center where she could touch down, but it wasn't a pretty landing. At least the old platform held. It wasn't even sinking into the sky, as far as she could tell.

"We could just stay here for a bit," I suggested.

"We can't," Resnick said. "My patients will die. Mr. Zhou doesn't have more than a few hours, and Mr. Achuthanandan is getting worse."

"Plus, we're still over seven hundred klicks away from rescue and nobody's recovered this platform in the last two hundred years," Moor said. "Nobody's likely to find us for years. Let's go see if we can get some power."

Easy for her to say. She didn't have to go outside.

The others didn't even have suits to go if they wanted to, because neither air lock on our chunk of metal had spare suits. And I was still in my suit. Did I mention that the bathrooms were upside down? Well, that was a real bit of a problem for the ladies, but at least I could pee in my suit.

I didn't really want to go out there. It was dark and hot. At our altitude, it hardly mattered whether it was day or night. It was always dark and hot. The temperature was about five hundred Kelvin and the pressure was pushing four hundred atmospheres. My suit would only protect me for a couple of hours before it needed to cool down.

Did I mention the wind? Well, it wasn't more than a variable breeze relative to the platform's float, but at that pressure, it was enough to bend me near sideways and shake me like a rag doll. I crouched low and used my magnetic boots, but I had to plan each step ahead to make sure I stepped on something solid.

Before long, I found an open air lock. Well, burnt out was more like it, and that confirmed the worst. This place was long looted of everything, including most of what had been bolted down. But at least the rig's emergency power was still working. I did a quick survey for radio equipment, but in those corridors and the few rooms that I could get into with all the damage and caved-in walls, there was nothing that looked like comm equipment. But there were power conduits. And I was right—the power plugs hadn't changed in centuries. All I had to do was drag our rack-mounted portable batteries to the working outlets in the burnt-out air lock and juice them up.

Yeah, well, portable is a relative term. The batteries massed fifty kilos each, and that's still more than forty kilos weight on Uranus. So first, we had to unbolt each of them from the rack, and then it took Moor and me both to carry them into our air lock. Then I cycled the lock and had to get them out, over the upside-down air lock's threshold, then lower and carry them across the ancient deck. On the wreck's surface, with holes the size of, well, battery packs, dragging was out of the question and carrying the suckers was pretty hard, too. And I couldn't see my feet when I walked. But at least the extra mass helped steady me against the wind.

Our recharge cables were only two meters long, so I had to get the batteries pretty close to the outlets. And recharging took time. I had four batteries going at once before the first was finished. We had eight total. It took me about four hours and strained every muscle I had. Being a liter down on blood didn't help.

Halfway through my moving exercise, I was back in our air lock, dragging batteries back into the corridor when Resnick called out to us. "Mr. Zhou is going to die in under an hour if we don't get him medical attention."

I'm not sure why she said that. It's not like we had any way of calling for a doctor, and it's not like I was hiding a medical degree or an operating suite in my back pocket. I suppose she had to vent to someone. Having just used power tools to disconnect those batteries, I offered my suggestion. "Well, if it's

351

pressure inside his skull, can't you just drill a hole and let it out?"

Long pause, then, "I can't do that."

"We have a large assortment of drill bits," I added, not too helpfully.

Not too tactfully, either. I think I made her cry, but then she said, "I can't just go drilling into his head. I'm not trained for that, and it will probably just kill him."

"Isn't he going to die in the next hour anyway? So it's your choice: active or passive." Okay, that was harsh, but I was getting pretty tired dragging the damn batteries back and forth to save us all and wasn't really interested in her problem.

I got no answer from her, but Moor hissed, "Shut up, genius."

So I did. Mr. Zhou was dead by the time I finished with the batteries. There was a hole in the back of his head.

When dawn came, we were ready to take off. Moor expanded the envelope, and even though it drained our energy fast, it got us back up in altitude. Just barely above the altitude we had before we descended to the station.

"Hey, at least it bought us six hours," I said.

"But it didn't get us any closer toward the last reported location of Caelus IV."

"So how far out does that put us?"

"We're still seven-eight hours away by my plot. Late afternoon," Moor said.

The latest track had us running out of power and

reaching broil depth about an hour and a half short of our target. Of course, that was a hundred and fifty klicks away—and a hundred down—so theoretically it was within line of sight of the rig, if the atmosphere was fairly clear. They might see us. If they had any instruments looking down into the gloom for a tiny spot. But that old platform we'd just left was evidence enough that mining rigs didn't spend a lot of time looking down into the sky.

No point in getting into a sulk, though. Kyla Resnick was doing enough of that herself, and with Lasko still out and her boss delirious with fever and blood loss, I didn't even want to try and talk to her. Moor and I moved Zhou into the one freezer she'd left running. Same place we'd stuffed those three dead bodies I'd found on my first look-around.

Nothing more I could do, so I crawled back up into that observation dome. At least I could die seeing the sky. Then I fell asleep. All that excitement, the strain of heavy labor and that missing liter of blood left me out for five hours. I woke up with the nurse standing above me with a tube and a needle.

"I need another five hundred milliliters," she said.

"Are you sure that's a good idea?"

"Well, I can either be active or passive, and if I'm passive, Mr. Achuthanandan will die for sure."

I hate it when they turn my arguments against me. So I let her take my blood, and I was pretty woozy when finally I got up and climbed down to see how Moor was doing.

"Good news is that I found us some thermals," she said.

JOEY JORDAN

"Bad news?" I had to ask.

"Not enough. We're fifty klicks below the rig's probable altitude and still two hundred and fifty klicks behind it. I can't find it visually. Wish we had radar or lasers or something. Anything more than a glorified camera."

"How's the power?"

"Bad. We can have velocity or lift, and right now, even if I could find them, we'd pass below them at a hundred down, or get us back to their altitude with no change in position. So we'll have to pass underneath them and wave at them as we cook. If I could find them."

"Do you think the 'Roiders hit them, too?"

Moor shrugged. "How the hell do I know? I doubt it. Tensions were high between Mars and the Belt. I figured there was going to be a war, because we both wanted a war more than peace. But picking a fight with the Venusians would be just stupid for them. Or us."

"I'm not Martian," I reminded her.

"No, but you're on Martian contract, so that's the same thing."

"Contract just got violated," I said. "Somebody owes me a termination package. Okay, poor choice of words. So what's the plan?"

"Keep scanning the skies and hope for the best."

"Great." I took a seat and worked a screen, scanning above us. The sky was a clear blue haze, just some streamers in the distance. Picking out anything was going to be hard. I turned the contrast up until I started to see spots on the screen. Or maybe it was my blood loss. I pointed them out to Moor.

"No, those are real."

"Debris? Do you think they blew up the Caelus platforms, too?"

"It's not falling. Cutting across the wind, too."

I kicked the magnification up high enough to get a pixilated mess and those spots turned into wiggles and disks. "I think that's the spring migration," I said. I'd seen pictures. There were murals of the swarms on the rig's main cafeteria walls.

"Well, that's not something you see every day," Moor muttered.

"Yeah. So what's the range? Fifty forward and twenty up?"

Moor nodded. "Looks about right."

"Well, can you get us up into them?"

"Maybe, but we'll start dropping or stall out after that. So what the hell good does that do? We still have no idea where that rig is, and flying anywhere near a migration swarm's been illegal for almost four hundred years."

"Exactly. You have a problem about being arrested?"

"You're kidding, right?"

"Got a better plan?"

So she did her best to get us up toward the swarm. The odds of hitting any creature were pretty low. Even though they didn't have central nervous systems, they had enough hard-wired instinct to keep their distance from each other and from us. I hoped. I also figured that this once-in-a-forty-year migration was interesting enough for the people up on that rig to be watching it.

An hour later, we buzzed through a line of gossamer tubes and disks, past giant translucent filter feeders up to twenty meters long. They really were beautiful creatures. Pale ghosts of the sky. Didn't hit a single one.

And then the power level went to red. The morph metal envelope began to collapse back into a wing. We had nothing but gliding and life support now. Four more hours and we'd be dead. Another hour and Achuthanandan would be dead. Kyla Resnick didn't even bother to ask if she could take any more blood.

Moor kept us in line with the migration, heading north and away from the Caelus track as we slowly dropped below the critters. I watched them recede from the observation dome. Whether I lived or died, I was never going to see anything like that again.

I went back to the tech room to help scan for the rig. Couldn't see it at all. Didn't even know if it really was in the neighborhood, but less than an hour into our final descent, Moor's phone crackled to life on the emergency channel.

"Attention, unknown vehicle! Under the authority Articles Two and Three of the Convention of Uranian Conservation and Protection, you are under arrest for gross violation of buffer zone restrictions. Prepare to be boarded."

I didn't answer, I just laughed. Hysterically, to be honest. Moor pointed at the dot growing on her screen, moving to intercept our glide path.

I picked up her phone and said, "Yeah, great, arrest us. Just hurry up. And we're going to need a medic. And blood. You guys better have some synthetic blood packs with you."

So Achuthanandan lived. So did Lasko, but he was never in any more danger than me. He probably had more blood left in him than I did. Our makeshift refuge—Moor's act of panicked genius that had saved us all—finally collapsed in the crushing depth three hours after our rescue. Those damn Venusian bureaucrats didn't want to drop the charges, but hell, worst they can do is deport me back to Earth. Only way I could afford a ticket, anyway.

When I get back, maybe I'll take up ballooning. Or not.

Creating Your Own Destiny

BY ROBERT CASTILLO

Robert Castillo is a storyboard artist who lives in Jersey City and works in New York City. He is represented by Frameworks, LLC.

Robert graduated with honors from the Art Institute of Boston and has a master's degree in computer arts from the School of Visual Arts. As a storyboard artist, Robert has created boards for films including Lee Daniel's Precious, the Christopher Reeve-directed animation Everyone's Hero, Queen Latifah's The Cookout and The Perfect Holiday and the award-winning cable television program The Sopranos. He has also done music videos for Alicia Keys, Ja Rule, Kid Rock, Lauryn Hill and Don Omar, commercials for Phat Farm, Adidas and And1, as well as promo work and music videos for MTV, Nickelodeon's Ironman and Fuse, VH1, Court TV and ESPN. Robert has done concept boards for shows like Lopez Tonight, Skins and Chopped.

Robert's talent has been recognized with various awards and honors including L. Ron Hubbard's Illustrators of the Future Contest and the Student Academy Awards in 2004 for his short film S.P.I.C. The Storyboard of My Life which has screened in fourteen festivals including Cannes and the Museum of Modern Art.

Robert has given back by auctioning his artwork for charitable foundations. He also volunteers his time with Ghetto Film School in the Bronx, NY, Mount Sinai Medical Center and the Automotive High School of Brooklyn, NY. He is married to Karen Latney and has four dogs.

Creating Your Own Destiny

I was born with a pencil in my hand, or so the story goes! Ever since I can remember, drawing has been a vital part of my life. It's something I have been doing all my life. Drawing was the tool which helped me communicate with others. In 1977, when I stepped off the plane from Santo Domingo, I knew not a word of English and drawing was how I communicated.

In school, my counselor told me that I should take up a trade like woodworking because artists did not make a lot of money, or else to be careful because I may end up a starving artist. When I applied to art school, I was torn between fine arts and illustration and was told illustrators worked for the quick buck and that fine arts were the way to go. My professors told me to loosen up, that I drew too much detail and that I needed to slow down because I was drawing too fast (traits that really come in handy today when I work on a storyboard job needed in twenty-four hours). Many of my friends who were artists changed their profession and got so-called "real jobs." It was perceived that only a lucky few would make it. Even today, I hear negative remarks from my peers about how hard it is out there. I'm sure many of you reading this right now have had your share of obstacles.

So, having experienced both the benefits of the Illustrators of the Future Contest and knowing what it is like to work from the bottom up as an artist, I have some points that I highly recommend to anyone wanting to make it as an illustrator in today's world.

People have asked me: "What is your secret?" "Why do you get the best jobs?" "Why are you so lucky?" Little do they know luck has nothing to do with it. You create your own destiny—along with some assistance from the Man above. To all aspiring illustrators out there, I offer this advice I have learned through the years. I have broken it down to ten key points.

1. *Believe in Thyself:* You need to have confidence in your work. If you believe in your work, others will believe in it also. The best artist you can be is yourself. You don't have to imitate someone else; there is only one of you and your style is your style. When I was in art school, there was a class where we needed to emulate another artist. I had a hard time doing this because what I ended up with was a cheap imitation of the other artist's work.

2. *Practice, Practice, Practice:* Athletes do it! Singers do it! Actors do it, at least the good ones! Then why shouldn't illustrators? Someone once asked the great Wayne Gretzky how a skinny little kid from Canada ends up being one of the greatest hockey players of all time. He remarked, "I go to practice!" Many illustrators don't draw every day. We have a tendency to procrastinate. Believe me, I know! You should keep a sketchbook or journal and sketch in it every

day, practicing drawing people in different poses or animals at your local zoo. If you don't get to draw every day, at least do it every other day. Some of the best illustrators in the world sketch at least an hour a day. It really makes a difference.

3. *Communication:* This is a big one! I know many talented people who are amazing at what they do, but there is one problem; they can't express themselves. Many illustrators work alone in their studios, and so this is a skill that is not practiced enough and it hurts their chances at great projects or jobs. It can also affect your income potential. Anyone can overcome this; I did! Many people don't believe me when I tell them I was a very shy kid in high school. The best way to learn this is to try it. Learn about public speaking; volunteer and work with kids in your community such as teaching them art. Take a class on public speaking or read a book about it. If you are from another country, learn the English language as it will open doors for you. I have received jobs just because I was articulate and spoke properly. These things are very important, but it is something that is not addressed in some art schools.

4. *Self-Respect and Respect for Others:* If you have respect for yourself, others will respect you. There might come a time when you will be asked your opinion on a fellow artist and what you say can very well come back and bite you! Think before you speak and find respectful words to express disagreement with the other person. Stay away from gossip, especially in a studio setting. You never know who is listening. I worked in a studio where I made the mistake of criticizing someone's work when he was

not present and the very next day I was confronted by that person. Of course, what I said was made even worse by the people telling him what I had said. Tell the person yourself. Most artists welcome constructive criticism from their peers. The professional way to disagree with someone is to say you have "creative differences."

5. *Positive Mental Attitude:* I've come across students and other illustrators who have a negative attitude about almost everything around them. They defeat themselves before they get started. Most of it comes from listening to other negative people. If you told someone you were going to start a business tomorrow, one of the first things they will say to you is how hard it is or that 90% of businesses fail in the beginning. We live in a world full of negativity—just turn on the news. It is up to us to see the positive results in our mind and know that things will eventually be all right. See yourself as a successful illustrator and you will be blown away by the results. Stay focused on what you want to achieve.

6. *Think Outside the Box:* I have had success with this one! If everyone is doing things a certain way, it doesn't mean you need to do them that way. For example, when I was at the Art Institute of Boston in my freshman year, I heard about an internship position at an animation studio. I knew that students were mailing in their portfolios and that the studio had a table with a pile of work from everyone wanting in. I decided to visit the studio and deliver my portfolio in person. I rang the bell and a woman answered the door. I told her I was in the neighborhood and just wanted to drop off my work. As I was speaking to

her, I saw the president walk by, and lucky for me I knew that the company had recently won an Emmy. I congratulated the president and he struck up a conversation with me. I told him that I was trying out for the internship and he asked me if I could come back the following day. I ended up getting the internship by showing up and thinking differently than anyone else. Einstein once said, "We can't solve problems by using the same kind of thinking we used when we created them."

7. *Self-Promotion and Networking:* It is very important to promote your work and to market yourself. In the beginning of your career, you have to act as your own agent. Technology and the Internet have made it possible to reach all over, so the sky is the limit on this one. You can put up a free website with your work or a blog, upload a video of you drawing on YouTube or a slide show of your illustrations. I have received many jobs because someone saw my work on the Internet or they did a search for a storyboard artist and my name came up. I now have an agent for storyboard work, but 95% of my work has come from my connections that I have made through self-promotion or word of mouth. You should always have business cards ready. You could be on a train or at the supermarket and be next to someone who is looking for an artist. I once went to a party I did not want to attend but passed out my cards and got a job that lasted me for a year. All because I walked around, introduced myself to people and passed out my business cards.

8. *Research:* One important thing that I like to do before every job or client I might meet is research.

Before I do a storyboard job, I gather references of the artist and subject matter I will be working with. It saves a lot of time and stress when you have what you need in front of you. If I will be meeting a new client or working with a new company, I research and read up everything I can on them. It helps you communicate better and make better decisions.

9. *Give Back:* Giving is one of the most important things you will ever do. It is something we all need to do! You can give by donating your time and artwork. For me it encapsulates all the other key things I've talked about. When I donate art to charities, it's a perfect combination. I'm giving back and at the same time, I am getting exposure for my art and meeting other people who could potentially hire me. Another great way to give back is to mentor and teach others. Advise your peers. We will all see each other again in this industry; it's a small world.

10. *Be Flexible:* The best way to survive in this illustration market today is to be flexible. Like the ancient saying, "Be like water." For example, I went to school wanting to be an animator at Disney Studios. I studied animation. Disney started laying people off and many animation companies went overseas. So I took a comic book and storyboard class. While in school, I started doing storyboards for students at first to make extra cash. Eventually one music video led to another and now I make a living doing storyboards. You might start out wanting to be an illustrator, but it doesn't mean you can't end up doing concept art for movies or comic books and graphic novels, maybe even directing films. Kurosawa was a painter. James Cameron was an illustrator and also a truck driver. So

be open to changes and you will survive. I still draw caricatures for kids' parties or an occasional portrait or mural here and there; art is art. It's all practice!

I believe that if you work hard and believe in yourself you can achieve your goals no matter where you come from. Your environment or economic situation does not define who you are or will be. It doesn't matter if you come from a poor neighborhood or had a hard life, or if you don't speak English. We have all had to struggle! It's part of the human experience. It's easy to say my life was hard so I couldn't make it. I try to do every job that I get the best way I know how. I go the extra mile for my clients and it pays off because they only want to work with me. I also try to live an honest life and do what is right when it's easy to do the wrong thing. Another area of my life that I enjoy is giving back, raising money for charities and helping underprivileged kids. It really does come back tenfold. It's a great feeling when you can help others. That is the secret of success: "To give!" As far as the job market, the jobs are out there, no matter what they say about the economy. Illustrators will always be needed. We put image to word, whether with pencil or computer. We are the creators of worlds. We are the unsung folks of the movie world. Along with the directors, we put the film on paper before it is shot. How great is that? So, go out there and create your own luck and make your own path. Life is an adventure! Every day is an opportunity to learn. Teach and pay it forward.

On a closing note, I would like to thank L. Ron Hubbard and the Illustrators of the Future Contest. Thanks to all the judges of the Contest who are artists themselves and are at the top of their game. They are a wealth of information and experience. I still carry with me the advice that I received from them. The Illustrators of the Future Contest is more than a contest, it is truly a great opportunity that could very well change your life. The Contest gives you the tools to think outside the box and create a niche for yourself. They have given me the opportunity to express myself in the way I do best—drawing!

Unfamiliar Territory

written by

Ben Mann

illustrated by

ERIK JEAN SOLEM

ABOUT THE AUTHOR

Born in England to parents from the US and Australia, Ben Mann started life on the move. After time spent in the US, his family returned to Australia. His earliest memories would become daydreams of flying to far-off places, daydreams which changed forever the day he was introduced to C. S. Lewis.

Fantasy and science fiction opened worlds of wonder, in which he could fly to far-off places he'd never imagined, live adventures with people he'd never met and come back at the end of it all changed somehow. Creative writing became a childhood passion, but faced stiff competition: a comprehensive education would unearth passions throughout the arts, mathematics and the growing field of computing.

Following school, the joy of exploring his imagination would wane, overcome by the challenges of chasing a mortgage and raising a family. Ben's career in software engineering would lead him through a number of industries, ranging from the military and aviation to business and government. Despite the travel this entailed, that flying to far-off places, there was always something missing. It would take reading C. S. Lewis to his children one evening to realize what it was, pick up a pen and start writing again.

Ben currently lives in Western Australia with his wife, two children and a Labrador who eats homework.

ABOUT THE ILLUSTRATOR

Erik Jean Solem is native to San Francisco, California, returning to the city to live and go to college, after growing up in the tiny Rocky Mountain town of Ward, Colorado. He started drawing and making all kinds of other art when he was very young: detailed visions of ants' villages, pencils that came to life, insects of various kinds; then later, pages of ninjas, beautifully modeled clay horses, hands and other figures would appear in his room. An interested and engaged student, Erik's art has inspired several teachers to make extensive commentary on his work and give him encouragement.

Now studying for his bachelor of fine arts in illustration, his interests range from science fiction and fantasy environments to depictions of contemporary urban life he observes around him. The Rocky Mountains provide a compelling backdrop for Erik's imagination: growing up on the trails in the woods of the high country, learning to cope with harsh weather, the elements and the eccentrics of a former gold mining town who fiercely practice and protect their home rule status.

After graduating from high school, he happily adapted to the downtown intensities of San Francisco, where he walks to his classes on streets populated by vastly different wildlife, just as fascinating and worthy of his attention and rendering. Erik has received a portfolio grant from his school, the Academy of Art University. He was represented in his school's spring art show, and his deepening love for illustration combined with a fan's devotion to science fiction, fantasy and futuristic concepts led him to enter the Illustrators of the Future Contest.

Unfamiliar Territory

The rhythmic pounding of her boots against the distressed and weathered metal was a meditation, a way to put damaged spacecraft, stolen cargo and missing crew into perspective. Mira wiped her brow with the arm of her jumpsuit. At two thousand paces, she was completing her spinward circuit of the station's outer ring and only just starting to break a sweat. Amidst this vast spinning construction of metal, with its Coriolis force twisting at her inner ear, she felt at home.

Mira's jog ended at the hatch to the company's rented offices. As she swung past the Empire Freight Corporation placard and into the adjoining corridor, her jumpsuit's intercom buzzed to life.

"You're late," it said as she opened the door. Harlan looked up from his desk as she entered, releasing his finger from his console. "Or you were about to be." The company's director, thin from a life in low gravity, head shaved as much for convention as utility, waved her to a seat in the metal box he called his office. "Still wasting time running?"

"Hello to you too. And it's not wasted time; I don't get to run when I'm away."

"I don't know why you bother, Mira. You've not been back planet-side since you started." He rummaged through a stack of papers on his desk, pulled out an envelope and tossed it to her. "Speaking of which, here's a letter from your parents. When you write back, tell them to get online so I don't have to act as postmaster or I'm going to start taking a redirection fee from your salary." He looked up at her and squinted momentarily. "And get yourself a haircut."

Mira rubbed her stubbled scalp, frowning. "They won't listen. They want me home." She pocketed the envelope, unopened. "I doubt my hairstyle is why I'm here, either."

"No." Harlan turned his console's screen so they both could see it. "I have an assignment for you. I know it's only been a week since Jake."

Mira met Harlan's eyes. "I don't want to talk about it."

"It's not your fault, Mira. Accidents happen."

She turned to face the console screen. "You have a new engineer for me, then?"

Harlan gave her a sideways glance. "Yeah, we'll get to that." He brought up a schematic on the console. It showed a small craft, a modular construction designed solely to freight ore in from asteroid mining operations. Conspicuously absent was the massive sphere of minerals the freighter would propel. "This is the *Lumen*. It dropped out of the net yesterday on its return journey from the asteroid belt. We can't raise any response."

"Is it intact?"

"Yes. I requisitioned some imaging time and the observatory says it remains on course, one big IR reflector coasting right where it should be."

"Intercept time?"

"The thrusters' reaction mass is reloaded on the *Nyx* so your little tin can will make good time. The *Lumen* is Earthbound, so with a standard initial burn you will intercept in fourteen days."

"Okay," Mira said. Fourteen days wouldn't be too challenging. "So who's the engineer?"

Harlan stood and motioned for her to leave his office. "Follow me."

Mira stepped into the small anteroom serving as the *Nyx*'s loading bay, its air lock hatch the only indicator the shuttle was anywhere nearby. Harlan stepped in and shut the access hatch behind him. A young woman with shoulder-length hair stood waiting by the hatch, guarding a duffel bag. Her orange engineer's jumpsuit bore trainee's bars on its epaulettes.

"You've got to be kidding," Mira said.

Harlan flashed her a hard look. "This is Rose, your engineer for this job."

"Hi," Rose said, offering her hand.

Mira ignored it and turned to Harlan. "I want another engineer."

He shook his head. "The candidate we have won't be here in time."

"But she's a trainee, Harlan."

"Actually," Rose said, raising her hand. She paused, seemed to think better of it and lowered it again. "I'm an intern."

373

"Mira, the company needs this. Exposure to the education system will help Empire's recruiting for a long time to come. Training's not so hard; it's time to expand your skill set."

Mira turned to look at Rose. "You'll have to shave your head."

Rose blanched and began to protest, but Harlan cut her off. "No, Mira, she doesn't. Spacer convention won't apply in this case; she won't be here long enough. She can tie it up."

"Rose, do you know what our job is?"

Rose brightened. "Repairs and salvage. Getting disabled craft working again. I have certifications in vacuum welding and diagnosis and repair of spacecraft systems."

"How much was done in free fall?"

As Rose shifted her feet and looked at the floor, Harlan interrupted. "They don't do free fall training on the planet, Mira. This is her chance to learn."

"Rose, what's my job?" Mira asked.

"Security?"

Mira looked sideways at Harlan. Her jumpsuit was labeled Salvage Security. Was this new kid really this dense?

"I've gotta protect the talent," Mira said, "like engineers with shiny tools which any lowlife with a spacecraft will try to run off with. If the ship we're repairing is overrun with armed scavengers, what are you going to do? What's your major?"

"Design," Rose said in a small voice. "But I can't graduate without this."

Mira turned to Harlan with raised eyebrows.

"And what was your major?" he asked Mira in a

raised voice. "Ah, yes," he said, aiming a thin smile at Rose, "exobiology. And you dropped out of studying theoretical mumbo-jumbo to work here." Harlan turned to give Mira an iron stare. "Maybe you shouldn't argue qualifications."

Mira ground her teeth. "When do we leave?"

"Now. I've had your away kit transferred onto the *Nyx* already." He thumbed the air lock controls and the door slid open silently. "Show me you're ready for a new engineer, Mira. This is your chance." He waved them in, then turned and left.

Rose turned to Mira and cocked her head to one side. "Where's your old engineer?"

Mira wished she could forget the last two weeks. Rose kept repeating the same questions: How had Jake died? How long had she been in space? Would Mira please stop making grunting noises when exercising? How many people had she killed? The questions inevitably ended at the unanswerable one: What was wrong with the *Lumen*?

Now, Rose was refusing to suit up.

Taking advantage of the pseudo-gravity of the *Nyx*'s final deceleration, Mira climbed down to the hold. Beginning to work through the routine preparations for a salvage job, she slipped into her gray armored suit.

"I'm not coming down," said Rose through the access hatch. "No one told me there would be dead people."

Mira leaned her head against the hold's lockers. "We don't know that, Rose. That's exactly the point. We don't know what to expect."

Mira opened her weapons locker. Her eyes flicked

over the dozen unopened letters and photo of an old, familiar orchard onto the tools of her trade. A nickel-plated handgun, a battered but serviceable machine pistol and several dozen rounds of nonstandard, high-powered ammunition were locked in place by elastic foam.

"You're going to use guns on a spacecraft?" asked Rose.

Mira turned to see she'd made her way down to the hold and was standing behind her. "Did you miss a class in grade school, Rose?" Mira strapped the guns to her suit.

The *Nyx* finished its burn with the ping of the maneuvering alarm and a jolt as the shuttle reentered free fall. As Rose grabbed at a handhold, Mira only bounced in place, her left foot already hooked beneath the weapons cabinet.

"No, I know about piracy," Rose said, stabilizing herself, "and that spacecraft carry defenses. I guess I never realized how real it was."

"It's why my job exists, Rose. Pirates don't play around once they find a company freighter coasting with no power. They aren't going to throw bouquets at you when you try and recover the company's equipment; they're going to fight to the death. Which is why," she said, pausing with her helmet ready, "you need your suit on. Decompression is not fun."

Her helmet sealed to the suit and she heard the quiet whine of the suit's reactor spinning up, its nanofibers flexing briefly all over her body as it powered on. Mira keyed the suit's intercom.

"I'm not going to wait for you," Mira said, her

voice reverberating inside the helmet's small space. Rose appeared lost in thought. "I've got a job to do and I'm going to get started. I expect you to be suited and ready to carry out repairs once I've announced the all-clear."

Rose shook her head and covered her face with her hands.

Mira frowned and slapped the air lock control, watching the access door open for her. Harlan knew she was no mentor. The only motivational technique she knew involved her trigger finger. Convincing Rose to suit up and leave her comfort zone wasn't in Mira's repertoire.

What she could do, however, was do her own job.

I'm aboard," Mira said, keying her intercom.

"Aboard," said Rose's voice in the earpiece. There was a shared silence before she spoke again. "What's happened?"

It took a moment before the dim scene this side of the closed air lock registered. Similar to the *Nyx,* the freighter was comprised of several windowless, cylindrical modules stacked end to end. The opposite side of the tiny cabin would normally feature bunks folded into its inner hull surface, but in their place now, amplified by the inky blackness of the unpowered living quarters, was a circular opening washed in stars. With the freighter's orientation stabilized by the *Nyx,* the starlight illuminated the cabin in a cold, steady gray light.

"Hang on," said Mira, turning on her auxiliary suit lights.

The cabin was clean. The gaping hole in the hull would have drawn out any loose contents, including the crew. The secured equipment, the navigation console, fixed furnishing and suits strapped next to the air lock all remained. In the absence of the daily clutter of life, it looked freshly commissioned.

Mira connected her tether to the inside of the air lock door and launched toward the gaping aperture on the opposite side. The hole ruled out a collision, but the valuable equipment that remained ruled out piracy.

She reached the edge of the hole and caught the lip with both hands, her legs continuing out into space, spinning her to allow an examination of its surface.

The edge of the hole scraped on Mira's armored glove. This didn't look like a hasty job. There was no obvious pitting or ablation from a welding laser, no scarring from a mechanical grinder, no tearing or burning of the sandwiched insulating material. The hole appeared to be a perfectly round circle. It was unlikely pirates would do such a clean job.

Mira followed her hand around its circumference. Earth's superpowers fielded only a token military fleet for political grandstanding. If this had been a military mission, there was no danger of further traps; a military operation would either have destroyed the *Lumen* completely or taken what they wanted and left her to rot.

Mira released more tether, floated out and away from the *Lumen* for an exterior view. "You'll need to make three hull repairs, Rose."

The three cylindrical modules of the *Lumen* hung

below her in the shade of the freighter's massive ore load: crew quarters, reactor and engine. Each bore an identical gaping circular hole, transforming the freighter into a full-scale cutaway model. Whoever had disabled the *Lumen* and killed or abducted her crew was long gone.

Mira paused over the *Nyx*'s console, unsure how to complete her salvage report's final question.

Cause:

Rose's voice chirped through the intercom. "Those poor people."

"That's why they pay big out here, sweetheart," Mira said, keying the console's microphone. Rose might be having second thoughts about life in space, but at least she was carrying out the repairs.

The console chimed with a communications message. Mira groaned, paused her report and played the message.

Though tinny and distorted, Harlan's voice was instantly recognizable.

"Mira, I realize you're repairing the *Lumen;* however, a situation has come up."

Mira grimaced.

"Another Earthbound freighter, the *Crucible,* has gone off the grid. This puts us in a bad situation, because if we can't transport freight securely we're going to start losing contracts. She's not too far from where you are now, about two days' standard burn homewards. Matters are further complicated because we only expected Rose to work one salvage job.

"So start a hard burn back here and drop off the

rookie. Pick up your new engineer and then hard burn back out for repairs before *Crucible* has to slot into Earth orbit. The schedule's tight, so hustle." The intercom pinged, announcing the end of the message.

Mira sighed and pulled her report back up on the console. Her hands paused over the keys. The company would want a definitive answer. With cargo and fixings still present on the *Lumen,* the only thing worth pirating would have to have been unlisted. The company would be even less receptive of smuggling.

But, whether ejected by decompression or abducted, the crew were gone and the ship had been cut open. She tapped in the only answer she was prepared to settle on.

Piracy

It wouldn't be a popular conclusion. No doubt the company assessors would find a cleaner explanation for their final report. But they had their job and Mira had hers. And hers wasn't political.

"All done," said Rose through the personal address system. "It was only superficial damage. I've powered the *Lumen* up and it's ready to separate." The intercom went silent for a moment before crackling to life again. "Do you think they're dead?"

Mira sniggered. Rose could repair a freighter, but she still needed a dose of real life. She opened up a reply to Harlan's message. A little more work experience wasn't going to hurt.

"Harlan, we'll do the new job on the way back. Send us a course to the *Crucible*."

The final gentle burn toward the *Crucible* passed in familiar routine. Mira checked her equipment and suited up, the rustling of Rose doing the same behind her making for a quiet, white-noise duet.

According to Harlan's report on the *Crucible,* two days ago the freighter was carrying out routine maintenance on a misaligned cargo linkage. Misaligned linkages were about as mild as problems got in the freight business. Most crews would be more worried about a blown lamp in the cabin.

Rose broke the mood.

"I want to come out with you on the sweep."

Mira stopped what she was doing. She realized she had been fitting the handgun to her suit and finished its last clasp. She turned to Rose slowly.

Rose was fully suited, helmet on. Her expression behind the cleared visor was hard, pained.

"That's out of the question."

"I don't want to be afraid any longer. I want to be there. If there's nothing wrong, I can start repairs immediately."

The shuttle's maneuvering alarm sounded and the sharp loss of gravity launched Rose into the open space of the hold. Mira tensed her foot to remain in her habitual position by the weapons locker.

"Just do the job, Rose," Mira said, watching Rose catch on a handhold and spin to hang upside down in front of her. "The job isn't to get the *Crucible* fixed quickly; it's to protect company interests. That means fewer resources lost, which means you stay here until I say it's safe."

"Company, company, job, job, company." Rose's

381

head wagged side to side inside her helmet as she spoke. "That's not living."

"If that's your best argument, then I think the point is settled."

"Don't you even care, Mira?"

"Just do your job," Mira said, punching the air lock panel and pulling herself through. "Five minutes."

"Five minutes," came Rose's disembodied voice in the headset as the hatch closed. "I don't have to like it though."

"Most people don't. That's the whole attraction." Mira felt her suit pull tight, countering the sudden drop in pressure as the air lock cycled.

Mira's headlamp illuminated the opening door, revealing a light spray of gleaming particles erupting from the gap. She had seen this before, a signal of what remained on board the damaged freighter.

"This isn't going to be pretty, Rose."

As the stream of particles slowly ebbed, Mira spun the manual air lock release as fast as she could. For all her effort, the unpowered hatch slid aside with agonizing slowness.

"I'm not sure I want to know," Rose said, her voice quiet in the earpiece.

Ochre dust fogged the hold, glinting silver where it crossed the suit's lamplight. Equipment racks ringing it were in various states of access, some locked closed and others open with tools splayed about. On the other side of the hold Mira made out a rack of suits.

"Only two suits are in the hold, Rose, but the job data said there were three crew. There are several crew modules here; I'm going to have a look through them."

"Hart, Remington and Kendrick," Rose said, her

tinny voice seeming somehow thinner, isolated. "Good luck."

The living space held two bodies in regular transit jumpsuits. One was strapped to the navigation console seat, the other tangled in exercise webbing. Mira tried not to look at the frozen gore beneath the suits, the mangled, gray-blue human shapes. The navigation computer and other potentially valuable equipment were all present and accounted for.

The cramped sleeping quarters on the other side of the craft held no third crewman. A circular portal cut into the hull revealed the dark, featureless cylinder of the *Nyx* outside.

Mira tethered to the cabin's entry and gently launched out of the *Crucible*.

The *Crucible*'s massive ore load, a huge mineral sphere which dwarfed the craft, appeared as a dim disk blocking the sun and swallowing a hemisphere of stars. In its shadow, the only light was a starry ambience reflected where distant cranes and tensors holding the cargo extended out and caught a few rays of light. The dimness rendered the two craft colorless, gray shadows floating silently among the stars, one whole and the other maimed.

Mira looked the *Crucible* over. A higher-capacity ship than the *Lumen,* her reactors and engine cluster were both significantly more substantial. Both modules also now had nonstandard dark circular patches on their hulls.

Mira keyed her intercom. "The damage is the same as the *Lumen,* Rose, but it's on the same side as the *Nyx*. Go ahead and separate and set the shuttle to a station-keeping position."

Mira retracted her tether and drew herself back into the *Crucible*'s cabin. She felt the nudge of the shuttle's separation through her handholds in the freighter's living space. The bodies of the two crewmen bounced elastically in their restraints.

Kendrick and Remington, their badges read. Frozen into awkward poses, she wasn't going to be able to bag them as they were. Forcing herself to look away, she removed the utility knife and body bags from her suit. She closed her eyes and sought focus.

She had to get it done.

A cut here, another there. Sawing, the snap of bone. Mira planned each separation, dispassionately watching the first crewman come apart. In her eyes, in the cold darkness, he became a blue-gray papier-mâché mannequin, brittle and fragile, jarring involuntarily beneath her manipulation.

It was disconcerting how little time passed before she bagged the last of the remains.

Sealing the bag, Mira looked about the cabin. Absent the bodies, it appeared truly lifeless now. The room flickered silver.

"How could you?" asked Rose, her voice hollow in Mira's earpiece. Mira turned to see Rose anchored outside the cabin's gaping opening, her face silhouetted by her suit lights, hidden beneath the reflections in her visor. Reflections of Mira holding a knife and two body bags.

"It's what has to be done," Mira said, her voice cracking. Rose pushed off and floated out of view, leaving a panorama of stars and the now-distant *Nyx*.

There was no reply.

Mira sat facing the console again, alone in the hold. The majority of the report was complete, a count of the deceased, state of the freighter, resources used. Now, the same bothersome question begged for a response.

Cause:

The answer should be the same, but she couldn't bring herself to type it. Piracy was just another predictable element to life in space. On reflection, the unexpected had always become understandable. But the *Lumen* had gone off the grid sixteen days ago, the *Crucible* only two. And they were practically on the same city block of the solar system. If they were attacked by pirates, where had they been hiding these last two weeks?

She keyed in her answer. The insurance guys were going to have a field day.

Unknown.

The intercom crackled to life with Rose's voice. "Mira, I may need your help out here."

Mira sent the report. Harlan could chew over the *Crucible*'s story while she dealt with whatever trouble Rose had found for herself. At least she'd remained suited.

"Go ahead."

"You only found two bodies in the cabin, right?"

"Yes."

"There's a tether anchored off the *Crucible*'s crew module. I can't quite make it out with my lamps, but it looks like there's a suit at the end of it, wedged high up in the cargo frame."

Mira pushed away from the console, retrieved her helmet and headed over to the supply cabinet.

385

"I'll be out in a moment," she said. A fresh body bag rustled cleanly in her gloves. Hopefully this would be an easier job.

"Can you believe we found a survivor, Mira?"

"It's not possible." The air lock finished its cycle and Mira launched out on the station-keeping guy wires toward the *Crucible*. Perhaps she had been an optimist too, once, but life in space had delivered a colder reality.

"I got him loose," said Rose.

The suit was faintly visible during the crossing to the *Crucible,* a gray shape descending toward the freighter from a distant edge of the cargo's visible disk. Rose appeared to have anchored to the cylindrical hull and tried to haul the crewman in by hand. She was pulling far too hard, accelerating the corpse even now. If it hit Rose and the hull at that speed, Mira would never be able to recover the pieces.

"Rose, stop."

Even as she said it, Mira was already in motion, heading toward where Rose was tethered. She wasn't ready to lose another engineer.

Rose was standing on the skin of the freighter, braced against her tether. In her hands, she held the slackening cable of the descending crewman. Mira caught hold of the anchor loop, quickly clasped her tether alongside the other two and spun around to brace her legs against the hull.

"Give me the tether," Mira said. Rose handed her the crewman's limp cable. Slapping her own tether's limiter to full length, Mira looked up toward the descending suit.

ERIK JEAN SOLEM

The crewman was clearly visible now, his blanked visor reflecting Mira and Rose's suit lights. Rose had managed to keep his tether from slackening completely. It made a lazy arc toward his approaching form. Mira took aim just off-side him and jumped as hard as she could.

The loose tether fed through a loop she made with her right arm, its low mass and substantial free length keeping her on course. It took mere seconds to reach and then pass the crewman. As he passed through her lamplight she saw his suit clearly for the first time, the usual engineer's orange, but fitted with a substantial harness for long-distance tether work.

As the tether tightened and shifted in Mira's arm, she abruptly snaked her arm around it, creating a brake. Locked, she was ready for the moment when both bodies, moving in opposite directions, snapped tight.

It came with a pop and an intense flare of pain, Mira's body swinging out against her arm. She let out an involuntary yelp.

Rose's voice was strained. "Mira?"

The wrapped arm was pulled out at an awkward angle from her shoulder. Mira tried twisting around to release the tether from her arm, but she was locked in place. She tried flexing the fingers on her right hand, but they stayed closed, a painful cramp spreading in her hand.

"Rose," she said, "pull us in. Very slowly this time."

"Okay."

"We'll both need help getting back to the *Nyx*."

Rose removed her helmet after the air lock door sealed and let it float away. "What can I do?" she asked.

Mira saw her arm brush against the interior wall of the hull, devoid of sensation. The *Crucible*'s crewman spun slowly on the other side of the hold. Mira shuddered. He'd go into the freezer later. Removing her helmet with her free hand, she tried to move her head.

"I think it's a dislocated shoulder. You need to pop it back into place."

Rose looked horrified. She didn't move.

"Do it, Rose. Now. It's numb, so I won't be able to feel anything."

"I can't. Are you sure?"

"If you don't do anything, I'll be worse off. Grab my wrist. Good. Now brace yourself around my shoulder with your knees."

Mira shut her eyes as the cabin spun around, her body reorienting with Rose's manipulations.

"Good. Now pull the arm out."

"Mira, no."

"Do it, Rose. Pull."

"Please."

"Pull, damn you. What the hell are you doing? Don't let go. Do you know how many engineers survive this job? Precious few, because when the going gets tough, they curl up and suck their thumbs."

"But I can't do it."

"Do you know why they send you out here before you can graduate? To learn the reality of what you build. This is it. Time to face reality, princess." Mira

389

heard a grunt of protest, felt the pressure against her side increase as Rose shifted position. "That's better, get a good grip. Now pull."

"What if it doesn't work?"

The hold's console chimed to announce a new comms message. Mira ignored it. "Pull it. Harder. Damn it, try and pull it out."

Accompanying Rose's rising scream, a sucking, tearing sound marked the realignment of Mira's shoulder. A flare of pain announced circulation and nerves coming back to life, offset by the relieved pressure on Mira's collarbone.

Rose screamed hysterically and released Mira's arm.

Mira clenched her teeth against the fire spreading from her shoulder and flexed her hand experimentally, giving Rose a thumbs-up with her good hand. Amid the sharp tingling of returning blood flow, it moved, but only a little. Rose would need to take over for a few hours.

Mira nodded at the console. Rose moved to it with a shudder and brought up the message with shaky hands. Harlan's voice eventually buzzed out of the intercom speakers.

"Mira, I've passed your reports on, but don't expect them to be popular. You're clear for early return with the *Crucible* crew's remains. Traffic control says your current return trajectory intersects with a United Mining support vessel in your area. It'll add an extra day, but I'm giving you an alternate course to loop out and around them on your way back."

Harlan paused, the white-noise background of his office continuing to play. "There's a lot of space out there. The chances our unusual pirate friends are on an identical course is nearly zero. But if they are, this trajectory will avoid them as well." The message cut out.

"What's a support vessel?" asked Rose.

"It's a frigate. United Mining uses a private military as insurance against piracy."

She looked at Rose, who had turned to stare absently at the crewman. How pleasant it must be, she thought, to not have been exposed to the reality of business. Rose didn't need to know. Perhaps in not telling her the full meaning of Harlan's response, that the company would be secretly hoping a competitor's frigate would come to grief, Rose could harbor a little innocence for the both of them.

Mira turned to follow Rose's stare, to the engineering equipment and crewman's suit bobbing about on the other side of the hold.

Mira jumped to his position, catching and anchoring herself with her good arm. She turned the suit around, wincing at her right shoulder as she pulled him to a halt. Its arm moved.

The suit's visor was glossy black, perhaps the result of having been blanked while the crewman was welding the *Crucible*'s damaged cargo linkage. The suit's badge, embroidered with the ship's name and designation, showed the crewman's name: Hart. Mira pressed a control on the chin of the helmet.

The visor flickered translucent, revealing a pale face, heavily bloodshot eyes blinking fiercely into the sudden light. Barely visible wisps of gray hair puffed forward across a male forehead, and a few days' worth of white stubble had etched its way across his chin. His jaw was working, its chapped, broken lips forming silent words.

Swearing, Mira found the clasp for his helmet and reached around with her good arm to remove it gently.

"Is he . . . ?" Rose said. She moved to a position behind Mira.

"Get water," Mira said.

A burp of foul air found its way around the seals of Hart's suit and into the hold's atmosphere. Mira gritted her teeth and tried to take shallow breaths.

Rose arrived and handed her a canteen. She appeared genuinely concerned, serious, transformed from her earlier hysteria into a regular Florence Nightingale. Mira handed the canteen back, shaking her head.

"No, you do it, Rose," Mira said, releasing Hart. "Take him up to the shower, get him out of that suit and clean him up." A look at Rose's concerned expression helped make her decision. "I have something to do."

As Rose gently tugged Hart and moved him up through the bulkhead door into the cabin, Mira found her way back to the navigation console. Ten days would be too long. Even if she burned the *Nyx*'s remaining reaction mass, the shortest route back to the station would take several days. If Hart had been exposed to enough radiation while dangling on his tether, he wouldn't last two.

Mira keyed up the communications system and started a new message.

The United frigate, fully equipped with a medical

center, intersected somewhere along her shortest route. Harlan had wanted her to leave it alone and for good reason, besides the obvious business motivations. An old shipping code of ethics which once guaranteed aid regardless of corporate affiliation was ancient history, forever changed by the growing threat of piracy.

Mira hoped she would be able to pay whatever price they placed on their hospitality.

Mira sat in the pseudo-gravity of the shuttle's thrust and watched silently for a moment as Hart snored in an elastic bunk.

"Do you think he'll make it?" Rose asked. She'd become detached, Mira thought, much less the bright-eyed undergraduate that joined her two weeks ago. It was a change she had secretly longed for and now that it had arrived, regretted; innocence was lost to both of them.

"Yeah, about that. It's not too late to change our minds, but I've set us a new course." Mira looked at Rose and winced. "If you really want to, we can return to the station as Harlan instructed. But we can make a choice. To go home will take over a week even if we don't avoid the United frigate. It will be several more days' journey than this guy—" Mira nodded at Hart "—can survive."

"Our alternative is not to go home at all. Protocol obliges United to render assistance. Their frigate will have medical facilities and will be the only vessel large enough to help between here and Earth."

"What does Harlan say?"

Mira shrugged. "I didn't ask him. I was planning on telling him once we had no way out."

"That's not like you," Rose said, smiling. "What happened to company and job? It's not going to go over well."

"Hart's here because of you, not him, so it's not his decision." Mira sat back and gave Rose what she hoped was a hard stare. "I want it to be yours. We're early enough in the burn that the navigation computer can compensate and put us back on Harlan's course to the station. What do you want to do?"

Rose turned and looked at Hart, snoring peacefully in the bunk. Color had returned to his lips and the hollows under his eyes no longer appeared blue, but his appearance was still pallid, the spacer hue of pale white and distinctive veins. She sat up straight, squared her shoulders and turned back to Mira.

"Save him."

Mira twisted her face into a wry smile. "I thought you'd say that." A month ago she would have put Hart on ice and returned to the station without a second thought.

"How long will it take to reach the United ship?" Rose asked.

"I can't be sure. We'll know when they hail us." Which they would. The militant wing of a primary competitor wouldn't take kindly to their paths crossing.

The message came the moment Mira had finally found a comfortable position in which to rest. As she went about the familiar procedure of unclasping the elastic cot wrapped around her, she watched Rose and Hart sleep through the bleating communications alarm. It had been a long time since she had slept deeply enough to tune out the ship's sighs, groans and calls.

Wincing at the lingering pain in her shoulder, Mira clambered over to the console and opened the waiting message.

An accented male voice rang from the console speakers. "Empire salvage vessel, this is United Mining security vessel *Prophet*. Your current trajectory intersects our restricted buffer. Alter course immediately." The message's "acknowledge" command blinked, signifying her expected response.

Mira strapped into the console seat, switched the console to its navigation mode and instructed the computer to commence an immediate deceleration. Though familiar with freefall maneuvering, Mira nonetheless felt a surge of nausea as the *Nyx* rapidly pivoted in place. Reoriented, it began its deceleration burn.

Harlan would have words with her about the indiscretion of burning so much reaction mass on this little escapade. That much was certain.

She brought the communications console back up, located the *Prophet*'s communication details and started her response.

"*Prophet,* this is Empire salvage shuttle *Nyx*. We have a medical emergency and request immediate assistance."

She sent the message. To have warranted a warning message, the *Prophet* was close enough that her response would be received immediately. She waited, counting out the time in her head. Any substantial delay would mean they needed to think about it.

The answer when it came was hesitant and deliberate.

"Empire salvage shuttle, we are unable to assist you at this time. Please modify your course."

Mira keyed her microphone immediately.

"*Prophet,* we have informed Empire of our intention to seek your aid. We request aid as guaranteed under our mutual shipping protocols." She sent her message with a violent stab at the communications terminal.

Harlan was going to have conniptions.

The response this time was delayed significantly. When it came, a different speaker, a resigned, unaccented voice, gave the shuttle clearance and details for navigating to its rendezvous with the frigate.

Mira muted the communications console. If they changed their mind now, she didn't want to know about it. She punched the navigation course through the console and grimaced. Bound for the asteroid belt, the *Prophet* was only two hours away on the *Nyx*'s hardest burn.

She glanced at Rose and Hart in their bunks. Hart's breathing was labored in the thrust's pseudo-gravity; he remained pale. In contrast, Rose's cheeks were flushed with warmth and her lips were pulled into a smile.

Mira massaged her scalp, numb with fatigue. Sleep was tempting, but in two hours she needed to do more than only face the crew of a United Mining ship. She needed to work out why she was acting against years of habit.

Mira swung away from them in a sudden flash of rage, a burning heat in her veins temporarily dispelling her exhaustion. She wanted to scream. Spacers were on their own, should be on their own. That was the nature of space, the nature of the job. It was how it always had been and everyone out here knew it.

Directing her anger and the fire in her shoulder into action, Mira climbed unsteadily down the ladder to the hold. Her suit and equipment were locked away where she'd placed them after sorting out Hart.

The *Nyx* was her shuttle, her home. At least it was now that Jake was gone. Now there was an engineer who knew what it meant to be a spacer. Together they had always completed the job and accepted the risks, no matter the cost. People had died, but spacers always died and the job still needed doing. And it was her job now. The responsibility rested on her shoulders and she would have to do it for the both of them.

Mira ejected the magazine from her handgun and absentmindedly rolled its topmost round with her thumb. It made a dull, threatening noise as it scraped the housing.

Her problem, she realized, wasn't really Rose or Hart. Rose was no spacer, and Hart should probably be dead, but that wasn't what hurt. It was the situation. Everything was different. Rose was playing by different rules. Different rules which forced Mira to question years of life-and-death decisions. Mira didn't want guilt or the paralysis of doubt. No, the job and the harsh realities of spacer life were clear. She'd been living it long enough.

Mira's breath caught in her throat briefly. Why was

she sending the *Nyx* to meet some damned United crew? No one ever crossed company lines anymore; no one had called on the mutual aid protocol in years. People set foot on her ship purely at her discretion. Mira tapped the unloaded gun against her head in frustration.

It was time to make a choice. She could give in, board the United ship and break all the rules she'd come to accept, or she could clear the board, bringing a hard stop to it and show she remained in control, the rules be damned. Both solutions would upset the boss, but she had to act.

Mira flipped over the pistol, reloaded the magazine and strode back to the ladder. She'd be damned if some wet rookie and a half-dead spacer were going to ruin her career and get away with it.

Mira emerged into the cabin to find the engineer and crewman still sleeping. Rose had turned over in her straps, facing away from her, her head hidden by a tangle of hair. Mira raised the pistol at the mess of hair, thumbed the laser sight.

There was another option, but this was the easy one, right? In the last four years she had shot and killed thirteen people. There was good reason. She filed all the paperwork and no one complained. Twelve were pirates, armed scavengers trying to strip Empire equipment before it could be officially salvaged. One was a survivor, fatally wounded already by a reactor accident and in more pain than her first aid kit could deal with. He knew what was happening. He even begged for it.

The cold metal of the trigger was warm beneath

her finger. All she had to do was pull, turn to Hart and pull again. Her problems would be gone.

Yet how could she? Explaining it wasn't the problem. The sleeping face, serene and unworried, was her, somehow, a shadow of the person she could never be again.

An unfamiliar wave of guilt turned her stomach. Mira released the trigger and thumbed the safety on. She'd have to resolve this the hard way.

She turned to Rose's suit, discarded beneath her cot. Strapped to the orange fabric of its legs were the box-shaped pouches dedicated to holding Rose's personal tools. Mira opened one, removed a bulky sublimation iron and inserted the pistol in its place.

United would know of Mira and the threat she represented. But a rookie unweathered by serious time in space would be another matter. Her lack of experience would also make United assume only a weak allegiance to Empire. With luck the *Prophet's* crew would disarm Mira but ignore her new crewmate. Should the situation turn bad, at least she would be armed.

Mira's heart thudded as she clasped the pouch shut and descended to the hold to place the iron amongst her tools. Her hand rested against the machine pistol, strapped in place in the cabinet. Inspecting it, she once again slipped into an automatic, meditative trance, disassembling the gun and checking the parts, removing a jot of residue here, applying a dab of lubricant there. It didn't matter that she hadn't used the gun since its last inspection; it focused her mind, this automated motion of her hands.

The routine promised stability. Yet even so, deep inside, a fear of vain routine and empty promises grew and tugged at her heart.

The shuttle's thrusters sputtered, shifting the deceleration rate and announcing the beginning of their final docking maneuvers. Mira had lost count of the number of times she had disassembled and reassembled the machine pistol. A glance at Rose's sublimation iron protruding from a tray of the weapons locker brought about a skipped heartbeat, a cold flush at her cheeks. She pushed it deeper, closed the cabinet and ascended to the crew compartment. She needed to get Rose busy.

Rose was already out of her bunk, examining the spacer. Hart appeared to be nearing death, his skin now an ashen gray. Mira handed her one of the *Nyx*'s spare suits.

"Get it on him," Mira said.

At the sound of her voice, Hart's eyes snapped open, turned and locked on her.

"You can't stop it," he said.

"We can't stop what?" Mira asked.

He seemed to stop and think about this for a moment, before knitting his eyebrows together and glancing around the cabin. "Where am I?"

The shuttle's thrusters chose that moment to cut out altogether and the cabin returned to free fall. As if on cue, Hart closed his eyes and his breathing fell into a rattling, steady rhythm.

"He's asleep," said Rose, bouncing into the air, one hand holding a support bar by Hart's cot.

Mira rolled her eyes. Only a couple of minutes remained before the shuttle docked with the *Prophet*. She pushed off and made her way down to the hold. It was game time.

The communications console gave a plaintive chime as she reactivated it, sealing her suit around her. Four outstanding messages from Harlan waited, blinking patiently.

Mira ignored them and hailed the *Prophet* as the shuttle's thrusters kicked in and out, settling them against the other craft. The crewman who answered sounded positively cheerful.

"Empire shuttle, welcome to United Mining support vessel *Prophet*. Please come aboard when you're ready."

Mira raised her eyebrows and turned to Rose.

"I thought they didn't like us," Rose said, sealing her suit.

"They don't."

"They could have changed their minds."

"No, they couldn't have. Get your helmet on and let's find out what they're playing at." Mira donned hers. "Because either way, we're here." She fingered the strap on her machine pistol.

Floating inside the air lock, Mira slowed her breathing and listened to her suit, waiting for it to stiffen and pop should the pressure suddenly change.

Instead, the exterior door slid open. Locked open, the *Prophet*'s air lock revealed a clear view into its hold.

The faces staring through at her confirmed that the *Prophet*'s crew were typical spacers, pale, gaunt and bald. Each of the three arrayed around the frigate's inner air lock hatch bore the same wry grin. Two were dressed in casual uniforms. The third wore his blue armored pressure suit unsealed, its helmet strapped to his back.

Each was armed.

"A weapon will not be necessary," the suited spacer said, his voice loud and crisp with authority. The sound echoed in Mira's ear, both amplified by her suit and transmitted by the ship's atmosphere between them. He waved a handgun at Mira. "Take it off and pass it through. Helmets off too."

"My weapon's a part of my uniform," Mira said, removing her helmet and clasping it to her suit. She nodded for Rose to do the same.

"Then leave." The spacer's smile widened.

Mira turned to Rose, whose furrowed brow and wide eyes were frozen into place behind her visor. Hart floated upside down next to her, unconscious, oblivious to the situation.

"Oh, fine." Mira unstrapped the machine pistol and tossed it gently to him. "Come on, Rose," she said, removing her helmet. "Let's get your boyfriend seen to before this whole trip proves a waste of time."

One of the spacers appeared to be the *Prophet*'s medic. As Rose towed Hart through the air lock into the *Prophet*'s hold, he took over. After first removing Hart's helmet and giving his vitals a cursory check, he left, towing Hart through one of several hatches into another part of the frigate.

What Mira could see of the *Prophet* was impressive. The hold's interior was a yawning cavern. Embedded with doors and shutters promising hidden storage, the ship would have a very substantial cross-section.

Finished in formed beige plastics, it made the tired and battered metal of the *Nyx* appear antiquated. The implication that United designed its ships, rather than assembling them out of inexpensive mass-produced modules, suggested more wealth than Mira was comfortable speculating.

"I'm Mira. This is Rose, my salvage engineer." She noticed the spacers hadn't holstered their weapons.

The *Prophet*'s spokesman glanced at Rose for only a moment. He snorted derisively. "Smells green. New recruit?"

"Intern," she said. A badge on his suit named him Warren.

"Figures," Warren said, giving Mira a hard stare, "but with twenty crew I'm not going to introduce you to everyone. Boss wants you to sit tight in the decontamination bay until Doc is done with your boy." He holstered his handgun and waved Mira's machine pistol. "Follow me."

Tailed by the remaining United crewman, Mira and Rose followed Warren through the same hatch the medic had used for Hart. The hatch opened onto a tubular, fluted access corridor that extended some fifty or sixty meters distant. Multiple access hatches were studded in rows along the corridor, and it was through one of these that Warren swung, followed closely by Mira and Rose. Mira caught one of several webbed seats studded around one side of the room.

"Boss will be down shortly," Warren said.

Mira tilted her head and raised an eyebrow. "I know you're not happy to have guests."

"You don't know nothing," Warren said. He

403

resumed his grin and waved off his colleague floating by the chamber's hatch. "Make yourselves at home. I'll stick around until Boss gets here."

"And my firearm?"

Warren smiled and patted it. "Who knows?"

They didn't have long to wait. Mira was settling into one of the bay's seats when a new crewman bounced into the room and wrapped himself around the seat next to Rose.

Tall and muscular, he imposed upon the room, shrinking its proportions in comparison. He wore a blue pressure suit similar to Warren's, lacking only the armor panels. Rather than the shaved head of a typical spacer, he maintained a short but thick black Mohawk. His smile seemed genuine, amplified by glittering eyes.

Mira had never seen a spacer like him.

"I see Warren settled you in, Mira, Rose." He nodded at each of them in turn. "I'm Deboss, the first officer."

"I thought the boss was coming," said Rose. Mira tried to stifle an involuntary laugh.

"No, that's me. The captain they call "sir." But that's all very much beside the point. I thought you'd like to know how your man is coming."

Mira saw Rose perk up at the offer. Deboss acknowledged her with an easy smile.

"Your crewman will be fine. He's sedated in the infirmary on the other side of the access corridor here. He's suffering mild radiation exposure and our medic is giving him a transfusion. He will be ready for your trip home in short order."

"You sedated him?" asked Mira. "He wasn't even conscious."

Deboss grinned and made a dismissive gesture. "What I'm really interested in, Mira, is something else."

Faster than she could hope to react, he reached out and grabbed Rose, turned her in her webbing and unclasped the engineering pouch. Trapped in indecision about why she was even here, Mira was unable to recognize the signals until too late. She was too slow to stop him.

Holding her handgun with an air of calm confidence, the glint in his eyes took on a new meaning.

"I'd love to know why an intern engineer is carrying a sidearm," Deboss said. The gun pointed first at Rose, then swung over to Mira. Braced against the bottom of her seat, she realized how futile her situation had become. She couldn't possibly reach him in time.

"Or maybe," continued Deboss, switching his gaze from Mira to Rose and back, "the engineer doesn't know anything."

Mira felt her shoulders slump. This wasn't how it was supposed to go at all.

"Maybe Empire can't afford to fit out its ships with basic security, but we're not so ill-equipped here. We imaged the three of you when you came aboard. So tell me, Mira." He waved the pistol at her again. "If you only wanted medical aid, why would you board us with a concealed weapon?"

Mira started to reply, wanted to say "for self defense," but found she couldn't. It wasn't really true, was it? She caught her hands shaking, pressed them still. No, the gun had been a way out, an escape. As Rose turned to face her with wide eyes, Mira looked away, biting her lip.

"I'm also curious to know why you lied to us about having called Empire," he said. "We checked, of course, and somewhere out there our people talked to your people, got your names and details and we heard that you'd made no change to your posted flight plan. It's a little unusual, wouldn't you agree?"

There was no right answer now, no plan. It was time to find a new starting point. Mira raised her head and furnished him with a quiet stare.

"You'll appreciate the irony," said Deboss. "We launched this ship only a month ago. United designed it with a single purpose: the eradication of piracy on mineral transportation. How fortuitous it is then that we capture a pair of pirates on our maiden voyage."

Mira laughed and shook her head.

"Tell him, Mira," said Rose. She waited for Mira to respond for a moment before turning back to Deboss, her expression somehow changed, clearer. "If we told Empire we were coming here, they would have ordered us not to."

"That doesn't explain this." He bobbed the weapon.

Rose appeared poised to answer, then paused and turned to Mira. "Mira?"

"You know," she replied, "I really don't know." She let out a deep sigh.

It seemed to reverberate around the room; she could feel the vibration in the seat. She jerked upright in alarm and Deboss turned to glance out of the decontamination bay. The ringing of the hull hung in the air, the diminishing, reverberating toll of a giant bell.

"You," said Deboss, raising the gun at her.

Alarms burst to life throughout the *Prophet,* accompanied by an impotent red warning lamp over the bay's hatch.

"You have to evacuate," Mira said, her head abruptly clear, as Deboss' expression changed from what had been a tight and calculating smile to a snarl of rage. She reached out to him, beckoning.

But she moved too fast. An instinctive awareness of Deboss' reaction began to twist her out of the way before the gun discharged. The bright flare of its detonation temporarily blinded her, its report registering as a devastating, ringing crack. A hard jerk against her right shoulder twisted Mira into the path of the ejecting gases from the gun's muzzle and she swung back against her seat's webbing, her ears ringing.

Her nose stinging with the smell of burnt propellant, she turned to see Rose launch at Deboss. Dismounted by the unexpected recoil of Mira's non-regulation ammunition, he was floating toward the back of the room. Rose intercepted the gun perfectly, wrenching it from his hands as he flailed trying to reorient himself.

Deboss recovered quickly, spinning in place and then launching back at Rose. There was a moment's hesitation before the gun flared in Rose's hands and Deboss spun past her across the decontamination bay, writhing.

The sound came from the wrong direction. It was

without emotion, a detached curiosity, that Mira realized the first blast had partially deafened her. She looked at her right shoulder where the armor had separated. A thick red liquid now pooled along a shattered seam. She felt it should hurt more, but the pressure in her ear overcame all other sensation. It took a moment to notice Rose grabbing her by the collar and dragging her toward the hatch.

It was Deboss watching them go that made her stop and detach from Rose's grasp. Having regained consciousness, he now held onto the base of a seat with one arm while clamping the other to his neck. His hand was slick with blood.

He's coming with us, Mira tried to say. Her voice seemed muffled behind the ringing in her ears, but Rose let her go. Reaching Deboss, she grabbed his free arm and pulled him toward the hatch.

Rose had the pistol trained on him as she approached. Mira hardly recognized her innocent engineer, her entire demeanor seeming to have changed in the last few minutes. Where her Earth origins and innocence were once exuded by every action, she was now the embodiment of cold calculation.

When Warren appeared at the hatch, Rose turned to train the gun on him.

"What the hell?" he asked, and then the world exploded.

The decompression of the *Prophet* wasn't instantaneous, a product of the frigate's massive size, but it was incredibly fast. Mira's reaction was trained. Ignoring Deboss, Rose and the growing pain in her shoulder, she freed her hands and donned her helmet.

Her suit spontaneously contracted, its nanofiber countering the growing pressure differential, pulling the broken seam at her shoulder back into place.

Rose was slower, but nonetheless managed to put on her helmet while retaining a grip on her gun.

Warren was gone, presumably sucked away from the hatch toward the hull breach.

Turning back to Deboss, Mira saw him struggling to right himself, his hands slick with blood, slipping on a nearby webbed seat. A vision of Jake blowing out of an air lock cut at her heart. Mira nodded across the hall and keyed her intercom.

"Get Hart," she said, pushing off toward Deboss.

"There's no time."

"It's not a negotiation, Rose. Get Hart."

Rose hesitated a moment and then launched out of the decontamination bay.

Deboss' skin had turned crimson as he struggled for breath in the increasingly rarefied atmosphere. Wrenching his hand away from his neck, she unclasped his helmet and strapped it on. His suit visibly pulled tighter around him, appearing to seal his wound in the process.

She dragged him out of the hatch and into the access tube as the *Prophet*'s primary lighting flickered and died. Red emergency lights, running on backup power supplies, blinked into life to illuminate the sudden darkness.

Across the access tube, Rose emerged from what must have been the infirmary with the suited Hart. Their eyes met before both swung out and into the hall.

From deep within the frigate, a flash caught Mira's attention. She turned to see a distant, suited figure float along the access tube toward her. Their source hidden from view, intermittent bursts of light revealed the figure in a stuttering silhouette.

The visible staccato of the automatic weapon was all too familiar; she immediately knew it was hers and who the spacer was. Propelled by its recoil, Warren was going to keep flying down the hall until he struck its side. Beyond him, in his line of fire, a black shape amassed.

Only it wasn't entirely black. Glinting in the weapon's fire, it reflected dull colors, a growing pool of onyx. Spellbound, Mira watched it coalesce into a sphere and then, so fast that Mira could not be sure of what she'd actually seen, it changed. Now a long, thin cylinder, following the path of the gunfire back to its source, reached and passed directly through Warren. Mira felt a noticeable tug in the hull in reaction to its motion.

Frozen in place by the black column, he hung stationary for only a moment. From both ends at once the column began folding back and congealing around him. Amidst the black mass, he disappeared.

Mira urgently signaled Rose to move toward the hold. They pushed off together, towing Deboss and Hart toward the hatch at the end of the access tube. A quick glance behind showed the black mass reshaping again, slowly this time, touching and then releasing the adjoining hull.

The shuttle's inner air lock had remained sealed. With the four of them inside, Mira cycled it as quickly as possible and launched into the shuttle. Rose wrestled the unconscious Hart aboard while Mira punched in a command on the *Nyx*'s console.

The shuttle's thrusters kicked in as helmets came off, but it was several minutes before anyone said anything.

"Are you okay?" was all Mira could manage.

Rose nodded. "Hart was already suited," she said. "They'd only slipped one of his arms out for the IV."

Deboss had a hard set to his jaw, one hand keeping pressure on his neck. "I don't know what to say," he said, turning to face them. "There were a lot of people on the *Prophet*. But thanks, I guess, and sorry. Despite what happened earlier, I'm glad you showed up."

"Gotta protect the talent," said Rose, turning back to check on Hart.

Mira felt her ears burn. She had some thinking to do.

Mira took one last look around the cabin, now bare of all traces of her inhabitancy. The station's curve was a now-imperceptible warp in the abutment between floor and wall, wall and ceiling. She had noticed it when first arriving here, but like so many things it had become a part of life, shaping her perceptions. Where once she'd seen a gently curving cell was now a straight-edged room. Mira hoisted her duffle bag onto her shoulder, nudged the door ajar and turned out the light. It was time to change perspectives.

Harlan was waiting outside. How long he'd been there, she didn't know.

"You can still change your mind," he said, falling in alongside her as she began walking the outer ring's main walkway. A number of spacers out on the path stopped mid-stride or gave her an odd look as they passed and talked behind their hands.

"Harlan, these last four years I had it all figured out. This was the only place for me. I didn't even open letters from family."

A spacer, dressed in a station technician's uniform, sidestepped over and interposed himself between them. Ignoring Mira's hesitant step backwards, he caught her hand and shook it, offering an effusive thank-you and grinning. Mira grimaced and took another step backwards. There had been too many weird encounters like this in the last few days.

As suddenly as his intrusion, a sharp moment of self-consciousness seemed to overcome him and he averted his eyes, his face and ears abruptly crimson. Mira withdrew her hand and stepped around him, shuddering.

"This will all quiet down," Harlan said. "They're just excited. Your encounter changes everything. Not only is there a reason for the companies to work together now, there's a reason for nations planet-side to take more interest in what is happening above their heads, something greater than commerce."

Mira kept walking, giving Harlan a wry smile. Catching sight of the planetary shuttle gates as they rotated into view on the walkway, she picked up her pace.

"And then," he said, straining to keep up, "I need you. Who am I going to replace you with?"

Mira nodded ahead to the Earthbound shuttle gates, where a number of security staff stood screening passengers. A familiar face was watching the crowd, filling out her new uniform with an air of authority, future studies forgotten. "You don't really need me anyway, Harlan."

Harlan saw where she was looking. "Are you sure about this?"

Mira stopped by the gate, nodded to Rose and laughed. She pulled a familiar envelope out from her jumpsuit, still unopened, and waved it at him. "No," she said and tucked it away to shake his hand. "And that's what makes it right."

Waving goodbye, she stepped through the gate.

Medic!

written by

Adam Perin

illustrated by

GREGORY J. GUNTHER

ABOUT THE AUTHOR

Adam Perin has a short attention span. In his adult life, he's been an artillery officer in the US Army, a waiter, a bartender, an associate on the help desk for Apple, an emergency medical technician and a field biologist for the Environmental Protection Agency. Along the way, he's earned two degrees: one in computer science and one in biology, neither of which he now uses. At times, he contemplated medical school, graduate school for marine biology and law school. He has taken the GRE, LSAT, GRE biology and almost every other standardized test in existence. But in the end, he ended up working as a diplomat for the US Department of State . . . something which has absolutely no relation to anything mentioned thus far.

Through it all, though, there was a desire to write. Taking bits and pieces from a lifetime of stunted pursuits, he now tries to stitch them together into stories that somebody might want to read. He placed third for the Dell Award for undergraduate science fiction in 1998, but then entered a long hiatus. Years later, after attempting to write screenplays for a while, he finally saw the light and decided to try his hand at short stories. This story is his first entry into the Writers of the Future and first professional sale.

ABOUT THE ILLUSTRATOR

Gregory J. Gunther has always been creative. He started storytelling through art and words from a young age, even winning the honor in junior high of having his children's books published through the Bay County Library System's "Be an Author Contest" three years in a row. That was just the beginning, however. Even through an eclectic history of career paths, he continued to pursue creative ventures and imaginative dreams—whether through design, illustration, writing or developing some new story, game or product idea, usually much to the chagrin of his friends and ever-patient wife.

He has been involved in freelance graphic and website design for over a dozen years and has great passion for the digital arts. Recently, he completed his master's degree in communications and digital media design. (Now he's enjoying teaching in that same graduate program.) He strives every day to turn his interests and creativity into a successful career as a designer/illustrator/teacher and creative entrepreneur through constant creative focus and work.

Personally, Gregory hopes to pursue his dream of working in the science fiction industry as an illustrator and writer, as well as doing freelance design work. Of course, he also has a few other projects in the works, like launching a board game development company, finishing some illustrated storybook ideas and a few top-secret original projects (on the side). He lives in Midland, Michigan, with his wife, Connie, and their pets (Bella, a Dutch Shepherd, and their two cats, Simba and Misty).

Medic!

Some guys go insane from being buried alive. I always get drowsy.

It's quiet down here, and dark. That's why I can't stay awake. The pale purple light from my head-up display weighs on my eyes, pulsing like a metronome. My suit is cold and clammy, and I tighten up, arms around my knees, head buried. Sometimes I'm here for hours, waiting, curled up in my little earthen cocoon.

I turn the radio down, far enough that it doesn't bug me, but I can still hear it somewhere in the back of my head. Like voices from ghosts, conversations fly back and forth between people I know but don't give a damn about. Bursts of static here and there, squelch beeping as the crypto kicks in. Over and over. My eyelids weigh a ton. The voices fade to garbled alien whispers.

"MEDIC!"

I'm awake. My eyes snap open. The HUD flares to life. The driller on my back whines eagerly, warming up. My hands move by themselves, moving before

417

my mind catches up. The training moves me like a puppet.

The driller belches as it fires up, emitting a dry roar. I'm already angling up, cutting through the rock like it's made of gelatin. The ground separates, molten, and slag drips off my suit, hardening behind me in wavy pools of deformed rock. My head's turned upward, eyes flickering back and forth, revving up the HUD. My mind fixates on one thing. Locate the injured.

Purple halos sizzle to life far above me. Casualties. That's Harare, the sergeant who always chews on kete leaves and walks around spitting out the residue. Over there is Moseley, the private who's set to marry some girl way too good for him. More halos pop up all over my field of vision, the names glowing above them with basic triage information fed to me by their nanosensors. I can already tell there's too many.

HARARE: Fractured femur. Compound. Blunt trauma to the chest. Possible hemothorax. He's done. Good riddance. Asshole always took two desserts in the mess hall anyway.

BORDEN: Penetrating wound to the head. Severed cervical-spine. Damn. I kind of like that kid. And he owed me money.

EDMUNDS: Burn damage to the upper back and chest. Double amputation below the knees. Airway blocked. Edmunds? He's not in my unit. Then it comes up. *LIEUTENANT GENERAL* Edmunds. A flag officer. What the hell's he doing out here?

I head for him. He was playing tourist out here where he had no business being, but the readouts tell me he's got a shot to live. A life's a life, even if he's an officer, and I need the credit.

I veer under him. Through the ground, I can see him lying supine, probably unconscious. I feel the ground tremble, and for a minute, I think it could be a gravity slammer, but I shake it off and try to focus.

The trick is to stop the driller at the right place. Just far enough and the ground gives way under the body. Too far and I'll impale the poor bastard and finish what the Jellies started. A lot of guys do that at first, usually because their hands are shaking from the adrenaline. But I've done this a million times.

The driller splatters molten rock everywhere, flowing down the tunnel I drill under the good general. I bore in from off to the side, tilting upward so the molten rock flows slowly down the tunnel wall's decline. By the time it reaches the bottom, where I am, it's already recrystallized. It makes the tunnel nice and slick so the body breaks through the top and slides right down to me.

He tumbles through and comes to a rest at my feet, the HUD giving purple highlight to his features. His eyes stare wildly up at me. Guess he wasn't unconscious after all.

"Thank you," he says through gritted teeth. I see tear tracks down his face behind his steamy faceplate. I hate it when they cry.

"Shut the hell up," I reply.

It's a little worse than I thought. The front of his suit is split open, and I can see mottled red and black inside. I turn him over. Ouch. Looks like burnt barbeque chicken. That's a Cnidarian weapon, no doubt. The wound resembles an electrical burn, but the air stinks of hot plasma and burnt rubber. I toy with the idea of letting him feel it a bit longer, just because. But no, there's no time. I give him a good dose of Damrovil painkillers. I hear him let out a relieved sigh.

"You owe me, asshole," I whisper to him.

My HUD links to nanosensors implanted inside his body. The vitals readout whizzes by my face, but I ignore it. I don't give a damn what his pulse-ox is right now, or that his BP is nosediving. I can see he's shocky with my own eyes. I'm just looking for anything that isn't immediately obvious. I send a command to deactivate his body armor. In an instant, the rigid nanoscale fibers in his suit become pliable and the material falls limp around his body. Now for my favorite part.

I slice his suit wide open with a laser cutter. Then I cover the burnt tissue with wet saline bandages out of the dispenser below my tricep. With my med-tool I squirt a thick layer of Plasticone Band-X over the damaged tissue. As I apply them, the synthetic peptides harden to the consistency of stiff plastic. The nutrient-rich material will be absorbed by the body in a few hours and staunch the bleeding until then. His breathing is really labored, so I do a quick fasciotomy with my laser scalpel, making long longitudinal cuts from the mid-clavicle to just beneath his ribs. It looks like hell, but the scorched flesh relaxes and he can breathe.

The HUD tells me he's sliding into cardiac arrest, so I inject a few picobot motors for good measure. The little buggers'll swim to his heart and zap him a few times, keep him out of ventricular fibrillation. Saves me the trouble of cracking open the breastbone, even though I kind of enjoy that part.

Now the legs. Nothing there below the knees, and they're clean cuts. I've seen the wound before and realize I was right to think it was a gravity slammer. Must've smashed his shins to a pancake about a millimeter thick.

"Bet that hurt, huh?" I say, chuckling.

I pull out two small plasticine tubes I fit snugly over the amputated areas. A single command from my suit tightens them and cuts off the blood flow. I throw a layer of Band-X over the open wound for good measure.

He's stabilized. Three sheets to the wind, too. I slap him across the face and he smiles. Asshole. He doesn't even notice the tube I stick down his throat. The end of it finds his larynx and slides in. These automatic tubes make it so easy. The other end expands and I hook him up to a portable oxygen pump. Finishing, I lash the whole thing to his side with some surgical tape. He'll live.

I hit the squelch on the command net.

"This is Angel-0-4, one for pickup my location. Staff officer with burns to the upper torso, about twenty-four percent coverage, double amputation below the knees, stabilized but tachycardic, over."

A burst of static. "Roger, 0-4, stand by. It's too hot right now. We'll get back to you for extraction, over." I recognize the voice. That damn female corporal up on the *Monongahela*.

"Roger that, darling," I say, grinning because I know that pisses her off. "For the record, that's a credit either way, out."

I flip off the radio, chuckling. That's a credit. A life's a life. Not my fault they're too chicken to pick him up. He dies now, it's on them.

"Guess no one loves you, sir," I say.

I smile. That's number nine hundred ninety-five. Five more to go and I'm done.

Days by the water are the ones I remember. The colony on Germonium was right beside the ocean, and it reminded me of growing up in South Carolina. Germonium is ninety percent water, clear and blue. It's where I met Kayla and where we fell in love. The waterways running between the marshes reeked of salt and stale brine, just like the pungent wetlands around Harbor Island, where as a boy I'd gone knee deep in marsh mud trying to startle soft crabs into a hand net. There aren't crabs on that alien world, of course, but the idea was the same. Kayla's a great student and took to it fast. When she pulled her first wriggling kractali out of those black waters and grinned at me with those little fingers of wet hair clinging to her cheek, I knew I'd marry her.

That was before the war. Before the Cnidaria. We were ignorant then, and I guess that's okay. The ignorant seem happier.

The *Monongahela* is a big ship, but it still seems like we're all on top of one another. People are everywhere, bumping into one another. Makes me miss my nice quiet hole down there on the planet.

I never eat with anyone. I'm not antisocial; it's just that watching someone chow down makes me nauseated. I can't watch the mush roll around in their mouths or hear the lips smacking. But it's too cramped in the mess hall to avoid that, and as I sit here, there's a sea of pea green overalls floating around me. I've seen most of them before; I just can't recall faces. After so long on this ship, they're just walking scars to me. Piles of injuries I've treated, dragged from the battlefield, patched together and sent back in.

I see the private over there and remember when I tucked his eyeball back into the socket when some shrapnel took half his scalp.

I see that sergeant, the big Hispanic guy with the tight gym shirt. One of his arms is slightly off color. It's cloned, and I bet it still smells like plastic and old leather. The one his momma gave him got disintegrated under a gravity slammer.

And there's that corporal over there, chatting with a nice-looking petty officer. The females are just drawn to him. But when I see him, I think of the day he had a certain body part blown off, and I'm amazed his libido doesn't seem to suffer. They can clone anything nowadays. But I just don't like the idea of cloning that.

Guys getting blown apart, crushed, burned alive, suffocated, vaporized, disemboweled, decapitated or smashed into pasty little bits of bone. It used to get to me a lot more than it does now. Maybe I felt more then, or maybe it's something else. Being underground is safer, and that's why medics make it their home. But it cuts you off, too, and gives you lots of time to think.

423

I can't help counting the days, though, until I go back down planet-side. In my hole, where it's dark and safe and quiet, and I don't have to suffer fools.

A young blond kid edges up to the table. I see his crutch, the sani-wrap around his leg, and I know what's coming.

"Sergeant Silk, I'm Private Hartlyn. I don't know if you remember, but you pulled me out of a burning glide tank three weeks ago. I just wanted to thank you. I hope I can repay you someday."

I remember him. I remember all of them. He holds out his hand, waiting for me to shake it.

"No difference to me, Private. I got credit for your life," I say, but I don't shake his hand. I only shake with people I respect. He holds his hand there for a long moment.

"My girlfriend made me promise to give these to you," he says and produces a small box. "They're cookies, real ones. She made them for you. Chocolate chip."

I stare at him. He puts the cookies on the table and fidgets. I keep staring.

"She prays for you every night, Sergeant. Here, look," he says and pulls his portable out of his pants pocket. "This is her."

He holds it out, beaming at me. Her photo is on the portable. She's blond like him, lithe and beautiful. So damn perfect that I hate them both. "Her name's Paige."

I knock the portable out of his hand and it flies across the room. "Get the hell out of here," I growl.

He hesitates, confused.

"NOW!" I yell, and the private retreats as fast as his crutch can carry him.

"That was great, Tom. Kid just wanted to thank you and you bite his head off." The voice is familiar. I groan.

"I didn't ask for any thanks," I say, "and I didn't ask to get a photo of his damn girl shoved in my face."

He takes a seat. "Another day and no messages, I take it."

I nod. "Not a damn thing." Kayla never writes me. Says it's too hard, and it just reminds her how far apart we are. I'd still like to get a letter once in a while, though.

"Well," he says, trying to sound way too sympathetic, "maybe tomorrow."

Normally an officer like him would make me stand and salute him, but I've known Captain Nirvelli for too long. He's one of our trauma surgeons and probably the best on the *Monongahela*. I play cards with some of the guys from the hospital sometimes, and I like Nirvelli because he's not very good.

"Nothing wrong with wanting to show a little gratitude," he says and takes a cookie.

"Not when I'm trying to eat."

He grunts and keeps chewing, as usual with his mouth wide open. I try not to look, but my food starts tasting like paste anyway.

"So what's it at now?" he asks.

"Nine ninety-five," I reply.

He whistles. "Close," he says. "You outta here, then? Back to that podunk planet?"

"You got it," I say, "fast as that transport'll take me."

"Shame to lose you, Silk. You know, I know the counselor on the *Bowditch*—" He stops abruptly, chews for few moments, then grins at me. "Hey, game tonight! New guys in from Earth."

"Officers?"

"Butter bars."

I smile. "Hell, I'm in." I'll always play with officers. They have more money to lose.

Medic!"

I'm awake. I sit up and bang my head on the bulkhead above my bunk. Sometimes I hear them scream in my sleep, and I forget where I am. But this time I was dreaming about Carolina, about walking along the tidal marsh. Things are always out of place in my dreams. I was a child, but Kayla was there. She was chasing the surf, in and out, playing a little game. The surf slid in fast and ran over her feet. She screamed. I ran after her, but in slow motion. When I got to her, I saw a jellyfish clinging to her foot. The gelatinous tentacles wrapped around her tiny foot, stingers lashing scarlet welts into her skin.

She screamed again, but her voice was the voice of a soldier. A soldier calling for help.

I seem to always dream about water. In liquid form, it's a rare thing in the universe. A lot of species need it, and there's just not enough to go around. So, if a planet has liquid water, sooner or later someone will fight over it.

The Cnidaria need water badly. I guess, on their planet, evolution decided it was better to stay in the ocean, so they built a civilization beneath the waves. At least that's what they tell us. Actually, few people have ever seen a Cnidarian in person. They always fight to the death, and so do we. I've even heard that the things we fight aren't actually the Cnidaria, but some kind of drones they grow in a lab and use for war. Soldiers trade stories like that to pass the time, and the more absurd the rumor the better. There's no doubt the Jellies need large oceans to live in, and any planet that has them is a fair target.

Ante up, boys," Nirvelli says.

He was right about the butter bar. The lieutenant looks like a baby to me. Did I ever look that young? He notices me watching him and shifts uncomfortably in his chair. I stare at him and watch him squirm.

The other butter bar walks in to our little poker oasis and huffs. He looks around, puts his hands on his hips and stares at me. I ignore him.

"Sergeant, I believe it's customary to stand when an officer enters the room," he says, and I hear Nirvelli stifle a laugh.

Oh boy. It's one of these guys. "Yeah, I believe it is," I reply with a giant eye roll, and I go back to my cards.

He stands there longer, staring, until Nirvelli tells him to sit the hell down. This kid's gotta be from the academy. They grow that kind of attitude there.

"First thing you should learn," Nirvelli says, lecturing the boy, "is to keep your trap shut until you know the deal. You pull that crap with the sergeant major and he'll have your ass for lunch."

I chuckle. It's true. I realize I'm no ray of sunshine, but the sergeant major is a genuine asshole.

"Lucky for you, Sergeant Silk is a real sweetheart," he says.

"No," I say, "I just never forget. You're already on the list, LT."

The kid broods and takes his seat, still shooting me dirty looks. Lucky for him, he's not in my company. Stupid kid like that's bound to get hit down there, and I might decide to take my time getting to him.

"Gentlemen, the game is five card stud. Deuces are wild."

"So start dealing, Captain," I say. "I need to get me some officer's pay."

"We have one more coming," he says, shuffling, "should be here any second."

I sit back, instantly suspicious. "Who's—"

The door slides open and the first thing I see is a colonel's bird glinting in the dim light. I stare daggers at Nirvelli.

"Ten-shun!" the kid shouts as he bolts upright. I get up slower, grumbling.

Colonel Perdomo walks in, and now I know this is all a trap.

"As you were, fellas," he says as he takes his seat. "Thanks for the invite, Captain. Haven't played in ages."

I seriously consider walking right out, but I know it's not that easy.

"Sergeant Silk," Perdomo says, "good to see you again."

I nod. You just can't trust officers.

Colonel Perdomo is the division retention officer. His job is to try to get young soldiers to re-up, whether they want to or not. It's not a hard job because most soldiers don't live through an entire tour of duty anyway, or at least the ground pounders don't. The colonel is a man with a good amount of free time on his hands.

But he can't play cards worth anything. And right now, I'm sitting on a few hundred credits' worth of his money. His thin face and hooked nose seem to be damp all the time, and his slicked-back hair looks like it belongs on someone in a casket. In the time we've been playing, I've learned his tell. He drums his fingers when he's carrying junk. I know it, and so does Nirvelli. A couple more hands and the poor colonel will go home a broken man.

Despite the fact I'm sitting on most of his paycheck, though, the colonel keeps peeking at me with ferret eyes that tell me he's got something to say. It bugs me, and I want to get up and bolt, but I decide to stay long enough to clean him out. I need the money, especially for Kayla and her kid.

"So, Sergeant," he says finally, clearing his throat, "Captain Nirvelli tells me you may not be with us too much longer."

"I think you could say that about any soldier on this ship, sir," I reply.

He laughs. "That's a bit morbid."

"Then maybe you're in the wrong war, sir."

He fidgets with his chips. Nirvelli deals and I've got two pair. Tens. The butter bar to my left looks at his cards and lets out a big sigh. Nice poker face.

"Your name's been thrown around in staff meetings," Perdomo says. "A lot of good things are being said about your work here."

I don't say anything, being too engrossed in my cards. I take three cards and get another ten and a wild two. Perdomo takes two and chews his lip.

"There's even talk of promotion, maybe a battlefield commission."

Nirvelli laughs. "Silk as a butter bar?"

Perdomo continues. "You two don't know him," he says to the butter bars, "but Sergeant Silk here is a medic who's saved almost one thousand lives on the battlefield. He's been in active service over four years."

They both look at me, their eyes wide. Suddenly they respect me, but that only pisses me off more. First impressions count, and I already decided they're both little pricks.

"What can I do to help you decide to stay on, Tom?" Perdomo says.

"You can start by not calling me Tom," I say. "I don't call you 'Javier' or whatever the hell you go by."

He flushes red, embarrassed. The butter bars shift in their seats. I'm sure they've never heard a sergeant talk to a colonel like that. I smile a little.

"Tom, he's just making small talk," Nirvelli says.

"If I want to chew the fat, I'll take a bite outta your wife's ass, Nirvelli," I say. "I'm here to play poker. Raise me three hundred."

Nirvelli chuckles. "Call."

Perdomo senses he's lost face. "Boys, we give Sergeant Silk leniency here because he's very good at his job. A lot of men owe him their lives, including me. But that only goes so far."

He goes all in. Then he drums his fingers. The butter bars both fold. I raise another hundred.

"Too rich for my blood," Nirvelli says and folds.

"Just you and me, Sergeant," Perdomo says. "Say, what are your plans for afterward, anyway? What's in Sergeant Silk's future?"

"I'm gonna spend it far away from here."

"Doing what?"

"No idea. Maybe I'll fish. Maybe I'll farm. Maybe I'll just lie around all day and get a tan. Either way, I'll live near the water and I won't waste time shooting the bull with retention officers."

"Live near the water? Sounds nice." He fidgets with his cards nervously. "You know, I think you got a rotten deal. I might've done the same thing if I was in your shoes. Any of us might have. The system stinks sometimes."

"It warms my heart to hear that, sir, but I won't change my mind."

He looks at me sadly, and I hate sympathy. "So it's going to be Germonium, then?"

"Yep."

"And your fiancée?" he asks.

"Gonna see her there. Maybe raise a family."

"On Germonium?"

"You heard me."

He smiles, sanctimonious. "I guess we all have our dreams. What about practicing medicine?"

"I step foot off this ship, I'm not a medic anymore. Never will be again," I reply.

"You have talent, Tom," he says. "Everyone here knows it. You could help so many more people. Good medics are hard to find."

"Sorry, sir," I reply, "but I thought this was a card game, not an intervention."

431

He stirs. "I'll raise you all I got." He puts in all his money. The pot's around nine hundred now. I try to suppress my growing glee.

"You got balls, sir," I say. "All in."

He grins, drums his fingers even harder. "Let's see what you got."

I show my hand. Full house. Aces full of tens. I smile and he deflates. I want to take a mental picture of this moment.

"You gotta stop drumming your fingers, sir. Maybe you'll win a hand once in a while."

He nods, resigned, and shows his hand. Straight flush. I stare at the cards.

"Kind of like right now," he says and sweeps the pot toward him.

He stands up, straightening his uniform blouse. "Thanks for the game, Capt. Nirvelli. It was refreshing to play with such skilled players."

He turns toward me, putting on his cap. "I heard about how you patched up General Edmunds. That's great work. Man like that could be really grateful for the effort."

Nirvelli laughs. "You don't know how stubborn Silk is, sir."

I sulk, and I know it's childish. Getting beat by this blowhard just burns me.

He nods to me. "I think sooner or later, Sergeant Silk may realize that, like this friendly card game, he doesn't have everything figured out quite right."

He bids farewell to all, then turns to me. "And God willing, if you make it back to Germonium, Sergeant, please give your fiancée my best."

This day just keeps getting better. I see him coming just as I'm stepping out of the chow hall. Some private, just like all the others.

He steps in front of me and stops. I immediately know this time is different. He's not smiling. We stare at each other.

"You Sergeant Silk?" he says. His mouth barely moves. He's young but there's something about him that gives me pause.

"That's right." I look at his name tag. I know that name.

I don't realize what's happened before my face slams into the steel of the floor. I taste blood and my vision goes awash in red. I don't feel any pain until he grabs my head and slams it down again. I hear a wet snap as my nose breaks.

I'm old, but these muscles still rally when I need them. I twist over and heave the kid off my back. He falls to the floor and I'm on him before he recovers. I pin his arms with my knees, digging in hard. He grunts and I know it hurts. Good.

I wipe my face and my hand comes away covered in blood. Son of a bitch. I'm about to rip out the kid's jaw when I see the name tag again. It hits me like a sledgehammer to the noggin.

"Atwell."

I take my knees off his arms and he's on top of me instantly. I feel his fists landing, I feel blood flowing but I do nothing. I hear him shouting at me, horrible things that I can't understand. His rage is boundless, but I don't fight back. I've wronged him, and I know it. Let him have his day. I can spit blood for a while.

433

I sit on my bed in the infirmary, cradling my broken face with a cold compress. The kid did a number on me. I'll avoid mirrors for a few weeks.

With my one good eye, I see Nirvelli coming toward me, already smiling. He whistles. "Damn, Silk, you just get more popular every day."

I smile. "If I'd known everyone was going to kick my ass, I'd never have come to this war."

He sits down next to the bed, puts his feet up. "You gonna charge him? Little bastard deserves it."

"I already forgot about it," I say.

"What? You kidding? Some enlisted bastard hits me and I'd—"

"It was Atwell's kid."

He stops and stares at me. "No way." We sit in silence a long moment, and it gets awkward.

"You don't have to get weird," I say. "Damn."

"No, I mean, I get it—"

"I'm not sorry for what I did to his old man, but I'm sorry it had to affect the kid. The universe isn't fair that way."

He nods. "Nope, I guess not."

He tries to change the subject, but I'm in no mood for talking. The beating I just took and seeing the name "Atwell" again has got me thinking.

Maybe I was hasty. Looking back, I don't regret it.

I sat before his desk, looking at a silver framed picture of his wife and children. His smiling, happy family.

"We've reviewed your petition for cohabitation," Major Atwell said as he stifled a yawn.

Cohabitation. An icy word for marriage. My palms were clammy and wet. I felt hot, and sweat trickled down my spine. I had waited over fifteen months for this meeting.

"This office has completed three interviews as well as neuroscanner veracity examinations on one . . ." Atwell shuffled through her file papers. "Kayla Marie Brulliard. I'm obligated to inform you that we conducted a thorough review and background investigation of every living member of her family. This is all standard procedure in these cases and is done for the good of the service member. That's you, by the way."

Her face filled my mind. This endless bureaucratic process was almost over. I feared the worst. Kayla was a widow with a four-year-old boy on a far-flung colony. She had no one. I had no idea what she would do if they said no. I couldn't bear the thought.

I have security clearances. My head is supposedly full of intelligence, though anyone who knows me may argue that. As a colonist from Germonium, Kayla was considered not quite trustworthy as a citizen, not like someone from Earth. Because of that, we needed government approval to marry. So, I did what's right and followed the rules. All colonists are viewed with some suspicion, maybe because they tend to have stronger streaks of independence. There's little left to chance in wartime.

"Your petition to marry the colonist has been denied," he told me, his eyes not even leaving the papers on his desk. "Markers in her veracity exams and/or her family history raised security concerns

435

with this office. For reasons of privacy, I cannot discuss these with you. Please be informed that this decision is final and there is no avenue of appeal. You have fifteen days to terminate this relationship under penalty of job termination or incarceration."

I sat there, paralyzed. I must have heard wrong.

"But—"

"This decision cannot be appealed, Sergeant. I'm sorry."

"She doesn't have anyone else."

"This decision cannot be appealed, Sergeant."

"So what—"

"Dismissed, Sergeant."

I still remember Atwell's dead and indifferent eyes. He dismissed me with a wave of his hand. This was a cold and pitiless man who cared nothing for me.

I sat there and stared at the perfect picture of his perfect family while he forever denied me the same thing. I started to crumble. The anger, bubbling inside for fifteen months, boiled over and I did what any man in love could have done.

I shoved Major Atwell into an air lock and spaced him. Maybe I was hasty. I don't regret it, though.

I was originally sentenced to life in prison. But it turns out that good medics are scarce and in war irreplaceable. I'm really good, so I was given a choice. Prison or service in the line companies until I saved one thousand lives. Then I could go back to Kayla. It was an easy choice.

They thought that it would take me decades. I did it in less than five years.

GREGORY J. GUNTHER

When I dream during faster-than-light travel, it's always about the past.

I had just proposed to Kayla. We were on her boat, a twin-sail sloop, gently bobbing up and down on the orange-tinged sea. She knows how to sail. She handles a rig like a real sailor, feeling the current in her bones. She put us perfectly on the far side of the sand bars where the ocean churned with hungry fish. We cast our rods until sunset, then grilled our catch on the bow. The perfumed scent of the sizzling filets wafted around our heads and drew in a family of hungry pipernets that hovered over us and cackled for a taste. Satiated, we tossed up bits of the tender meat to the fleshy beaks as they clacked in gratitude.

As the twin moons of Germonium rose like flames from the black horizon we reclined across the bow on a blanket, opened a bottle of sweet bourbon and I pulled the ring out of my pocket. Kayla melted and we lay embraced while turtle-shelled tungs, blinded by the moonlight, bumped softly against the hull. The boat swayed along with the trade currents and a warm breeze hugged our bodies as we drifted off to sleep.

It was the birth of our new life, and the water was our womb. I dream often of that night of nights, and I wake up smelling the sea.

The transport decelerates rapidly, lurching out of FTL travel. My face feels hot, and my sleeve comes away damp as I wipe my forehead. My pummeled face aches and my stomach is doing somersaults, angry at me for being empty now almost twenty days. I stretch and try to shake the sleep from my head, taking a few uneasy steps. I'm not authorized to be here, but there comes a point when you've had enough and don't give a damn. I've decided to take the bastard's advice.

Fort Dempsey is a huge orbital hospital. We're well behind the lines now, protected by a large chunk of Earth's naval forces. It's a bustling place, full of white-clothed people going back and forth, busy in their tasks. After passing through the biofilters and security checkpoints, I'm directed toward the hospital's VIP ward where all the high-ranking officers are housed. Coming off the elevator, the cold, sterile environment of the general ward gives way to something far more welcoming. I step into another world, surrounded by soft carpeting, wood panels and crown molding. So this is how the other half recuperates.

General Edmunds has his own suite, of course. The guards by his door menace me as I approach, but wave me by with the flick of a hand. I'm expected. The door opens and I see a cluster of doctors hovering around a large plush bed. They chat away, talking on top of one another, and I know it's because each wants to get his own insightful comment heard by the general. Everyone's a suck-up.

The swish of the door alerts them, and they look up at me in unison. One, a dark, plump man with a goatee, hurries toward me to shoo me away.

"Let him be," a weak voice says, and I know it's the general. "And the rest of you, get out."

They exit, measuring me up as they go. I give them a cocky smile and nod. Their scowls tell me I've hit home.

"Come here," the voice says again, and I can hear the labored breath pushing back, "next to the bed."

I see the general for the first time since the day I patched him up. He was probably a powerful figure before he was injured. But the thing on the bed is being held together by tubes and silicate castings. A wall of machines next to the bed hums and beeps away, pushing his lungs, pumping his blood, keeping him alive. His head is encased in some kind of helmet that hides his eyes, and I wonder how he can identify me. I edge close to the foot of the bed, hesitant.

"Stand before me, Sergeant," he says, his liquid-filled lungs gurgling. "I believe we're still in the service here."

I snap to and pop him a crisp salute. His skeletal hand, tubes dangling, returns the motion with surprising dexterity.

"Somehow I thought you'd come. I understand you've made some mistakes," he says. I can feel his unseen eyes piercing me, peering into dark places. "But hasn't everyone?"

I owe you my life," General Edmunds says in his raspy voice, "such as it is."

He utters a strained chuckle, and I smile uneasily. We both know it's not as bad as that. I'm sure a cloned body is being grown for him as we speak. "Just doing my job, sir."

He nods. "Yes, I agree. And nobody ever thanked me for doing mine. But we're soldiers, Sergeant Silk. That's how it is."

"I agree, sir."

"You've been through it, haven't you, Sergeant?"

"I guess you could say that, sir."

"Five years in. Wounded?"

"A little banged up, sir."

"You're modest, Sergeant," he says. "You'd never make a good officer." He laughs, and I know that wasn't meant as an insult.

He shifts in the bed, and I see that the sheets are soaked through with sweat. "I should never have been down on that planet, gawking around like a tourist. I've become the thing that I abhorred as a young officer."

I nod, not quite understanding.

"You'll see, Sergeant, if you stay in the service long enough and rise to a high enough rank, that it all goes to your head. The power. The privilege. You get used to being catered to. You get used to thinking of yourself as something special."

I nodded. The ego of a general. He was right about that. Goes double for politicians.

"There I was, strolling around a war zone to 'inspect' the troops, sticking my nose into places I had no business in. Watching the young officers scramble to fulfill my every whim." He laughed again and was wracked with a fit of coughing. "I thought even the enemy couldn't touch me. Maybe the universe saw my arrogance and decided to knock me down a few notches. I deserved it."

I shift back and forth on my feet, my eyes darting to the clock. Shocking talk from a general, no doubt, but I have no idea why I'm being forced to listen to it.

"Just as the gravity slammers were hitting, Sergeant," he says, "my mind became very clear. Just two months from now, my daughter will be graduating from the Naval Academy, and I would've been dead. Dead because I was an arrogant ass. That's all I could think."

He's silent for a long moment. "But now, even in my condition, I will see her graduate. I'll be alive to see my child again. I cannot tell you how that makes me feel."

His hand goes to his face, disappears under the helmet. I hear his voice crack. "You gave that to me, Sergeant. When you pulled me under the ground and put me back together. You gave me the greatest gift I've ever received."

I shuffle a bit. "Just doing my job, sir." I don't know what else to say.

He huffs. "You're known as quite the hard-ass, Silk. Oh, yes, I've asked around. I can't do much from this bed, but I can read personnel files. I can talk to people."

I straighten, getting even more uneasy.

"You know, I'm in pieces in this bed. My legs are a splatter somewhere on Luyten, and even with implants, I'll never be the same. But I don't begrudge you because you can walk, and I can't."

He breathes heavily, and I hear the phlegm down in his lungs.

"Envy will eat a man up, Sergeant. If all you want in life is rage, it'll be easy to find. But cursing others for what they have, and you don't, is no way to live."

I rock back a little, his words striking near home.

He straightens, regaining a touch of military decorum. "That's all I'll say about that. Now, name your pleasure, Sergeant. Whatever it is, it's yours."

I listen, but don't hear him. "Not necessary, sir. I—"

"Anything. I don't care what it is. Just tell me. I will give it to you."

"Really, sir—"

"Sergeant, you won't walk out of here without asking me for something. And I think we both know what you want to ask."

I stand there, dumb, fidgeting. He's done his homework and knows me. There's something incredibly uncomfortable about that. I just want to run out.

"You're only five short, am I right? I think a general's life is worth at least four credits, don't you?" Again, he chuckles. I don't know if he's being sarcastic or not.

"For chrissakes, Sergeant, ask me to release you from your sentence. Ask me to let you go to your fiancée. We both know that's what you want. Ask me and I'll give it to you."

I want to ask more than anything in the entire world. Every fiber in my soul wants to, but my mouth won't make the words.

"Sergeant, ask someone else for help, for once in your life."

I nod. Kayla's face swims in my mind, and something breaks. I feel warm, salty tears on my lips, and I smell the sea. With all I have left, I make the words. "Help me, sir."

He leans back, the skeletal hand rests on his lap. The liquid lungs settle to an even rhythm. "Okay, then. The last soul you save will be your own."

I stand on the beach and look over the ocean. Enormous dust devils dance back and forth across the horizon. The beach, with its pristine red sand, is blackened and riddled with spiderweb cracks. I look out to the sandbars, past the point where whitecaps played with Kayla's boat, and see thundering clouds spewing blood-red rain.

The ocean is gone. The colony is a memory, blasted into the next world by weapons that stink of hot plasma and burning rubber. My eyes sting as the dust invades them. The dust bowl that was this great sea, full of life, beckons me and my digger. I want to burrow into it and forget. Go down and never come back up. Bury myself with her.

Kayla appears before me. She's just as I remember. Her long black hair, tossed over her shoulder, flows with a harsh wind. Her smile, directed at me, makes me weak. It's been five long years. The images in my memory don't do her justice. Her beauty impales me on its spearhead, and my heart tears in two.

I fall into her arms and cry.

"Shhh, quiet, Thomas," she says, stroking my head. I feel her warm breast against my cheek and squeeze her tighter. The tears come too fast.

She holds my face firm in her hands and looks into my eyes. Her gaze levels me. "What's happened to you, Thomas? You're so angry."

"They took you," I whisper, because I can't summon more words.

"That's over, love. Now you can help people. You can save lives."

"I don't care about them," I say. "I want to stay with you."

"You can't, love. I'm gone. You know I am. This isn't you, Thomas. You're not the man I fell in love with. You have to move on. Please, for me, you have to be a good man."

I know she's dead. I've known for years, but refused to accept it. Maybe that's why I wanted to come back here, to force myself to admit it. She was the only thing that ever made me a good man. The only reason I ever wanted to be a good man, and if I couldn't save her, then what the hell do I care about the rest?

"Thomas, you have to promise me. Help those men. Save them. Use the talent God has given you. Do it for me. Promise me, love."

Her words cut me. I fall to my knees. All the battles of five years, all the horrors I've seen come rushing back. I see the men I've saved, all of them, alive again. Their wounds healed and bodies whole. And I see their children, their wives and their families. I see their families.

Something inside me breaks. "I promise."

The anger melts away like water running off a mountain. Jealousy runs down my spine and into the tortured ground. I can't be angry, not anymore. My sweet Kayla was taken, but those men have a chance to be happy. I gave that to them.

Kayla smiles and I fall in love with her all over again. "Goodbye, Thomas. I'll be waiting for you."

She hugs me, and I try to hug back but there's nothing there. I sit on my knees for a long time, eyes closed.

Water is a rare thing in the universe. It gives life, and it takes it away. It brought the Cnidaria to

Germonium, and they took everything I've ever loved away from me. Now I stand in the ruin they left behind, talking to ghosts and hiding behind denial.

But I can't lie to myself anymore. I'll try to put away the anger, at least for now, and be the man she thinks I am. That's what Kayla wanted.

I stand up and turn toward my transport. In the back of my head, they call for me. In the far reaches, I hear them.

Vector Victoria

written by

D. A. D'Amico

illustrated by

RYAN DOWNING

ABOUT THE AUTHOR

David grew up as the son of a fisherman and commercial clam digger, and spent much of his youth on the ocean. The hard work and long backbreaking hours gave his mind plenty of time to wander, so he's never been truly surprised at some of the places it's been.

As with many aspects of the author's life, David's writing skills are almost entirely self-taught. He has been writing speculative fiction as a hobby for many years, but has only recently begun to annoy others with it. He spends his days building computers, and at night he writes. One of his recent hobbies has been collecting and reading the Writers of the Future anthologies, and he can now proudly say he owns and has read every one of the twenty-six volumes, as well as the twenty-fifth anniversary coffee table edition.

He is currently working on several projects, including a novel-length version of his award-winning story "Vector Victoria" and a lengthy piece of very dark fantasy.

David currently resides in "The Witch City," Salem, Massachusetts, with his lovely wife and four black cats.

447

ABOUT THE ILLUSTRATOR

Ryan's interest in art started early, growing up watching TV programs like Wildcats, He-Man and Teenage Mutant Ninja Turtles. They were his first taste of fantasy art and stories and his interest grew as he got older. When Ryan was old enough to read, he discovered comic books. The artwork impressed him so much he wanted to learn how to do it himself, but back then there was no such thing as an action comic artist in South Africa. Newspaper political comedy and Garfield were the best there was. There were no local X-Men, Spiderman comic-type artists, let alone schools which would teach it (which is what he wanted) so he had to train himself. Ryan spent years learning how to draw comic art from copying the artwork he liked. As Ryan got older and discovered more intricately detailed fantasy arts, he discovered digital art (computer art) which allowed him more creative freedom than any other traditional media could permit him. He continued to teach himself the ins and outs of technical expertise as well as extending his art styles with different types of digital painting including even those found in video games. He studied the philosophies and laws of art from L. Ron Hubbard's book Art which he credits as invaluable to any artist.

While the digital and comic art industry remains very small in South Africa, he still hopes to publish some of his own stories and move into the movie business to do conceptual arts and even direct a movie or two himself. Even developing video games is something he would love to do one day.

Vector Victoria

Victoria tossed herself into the chubby stranger's arms and kissed him hard on the lips right in front of his red-faced wife. She danced playfully away, enjoying the open-mouthed look of surprise on both their faces. Shamus, watching from a distance, smiled as the infection began to spread.

"Oh, you're wicked." Shamus, his voice an echo from the button phone on her right temple, laughed.

"It's more fun this way," she sub-vocalized. "And a whole lot better than just sneezing on them."

Then she twirled away, rubbing a moist palm against the cheek of a gray-haired man, stopping briefly to lick her finger and tuck it into the ear of a small dark-skinned woman who had just stepped off the pellet platform. They yelled. The man complained loudly, and the woman actually flipped her off. Victoria just laughed and danced. She knelt in front of a passing stroller, leaning in to pick up and hug a pale-skinned little girl in a pink bonnet. Victoria loved children and made it a special point to give them all a big dose.

449

She somersaulted away from the crowd, leaping onto a raised dais filled with decorative palm trees. Her handiwork wouldn't take long to spread. The man she had kissed, the chubby one in the garish orange hula shirt, struggled to explain to his wife what had just occurred.

"Who was that?" the wife demanded sharply.

"Nobody—I don't know," the husband stammered. "I never saw her before in my life."

The wife slapped him across the face, and Victoria winced. "So, naked girls always throw themselves at you?"

Victoria frowned, glancing down at her lean brown body. She wasn't exactly naked, just tastefully undressed in a pale yellow belt-skirt and a few fiber-optic tattoos called shimmies. Spreading a virus took skin contact and lots of it.

W ell?" Shamus dropped down beside her, folding his long ebony legs beneath him like one of those tables that hucksters used to flash their card tricks on. He tipped that ridiculous gray fedora he had been wearing lately into a more rakish angle and smiled a broad, thin-lipped smile. His body shone, glistening with an olive-toned iridescence that only Victoria could see. It radiated a cold fire, tiny sparks sliding liquidly along his black skin as he moved. Her skin held a similar radiance, tinted in shades of the sun seen through the canopy of a rain forest and visible only to the inoculated as a layer of oiled microdiamonds.

"You like my technique?" She winked and pursed her lips, making fish faces in his direction. He leaned over as if to kiss her, but stopped a chaste distance away. His breath smelled of licorice.

She wished she could taste him, meet his body with her own, but that would only provide a "Romeo and Juliet" type ending to a promising day. Instead, she watched the color shift in liquid splashes, in leaps and arcs across his skin, as the battle was waged and lost across the landscape of his body.

Their work out on the streets came with a price. They couldn't touch, not until long after a session like this, not until days of gene therapy, enzyme replenishment and other uncomfortable things she tried not to remember. In fact, even a caress would mean death to either of them. The same was true for her and any of the post-infected strangers who wandered unknowingly through the gardens and walkways of the ring-shaped pellet train platforms. With each transition along the vector, the virus altered slightly. It mutated along a spectrum that would not vary its purpose, but would allow it to creep back into her skin and infect her as readily as she infected the many fresh faces that traveled throughout the Las Vegas area.

To a Vector, with their compromised immune systems, an unplanned infection meant a quick and painful death. So Vectors touched, or breathed or sneezed very carefully—or else.

"You enjoy this, don't you?" he laughed.

She smiled. "Why can't saving the world be fun?"

"That's why I wear this hat. Styling . . ."

She giggled and stuck her tongue out. "Funny and *funny looking* are different."

Shamus had been her partner—as well as her lover, her mentor and her boss for nearly a year. They had originally met in Kyoto at a G12 protest to stop the emission of some deadly toxic gas that giant nations were producing. The exact cause hadn't been important to her then. She was fighting the good fight, and that's all that mattered.

Shamus hadn't registered on her radar. He had been just another pretty face among the hundreds struggling to change the world.

She'd hopped around a bit after that: Save the North Atlantic Cod up in Reykjavík, stop the encroachment of deserts down in Cameroon, free Tibet, Chechnya, Hawaii at a Tiananmen Square rally in Beijing. The last had gotten her thrown in a holding cell that smelled like lemon-flavored urine. It had been two days that had seemed like two years. It had been the scariest experience of her life with constant interrogation, threats of torture and worse. She had cried the whole time, begging to go home. On the second night, the local authorities thought they had scared her enough, so they put her on the first plane out of the country.

Later, she had returned to the States and eased up for a while, passing out leaflets for Greenpeace for a month before hooking up with a couple of other girls who were doing the shimmy thing. They had already gotten some serious grafts, large patches of skin oversewn with the thin twisted fiber optics which made them walking advertisements, and they were dancing in front of the big-name casinos. Victoria had chickened out after only a few shimmy clusters, finishing her obligation with semi-permanent inks. She danced for a while, but it had been too much like selling out. Her sponsors had her promoting flashy First World excess items like deodorant and cars which burned honest-to-god gasoline.

She had refused to do it. They had fired her. She went back to PETA. At a rally against the murder of white lab mice, she had met Shamus again. They dated, kind of. Shamus never touched her that first night. She thought it wonderful, strange and unusual. It made him seem different from other men, exotic in a chaste sort of way. She didn't find out the truth until months later.

She gestured to the line of people exiting newly arrived pellets. They moved in small packs through the circular platform and up past the thin strips of shrubbery the city called a park. From her vantage on the top ring of the bull's-eye-shaped concourse, she could see it all. The chubby man, still arguing with his wife, had begun to turn a pale shade of green. The infection had blossomed out from the point where Victoria's lips had met his, spreading like hot tar from his head and down across his shoulders. His wife still wagged a finger at him, but it dripped a verdant honey that crawled along her forearm and over her body like a troop of glowing malachite ants.

The gray-haired man she had caressed and the tiny black woman she had given the "Wet Willie" to had gone their separate ways, faint patches of glistening emerald that formed a lopsided triangle in conjunction with the first couple. The old man, his

453

face scrunched into a tiny oval as he squinted in the sunshine, absentmindedly took one of the flyers being circulated by the minions of some religious cult on the prowl. Olive-colored diamonds passed through his infected fingers, oozing like mucus onto the toga-clad boy holding the flyers—who in turn spread the virus to fellow members of his sect as they maneuvered and traded packets of leaflets to accost the maximum number of tourists.

The woman, short but quite hefty, leaned heavily on guide rails, plant pedestals, trash cans and sometimes other commuters as she ambled her way to the mobile walkways. Every place she paused, she deposited a small puddle of jade liquid, visible only to Victoria and Shamus. Each one of those hot spots became a brief reservoir, a starting point for the induction of the virus as new hosts came into contact.

Within a few minutes, the entire lower platform had been engulfed. As new pellets arrived from the Strip, Fremont Street, the Boadd, a themed adults-only play land, and points around the greater Las Vegas area, they dislodged uninfected passengers and accepted a cargo of freshly created Vectors that sped off in all directions to propagate the virus.

What was this one?" Victoria asked as she watched the last island of unaltered people merge into the pearly green sea of humanity. It was good to actually speak. She found it difficult to carry on a conversation through throat movements alone. The button phones were necessary if they were to keep a low profile, but she had never liked them.

"You didn't ask?"

"No," she giggled. "I figured you'd tell me later. You always do."

And he would. Since he had first indoctrinated her into the movement, Shamus had made it part of his duty to try and educate her about the variations of the virus they spread: their origins, their effects on the general population and the occasional unintended mutations which it was their job to squash. They both knew his tutelage was a waste of time, but she loved him for treating her as an equal and not just a stupid girl. Even after nearly a year together, she still sometimes thought of herself as an imposter, as nothing but a troubled outsider pretending she was part of the big picture.

Shamus knew it all, and that was enough for her. He had been a doctor once, or so she thought. He never admitted it, but he talked like one all the time. He still kept much of his early life a secret from her, and she had never pushed him, not yet. Someday he'd open up, share those early years which must have held as much pain for him as her own held for her. She liked to joke that someday she'd know him better than he knew himself.

"This Vector has a whole new topology. The infection process is the same—the capsid uses some of the same proteins, and the antigens are real close. It's a retro, though, RNA based. It'll fool the body into making a wide spectrum of antibodies to counter what *they're* putting out there. It's one of the most ambitious deliveries we've Vectored yet. A majority of the population will never know they've been infected,

455

and those who can be helped by it will experience only mild flu-like symptoms for a couple of days."

She smiled. The doctor was leaking out of him again.

"And this will counter it? We'll break the FIT program?" she asked.

"We're getting closer," he said. "The government will either have to stop their 'Forced Inoculation Terrorism' or come clean and admit it to the public."

She smiled. The passion in his voice was so out of character with his usual casual demeanor. This was his love, his true calling. The "Federal Initiative To Cure" program (the real name of FIT) didn't have a chance.

He trailed off, his dark eyes wandering over the crowd. Something was wrong. Victoria followed his gaze. Among the infected passengers leaving the pellets headed toward the airport stood an inconspicuous man of indeterminate age. He could have been a father, a brother or a husband. She wouldn't have said he was fat or thin, short or tall. He appeared to be a little of everything, a human average, completely unremarkable.

Except that his body appeared bathed in an angry shade of blood-colored diamonds.

Victoria watched in shock as the man sneezed into the crowd. A red fog spread from his lips, visible she was sure, only to the inoculated. He looked like a firebreather, one of those Polynesian-style performers who stood outside the Grand Hawaiian Casino and fascinated passing tourists with bright jets of flame. But what this man spat was far stranger than any fire.

"Who is that?" she asked. He wasn't part of their movement. She didn't recognize him, and he looked too clean.

Shamus hopped from the dais. He began to wander in the direction of the newcomer, acting casual, blending in. Vectors were like shadows, always there in the light, but seldom noticed.

"Stay here a minute," he sub-vocalized.

At first it was merely odd. Then it became frightening as she watched the man spraying germs like a flamethrower. A crimson-colored tsunami washed over the crowd, spreading faster than the eye could see. It began as an intense blaze of bloody light, studded with garnet and ruby, which broke like a wave onto whatever the Vector touched, breathed on or came in contact with, covering them like a blanket—and then, nothing. No green radiance, or even red, just people the way they were before either Vector got to them. The two diseases simply canceled each other out.

There shouldn't be any other Vectors. She and Shamus were exclusive. They operated west of the Rockies, moving from city to city, sowing infection like farmers sowed wheat. Always, the infections manifested as greenish to the inoculated. The strange red glow made her uneasy, as if it were intended to stand out.

"I'm coming with you," she said as she somersaulted from the dais, dancing her way quietly through the crowd, careful not to touch or be touched. This was the part she hated. The "germy cold shoulder" she liked to call it. Until she went through her cleansing, she'd be susceptible to the mutated touch of her own Vector.

Shamus glanced quickly back. His long dark face was carefully neutral, but his eyes glittered like obsidian shards. "Stay back, Victoria. I'm serious." His lips never moved, but his voice came through her button phone loud and angry. It was the stern older Shamus, the "Doctor" Shamus, and not the quiet, amused, lover-Shamus who spoke.

But Victoria, ever petulant when accosted by authority, ignored him. Instead, she picked her way through the thickening crowd with superb agility and great care, conscious of their closeness, but outwardly casual and energetic. She was, after all, supposed to be merely a shimmy girl, a walking, dancing piece of eye candy, an advertising gimmick meant only to display merchandise on the glowing patches of fiber optics tattooed to her naked skin.

The chubby man arguing with his wife still occupied a place on the platform. Victoria watched as the ruby-colored wave engulfed them, flaring through her hard-wrought work in an instant, sublimating the greenish shine with a burst of bright cherry— and then, nothing. What was this process doing to them? She hadn't any medical training, but she knew that Vectoring triggered the immune response. What happened when you turned that response on and off like a light switch?

"Whatever he's doing, he's doing it fast," she said.

"Keep away from him. Don't touch anyone showing red," Shamus growled.

Was this her first day as a Vector? She knew how to handle herself, and she didn't need to be protected like a child. She knew better than to touch the forest of green hosts buzzing through the courtyard, as well as the new red ones who erupted like mini volcanoes, blazing briefly with infection and then dying out.

"Who is this guy?" she asked again. Shamus knew, she could tell. He just wasn't saying.

"Come on," Shamus said suddenly. "We've got to go."

He started back toward her, and for a moment she thought he was going to grab her by the hand and drag her physically out of the pellet station.

"Wait!" she shouted, forgetting to use the button phone's sub-vocals. A few of the closer tourists glanced over.

The unknown Vector jerked in surprise, noticing Shamus. Victoria watched the man's round face as he casually swept the platform with his eyes, maybe checking to see if there were others. Shamus had frozen beside a young couple pushing a covered stroller, blending in. But the stranger had locked onto him.

The tone in Victoria's ear changed to indicate a connection had been added to her button.

"I am the fluoride in your water. . . . I am your polio vaccine. . . ."

Victoria heard the man's smooth high voice recite the familiar words as if they were poisonous, spreading like smoke from his fingertips, and she *knew* who he was. He had to be a government man, a Vector from the FIT program. He was the source of the problem, the plague rat.

RYAN DOWNING

If the program had been out in the public eye, it might have been given a motto, and those words would be it, like the "to protect and serve" of the police, or the "through driving wind and pouring rain" of the post office. She knew the words, and she didn't believe them for a moment. The government may have started out on the right side, but they never stayed there long. Power corrupts.

"Who are you?" Shamus sub-vocalized as he pretended to be interested in the child shaded beneath the blue-striped awning that covered a small wheeled cart. "What do you want?"

"Don't you know me? I know you, Shamus."

"I do not." Shamus, suddenly unsure, moved swiftly through the crowd away from the stranger.

The man laughed loudly. He began shaking hands with everyone around him, clapping people on the back, breathing out his red smoke. Crimson flashed in waves of all sizes, cascading rapidly through the crowd as people jostled each other in a hundred different ways. Victoria had never realized before becoming a Vector how much unconscious intimacy occurred among humans as they shuffled through life, unaware of each other, but in constant contact.

"I've seen your picture a hundred times," the stranger said. "You're famous, or should I say infamous."

"Know thy enemy. . . ."

The man chuckled. "You're on a lot of watch lists. You've been causing trouble for a long time."

It was Shamus' turn to laugh. "Glad I'm getting through to you."

"You are, really," the man said as he moved closer.

"In fact, I'd be happy if you would come with me. We can debate points of view if you'd like. I have a car on the way."

Victoria gasped. She hadn't realized that she'd been holding her breath. When the stranger had said car, he really meant *police* car. Were they going to be arrested? Shamus claimed that they'd never do it, that they wouldn't want the publicity. Thoughts of that tiny cell in Beijing returned. She couldn't do that again.

"I don't want to go to jail," she whispered.

Shamus spun around, waving her down, trying to tell her without words to shut up and keep out of it. But it was too late.

The unknown Vector had noticed her. He began moving through the crowd as if he hadn't a care in the world, but his casual saunter had altered. He strode almost directly toward Victoria now.

"And who might this be?" The man's tenor had turned icy, almost mechanical. He staggered a bit as he walked, feigning drunkenness in order to jostle and infect more people as he came toward her.

"Nobody you need worry about, Attie," Shamus replied.

The man hesitated, off guard. Then he smiled. "Character profiling software is illegal, my friend. I could have you brought in just for that."

"But you won't," Shamus replied. He motioned for Victoria to work her way around the wedge-shaped park opposite.

"Can he see what we see?" she asked.

"No, he can't," Attie said as if the question were meant for him. "But I can tell that you're different somehow, and I know you're involved in something you can't possibly understand."

Victoria danced away, laughing and tumbling like a clown—pretending to be a shimmy girl playing the platform, performing for attention—but inside she trembled, more afraid than she'd been since that day in China. Distraction would make her sloppy, so she took her time, calculating her way through the crowd. A chance contact now would be deadly.

She'd spent so much of her time trying to find clever ways of putting her skin next to the skin of others that it took concentration not to simply wade into the passing bodies like a dolphin plunging through pristine waters. Her heart fluttered, beating swiftly. Her knees threatened to buckle and dump her on her ass at every turn, and when a fat woman dressed in a bright yellow snow parka (in July? in Las Vegas?) nearly collided with her, she lost it. She actually squeaked in panic and ran the other way.

"He can't really take us in, Shamus?" she stammered as she found an island of empty space in the sea of bodies. "Can he?"

"They don't want the publicity," Shamus replied. "There's nothing to fear."

The man laughed, his voice echoed like the sound of a dog barking in her ears.

"Ignore him. Come my way, Vic," Shamus whispered through the button. She could almost hear the "calm down and relax" he should have added.

He was right, whether he said it or not. She needed to slow down and get a grip. They weren't technically doing anything illegal—at least not anything that hurt anybody.

She glanced through the middle level of the pellet platform, at the trains coming and going. The small capsules rested on magnetically charged plates that would slingshot them away on spiral trajectories through underground channels, like pills delivering vital medicine through the arteries of the city. People meandered, going about their business unaware. None of them had suddenly dropped dead or even looked ill. In fact, they should be getting better. After all, Victoria and those like her were correcting a wrong, fixing the problem that this man represented.

"You're the bad guy here," she said abruptly. "You're the evil representative of a government that can't stop meddling in the lives of its citizens."

"Where do you get this stuff from? Who's writing your propaganda these days?" Attie replied calmly. "I'm not evil, and FIT isn't a new program."

"But its Vector component is," Shamus said.

"True." Attie had moved in, passing the raised gravel at the edge of the neatly manicured park, stalking them. The small rocks bubbled, a thin mist rising from beneath them as sprinklers below the surface struggled to keep the foliage lush in Nevada's one-hundred-and-nine-degree summer.

"But *we are* doing the good work," he said, his voice becoming more forceful. "It's FIT who prevents the flu, stops the flareups of random HIV strains and pushes polio and tuberculosis back to mere memories. *We* do it, not you. You protestors do nothing but complain, and when nobody listens to your whining, you start sabotaging things."

"It's our right to protest," Victoria said.

"But not your *right* to spread this killing filth," Attie spat back. "It's only because the law is two steps behind technology that you're not in prison right now!"

Victoria snorted. "I've listened to guys like you at a hundred rallies. You come, but not to talk or express real opinions. You only come to incite trouble. Then, when some poor bastard takes the bait, you point and say how irrational we are. The status quo is always correct. The government will always save us. God bless America. . . ."

She stepped back, away from the park and closer to the broad coal-colored pavement. Foot traffic was heavier here, but it was farther from Attie. She couldn't even stand to look at him.

"You're all the same," he said as he vanished behind the wide trunk of a palm tree at the other end of the park. "Authority is always wrong, always out to hurt you. Why? Why would the government deliberately try to poison its own people?"

She sputtered. She didn't have to know why; she just knew it was happening. The red tinge in the distance proved he was doing it right now.

"Control," Shamus said.

"Yes." She was losing control of herself, speaking out loud when she meant to use the sub-vocals. Attie had gotten under her skin.

"A sick population depends on socialized medicine," Shamus explained. "The larger the demographic, the more the government gets involved. An involved government is a big government.

"Didn't Thomas Jefferson say that 'a government

big enough to supply everything you need is big enough to take everything you have?'"

Attie laughed. A harsh cackle filled his voice. "Yes, I've heard the quotes, Shamus. I *know* you don't really believe them. You're too smart. But does she?"

"Hey!" she shouted, drawing a few looks. She turned with a self-conscious smile and walked the curved sloping ramp to the upper platform. "I believe that you're poisoning people, that's what I believe."

"Just saying it over and over doesn't make it true," Attie said as he casually followed her up the ramp. "Do you even know what's in the Vector we spread? Do you know what's in *yours*?"

"It's RNA based, with proteins and . . ." And she felt very, very stupid as she said it. She wasn't dumb, damn it. She may not know the details or the science behind the Vector, but that didn't mean she couldn't understand what was going on. He was twisting her around with his words, and it was making her flustered.

"He's messing with you, Vic," Shamus said. "That's what they do. They work you with their political skills until you begin to doubt yourself. Come on, come to me. We're getting out of here."

"Wait!" Attie lurched forward. He was still a good hundred yards away from Victoria, but in this crowd she couldn't run. If he chased her, he'd catch her.

"You really don't know what you're doing?" he asked. His tone was unexpectedly urgent, his face suddenly concerned.

"I know more than I need to," she replied. She reached up to her temple and tapped the button phone stitched into her skin. It sounded a double low tone. She tapped it again.

"Shamus, I can't get him off my line," she said nervously.

"No, you can't," Attie said. "I have you locked in. I want you to hear me."

His voice slid over her like snow sliding down a mountainside, leaving her feeling cold and exposed. Shamus had moved casually up the ramp, swinging around to put himself between Victoria and the other man.

"Do you know where your Vector comes from?" Attie asked unexpectedly. "It comes from China. Their government builds it, and they build it exclusively for protest groups. They don't use it on their own people. They don't offer it to the United States government. They don't mention it to the press. They make it solely to distribute to the troublemakers and the discontented in *this* country."

He sauntered a little closer. She could see the gleam in his brown eyes now. "Why do you think they would do that?"

"I don't know," she stammered softly, lowering her eyes. The mention of China had thrown her. Did Attie know who she was? Was he using her memories of Beijing, her fear of that episode, to make her crumble?

"Shamus?" Attie asked.

"It has to be made somewhere," Shamus replied quickly, closing the gap between Attie and himself. "Science has come a long way since bacteria were first isolated, but you don't suppose we can produce something like our Vector at home, do you? As

467

far as I know, the assembly can't be done without some really expensive equipment. You need a big lab, something capable of churning out tailor-made viruses, producing cultures, extracting and mixing DNA or RNA."

Attie had retreated at Shamus' approach. He chose to spread his infection among a group of school children playing some game with colored chalk on the dark pavement. Nearby, grizzled cabbies hawked rides in foot-propelled carts, trying to lure fares away from the main streets to back-alley casinos and amusements.

"I don't know what to think," she said. She didn't know how they'd gotten into a debate, but she already felt like the loser. Why was she suddenly so confused?

She moved west, slowly heading for the Fremont Street ramp. That was the quickest way to get lost if she needed to.

"Why didn't you tell me where it came from?" she asked.

"Would it have made a difference?" Shamus replied. "Nobody ever asks where the posters and pamphlets come from. Nobody cares where the websites are programmed or from what computer they originate. It's incidental, unnecessary information. Stuff just happens."

"But . . ."

"No buts," he said. His voice held a thick quality, a hardness she had never heard before. "We're still doing the right thing."

"No, you're not," Attie whispered.

"Are *you*?" Victoria said. Her voice sounded so

much calmer than she felt. She was perspiring. Her tan flesh glistened with moisture, roiling with an olive-colored combination of her Vector and sweat.

"Yes."

"Then why do you do this in secret?" she asked.

"We don't," Attie replied. "FIT is a registered and publicly available government agency. My rank is the same as a GS-7. I make as much as your average letter carrier for the post office, and let me tell you that's not a whole lot."

"You're not delivering mail, buddy," Shamus cut in.

"But I *am* doing a valid service for the citizens of this country, and that's more than I can say of you!"

Victoria glanced around. People strolled through the parks and across the platform. Most looked like tourists, and they were either enjoying the sunshine or excitedly on their way to one of the ubiquitous casinos. A young couple ambled by, both wearing huge smiles and holding each other tightly. The man grasped one of those purple buckets from the Rio, and Victoria could hear the coins sliding musically around inside. Everything seemed so tranquil.

When she glanced back, she stared at a collection of jeweled dolls, mannequins dressed in churning films of disease, some sparkling green, others flaring red before evaporating back into the normal spectrum. The words they were throwing back and forth were something like that. On the surface they sounded so rational, but when seen though the filter of lies and deception, they mutated into something else entirely.

"Why isn't the press here?" Attie interrupted her thoughts, apparently changing the subject.

"Who?" He'd lost her. What was he asking?

"The press," he said. "The news trucks, the reporters, the cameras . . . Where are they?"

"I don't understand," she said.

"If FIT is doing something dirty, something deadly, shouldn't the public know?" Attie made a show of spinning around, arms wide, as if searching.

"Where are they?" he asked. "You people and your protest groups, you're like actors. You're always in front of a camera somewhere. And if something as terrible as you say is being perpetrated, then you can bet that Shamus or someone just like him would be at Channel 7 in a heartbeat spilling his guts. But, no. How come?"

Actually, that had occurred to her. She'd asked and been given a reasonable answer.

"Publicity would lead to panic," she replied. "If the public only knew what you were doing to them . . ."

"Enough!" Attie shouted. "What *you're* doing should be called murder, and you know it."

His voice became low and frosty. "You two are doing more harm in this pellet station than a battalion of soldiers could."

"Lives are saved here," Victoria said. "We're shielding these people from future infections. How can that be bad?"

Attie chuckled, an evil sound. He shook his head as if she had suddenly told a joke.

"We're still doing more good than harm," Shamus replied. "Come on, Vic. Let's go."

"Wait a minute," she said. "More good than harm? What kind of harm?"

Somehow the conversation had gotten away from

her. Was there something wrong with their Vector, something she hadn't been told about? Or was Attie twisting them both around, trying to play one against the other?

"She doesn't know, does she?" Attie circled, shaking hands and patting backs as he moved, like a politician whoring for votes. Unsuspecting people lit up like fireworks under the man's skillful fingers, bright streamers of red that flared and multiplied, and then faded in an instant.

One woman, a thin Caucasian with tight, pinched features, shone like a newly polished apple as she bumped an elderly gentleman. He began to glow like a freshly cut ruby, and then accidentally leaned on the shoulder of the man beside him. It went on from there, like a rising tide in cotton-candy colors, as people bumped, jostled and breathed crimson fumes all over each other.

"What don't I know?" Victoria tried to make her voice as cold as Attie's. She now realized there was far more going on here than she had originally thought, and she wasn't very happy about it.

Shamus had been her hero from the moment she had met him. She had trusted him instinctively. He had all the right words and all the right moves. Had she been mistaken? Had he been using her? Was their protest actually *bad,* the kind of wrong she had dedicated her life to overcome? Or was she jumping to conclusions?

She took a deep cleansing breath, shaking herself, opening her mind. She'd learned the calming technique in New Delhi at a sit-in to save the Ganges, and she felt it really helped when the world got complicated. But thoughts rocketed through her mind so fast that nothing could slow them down. She had been lied to—she was being lied to now—and, somewhere inside the splitting headache that had begun to force itself on her already-throbbing skull, she was pissed off about it.

"We're not the bad guys here, Vic," Shamus said.

A horrible sour feeling formed in the pit of her stomach. Part of her didn't want to know the answer, but she had to ask. "What have you been keeping from me?"

"Tell her," Attie said venomously.

Shamus sighed. Victoria saw his shoulders slump, and he dropped heavily onto the hot pavement, collapsing into a heap like an imploding building. His body looked like one of those old statues that they used to place in parks, hard copper with a deep coat of bright jade patina.

"What do I need to know that you haven't told me?" she asked softly as she backed away, away from the stranger and away from her lover.

The first Vectored infections FIT produced were simple piggybacks, genetic tags added to HHV6. That's a variant of the herpes virus which infects more than 95% of the population at a young age. It doesn't cause any serious health problems, so it was perfect as a delivery system. That was the whole project, at first. Nobody had a problem with it. But then they began to get ambitious. They started adding elements, selecting for specific and sometimes disturbing things. A group of doctors and scientists saw where this was headed, saw that this might lead to not just cures but modifications to the human genome, forced genetic homogenization."

"Wait a minute," Attie interrupted. "Nothing like that was ever planned. Nobody's trying to take over the world. That's just paranoid propaganda. Vectoring is a tool, a means by which we can improve our whole species."

"How?" Shamus said. "I have documents that clearly show proposals for several radical alterations to the human genome, documents given to me by reliable sources."

"I don't believe you."

"Stop!" Victoria shouted. Her head wanted to explode. "I can't take this all in. Let Shamus finish."

"Okay—so we recognized the potential for abuse and we petitioned for a halt to the program," Shamus continued. "Typical bureaucracy, they ignored us. We shouted louder. We even made some headlines, but nobody really cared.

"Things used to be different in the old days. There was a time when the people would have stood up and fought with us. I'd been in marches where the streets had undulated like a living carpet with the sheer press of bodies, and the sky was dark with news copters. People cared. They didn't let the government make all the decisions for them, and they cherished their freedoms. Now . . ."

Shamus waved listlessly to the east, toward the towering glass and plastic structures of downtown. He seemed so dejected that it nearly broke her heart. Victoria suddenly wanted to run to him.

"Now nobody cares. As long as they're plugged

into a phone or a streaming media source, the rest of the world can go to hell. We're becoming isolated, islands in the sea of humanity," he said.

"After we realized the news media couldn't be counted on, we decided to fight fire with fire. We found backers overseas—and you'd be surprised at how easy it was. They agreed to do the work. All we had to do was tell them how."

"You did? You, personally?" she asked. She hadn't realized that he'd been the driving force behind the protests. That in itself was frightening, to think that Shamus had been responsible for all this.

"I was on the original team," Shamus said. "We took HHV6 apart and rebuilt it protein by protein. We did a damned good job, too. The tests were so promising. Our virus ate the government's variant for breakfast along every mutation. Absolutely no side effects. It appeared to be perfect, so we unleashed it. I Vectored it myself."

"I don't understand," Victoria said. "What were you trying to accomplish?"

"It's complicated, but we thought that if we could block the base code of the virus FIT was distributing, we'd be able to keep them from dispensing more updates."

"But that's not what happened," Attie interrupted. He glanced up as a disk-shaped helicopter passed by overhead, its rotors encased in a carbon mesh shield that made the machine look like a 1950s-era flying saucer.

The expectant way his attention moved to the copter made Victoria realize that he must be waiting for something like that. Despite what Shamus thought, someone was coming to arrest them. Attie was just stalling for time.

"We couldn't understand why our own virus seemed to become impotent," Attie said, his awareness returning to the plaza. "Several varieties were Vectored without success. My people suspected that it might not be a natural immune response, and that something like your group was responsible. We could never prove it—until today."

"Good."

"Not good," Attie snapped. "You've compromised nearly the entire population. You and your group have weakened all of our immune systems to the edge of collapse, and our attempts to circumvent the problem have proven ineffective. We can't fix this, not without knowing more about the topology of your variant."

Victoria could hardly think. There was so much new information flooding in, so much she hadn't understood and still didn't understand. The sunshine and the heat, the small clusters of people flaring through the spectrum of reds—from cherry to oxblood, to brick and ruby—as Attie weaved his way across the wide curved pavement; they all distracted her. She desperately wanted to run, but couldn't pull herself away. If she left now, she'd never know it all.

Shamus had continued to speak, shaking his head as if willing the information to become unreal. "It should have worked."

"But it didn't." Attie had changed his course, moving away from Victoria and toward Shamus. He casually brushed against a trio of college kids. The largest man, a dark kid in a slashed silver shirt and a black kilt, paused momentarily to give Attie a dirty look. Then he turned and dived on his friends, whispering something Victoria couldn't hear. They all laughed—and they all brightened with the red glow of infection.

"No, it didn't. Our variant somehow interfered with the mechanism the body uses to prevent the synthesis of viral proteins in infected cells."

Shamus paused. His head tilted to one side as if he was listening to another conversation. Attie had circled around. He stood a dozen or so meters behind Shamus, pretending to stare at the screen of his wristbook.

"This explains so much," Attie said. Victoria could see him stealing furtive glances at the sky while at the same time trying to keep an eye on Shamus. "You do understand that everything you say can be used against you in a court of law. . . ."

"I don't care anymore." Shamus sighed. "Vic, take off. Get the hell away from here."

"I'd prefer it if she stayed right where she was," Attie said.

"Go, Vic. This guy won't leave me, and he can't trace you. Get away."

"Wait!" she said. She couldn't even breathe anymore. Her stomach churned and her legs had begun to tremble. She felt like the conversation had left her far behind. "I need to know. . . ."

"Go, just go."

"No!" she yelled. "Answer me, damn it! Yes or no—no debates, no quotes from dead presidents, no technical terms to confuse me—*are we still making people sick?*"

She held her breath, waiting. A long silence followed.

"Technically, yes," Shamus finally whispered. "Yes."

Victoria staggered back as if he'd punched her in the face. She'd been a fool for his good looks and smooth words—and his talk about saving the world. How could she have been so stupid?

"All this talk about how the government was killing people and it was us! How could you!"

She felt herself beginning to cry, but she forced it back. There'd be time for tears later. Instead, she concentrated on the anger. Shamus had betrayed her. He'd used her, letting her believe the whole time that she had been doing the right thing. It made her sick to think of how many times she'd spread his Vector.

"We're *not* killing people," he growled. "Never say that! I've put my soul into turning this around."

"Maybe if we knew exactly what you did, we could fix the problem," Attie offered. "It will go a long way toward mitigating the penalty for what you've done."

"No," Shamus said.

"But . . ." Victoria began.

"Don't you see? Just because we screwed up doesn't mean we were wrong. I'm still convinced there's a plot out there."

Her whole world was falling apart. Months of being with him and she thought she knew him, but now he seemed like a stranger, a paranoid stranger.

It had all started so playfully, so carefree. They had shouted together in San Francisco while waving signs and screaming for the rights of mice. Later, they talked. He hadn't tried to sleep with her or even kiss her. He spoke with her as an equal, and she respected that. He never talked down to her, never tried to change her. They laughed. She fell in love.

But it was all a lie. Shamus had already been spreading his Vector even before they met. That summer night at the PETA rally, he had already been infected then, glowing in emeralds. If she had only been able to see it . . .

"So what have we been doing this whole time?" she asked. She'd been carrying the Vectored infection off and on for more than half a year now, deliberately targeting others. She'd become an accomplice to a crime she hadn't realized she was committing.

"What we have to. There's nothing else we *can* do," he added hurriedly. There was a note of pleading in his voice. "You don't understand."

"I think she's beginning to understand," Attie said. His voice had softened. It held a note of sympathy that seemed to churn inside her, making her even angrier.

Her mind spun. Up was down, black was white, truth was—was just something that didn't seem to exist anymore. Could Shamus really have kept this from her this whole time? Could she ever trust him again? He was a stranger to her now.

"What do you want from me?" she said coldly. "Do you want me to go on infecting people? Do you want me to dance, to smile, to laugh while I poison people? I thought we were trying to stop others from doing that. I can't do it, not now. I can't be your puppet, Shamus. I can't be your Typhoid Mary any longer."

Tears had begun to fall. Embarrassed, she turned away. She hugged the raised wall that marked the boundary between the pellet train station and the busy streets of downtown Las Vegas.

"We're not poisoning people, Vic." Shamus stood. He rotated slowly until he spotted Attie. "The reason we—you and I, the others in our group—continue to spread this Vector is to save people. We're committed to that. We always were. I never lied to you."

"But there was so much you never told me," she said.

"You never asked—and I know that's an evasion. I should have told you. I should have explained all these things. But you were so innocent, so . . ."

"Naïve," she said.

"Yes, naïve—but in a good way: unspoiled and not contaminated by the darker side of what had happened. You brought a joy to this disaster, and it helped me to feel as if it would all turn out okay. I was convinced—I *am* convinced that it's only a matter of time until we Vector a cure for what we've done. Then we'll be heroes."

She felt betrayed. She didn't know what to think. She should have been told, allowed to make her own decisions. He'd treated her like a child. The whole time she had thought his dark past involved merely an old girlfriend or even an ex-wife. It had been cute, almost chivalrous at the time, when she thought he had only wanted to protect her. Now she had nothing, a hole in her heart where the truth used to be.

"There are a lot of people who are going to need to know exactly how you managed this, Shamus,"

Attie said. "What alterations you made, how many variations you've spread and where you've spread them. The CDC will have to be involved. We'll try our best to turn the clock back on this, but . . ."

"No. We can only move forward," Shamus said. "The government will take this and corrupt it. Trust me. I know things, things that aren't part of the public record. We can't rely on FIT, or the CDC or any branch of the government connected to the Vectoring project. We need to stick together and work this out for ourselves, Vic. I don't want to say it, but we need to keep dancing before the flames."

Victoria felt the strain tugging at her, threatening to rip her apart. Her heart wanted to go with her lover and his ideals, but her conscience felt the weight of the other man's argument that it would have been better if they hadn't tampered with nature. Shamus had lied to her. He'd told her that she would save the world, but right now she felt more like an accused mass murderer. His words disturbed her, but she believed in the sentiment behind them. She'd been taught that the government was uncaring at best, intentionally evil at worst. That's why she always took the counterpoint. But where was the opposite pole here? Which way could she turn when each side seemed wrong?

"There's no way out," Shamus said. "If we continue, there's no guarantee we'll be able to put things right, but if FIT or the CDC get hold of our Vector, they'll use it to unlock their virus and start all over."

Attie sighed. Victoria could tell his impatience was growing. His backup must already be overdue.

Cars full of agents would be coming soon, maybe even helicopters. They'd arrive in gangs, sirens shattering the serenity of the station. They wouldn't ask questions or wait for complicated answers that required a moral epiphany to make a choice. They'd use cuffs and pepper spray. She didn't know if Shamus would go quietly, but she would.

Victoria glanced at her fingers, at the lime-colored flecks as they caught the sun. She felt harmless. Would her feelings change? Were her hands really deadly, and did they carry a bacterial Midas touch?

It was time to go—but where, and with whom? And could she even leave knowing what she now knew?

What do I do?" she cried out loud.

"Forgive me," Shamus whispered from behind her.

She spun quickly, panicked at the unexpected sound of his voice so near. He reached out to her, his arms strong, welcoming. She yearned to fall into them, to let him take her away, take her back to the morning, or the previous day, or any time before she had learned the world wasn't the place she thought it was. But touching was forbidden.

"Don't do that!" she shrieked. A couple in their early thirties, dressed in identical Hawaiian shirts and baggy blue shorts, paused. Concern played over the man's fat sunburnt face.

Victoria noticed them staring and laughed. She swung her arms in the air, twirled and giggled. She nearly touched Shamus then, but only knocked his silly fedora askew instead. She put on her best "happy

481

couple just having a little spat" face and winked at the tourists. They waddled off, shaking their heads in unison like two bobblehead dolls.

The moment they had moved on, Victoria's smile vanished.

"I never meant to hurt you," Shamus whispered as she drifted back through the crowd.

But you did, she thought. Could it have been as little as an hour ago that she had been happy? What had happened to all that? She could no longer trust Shamus. Did that mean she no longer loved him?

"I wish I could believe you," she said.

Shamus followed her, trailing behind like a poodle on a leash. He stood just beyond her reach, his face mostly hidden by the dumb hat. "Believe that I love you, and we'll figure out the rest."

She couldn't make the choice. Neither option made her feel good. She wasn't God. She didn't want the responsibility of deciding who lived and who died. It made her skin crawl to think that it was exactly what they *had* been doing, changing the world. What had they been trying to change it into?

Maybe she wouldn't make a choice at all. Maybe she should just turn and walk away. Let them fight it out, let Attie take Shamus to jail. She could go back and become a real shimmy girl, get the full fiber optics sewn under her skin and become a walking billboard. But then she'd have to face the crowds, the teeming masses of mothers and fathers, brothers and sisters, all unaware they were either about to die or were one Vector away from death.

And the babies . . .

She couldn't give up on them. Some hope was better than having no hope at all, wasn't it? But she was through taking things on faith. That had to stop. The little girl who followed her big strong boyfriend around and treated controlled contagion as a game was gone. She'd have to learn now, study the Vector process from both sides and decide for herself if what they had done could be corrected or not. She'd have to ask questions, questions she should have asked from the beginning. Instead, she'd let herself be led around like a toy balloon—an empty-headed, helium-filled balloon.

She'd have to find out about those documents too, the ones Shamus had mentioned. If he could prove to her that the government was up to something, it would go a long way toward making her feel better about her choice. If not . . .

"I want to go now," she said. "I'm ready. Take me home."

Shamus had been waiting, hoping for her to make a quick decision. He started forward, a wide smile forming on his lips. He looked suddenly younger, more vibrant. This must not have been easy for him either.

She wondered what would become of the people passing through the concourse. Would they live? Would a Vector—possibly even her—reinfect them with the necessary immunities to keep them healthy and blissfully unaware? And what would Attie do? He couldn't stop them, not physically. Others could, agents not currently compromised by either version of the Vector, but none had yet arrived.

Their luck ran out at the same instant that the thought entered her mind. Sirens, distant shrieks, high-pitched and mechanical, sounded from the direction of the Boadd. At this time of day it would take a while for wheeled vehicles to navigate the crowded streets of Las Vegas' new sin preserve. They still had time, but only a little.

She turned, expecting to find Shamus nearby. Instead, Attie stood within a foot of her.

He smiled. She screamed.

"Boo," he whispered. His face smiled, but contempt gleamed behind his small eyes.

So she spit on him.

She didn't think about it. It was an instinctive reaction. The little blob, shining green with her Vector, landed on the ruby skin of his cheek, like an olive in a bowl of cherries—and it began to spread. Her Vectored virus began to infiltrate Attie's body. He reacted as if shot, stumbling back. His fingers moved to his cheek, coming away with a dusting of molten emeralds.

"You bitch!" he hissed. His right hand balled into a fist, and he swung. Victoria closed her eyes, expecting pain. Nothing happened. Trembling, she peeked. Shamus stood between her and the other man. He held Attie's small fist tightly in his massive hand.

"That is no way to treat a lady," Shamus growled ominously. His skin, once the color of darkened sea glass where the avocado shimmer of his Vector covered his natural chocolate tones, began to bleed. His arm to the elbow became engulfed within a crawling wave the color of burgundy. Attie's skin, bright as a stop sign, now appeared mottled like jungle camouflage. The two distinct viruses, at war, passed between the men in bursts and cascades, packets of green and red that blurred, collapsed and coalesced almost too quickly for the eye follow. They burned themselves out within moments, leaving the two men standing in the sunlight, blank, drained. Neither of the Vectored viruses remained to stain their flesh.

"Shamus!" Victoria cried.

Shamus raised his right hand, momentarily confused as he inspected himself. Then the enormity of his actions sank in, and his face twisted in distress. It lasted only a moment before he spoke, but Victoria had seen the hopelessness in his eyes, and it crushed her soul.

"Don't worry, Vic. Everything's fine." He smiled, but there was no joy behind it.

She leapt into his arms, tears the color of summer meadows splashing from her eyes. They struck his cheek, his shoulder, his chest—but with no potency. The drops melted against his skin like ice on hot pavement, as did her hopes. Her Vector wouldn't stick.

"You can't die on me. Don't," she sobbed.

He shrugged. There was nothing he could say. They both knew what would happen, what was probably already happening. His body would begin to tear itself apart. Foreign organisms flooded through his blood stream, encountering no immune response. Every system in his body would begin to react, like an organ transplant patient gone horribly wrong. Healthy cells would be eliminated, healthy organs rejected. Every one of the hundreds of molds, bacteria and viruses that harmlessly enshroud people every

485

day, living within us and floating around us, would instantly become a lethal enemy. His own white blood cells would start to turn against him, and he'd die. Quickly and terribly.

If he hadn't been a Vector, he might not even have noticed what Attie had done to him, but his own choice had doomed him.

Suddenly, all the confusion and betrayal was behind her. She felt so young and vulnerable, and so very much alone.

"Please don't leave me," she begged. "I don't know what to do."

His lips formed into a sad smile. "You're strong, Vic. I know you, maybe better than you realize, maybe even better than you know yourself. You'll keep trying to save the world."

A moment ago he had her believing that she was partly responsible for wrecking it. Now, she just didn't care. The rest of the world seemed small and unimportant. She wanted things back the way they were, back the way they could never be again.

"But I can't. Not without you."

"You can," he said firmly. "Remember, I love you."

Then he grabbed Attie by the shoulder and spun him around. The smaller man had stood there through the whole exchange, pale and stricken. A look of disbelief mixed with growing horror covered his face and his flat, lifeless eyes. As a Vector, he'd share Shamus' fate. Nothing could cure what was already happening inside them.

"Let me buy you a drink," Shamus said as he maneuvered the man up the ramp and toward the closest walking sidewalk headed downtown. "Your friends can pick us up at the Shamrock. How's that sound?"

He glanced back briefly to wink at Victoria and then was gone.

She stood there in shock, unable to move as the growing swarms of people ambled around her like water past a boulder in a stream. Without Shamus she had nothing. Her soul had been ripped free with his departure, leaving a very thin, empty shell. How could she go on? What would she do?

The passage of bodies flowed around her as she remained transfixed, unable to step outside her pain. Time passed, but she wasn't aware of it. Thoughts and images came and went within her mind, but they flitted though her subconscious with such dizzying speed that she could concentrate on nothing. Part of her heard the sirens scream past, headed uptown. They'd be coming back this way soon enough, but she no longer cared.

The past emerged as an intense light, brilliant and bright, jammed full of happy memories and laughter. She remembered the first day she and Shamus had met. She remembered his smile, and his loose confidence and the affectionate way he always called her Vic. That was all gone now, lost in darkness and despair.

She felt as if she should move, run, escape, but that would take focus. Focus would be thinking, and thinking was bad. Maybe she'd just stand here, wait until her Vector died out, or they came for her, or until her own immune system collapsed. She could join him then. They could be together again, together forever.

Something soft caressed her thigh. "Lady . . ."

Victoria glanced down, slowly shifting her center of attention from her pain to the young girl standing in front of her. The child must have been only six or seven years old, a chubby little dark-skinned cherub with tightly curled black hair held in asymmetric clumps by glowing rods in primary colors. In her hands was Shamus' ugly felt fedora. The girl had been pressing it against Victoria's leg.

"A big man told me to give this to you," the girl said as she held the dreadful gray lump out for Victoria to take. The air seemed to thin around her. She couldn't catch her breath, let alone talk. It seemed like forever before she was able to reach out and touch the fedora.

"Thank you," Victoria stammered, unable to think of anything else to say.

"He said 'there are things worth fighting for,'" the little girl recited. "He told me you'd know what he meant."

And then, in a tiny whisper, she said, "But I hope you're not fighting about that hat. It's ugly."

Victoria began to cry again.

"No," she said. "It's not about the hat."

She gazed down at the girl, at her beautiful big eyes and innocent smile. She loved children. They were hope and happiness all rolled into one, and Shamus knew just how to get her going again. It was just like him to worry about her, to make sure she didn't get locked into self pity.

488

She knelt down and took the child's face in her hands. The girl's skin was warm. Victoria kissed her on both cheeks and then once on her forehead. "Thank you."

The girl giggled and then skipped away into the crowd. Victoria watched her go, a brightening emerald glow enfolding her small body. She ran up to a heavy woman and wrapped her little arms around one thick pillar of a leg. The green film slithered from the girl's fingers, covering the older woman—who in turn spread it to yet another woman and two men who stood nearby. The Vector fanned out from there, sprouting a forest of shimmering bodies in tints of green ranging from olive, to jade, to lime and shades she couldn't put names to.

Victoria smiled and wiped one last tear from her eyes. It wouldn't be the same, not now. She wasn't the naïve girl who had danced into the public concourse that morning. She was a Vector, and now she'd have to learn what that really meant. She'd have to find the documents Shamus mentioned. With those she could choose a side, make a decision. There was a lot to do. She needed to organize, but most of all she needed to learn. If she was going to change the world, she couldn't simply stand by and protest anymore.

She looked down at the fedora in her hands and almost put it on. No, she thought, she'd do it her own way.

The Sundial

written by

John Arkwright

illustrated by

IRVIN RODRIGUEZ

ABOUT THE AUTHOR

John Arkwright's mother paid for his birth by digging potatoes during the final stages of her pregnancy. His father was in a body cast due to a train wreck. Mom recited "The Raven" to put John to sleep at night. The soles of his feet were thick and hard from going barefoot for eight months per year; his back was tanned from going shirtless. John loved tic-tac-toe and checkers, which his grandfather, Cricket, taught him. Later he enjoyed chess and impromptu wrestling at his country school.

Poe continued to thrill John with "The Tell-Tale Heart" and "The Black Cat," but in his teens and twenties John found Asimov, Tolkien, Orson Scott Card and William Gibson. John met Julia at a Dungeons & Dragons game in college and they married about the time he earned his first degree. Later, he earned a doctorate in economics from the University of South Carolina with a dissertation on terrorist bargaining. John and Julia now live in a small southern mountain town with their three sons.

John works hard to show his students how they can use rational decision making to enrich their lives. Julia works hard to raise three sons and an aggravating husband. John writes when he can, his imagination fueled by his rediscovery of Mark Twain and his belated discoveries of George R. R. Martin and Elmore Leonard.

Julia, the world's most voracious reader, edits his work. His creative writing professor, B. J. Robinson, and his writing friend, the computer goddess, Barbara Seaton, form their Gang of Three writing group. They have taught him well. Stonepile Writers, located at his university, also nourishes his craft and creativity.

John's mother is now deceased. His hero is his father, Scotty.

ABOUT THE ILLUSTRATOR

Irvin Rodriguez is also the illustrator for "The Truth, from a Lie of Convenience" in this volume. For more about him, please see page 66.

The Sundial

The moon looked up at Hept from the water of the washtub. "Bess, do not put those sheets in yet," she said.

A thin breeze set the glowing surface aquiver. Bess said, "Miss Hept, what you see in the water?"

"A man is on my property, Bess. He bleeds. He aims for the old stables behind the trees."

Bess dropped the woven basket of clothes. "Is he a outlaw? A soldier man? Is he running to or running from?"

Hept frowned. "He is running from. Another man, one of Mosby's cavalry, just crossed the fence line at the lower forty, by the creek. I am going into the house to gather my bag and my shotgun. You hide inside."

The whites of Bess' eyes shone. "Don't you go out there with them men, Miss Hept. We both hide inside, up high in you room where you can pick 'em off with you rifle if they comes close."

"Obey me, Bess."

Inside, Hept took her leather satchel and the Lenderhaux shotgun from the chifferobe and waited for Bess to situate her thin black body inside, butcher knife in hand.

Outside, Hept knelt at the tub and stared into the reflection of the moon. One man lay in the abandoned stable while the other followed the trail the first had left in the expansive hayfield. She murmured a prayer to Thoth and aimed her steps for the stables, past her stone sundial, an obelisk spire as tall as Hept, but useless in the dark.

At the tree line, Hept took a pinch of the powdered blind rat eye out of her satchel, blew it into the air and walked through the cloud, whispering in the old tongue. The men would not see her now unless she walked through a moonbeam.

Down the hill, no one moved outside the stable. The mossy door was ajar; the frame bore fresh knife scars. The man inside had exposed wood that had never seen this world before and had now dried up, with nary a drop of sap. "Nary," she thought. Bess would have said it that way. Hept was becoming comfortable with the language of this time and place.

She smelled the blood of only one man. She crept inside, quiet as a snake, lifetimes of practice, feet inching their way, avoiding dapples of moonlight shining between boards, through knotholes and through cracks in the shutter of the hayloft window.

The man was in the last set of stalls, sitting back against the wall. She slunk to the opposite stall and crouched, the steel of the shotgun comforting her as her eyes adjusted to the darkness.

He had removed his shirt and held it against his

upper chest, nearly under his arm. Only a fold of the cloth was not soaked black. She did not see a gun—perhaps that was a knife beside him. He might live, if the other man did not kill him. But, no, he was too weakened to prevail.

The bleeding man whispered to no one, "I'm sorry I didn't finish bricking the footpath. It was your birthday present. I saved money for half a year and worked for three days. I probably had another two days to go. I wanted you to be able to walk from the carriage house to the back door without getting mud on your skirts." He took a shuddering breath. "I would have finished, but I was due at the regiment and they came for me. I couldn't linger until you got back. I wanted to see you on your birthday. I don't mean to complain. I just want to say, 'I'm sorry.' And 'I'll miss you.'"

Hept blinked. Few men were worthy of women. Most of them were not worth the effort that it took to pour boiling oil in their ears—to say nothing of the value of oil.

She winded the other man—Mosby's raider. She wanted to talk to this man—this creator of pathways—who truly loved his wife. The creator of pathways coughed. His throat was surely dry from loss of blood.

Mosby's man called, "Come on out, Yank. I'm not gonna shoot you—just take you into custody. Walk out slow now, so I don't get jumpy and shoot you by accident."

"Liar," the bleeding man breathed. His left hand went to the knife. He was left-handed. He was bad luck. He struggled to his knees.

"Easy, Yank. Nobody's gonna get hurt." Mosby's man sidled through the door.

The bleeding man crouched on one knee.

Mosby's man crept onward. Hept wanted to warn the bleeding man that he was breathing so hard that he could be heard—that before he could spring with the knife, Mosby's man would hear him and shoot him dead. It was not fair, but it was the way of things. She was torn inside. But her mind was her master. She would not interfere.

The breathing turned to panting.

The hammer clicked back. Mosby's man's gun wavered, aimed in her direction. The panting—it had been her own!

The Creator of Paths sprang at Mosby's man from behind.

The revolver thundered. The muzzle flash blinded her. The ball slammed into her forehead. Bone shattered. Flesh tore. Blackness enveloped her.

Way down yonder, down in the meadow,
There's a poor wee sweet little lamby.
With the bees and the butterflies peckin' out its eyes,
The little thing cried for her mammy.

Hept's black world spun.

Hush-a-bye, don't you cry.
Go to sleep . . .

She reached to lay hold of something in the nothingness, guided only by Bess' song.

"Miss Hept!" Bess cried. "I thought you was dead!"

Hept tried to speak. "B . . ."

"Praise the Lord! You gonna be all right. I'm gonna set you up now. Gonna set you up nice." Scorching fingers gripped Hept's upraised hands. She struggled, but the hot iron fingers clamped tight.

Hept tried to tell Bess to let go. "F . . ."

Bess braced one arm behind Hept's back and pulled her upright.

"F . . . fire . . . stop."

When Bess released her, Hept sank back onto softness. She pulled her seared fingers to her breast and looked around in the dark.

"That's all better, Miss Hept. Let's give you some water. Good Lord, I done some crying about you."

"Dark. I am blind."

Bess said, "You not blind. I stuck liberty dimes to you eyes with sweet gum because I thought you give up the ghost. My, you are cold as a stone. I get you warmed up and you be just fine."

Bess removed the dimes, washed Hept's eyes and hurried into the house. Hept could see. She lay on a blanket on the porch.

Bess brought teacakes and cold coffee, then knelt beside Hept to assist her. Hept lifted a teacake with trembling fingers and tasted. "Too sweet, Bess."

"I know you don't like 'em that way. But since you was dead, and you got lots of sugar laid up, I figure it didn't make no difference."

When Hept spilled a drop of coffee, Bess took the cup. Hept said, "How long since . . . ?"

"You was shot night before last. I was worried somebody would come around and steal me because you was dead. I would have buried you last night, except you was too heavy for me to carry. I didn't want to dig a hole beside the porch and roll you in it because someone might see the grave and know you was dead. I made up my mind to cut you up in little pieces and bury you down the hill in the woods. Made up my mind a few times, but I kept unmaking it."

"How did you carry me from the stables?" She guided Bess' hand holding the bitter coffee to her mouth—Bess had been making it from roots since the second year of the war.

"I ain't carried you, Miss Hept. You walked."

Hept studied her. "I walked? Did you see me walk? Are you sure the soldier did not carry me?"

Bess crossed her eyes as she did when frustrated. "I seen you, Miss Hept. I kept peeking out after I heard the gunshot. And that soldier wasn't carrying you. You was carrying him."

Hept's hand spasmed, knocking the cup from Bess' hands, spilling the cold liquid on the sheet that covered her breasts.

"Oh, my," Bess said. She scurried toward the kitchen and called back, "You carry him up to the porch, put him down, then lean on the porch rail and die."

Hept tried to collect her thoughts. Bess returned and dabbed at the coffee. Hept tried to keep the quaver from her voice when she said, "Is he alive? Where is he?" She sniffed, and caught a whiff of his blood. She saw a dark stain on the porch. "Oh, Bess, did you cut him up?"

"No, Miss Hept! I ain't cut no white man up! I took care of him and he drug hisself off the porch."

"Which way did he go? You have to find him!"

"You know I ain't a tom fool. He's laid up in your room."

Hept's body went slack. Her head hit the pillows and her hands thudded against the board floor. She had not realized she was straining upward.

Bess continued, "Got a tanned hide and a blanket under him so he won't bleed through to the bed. I figured since you was dead and you don't have no childrens . . . well, I thought maybe he could be the new master and he'd be pleased with me for saving his life."

"I want to see him." Hept felt her forehead for a wound and found none.

Hept bathed in a washtub in the corner of the parlor, enveloped by the scent of rosewater. After she chased Bess away, Hept found that her legs could support her. She wrapped in a white sheet from the chifferobe—pleased that Bess was keeping up with the wash. Bess had turned the mirror to face the wall, but Hept turned it around and saw by the lantern's light that her bronze skin was unbruised. No puffiness distorted her slim features and her eyes were not blackened or swollen, as always happened to her immediately after suffering a jarring facial wound.

She sat on her bench, combed her hair and worked out the details of the conversation she would have with the man. Then she lit a candle and went up to her bedroom, where he lay.

She slipped in, wanting to look him over for a while, but he woke and said, "Bess?"

"Hept," she replied.

He shifted in the bed and grunted with discomfort. "Bess said Miss Hept died. Are you her daughter?"

The cotton sheet that covered him glowed in the moonlight, as did her own sheet. Hept blew out the candle and sat on the cedar chest at the foot of the bed.

"Ma'am? What do you . . . ?"

She laid her hand on his foot under the sheet. His body stiffened. Hept said, "Bess should not have told you that I died. You would be emboldened to harm us if you were inclined."

"The thought never occurred to me." He relaxed under her hand, but did not move his foot as she squeezed it rhythmically.

She said, "You are so innocent. I do not wonder that you are not a competent warrior." Would he rise to the bait?

His body stiffened. "Not a competent warrior?"

"If I had not distracted Mosby's man, he would have killed you." She brushed his foot with the tips of her fingers.

He swallowed. "That was really you in the barn? It couldn't be. That woman's head was half blown off."

"My wound was not as serious as it looked in the darkness."

His hair was white in the moonlight. He strained upward from the pillow. She kneaded the arch of his foot. "Calm," she said. "I will depart if you cannot rest in my presence."

He lay back, still looking at her. With his hair tousled, he resembled a little boy—in youthfulness, he resembled a darker-hued young man, the only man for whom, in her long life, she had felt love.

He said, "You're right about the barn. I didn't show myself well. If you hadn't distracted the reb, he would have killed me. Thank you, Miss Hept. I have people counting on me to come home after the war is over."

Impressive. The Creator of Paths had not risen to her goading. She breathed in the night air and began to massage again. "I heard your prayer in the stables."

"Prayer?"

"You apologized for not finishing a path."

He cocked his head. "It weighs on me. Nothing frets me more than not to keep faith where it's due."

"You are rare," she said. "Facing death, your only thought was for a small duty that you had not fulfilled. Your wife is fortunate."

"My wife?"

"To whom you apologized in the stables."

"Oh. I was talking to my mother. I didn't finish the path for her."

She exhaled. She had not dared to hope that this one thing could be right.

She wanted to declare herself. He might leave in days. How could she say it? Women in this age could not speak freely. She said only, "Will you tarry here?"

His breathing was irregular as he said, "I need to go tomorrow. If Mosby finds me, I don't want him to hurt you for saving me."

She closed her eyes. "Perhaps that is best."

When she opened her eyes again, he looked straight at her. "I don't ask you to protect me. But if they ply you, would you say that you had not seen me?"

Tears welled and spilled down her cheeks. She heard the same words from four ages ago. A beautiful young son of Pharaoh stood before her, his eyes locked on hers, his tousled hair stirred in the wind, his hands dripped blood. He said, *"E' mem ght'bi en osi. Sama mem bh'gti nefti'm Phol mamin tathtalm E'."* Her heart broke with love for that dark-skinned young man—and, by the god's alchemy, her heart now broke with love for this light young man.

She whispered, "I must go," and stood. But out the window, she glimpsed the stone sundial on the grounds. Though there was no sun, the spire's shadow lay across the hour of death. The god was showing her the path toward what she had so long desired. He demanded a sacrifice, to atone for her ancient indulgence.

She rushed, sobbing, from the room. Bess jumped away from the other side of the door as Hept shoved it open.

Miss Hept?" Bess' voice died on the dirt floor of the root cellar. Hept felt Bess' arm around her shoulder. "You was down here all night. You gonna freeze to death in that sheet."

Her body spasmed with a suppressed sob.

"I would have come sooner, but black folks don't like to go in a cellar at night because of the haints, so I waited 'til the sun come up. You ain't none scared of the dark."

Hept swallowed.

"What's wrong, honey?"

She shook her head.

IRVIN RODRIGUEZ

The house above them creaked. Water dripped nearby.

Bess said, "I thinks a lot about how you ain't scared of the dark, since I know you ain't strictly white. You free, naturally, and you can pass with white folks, but I can see it and Jim from the Henry farm could tell, too. When he tell me, 'Your woman, she got more than a drop of the black,' I tell him he was full of John's barleycorns and to git along to Mister Henry. Ain't none of his worry."

Bess patted Hept's shoulder and hugged her close. "If you talk to me, you feel better, honey. I bring you back some coffee."

Bess returned with the lantern and set it on a shelf beside some fig preserves. Hept sat back against the wall, eyes on the ground. She took the hot cup and whispered, "Coffee does not solve everything, Bess."

"It ain't so bad. We give that man upstairs to Colonel Mosby and that solves it."

Hept shook her head.

"Honey?" Bess leaned close to Hept. Bess had flour on her hands from making breakfast. "Oh. You done taken a shine to him?"

Hept closed her eyes and sipped the bitterness.

"Miss Hept, he's just a man. There plenty of mens out there. Mosby's Raiders skin us alive if we don't give him up when they come. They burn you house. They steal me and sell me down the river—go to Alabama where they whips me every morning and every night."

Hept's face tightened and tears squeezed out from the corners of her eyes. "He's not just a man. Oh, Bess, he is *the* man."

"No. No, there ain't no *the* man. There's just one man and then another, and most of them dogs that beats their womens like they was the master."

"A long time ago, there was another man—a friend of the God—the One God. I saved him." Hept took another sip to dissolve the knot in her throat.

Bess said, "Ohhhh. Oh, I knowed you was older than anybody else. Just from the way you says things and from the way you looks at everything like you was riding by it in a wagon and everything you seen was going to turn to dust before you could stop the wagon."

Hept nodded. "It shows. It has always shown."

"You can't pass."

"I cannot."

"How did you save that man—the old one?"

Hept took a deep breath and let it out slowly. "I saw him kill a man. I was questioned in the matter, but I lied. I was in love with him. I did not tell the king."

"King?" Bess' eyes widened and shone. "Oh, this *was* old. What king was he—King Solomon or King Caesar or King Feeberum?"

Hept looked into her eyes. "Bess, if you tell anyone about this, you know I will sell you down the river for a lying slave."

"Oh, Miss Hept. You can do all that and you can beat me morning and night 'til I go. Who was he? You got to tell me."

Hept decided that it did not matter. Anyone would take Bess for an imaginative black woman. Then they would begin to look more closely at Hept, and they would know. But with Mosby's men sure to find her, she would soon face even worse scrutiny. "His name was Thutmose."

"Thut . . . mose? I never heard of no king like that. Why did your man kill the other man?"

"He killed the man to prevent him from killing a slave. And since the man I loved and protected was a friend of the One God, the God gave me this long life."

Bess nodded. "Well, your man sounds right nice. But I can see how King Thutmose don't want nobody killing his overseer . . ." Bess' mouth gaped open.

Hept sipped a long draught of the coffee. Bess sat like a bug-eyed statue.

Bess said, "No. It wasn't. He kill the king's overseer. It wasn't Moses that kill that overseer, was it?"

Hept nodded.

"And you saved him! Moses is the best man in the world, except for Jesus and maybe Adam. No, Moses is better than Adam. I see why God loves you. And I love you, too. You the best woman in the world, and you my mistress."

Hept finished the coffee.

Bess said, "I just can't believe it. But I do believe it. I always knowed you looked young but was way much old. God let you live forever just like Moses did because you saved him. But, Miss Hept, what does this have to do with that Bill Yank soldier upstairs?"

"That soldier." Hept realized that she did not even know his name. "That soldier killed a man who fights with Mosby's men, who defend slaveholders. Just like before, I can give the man up for killing the king's man, or I can protect him."

"Then this is as easy as hoe cakes. You protects him like you done to Moses. And God is gonna bless you again. He bless you the first time with living forever. What you think he's going to bless you with this time?"

Hept breathed out slowly. "The same blessing."

Bess beamed and patted her on the shoulder. "Then we all set."

Hept shook her head. "No."

A wave of exhaustion washed over Hept. Her lids fluttered. What was this? Was she exhausted from her night of heartbreak? Bess drew close and studied Hept's face.

Hept knew Bess would not understand, except for the pain. "King Rameses was my first husband. He wished to partake of my blessing, which only the One God could bestow. Because I could not share with him, he flayed my back with the whip and sowed ants in my wounds, but I healed every night. Cyrus, his sons, and grandsons chained me in the passages beneath the temple to force me to reveal the secrets of life. Tiberius tortured me for his amusement for over two years. He nailed my severed body parts to a wall, saying he would build another woman from them. In another age, Dwenth, my little brown-skinned girl, died from plague. She retched blood until her twisted body ceased shuddering. I was adjudged to be a witch in Copenhagen. My friend, Ebba, was burned for her friendship with me. I still smell her hair as it crackled and the odor of her peeling skin roasting."

Her tongue was sluggish. Her eyes closed. "I would have given the God's gift back to him, but he would not take it. I have prayed to him for an end."

"Shhh, Miss Hept. It's all right. All that can't hurt you now." Bess pulled Hept's head to her shoulder.

"It does not end until death."

Bess kissed her hair and rocked back and forth. She said, "When I lived on the Lawson farm, sometimes I thought about dying, too—going to my rest. I'd feel the same way if I was you. But that man sleeping upstairs don't change none of that. Why you so brokehearted?"

"Long ago, the man I saved had dark skin. This man is light. Then, life opened to me for saving a life. Life will now close to me for ending a life. The God showed me last night on the sundial. Long ago, the hour of death showed clear, though the spire's shadow pointed toward the sun. Last night, the hour of death showed, with the spire's shadow pointing toward the moon. The God told me. I know his voice. I may now choose to rest."

Bess whispered, "If you kill him?"

Hept replied, "If I kill him."

She relaxed into the warm darkness of Bess' bosom.

Hept woke, alone in her bed. The moon was just beginning to wane. Just now, she had been in the cellar—Bess had said it was morning. She refused to look at the sundial.

"Bess!"

Bess bustled in. "You awake already! Well, ain't that nice."

She sat up in the bed. "Where is he? He was in this bed. He has not departed, has he? Bess! You did not give him to Mosby!"

Bess turned the sheet back. "He's fine, Miss Hept. He's downstairs in the parlor. He was ready to leave, saying he thought you was a fine woman and he wasn't gonna make trouble. But I told him that you was so smit with him that you swooned in the root cellar and he had to stay and make sure you lived, since you save his life in the first place."

Hept looked up at the darkened ceiling and took a deep breath. "Why did I swoon in the root cellar?"

Bess squeaked, "I put some tonic in you coffee so you can sleep. You was awake for too long."

Hept clenched her jaw. "By rights I should lay a curse on you for being a meddling slave." She reached out. "Help me down the stairs. The poppies have loosened the sinews of my legs."

When she turned her back to the bedroom window, she staggered, and Bess buoyed her up. A sob convulsed her. Bess said, "You not good to walk yet, Miss Hept."

"No," she said. "I can walk. I only realized that I have given up."

"What you give up on, honey?"

"I am rushing downstairs to meet him, like a girl." She took a breath. "How can I? The God has sent a worthy man to me and I will not sacrifice him. I have given up on taking my rest."

Bess kissed her cheek and whispered in her ear. "Miss Hept, my momma and daddy had some love in them. When Daddy got sold over to Chattanooga, Momma just wanted to die—but she didn't. She kept living, for her babies that she love. And my brothers and my sister got sold, too. And now she's just living for me. Love keeps you living, Miss Hept. Love gonna keep you living, too."

Hept nodded. "I should go down to him. He is

prepared to depart and this may be my last chance to hold onto him."

When they approached, the man woke in the light of Bess' candle. He rose and took Hept's arm, guiding her to the divan. Bess lit the lantern on the parlor table, trimmed the wick, then went into the kitchen.

He sat beside her and said, "When I carried you to your bed, I was afraid you were sore stricken."

Hept was touched—though he had been wounded three days ago, he had carried her—perhaps he really cared for her. She was surprised by the calm that replaced her distress. "Bess dosed my coffee. She thought I needed rest."

He nodded. "You *have* had a difficult time, what with being shot . . ." He leaned forward, peering at her. His breath smelled of strawberries. "Miss Hept, you could not have been shot."

"Call me only 'Hept.' If you will give me your name, I will tell you of myself."

"I'm Ammon. Ammon Granger." He paused. "You're smiling."

"Take no offense, Ammon."

"Oh, no. You have a beautiful smile. You are just so reserved. I didn't expect it."

She felt her smile widen of its own accord. "Nor did I. I was amused by your name. In the ancient days of a people long dead, Amun was the creator— The Hidden One."

"Why is that funny?"

"Because, above all, when faced with death, you regretted such a small thing, a hidden thing—caring for your mother."

"It wasn't a small thing."

"It was not. But the world sees it as small."

He shrugged. "I suppose so." He tugged on the sleeve on his wounded side. "You said you would tell me—before I collapsed, I saw that Mosby's raider shot a hole in your forehead. It couldn't have been you."

Bess entered with the service tray, glasses tinkling. She set the tray on the table and poured dark wine in glass goblets beside fragrant bread and cheese. Bess paused and Hept waved her away, knowing that Bess would listen from the kitchen door.

Hept cut bread and cheese for Ammon, then for herself. When she replaced the bread knife, she nicked her thumb. She used the dishtowel, rather than the lace napkin, to staunch a few drops of blood.

He reached out to help, but she waved her other hand at him. Hept said, "We have a bargain. You have given me your name. I will trust you with my secrets, Ammon Granger."

"Secrets, no." He held out a hand, palm forward.

She continued before he could protest further, saying each word distinctly, "I know you. I trust you."

"All right. You can," he said. "You can trust me."

"I was shot in the stables, and lived, without a scar." She took his rough hand in her slim fingers, raising it. She gripped his fingers and ran their tips over her forehead.

"Five years ago, when field hands hired from the Henry farm helped me clear another acre, a rope that bound a stump snapped and lashed my throat. They carried me into the house, bleeding." She folded the rug back at the corner with a pointed toe and tipped the lantern toward the spot with her free hand.

"That is the bloodstain on the floor. Since I did not want my woman to notice my swift recovery, I left a bloodied bandage on my throat, whispered for a week and sold her to a reverend in Tennessee."

She exposed her throat to him and moved his fingers, tracing along the smooth skin of her neck and jaw. With her other hand, she steadied herself. He wet his lips with his tongue. "Do you feel the scars?" she asked.

"There aren't any."

She took his hand and pulled up the hem of her skirt. He pulled his hand back.

She whispered, "It is all right. You must see." She placed his palm on her bare knee. She looked into his eyes, but he was looking downward at her bronzed leg and lower thigh. "I was thrown from my horse ten years ago. This knee was smashed on a rock, bone ripped through skin. Did you see the scar? Do you feel it?"

He shook his head, his mouth open as he stared.

She took his other hand in both her hands and pulled the skirt's hem up again, exposing her other knee. She placed his hand there. "Nor any flaw with this leg?"

He passed his shaking hand over her knee. He squeaked a broken syllable. She placed one hand on each of his hands and said, "Look into my eyes, Ammon, Creator of Paths, Hidden Creator of All Things."

His pupils were gaping wells. His shoulders rose and fell with each labored breath. He said, "Those—those could be tales."

She whispered, "You do not trust me?"

"I . . ."

She raised her hands, palms up, to him. "Which thumb was wounded by the knife?"

He shook his head slowly, glancing down to the drops of blood on the towel.

"This one." She placed her thumb on his lips. He kissed it.

The pit of her belly burned for him. He kissed her palm as if feeding from her.

She said, "Do you trust me?"

He whispered, "I do."

Thunder rumbled from afar, waking Hept. Lying on the divan, she listened to Ammon's heartbeat against her ear. She planted a single kiss on his breastbone. A sheet covered them—Bess had been stealthy. She was an intuitive slave. How many masters in this age would beat a slave who eavesdropped on their lovemaking and covered them afterward? Bess somehow sensed the customs and views that Hept retained from ancient days.

"Miss Hept!" Bess whispered intently from the kitchen.

"Not now, Bess."

"Livia from the Randolph farm just woke me up and tole me that a man rode up looking for that Mosby soldier."

Hept shoved upward from Ammon, minding the healing wound in his side. He roused. "Ammon, love. Mosby's men are nearby."

"No," he whispered. "I should not have stayed so long." He sat up and began pulling on the loose clothes that Bess had bought from Jim Henry.

513

"We can leave quickly," Hept replied. "They may expect us to travel north, so we will cross the Rappahannock to the west. There is no fighting to the south around Charlottesville—they would not expect us to venture in that direction." She glanced at the clock. Two o'clock—plenty of time before the sun rose.

Hept sent Bess to the cellar to pack supplies, but she would not go at night without accompaniment, so Hept sent Ammon to assist her. Hept went to her room and stuffed a fresh sheet into her carved apothecary box, so that the tins would not rattle and the bottles would not break when placed in the wagon. From her satchel, she drew four vials and one tin of powder to carry in her pockets.

There was a loud knock at the front door. Whoever was there would have seen the light in the bedroom. She took a deep breath. Ammon would not answer the door, but Bess might, and might unknowingly reveal Ammon's presence. Hept hurried down the stairs.

The lantern illuminated a young man, dressed in dark gray, hat in hand. His beard ended in two points jutting from his chin. "I apologize for calling at this indecent hour. You are Miss Hept Hawthorn?"

"I am. And you are?"

"My name is Chapman, ma'am."

"Please come in, Mr. Chapman."

As he walked in, she saw two pistols on his belt. He paused and surveyed the dimly lit room. She placed the lantern on the table.

He said, "You dined in the parlor this evening."

"Please sit down. The bread is good. I confess my

woman is not the best at making cheese, but it is passable. The wine is from the Grayson farm. Their scuppernongs made well last year."

She leaned over and filled the glass that Ammon had drunk from, spying the pistol grip protruding from Chapman's boot top. She set the wine down, pointing at his boot with her left hand and reaching into her pocket with her right. She thumbed the cork off a bulbous little bottle. Still pointing to his boot, she said, "Is it safe to carry your gun like that? It must be uncomfortable."

As he looked downward to his boot, she passed her hand over his wine, dosing it from the bottle. He said, "I reckon that gun in my boot is more comfortable than the grave that a Yankee would shove me in if he bested me."

She filled her glass and adjusted her bottom on the couch, dropping the bottle behind her as she did so. He raised his glass. "You have my thanks for the refreshments."

She cut bread and cheese for them and lifted a piece. "You are quite welcome. What brings you to my home at this late hour, Mr. Chapman?" She took a small bite.

"Miss Hawthorne, do you always ask questions that you know the answer to?"

She sipped the wine. A tinkle of breaking glass came from the cellar. Chapman cocked his head. She ran her finger around the rim of her wine glass, making it sing, hoping he would not investigate immediately.

His dark eyes bored into her. He said, "I found your home lit at this ungodly hour, and further, you,

515

an unmarried woman, asked me in and sat with me, unchaperoned. Now I find that you have prepared an excellent morsel for a guest, but there is no guest about." He smiled and tasted the wine.

"My woman and I work during the night, when it is cooler. It is a habit that we have always observed. You may confirm that fact with the slaves from other farms who know her."

He took a bite of cheese and washed it down. "This cheese is much better than you let on. For whom was my place set? Surely you do not take your meals at the parlor table with your woman."

"I do. It has ever been our custom. We discuss the management of the house as we eat."

He raised his eyebrows. "That is a tidy story. But I am afraid it is too unusual for me to credit. Would you mind if I spoke to her? Her name is Bess, isn't it?"

"You are thorough, Mr. Chapman—you have even taken care to question the neighbors about my slave. She is sewing in her room. We can speak to her now. May I replenish your glass?" She reached for it.

He handed it to her. "No, thank you, ma'am. I must keep my wits about me."

"Look at me, Mr. Chapman."

He squinted at her in the lantern light.

She drank the remnants of his wine and whispered, *"Eld sfir t'nhali. H'she nens khiw'epta. M'em phot'th."*

"I don't . . ." he said.

She stared into his eyes and said, "I woke Miss Hawthorne from her sleep and found nothing suspicious. She and her woman survive as best they can."

He stared into her and worked his jaw, the twin spikes of his beard making circles.

She repeated the words twice more.

He replied, "I woke Miss Hawthorne from her sleep and found nothing suspicious. She and her woman survive as best they can."

"*Eph'ta,*" she said and kissed him, mingling the essence of the potion on her breath with his. "You may leave, Mr. Chapman."

He walked to the door, replaced his hat and left.

She collapsed onto the couch. The potion she had dropped in the corner wet her backside.

"You kissed him?" Ammon said from behind her. "Have you betrayed me to them?"

Hept rose. "You said you trust me, Ammon Granger. If I had wished to betray you, I would have led him to you and not sent him on his way."

"But . . ."

She retrieved the bottle from the stained divan. "This is an old medicine which makes men pliable, as if it were liquor, but with no drunkenness. I dosed his wine."

He approached her and took the bottle. He looked at it, then at her.

Hept placed her hand on his chest and said, "Ammon, I have shown you that I care for you, that I trust you, that I love you."

He nodded and looked down.

"I have shown you that I cannot be harmed, and you believe what your eyes have seen."

"I do." He placed his hand on hers.

"I have one more secret to reveal."

517

With his head lowered, his blonde hair obscured his eyes. "Tell me."

"I am older than your father and your grandfather. I am older than this nation and this nation's mother. I have served the One God and am favored of Him. He has given me abundant life. I have wished to give that life back to him for ages, but he would not have it. But now, I wish to live, for you. If the God suffers that I tarry here, I will care for you, for our children and for our grandchildren, through whatever ages remain in this world. It will be my work, if it pleases you."

Ammon looked up. He searched her face. "It's true, isn't it?"

"It is true."

"Then I will care for you. It pleases me."

She hugged him close.

She said, "We must leave this house soon. Mosby's man's drunkenness will not endure forever. We will cross the Rappahannock at the Kellysville Ford."

They hitched the wagon and piled in their most important possessions. Hept and Bess loaded the cedar chest that had stood at the foot of her bed for years. When the women could not pry the lid up, Ammon pitched in, laying it on its side, kneeling on it with one knee and pounding the lid back with the heel of his palm until it popped open.

Hept said, "As if it were sealed for the ages."

They removed surplus linens that Hept had not needed for years. In one corner, Hept placed the urn with the fused lid where she kept the gold that had sustained her household in this land.

After all was packed, she spoke to Ammon. "We may be seized by Mosby's men, or by others. If they find you, they will kill you. You should ride in the cedar chest. If you hear that we have been found and the wagon is being searched, swallow this medicine." She handed him a thimble-sized vial, etched with the setting sun. "You will sleep deeply, so that you will be mistaken for dead." She held up another vial with the lotus flower inscribed. "With this, I will wake you."

He swallowed hard. "I trust you."

He climbed into the chest and curled on his side. As she shut the lid, he said, "Wait."

She peered in at him, shadowing him with her body.

"This may not go well for us. I don't want us to part in fear. So kiss me," he said, turning his head up to her.

Their lips touched. He extended his free hand out of the box and snaked his fingers through her hair, pulling her body closer. His mouth sucked at hers, as if feeding, taking her life to him. Moaning, Hept gave, silently praying that the One God would allow her to give more.

Afterward, she and Bess stacked large-folded linens onto him, taking any small opportunity to avoid detection. They closed the lid and stretched a tarp over the wagon. As they rode out Hept looked toward the sundial and, again, saw the hour of death.

Hept gripped the side of the wagon with one hand and snapped the reins with the other, calling to the horses in the ancient tongue so loudly that they could hear her over the tumult. The wagon thundered down the road leading to the ford. There were lights in the mill on the other side of the river. Beside her, Bess gripped and yelled, "I can see them riders back there! Must be five or six."

Hept did not look back. Either the potion she had given Chapman had not lasted, or Mosby's men had been watching the road to the ford for some other reason.

Hept's horses slowed as they approached the water, high for summer, and Hept knew that the riders would be on them all too soon. When they were halfway across, Hept stopped the wagon and handed the reins to Bess.

"Miss Hept! You done gone crazy!"

Hept stepped into knee-deep water. "Ride to dry land."

Bess protested.

Hept repeated, "Ride!" She drew her rod of acacia, shod in gold, from under the tarp that covered their possessions. The wagon pulled away.

She turned toward the riders, now approaching the water, planted the rod, and chanted in the old tongue,

"Hail to thee, oh Rappahannock!
Who manifests thyself over this land!
Hail, oh Hap, come and prosper!
Oh, you who gives man life,
through his flocks and through his orchards!
Hail, oh Hap,
Come and prosper!"

Hept raised the staff slowly and the water rose with it. Her knees quivered as the River God drank from her spirit. She stumbled in the swelling current. She pushed herself upright with her staff, hearing only the rushing voice of the God.

In the moon's light one rider took aim. The crack of the shot and its answering splat against the bank behind her focused her mind on her surroundings. One of the gunman's companions yelled and backhanded him, then they spurred their horses into the flow.

Hept struggled toward the bank, leaning against the current, stumbling, righting herself with the staff, water now above her navel. The wagon was on dry ground. Bess' cries were lost in the wind.

From the dark water, a driftwood log struck her right hip. The staff slipped and she plunged below the surface. She lifted her head above the water, coughing and sputtering. The current unbalanced her and her knee hit the bottom. Something stabbed it. She lost her staff and went under again.

She tried to regain her footing, but she was below the ford and the water was deeper. The Rappahannock rushed her into darkness near the west bank. Her left shoulder exploded with pain as she smashed into a tree. She clawed at it with her right hand.

She found the bottom and dragged herself onto the grass on the bank, too far to see the lights of the mill that stood near the ford.

Hept wept with pain. The River God had taken much. She shivered with exhaustion. Wet hair plastered across her face.

She shoved herself up on her good arm. It trembled. Only her left elbow and left knee worked properly as she dragged herself upward toward the crest of the bank. Her wet dress tugged at her. A stand of tall weeds spread before her. She crushed them under her. Her good arm collapsed.

She lay in the weeds. A shaft of moonlight revealed lambent purple clusters of Dead Men's Bells on the end of the stalks that she had pressed flat. Their sweetness of death played in her nostrils.

"Bess," she meant to scream, but only whispered. Her body wanted to sleep—to heal. Hept growled in frustration, pulling her arm under her and inching onward.

The road was on the downhill side of the bank. She lay on the grass beside it, panting. Bess would not know to find Hept here. But Ammon was safe. The two were heading south, toward Charlottesville. She ran her hand over her swollen, seeping knee.

A horse cantered from the south, its rider calling to her. She cursed herself under her breath for not hiding. The uniformed man dismounted and bent over her. A pistol's ivory handgrip protruded from the top of his boot, but this was not Chapman.

"First I thought you was a pile of rags," he said. "Then I thought you was dead." She cursed herself again, this time for not playing dead. He reached down. "Are you Mistress Hept Hawthorne, that bought the old Whitehall farm?" He knew who she was.

Hept said, "I was taking stored grain to the mill. My horse spilled me into the river. I either climbed out—or someone pulled me out. I woke and could not walk." She showed him the bloodstain on her skirt. "Only now did I find the strength to crawl to the road." She felt her dress pocket for the vial with the lotus flower inscribed. But the Rappahannock had it now, taking her last chance to set things aright, should they go wrong. She could only hope.

He helped her onto the horse and led it back toward mill. As she swayed, still sapped by the River God, she tried to plan.

The rider had come up the road that Bess was supposed to go down. If Bess had been caught she might depart from the story she should be telling them. Ammon might not have followed her instructions. Mosby's men might kill Ammon— they had shot Yankees before in retribution for the execution of their men. She could try to steal this man's horse and find them quickly, but she might not have strength to ride.

Then the mill came in view. Hept's wagon was still there.

Her horses were tied to a post, along with others. The four men who stood around the wagon, illuminated by a lantern, fell silent as she approached. The man leading her horse said, "I found Mistress Hawthorne down the road."

A tall one cut a wedge of tobacco and shoved it into his cheek. "I blacked Newell's eye for shooting at you, ma'am."

"I told you I wasn't shooting at her," Newell said.

"Hard news about your cousin," said the first man.

"He's dead!" Bess cried. "He run outta air in that cedar chest with them clothes." Bess covered her eyes and said, "I'm so sorry."

523

Hept's voice quivered. "No." She put out a hand to the man who led her horse, and he helped her down. She leaned on him for assistance and approached the wagon, seeing that the tarp was thrown back. The cedar chest was open. The folded sheets had been unpacked. Ammon lay in the box, not breathing.

Hept clutched the side of the wagon with one hand. Her other hand explored her empty pocket, though she knew the lotus flowered vial was gone. Her body spasmed with sobs. "Why?"

"You have our sympathies," said a smaller man, who stood across the wagon, studying her. "When this man separated from his unit, we assumed he was a Yankee agent. But since your woman told us that he is your cousin's husband, it is clear that he simply deserted and sought your farm. He killed one of ours, and we would have tried him for that. But he is gone. Since we have an interest in pursuing Yankee agents, but no interest in pursuing Yankee deserters and their relatives, we needn't trouble you more."

She shut her eyes and put her forehead against the wagon.

The men mounted up. She heard their horses' hooves as they galloped back through the ford. Bess hugged her and cried against her. "I should of knowed better than to put him in that chest. I should of told you not to."

"No." Hept sobbed. "I am responsible. He drank from an elixir that took him into the realm of Osiris. My poison—my potion to bring him back—it is in the river. Without it, he is under the power of the Lord of the Dead."

Hept rocked against Bess.

Bess took Hept's wrist and said, "Let's go back home and get some more of that potion. You can save him."

Hept shook her head. "Osiris took him. We had minutes, not hours."

"We just got to give up? Hell's bells, Miss Hept! Can't you make some more?"

Hell's bells?

Hept's head snapped up. Her eyes locked on Bess. Bess said, "What?"

"I am injured. Quickly, help me into the wagon."

Hept lay against Bess as the wagon jostled down the road that ran along the river. "Here," Hept said. "I think it is here."

Bess twined her arm under Hept's and they staggered up and over the bank. There, to one side, Hept saw the shoulder-high stand of purple flowers, some pressed flat. Hept fell upon them and ripped the blossoms from the stalks.

Bess said, "You know them's poison, honey."

Hept stuffed her pocket full of the sweet scented blossoms.

Back at the wagon, Ammon lay on his side in the chest. "Push the chest over!" Hept said.

"There's too many things in the way!"

"Shove them out!"

Bess released the catch on the wagon's gate and shoved at their possessions, which spilled over the edge and clattered into the road.

They pushed the chest onto its side and tipped Ammon into the bed of the wagon. Hept hovered over him, rolling him onto his back. She grabbed a handful of Dead Men's Bells and stuffed them into her mouth. Her eyes watered as bitterness flooded her. She chewed.

"Oh, Miss Hept," Bess said. "I hope you know . . ."

Hept swallowed a measure of death's astringent. Her breathing quickened. Her heart shuddered. The world dimmed. She descended slowly.

Darkness. Standing in the boat, moving slowly onward. Fireflies gathered before her, illuminating the two bearded men who framed the entryway, groaning under the impossible weight of the sandstone crossbeam. Fireflies flared into fire, filling the corridor between the men, their names scribed on their foreheads.

By instinct, not sight, she tipped Ammon's lips to hers. They were cold. She kissed him. The bitter juice dribbled down his throat. She must give enough. Just enough. So cold.

Lit by flames, the bearded one named Right of Heart said, "He is here." Hidden of Heart said, "He must be judged." Hept stepped from the boat to the landing. Heat, as from a furnace, pressed against her. Scalding tears streamed back, tickling her earlobes.

She said, "He is mine."

Through the flames, the passage opened into the judgment hall. Heads of gazelles, horns pointed downward, dangled on ropes. Chained in the far corner, to her right hunched Ammit, the devourer, who glared, the rictus grin of his crocodile teeth grinding, one lion's foreleg working rhythmically, claws scraping the stone floor.

On the dais, above the throne, the stone proclaimed, "Osiris, Master of Hades, Earth and Tanen." Ammon stood on the topmost step before the throne, a stave across his shoulders supporting the hanging brass basins of the balance.

In the wagon, she kneaded Ammon's cold lips with hers. A sob wracked her. Too much juice poured over his tongue.

Before Osiris, she sank to her knees, but did not avert her gaze. She put forth her hand. Blood dripped onto her fingers from the roof above. "He is mine, Lord. Into your hands I trusted him and now retrieve him."

The rumble of the god's words reverberated in her bones. "He will be judged."

Tears slid from her face to Ammon's. She was bidding him farewell, into the realms.

Osiris' gaze impaled her. She gritted her teeth against the pain. "He is not yours, Great Osiris. He belongs to The One God. And by the favor of The One God, he belongs to me."

Still, she kissed him. A knot in her throat tightened for all the warm kisses that he might never return.

From the top step, Ammon raised a hand toward her. "Hept, love. It's too late. Save yourself."

She broke the kiss. "Live!" she whispered to Ammon. "Live, Ammon. Live, Creator of Paths. Live, Hidden One."

Osiris said, "Begone, woman. You have no place here, wretched wanderer of the ages."

She stood, straining under the weight of His gaze. She struggled to step forward, oppressed by the might of His dominion. Her foot found the bottom step. She heaved forward. Sweat ran freely. Step by step, she climbed. Blood welled in her eyes. She stood on the top step. She reached

527

for Ammon's hand, draped over the stave. He withdrew his hand.

"Ammon. If you are attempting to save me, do not. I have no wish to live, except for a life with you."

Tears dripped from his eyes. "I feel it—I know this is hell. There is no hope for me. You died for me in the stables and I won't let you die for me again."

Osiris roared. She turned her back to Him.

She knelt before Ammon. "Osiris has no authority over you, who belong to the One God, through me, unless you yield authority."

Osiris' voice thundered. "Your wish for death has led you here, unworthy servant of Thutmose. You cannot deny your flesh to the jaws of Ammit. Run to him now and find the oblivion that you seek."

Ammit growled from the corner and lunged upward, yanking his chains taut. Osiris had spoken truly. She could find death in those jaws. If she gave herself to the beast, the One God would not save her in this realm. She teetered on the top step, her world focused on the knives of the devourer's teeth.

Ammon said, "Hept?"

She could not let Ammon die.

Her body throbbed with the drumming of her heart. Her lips crushed against his again. Holding the kiss, she said into his mouth, "Live. Even if I do not. You must live." His lips sucked at hers. The bitterness of the flowers became sweet.

She screamed and cast the stave of the balance away from Ammon. The brass basins and wood clattered down the steps. "He cannot judge you. You do not belong to Him. I sent you here before your time. Run! Live!"

He ran. But he grabbed her hand and pulled her after. At the bottom of the stairs, her feet, of their own accord, sought the void that Ammit offered. Ammon jerked her forward, catching her in his arms as her legs collapsed.

He scooped her up and ran through the fiery corridor. Osiris rained curses on them. They ran past the bearded men. Right of Heart and Hidden of Heart entreated, "He must be judged."

Ammon leapt into the boat and shoved away from the shore. He lay with her under a canopy of reeds and enfolded her in his arms.

Her lips parted from his.

"No," he murmured. "More."

"Wait."

She spat the flowers out.

Then she gave more.

Hept opened her eyes. It was daylight, somewhere along the edges of her vision, but was dark and cool, here, lying in Ammon's arms. His heartbeat was strong against her.

From somewhere, Bess said, "Miss Hept. You gotta wake up."

"Where am I?"

Ammon said, "In a wagon."

Bess said, "I stretch the tarp when I seen you wasn't gonna answer me and I seen you need to be alone. You got to get ready now so we can reload the wagon."

Hept reached back and groped behind her. The cedar chest was there. The sealed crock filled with gold was there.

"Just take us home, Bess."

"But we got to get our butter churn and our spinning wheel."

Hept sighed against Ammon's chest. He laughed.

"Bess, I am comfortable here in the dark."

Ammon reached over her and unhooked the corner of the tarp. He folded it back. From just above the bank of the Rappahannock, the sunlight slanted down on them.

The Year in the Contests

The biggest change for the L. Ron Hubbard Writers and Illustrators of the Future Contests this year was our decision to take electronic submissions, starting with Quarter Two. Details can be found at www.writersofthefuture.com/submit-your-story and www.writersofthefuture.com/submit-your-illustration.

In news, the latest Pirates of the Caribbean movie is based on Contest Judge and Lead Workshop Instructor Tim Powers' book *On Stranger Tides* and is due out this summer.

One of our newest Illustrators of the Future judges and a past winner from 1991, Shaun Tan, won an Oscar for his short animated film *The Lost Thing*. He also won the 2010 Hugo Award for Best Professional Artist as well as the world's largest prize designed to promote interest in children's and young adult literature and in children's rights, the Astrid Lindgren Memorial Award for 2011.

Writers of the Future winner Patrick Rothfuss' second book, *The Wise Man's Fear,* hit the #1 position on the *New York Times* bestseller list. His first in the series, *The Name of the Wind,* was also a *New York*

Times bestseller. Both books are based in the world created for his winning *Writers of the Future* volume XVIII story, "The Road to Levenshir."

Writers of the Future winner Jo Beverley's latest book, *An Unlikely Countess,* debuted on the *New York Times'* bestseller list.

Three of our Writers of the Future winners are on this year's Nebula ballot: J. Kathleen Cheney, Eric James Stone and Aliette de Bodard. Published Finalist Nnedi Okorafor is also on the ballot.

Writers of the Future Contest Judge Robert J. Sawyer received a Hugo nomination for his novel *Wake.* One of the episodes of *Flash Forward,* the series based on Sawyer's novel, was nominated for a Best Dramatic Presentation—Short Form Hugo.

Writers of the Future Contest Judge Mike Resnick received a Hugo nomination for his short story "The Bride of Frankenstein," published in *Asimov's Science Fiction.*

Illustrators of the Future Judge Bob Eggleton was nominated for a Best Professional Artist Hugo.

In addition to Shaun Tan, award-winning science fiction and adventure artist, Dave Dorman, and Illustrators of the Future winner from 2002, Robert Castillo, became Illustrators of the Future judges.

For Contest year 27, the L. Ron Hubbard Writers of the Future Contest winners are:

FIRST QUARTER

    1. Brennan Harvey
    THE TRUTH, FROM A LIE OF CONVENIENCE

    2. D. A. D'Amico
    VECTOR VICTORIA

    3. Ryan Harvey
    AN ACOLYTE OF BLACK SPIRES

SECOND QUARTER

    1. Patty Jansen
    THIS PEACEFUL STATE OF WAR

    2. Ben Mann
    UNFAMILIAR TERRITORY

    3. Van Aaron Hughes
    THE DUALIST

THIRD QUARTER

    1. R. P. L. Johnson
    IN APPREHENSION, HOW LIKE A GOD

    2. Geir Lanesskog
    SAILING THE SKY SEA

    3. Keffy R. M. Kehrli
    BONEHOUSE

FOURTH QUARTER

    1. Patrick O'Sullivan
    MADDY DUNE'S FIRST AND ONLY SPELLING BEE

    2. Jeffrey Lyman
    THE UNREACHABLE VOICES OF GHOSTS

    3. Adam Perin
    MEDIC!

    Published Finalist: John Arkwright
    THE SUNDIAL

For the year 2010, the L. Ron Hubbard Illustrators of the Future Contest winners are:

FIRST QUARTER
> Vivian Friedel
> Scott Frederick Hargrave
> Erik Jean Solem

SECOND QUARTER
> Meghan Muriel
> Irvin Rodriguez
> Dustin D. Panzino

THIRD QUARTER
> Frederick Edwards
> Joey Jordan
> Nico Photos

FOURTH QUARTER
> Gregory J. Gunther
> Fred Jordan
> Ryan Downing

Our heartiest congratulations to all the winners!
May we see much more of their work in the future.

NEW WRITERS!

L. Ron Hubbard's

Writers of the Future Contest

Opportunity for new and amateur writers of new
short stories or novelettes of science fiction or fantasy.
No entry fee is required.
Entrants retain all publication rights.

ALL AWARDS ARE ADJUDICATED BY PROFESSIONAL WRITERS ONLY

*Prizes every three months: $1,000, $750, $500
Annual Grand Prize: $5,000 additional!*

Don't delay! Send your entry now!

To submit your entry electronically go to:
    www.writersofthefuture.com/submit-your-story

E-mail: contests@authorservicesinc.com

To submit your entry via mail send to:
    L. Ron Hubbard's
    Writers of the Future Contest
    PO Box 1630
    Los Angeles, California 90078

WRITERS' CONTEST RULES

1. No entry fee is required, and all rights in the story remain the property of the author. All types of science fiction, fantasy and dark fantasy are welcome.

2. By submitting to the Contest, the entrant agrees to abide by all Contest rules.

3. All entries must be original works, in English. Plagiarism, which includes the use of third-party poetry, song lyrics, characters or another person's universe, without written permission, will result in disqualification. Excessive violence or sex, determined by the judges, will result in disqualification. Entries may not have been previously published in professional media.

4. To be eligible, entries must be works of prose, up to 17,000 words in length. We regret we cannot consider poetry, or works intended for children.

5. The Contest is open only to those who have not professionally published a novel or short novel, or more than one novelette, or more than three short stories, in any medium. Professional publication is deemed to be payment of at least five cents per word, and at least 5,000 copies, or 5,000 hits.

6. Entries submitted in hard copy must be typewritten or a computer printout in black ink on white paper, printed only on the front of the paper, double-spaced, with numbered pages. All other formats will be disqualified. Each entry must have a cover page with the title of the work, the author's legal name, a pen name if applicable, address, telephone number, e-mail address and an approximate

536

word count. Every subsequent page must carry the title and a page number, but the author's name must be deleted to facilitate fair, anonymous judging.

Entries submitted electronically must be double-spaced and must include the title and page number on each page, but not the author's name. Electronic submissions will separately include the author's legal name, pen name if applicable, address, telephone number, e-mail address and approximate word count.

7. Manuscripts will be returned after judging only if the author has provided return postage on a self-addressed envelope.

8. We accept only entries that do not require a delivery signature for us to receive them.

9. There shall be three cash prizes in each quarter: a First Prize of $1,000, a Second Prize of $750, and a Third Prize of $500, in US dollars. In addition, at the end of the year the winners will have their entries rejudged, and a Grand Prize winner shall be determined and receive an additional $5,000. All winners will also receive trophies.

10. The Contest has four quarters, beginning on October 1, January 1, April 1 and July 1. The year will end on September 30. To be eligible for judging in its quarter, an entry must be postmarked or received electronically no later than midnight on the last day of the quarter. Late entries will be included in the following quarter and the Contest Administration will so notify the entrant.

11. Each entrant may submit only one manuscript per quarter. Winners are ineligible to make further entries in the Contest.

12. All entries for each quarter are final. No revisions are accepted.

13. Entries will be judged by professional authors. The decisions of the judges are entirely their own, and are final.

14. Winners in each quarter will be individually notified of the results by phone, mail or e-mail.

15. This Contest is void where prohibited by law.

16. To send your entry electronically, go to:
www.writersofthefuture.com/submit-your-story
and follow the instructions.

To send your entry in hard copy, mail it to:
    L. Ron Hubbard's
    Writers of the Future Contest
    PO Box 1630
    Los Angeles, California 90078

17. Visit the website for any Contest rules updates at www.writersofthefuture.com.

ILLUSTRATORS' CONTEST RULES

1. The Contest is open to entrants from all nations. (However, entrants should provide themselves with some means for written communication in English.) All themes of science fiction and fantasy illustrations are welcome: every entry is judged on its own merits only. No entry fee is required and all rights to the entry remain the property of the artist.

2. By submitting to the Contest, the entrant agrees to abide by all Contest rules.

3. The Contest is open to new and amateur artists who have not been professionally published and paid for more than three black-and-white story illustrations, or more than one process-color painting, in media distributed broadly to the general public. The ultimate eligibility criterion, however, is defined by the word "amateur"—in other words, the artist has not been paid for his artwork. If you are not sure of your eligibility, please write a letter to the Contest Administration with details regarding your publication history. Include a self-addressed and stamped envelope for the reply. You may also send your questions to the Contest Administration via e-mail.

4. Each entrant may submit only one set of illustrations in each Contest quarter. The entry must be original to the entrant and previously unpublished. Plagiarism, infringement of the rights of others, or other violations of the Contest rules will result in disqualification. Winners in previous quarters are not eligible to make further entries.

5. The entry shall consist of three illustrations done by the entrant in a color or black-and-white medium created from the artist's imagination. Use of gray scale in illustrations

and mixed media, computer generated art, and the use of photography in the illustrations are accepted. Each illustration must represent a subject different from the other two.

6. ENTRIES SHOULD NOT BE THE ORIGINAL DRAWINGS, but should be color or black-and-white reproductions of the originals of a quality satisfactory to the entrant. Entries must be submitted unfolded and flat, in an envelope no larger than 9 inches by 12 inches.

7. All hardcopy entries must be accompanied by a self-addressed return envelope of the appropriate size, with the correct US postage affixed. (Non-US entrants should enclose international postage reply coupons.) If the entrant does not want the reproductions returned, the entry should be clearly marked DISPOSABLE COPIES: DO NOT RETURN. A business-size self-addressed envelope with correct postage (or valid e-mail address) should be included so that the judging results may be returned to the entrant.

We only accept entries that do not require a delivery signature for us to receive them.

8. To facilitate anonymous judging, each of the three photocopies must be accompanied by a removable cover sheet bearing the artist's name, address, telephone number, e-mail address and an identifying title for that work. The reproduction of the work should carry the same identifying title on the front of the illustration and the artist's signature should be deleted. The Contest Administration will remove and file the cover sheets, and forward only the anonymous entry to the judges.

9. There will be three co-winners in each quarter. Each winner will receive an outright cash grant of US $500 and a

trophy. Winners will also receive eligibility to compete for the annual Grand Prize of an additional cash grant of $5,000 together with the annual Grand Prize trophy.

10. For the annual Grand Prize Contest, the quarterly winners will be furnished with a specification sheet and a winning story from the Writers of the Future Contest to illustrate. In order to retain eligibility for the Grand Prize, each winner shall send to the Contest address his/her illustration of the assigned story within thirty (30) days of receipt of the story assignment.

The yearly Grand Prize winner shall be determined by the judges on the following basis only:

Each Grand Prize judge's personal opinion on the extent to which it makes the judge want to read the story it illustrates.

The Grand Prize winner shall be announced at the L. Ron Hubbard Awards Event held in the following year.

11. The Contest has four quarters, beginning on October 1, January 1, April 1 and July 1. The year will end on September 30. To be eligible for judging in its quarter, an entry must be postmarked no later than midnight on the last day of the quarter. Late entries will be included in the following quarter and the Contest Administration will so notify the entrant.

12. Entries will be judged by professional artists only. Each quarterly judging and the Grand Prize judging may have different panels of judges. The decisions of the judges are entirely their own and are final.

13. Winners in each quarter will be individually notified of the results by mail or e-mail.

542

14. This Contest is void where prohibited by law.

15. To send your entry electronically, go to:
www.writersofthefuture.com/submit-your-illustration
and follow the instructions.

To send your entry via mail send it to:
    L. Ron Hubbard's
    Illustrators of the Future Contest
    PO Box 3190
    Los Angeles, California 90078

18. Visit the website for any Contest rules updates at
www.writersofthefuture.com.